"Ms. D'Alessandro has the nimbleness of a thief when it comes to crafting relationship dynamics."

—*Heartstrings Reviews*

RAVES FOR JACQUIE D'ALESSANDRO

"On par with some of the best works from seasoned authors like Julia Quinn and Stephanie Laurens."

—*Publishers Weekly*

"A delightful tale of honor and duty, curses and quests, treachery and betrayal, love and passion."

—*Romance Reviews Today*

"A delight from start to finish . . . Romance at its enchanting best!"

—Teresa Medeiros, *New York Times* bestselling author

"Overflows with romance, passion, humor, and danger."

—*Huntress Book Reviews*

"An entertaining, often humorous Regency romantic romp that also provides a lesson in sticking to one's values even if it hurts to do so."

—*The Best Reviews*

"Ms. D'Alessandro's books are not only keepers—they are treasures."

—*Affaire de Coeur*

"An engaging tale, combining witty dialogue with charming characters . . . Jacquie D'Alessandro is always a solid read for me."

—*Night Owl Reviews*

continued . . .

Summer at
Seaside Cove

Jacquie D'Alessandro

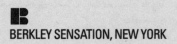
BERKLEY SENSATION, NEW YORK

THE BERKLEY PUBLISHING GROUP
Published by the Penguin Group
Penguin Group (USA) Inc.
375 Hudson Street, New York, New York 10014, USA
Penguin Group (Canada), 90 Eglinton Avenue East, Suite 700, Toronto, Ontario M4P 2Y3, Canada
(a division of Pearson Penguin Canada Inc.)
Penguin Books Ltd., 80 Strand, London WC2R 0RL, England
Penguin Group Ireland, 25 St. Stephen's Green, Dublin 2, Ireland (a division of Penguin Books Ltd.)
Penguin Group (Australia), 250 Camberwell Road, Camberwell, Victoria 3124, Australia
(a division of Pearson Australia Group Pty. Ltd.)
Penguin Books India Pvt. Ltd., 11 Community Centre, Panchsheel Park, New Delhi—110 017, India
Penguin Group (NZ), 67 Apollo Drive, Rosedale, Auckland 0632, New Zealand
(a division of Pearson New Zealand Ltd.)
Penguin Books (South Africa) (Pty.) Ltd., 24 Sturdee Avenue, Rosebank, Johannesburg 2196,
South Africa

Penguin Books Ltd., Registered Offices: 80 Strand, London WC2R 0RL, England

This is a work of fiction. Names, characters, places, and incidents either are the product of the author's imagination or are used fictitiously, and any resemblance to actual persons, living or dead, business establishments, events, or locales is entirely coincidental. The publisher does not have any control over and does not assume any responsibility for author or third-party websites or their content.

SUMMER AT SEASIDE COVE

A Berkley Sensation Book / published by arrangement with the author

PRINTING HISTORY
Berkley Sensation mass-market edition / May 2011

Copyright © 2011 by Jacquie D'Alessandro.
Excerpt from the next Seaside Cove novel by Jacquie D'Alessandro copyright © by Jacquie D'Alessandro.
Excerpt from *Seduced at Midnight* by Jacquie D'Alessandro copyright © by Jacquie D'Alessandro.
Cover art by Jim Griffin.
Cover design by George Long.
Interior text design by Laura K. Corless.

ISBN: 978-0-425-24149-3

BERKLEY® SENSATION
Berkley Sensation Books are published by The Berkley Publishing Group,
a division of Penguin Group (USA) Inc.,
375 Hudson Street, New York, New York 10014.
BERKLEY® SENSATION and the "B" design are trademarks of Penguin Group (USA) Inc.

PRINTED IN THE UNITED STATES OF AMERICA

10 9 8 7 6 5 4 3 2 1

This book is dedicated with my love and gratitude to Jenni Grizzle. Thank you so much for keeping me on track and for being such a great friend. And especially for being older than me. ☺ And to Wendy Etherington, for always lending an ear and support.

Also, to all the men and women serving in our Armed Forces. Thank you so much for the sacrifices you and your families make every day to keep our country safe.

And, as always, to my wonderful, supportive husband, Joe. You're like a fine wine, getting better and better as time goes by. And our terrific son, Christopher, aka Fine Wine, Junior. Love you guys! xox

Acknowledgments

I would like to thank the following people for their invaluable help and support:

All the wonderful people at Berkley, including Cindy Hwang, Leslie Gelbman, Susan Allison, and Leis Pederson.

My agent, Damaris Rowland, as well as Steven Axelrod, Lori Antonson, and Elsie Turoci.

Many thanks to Steve, Michelle, and Lindsey Grossman and Jeb Kehres for the brainstorming session that resulted in the restaurant at Seaside Cove.

A very special thank you to Lisa Stone Hardt for putting me in touch with Princeton graduates Bill Hardt (class of '63), Josh Hardt (class of '95), and Adrienne Rubin (class of '88). Your help with my research of the school was invaluable. I hope I got it right—if not, the mistakes are mine. You all were wonderful. Go Tigers!

Thanks, as always, to Sue Grimshaw, Kathy Baker, Kay and Jim Johnson, Dick and Kathy Guse, and Lea and Art D'Alessandro. Thanks also to Serena and Jeremy Wray, Kendra Fogelberg, Brenda D'Alessandro, Anna Lynksey and Anthony, Michele Lynskey, Danielle Lynskey, and Robert, Toni, and Isabella D'Alessandro. Thanks as well to Susie Aspinwall, Sandy Izaguirre, and Melanie Long, and special thanks to Melissa and Ned Windsor for introducing me to the real Godiva.

A cyber hug to my Looney Loopies: Connie Brockway, Marsha Canham, Virginia Henley, Jill Gregory, Julie Ortolon, Julia London, and Sherri Browning. And my Whine Sisters, Julia, Sherri, Julie Kenner, Dee Davis, and Kathleen O'Reilly. And to our missing sister, Kathleen Givens, who is missed every day.

And finally, a very special shout out to all my readers who have been so supportive through the years. Thank you so much—I really appreciate it!

Chapter 1

The decapitated, plastic pink flamingo, standing ass-feathers deep in what looked like poison ivy, was Jamie Newman's first clue that doom had followed her from New York. The pictures of the "cheerful, cozy, inviting" beach house posted on the rental Internet site for the North Carolina coastal barrier island of Seaside Cove must have been seriously Photoshopped.

There was absolutely nothing cheerful, cozy, or inviting about this ramshackle bungalow, which sported peeling paint, grimy windows—two of which bore jagged cracks—and a second-story porch whose screens drooped like a flag on a windless day. The ten-foot stilts raising the house off the ground resembled weathered toothpicks and the entire structure looked a single ocean breeze away from dropping into a pile of rubble. The headless flamingo's faded color was the only bright spot in the tiny yard choked with weeds and thorny bushes.

Like all the neighboring dwellings, a plaque hung on the front of the rental proclaiming the house's name. She turned and read the names of several homes across the street—Beach Music, Kickin' Back, It's Five O'clock Somewhere. Unlike those colorful, beautiful plaques, however, her cottage sported a splintered oval of wood bearing sun-faded sand dunes and the words Paradise Lost. It hung at a drunken angle above the cracked front window.

While "Lost" was appropriate, someone clearly didn't know what "Paradise" meant.

"More like Hell Found," she muttered.

"Good luck, ma'am," came a male voice.

Jamie yanked her gaze away from the house of horrors and saw that while she'd been gawking, the cab driver had set her luggage at the end of the driveway. He made a beeline for the driver's seat.

"Whoa—you're not leaving me here," she said, hurrying after him.

"My shift ended twenty minutes ago, ma'am, and I promised the wife I wouldn't be late. As it is she's goin' to be hoppin' mad."

"She's not the only one. There's obviously been a mistake in my accommodations, and I'll need a ride once it's straightened out."

"I'm afraid you'll need to call the cab company and arrange for another driver. Don't worry—they'll send someone quickly if you need them to. You have a good evenin' now, ya hear?" With that he slammed the door and took off like his gas tank contained rocket fuel.

"*If* I need them to?" Oh, she'd definitely need them to send someone else. There was no way in hell she was staying in this tumble-down shack. "We came to Seaside Cove to get *away* from disasters, not take on any new ones, right, Cupcake?"

She looked down at Cupcake, who glared at her through squinty eyes from the confines of her cat carrier. Poor kitty. Jamie hated putting her in the carrier as much as her beloved pet hated being in it, but safety first.

"Don't give me that look. Believe me, it's no better out here."

Cupcake answered with a pissed-off hiss.

"I know exactly how you feel." In fact, pissed off didn't begin to describe her mood as anger and frustration burst through the wall she'd so carefully erected around her emotions since her life had fallen into a sinkhole a week ago.

With a muttered curse she sat on one of her three over-weight suitcases that had cost an arm, leg, and part of a kidney to check in at the airport and pulled her cell phone from her pocket. Ignoring the flash that announced three missed calls, two voice mails, and seven text messages, she scrolled through her contacts until she found Jack Crawford. Right now the Re-altor, from whom she'd picked up the keys to Paradise Lost less than ten minutes ago when the cab had stopped at his of-fice, was number one on her hit list. Jack Crawford had *seemed* like a nice man—fatherly and oozing Southern hospitality—but clearly he was insane, not to mention severely mistaken, if he thought he could pawn off this dump on her.

After two rings, Jack's cheery voice came through on his voice mail stating he wasn't available but would return "y'all's call as soon as possible."

"Mr. Crawford, this is Jamie Newman," she said through her clenched teeth. "I picked up a key at your office a few minutes ago. I need to speak with you immediately as there's been a mistake with my rental. Please call me as soon as you receive this message."

She ended the call and heaved out a disgruntled breath as she glared at the house. The absolute last thing she wanted to do was go inside, but given that she had no idea how long she'd have to wait for Jack Crawford to return her call and the bottle of water she'd sucked down during the hour-long cab ride from the airport had made its way to her bladder, she was going to have to brave it. Not to mention that Cupcake could use a few minutes of freedom.

Pulling in a resolute breath, she grabbed the carrier, then picked her way up the crushed-shell pathway—a construction material that should have come with a warning label, as she discovered when a piece of shell found its way inside one of her flat-heeled sandals.

"Youch!" She shook her foot to dislodge the sharp shell and tried to recall if her tetanus shot was up to date. "Clearly I should have worn Nikes," she mumbled. "And a hazmat suit."

She cut across the cracked cement of the carport, pray-ing with each step the house wouldn't collapse on top of her, then stared at the steep wooden stairs leading up to the door. The two bottom treads were missing. Not even broken—just completely gone. Like giant termites had come and hauled them away.

"Perfect. Really adds to the ambiance. Hold on, Cupcake. This first step is gonna be a doozy."

Jamie hauled herself and Cupcake onto the third step, then carefully climbed up, testing each tread before putting her full weight on it. Holding the screen door open with her elbow, she inserted the key in the lock, then pushed the heavy, wooden inner storm door inward. And was immediately enveloped in a noxious cloud of hot air that reeked of something fishy. Something *dead* and fishy.

"Holy Stink Almighty!" Jamie said, wrinkling her nose. Breathing through her mouth, she shouldered her way in and rolled her eyes at Cupcake, whose quivering nose was pressed against the carrier.

"Yeah, sure, that's *your* favorite smell but Eau de Old Man and the Sea doesn't make my top-ten fragrances. There's fifty bucks in it if you find whatever that stink is and drag it outside."

Leaving the storm door open so she wasn't asphyxiated by the stink fumes, she unlocked the carrier. Cupcake shot out so fast Jamie was shocked she didn't leave a vapor trail behind her. Knowing her pet was simultaneously pouting over her confinement and scouting out potential hairball hacking locations, Jamie looked around the shadowed interior, which was—no shocker—as shabby as the outside.

She stood in a small, dingy kitchen complete with a linoleum floor that peeled up in the corners and a chipped Formica countertop. The appliances—which she noted with horror didn't include a dishwasher—screamed circa 1958. Beyond the kitchen was the living area, furnished with a dirt-colored sofa, two folding chairs, a cracked-leather beanbag chair, and a coffee table made out of two plastic crates emblazoned with the United States Postal Service logo topped with a piece of swaybacked, splinter-ridden plywood. A pair of doors, both ajar, one on each side of the living area, led, Jamie presumed, to bedrooms, and hopefully a bathroom.

"Probably there's a frat boy somewhere who would think this is very chic," Jamie grumbled. "No doubt the bathroom has all the elegance of a Porta Potty."

She crossed the living area and opened the nearest door. As she suspected, it led to a bedroom. She hit the light switch. Nothing.

"Perfect." Probably whoever owned this dump forgot to pay the electric bill. Although that could be a blessing as the room definitely benefited from a lack of illumination. There was no headboard or bedspread on the bed, and the dresser was missing three of its four knobs. Clearly a garage-sale find. No blinds or curtains covered the windows, but given how dirty the glass was, privacy probably wasn't an issue.

She stuck her head in the tiny adjoining bathroom and groaned. Porta Potty with a shower. It had looked way larger in the Internet photo. The Internet photo had also featured a shower curtain. Now there was merely a liner of dubious cleanliness that drooped off the curtain rod, as half the hooks were missing.

Her jaw clenched. How could anyone possibly think they could get away with renting something like this? And so grossly misrepresenting it on the Internet? It was fraud! By God, when Jack Crawford called her back, he was going to have to offer her the damn Taj Mahal of Seaside Cove to make up for this snafu.

Because the pressure on her bladder had reached emergency proportions, she made quick use of the facilities. When she finished, she explored the rest of the house. The door on the opposite side of the main living area yielded an identical bedroom/tiny bathroom/no light situation. The only difference was this bed did have a bedspread—depicting the New York Mets logo. Figures. She was a Yankees fan. Cupcake had taken up residence on the bedspread and currently had her hind leg hoisted in the air to clean her lady bits. She spared Jamie a single glare, then resumed her cleansing ritual.

"Feel free to hack one up on the Mets," Jamie said, sitting gingerly on the edge of the bed.

Her cell phone buzzed and she quickly pulled it from her pocket. When she saw the caller's name, she was sorely tempted to hit ignore—as she'd done the last two times he'd called—but since he obviously wasn't taking the hint, she might as well get this over with.

"Hi, Patrick—"

"Thank God you picked up." Patrick Wheeler, the normally unflappable maitre d' of Newman's restaurant, sounded like he was about to cry. "Everything has gone to hell in a handbag here. The seafood delivery truck hasn't come because the drivers are on strike, which could continue for God knows how long. Laurel pissed off both our beef and vegetable suppliers and they're now refusing to deal with anyone other than you. Not one, not two, but *three* waiters *and* the new hostess have all called in sick—yeah, right, like they're not out in the Hamptons and just don't want to come back to the city during the worst heat wave in a decade. And don't even get me started on Eduardo! He's simply impossible. Why do we have such a diva chef? Plus—"

"Patrick. Stop. Deep breath."

She heard him pull in a shuddering lungful of air. "Okay. I breathed. Look, I'm keeping things afloat here as best I can, but it's like the Titanic after the iceberg—only a matter of time before we sink. You need to come back. Now."

"Patrick. I told you. I'm not coming back until the end of summer. Consider me temporarily resigned."

"You can't temporarily resign. Newman's belongs to your family."

"I'm not the only Newman."

"But you're the only one capable of running the restaurant. God knows I love your mother, but a manager Maggie is not."

Jamie couldn't argue with him on that point. Maggie Newman was a perfect hostess for the busy, upscale restaurant located in Manhattan's theatre district. But she had no talent—or interest—in anything managerial or financial.

"Nathan is perfectly capable of handling things," she said, referring to her assistant manager.

"Yes, but he's off for the next two days."

"Then call him at home."

"I already left him two voice mails."

"Then you'll need to speak with Laurel about these problems, Patrick."

Her voice caught on her half sister's name, and the sense of betrayal that she'd fought so hard to swallow rose up and grabbed her by the throat.

"Laurel is part of the problem. She's great when it comes to

schmoozing the patrons and getting her rich, fancy friends to
frequent the restaurant, but she doesn't have the rapport with
the staff or suppliers that you do. I told you—she's completely
pissed off the beef and vegetable suppliers with her attitude."

"I know she can be difficult"—*difficult, abrasive, snobby,
and oh, yeah, a backstabbing Judas*—"but you need to find
a way to deal with her because for now the restaurant is out
of my hands."

"Your father is turning over in his grave to hear you even
whisper such a thing. You know that's not what he wanted."

Jamie gritted her teeth. Her mother had already heaped
a ton of guilt on her. The last thing she needed was more
guilt—and pressure—from Patrick. Nor did she need any re-
minders of her dad.

Even after three years, grief still wrenched her heart at
the mention of him. The pain had dulled with time, but it still
cut deep. And no, Tom Newman wouldn't have wanted her
to walk away—even temporarily—from the restaurant he'd
founded thirty-five years ago and where she'd worked in one
capacity or another since she was fourteen. Just one more burden for her to deal with. Which was why she'd had to get away.

"Dad's not here," Jamie said quietly, "and I have to do
what's best for me." *For the first time in my life.* "I'm sorry,
Patrick, but I'm off the clock until the end of August. Call
Nathan again. Call Laurel or my mother. But don't call me."

"But, Jamie—"

"I can't help you. Good-bye, Patrick." She ended the call,
then pulled in a slow deep breath. Before she'd even fully ex-
haled, her phone rang again. The only name she wanted to see
on her caller ID was Jack Crawford. Unfortunately that's not
what she saw. That's what she got for turning the damn phone
back on. She was once again sorely tempted to ignore the call,
but she sucked it up and answered.

"Hi, Mom." She braced herself—Maggie Newman attracted drama like bees to honey, and this phone call no doubt
would bring some form of commotion.

"Jamie! Finally. I've been so worried, honey. I sent you
half a dozen texts. Are you all right?"

"Of course. I texted you when I landed."

"Yes, but that was ages ago. Are you in Seaside Cove yet?"

"I just arrived."

"How's the house?"

"It's"—her gaze darted around the bedroom and she winced—"perfect." In her mind's eye she pictured the decapitated flamingo. "Gorgeous. A veritable palace."

She looked upward, praying she wasn't about to get sizzled by a lightning bolt for that whopper. But there was no way she could tell her mom the truth. One of Mom's many, many arguments against Jamie leaving New York and going to Seaside Cove for the summer had been that any rental available on such short notice and for such a cheap price had to be a dump.

Damn it, she *hated* it when Mother Knew Best. Granted, it didn't happen often, but still. Galling. Especially in this case.

"Oh, well I'm glad," Mom said, not really sounding glad at all. "I was afraid it would be awful."

"Nope. It's great. How are you doing?"

Her mom hesitated. Uh-oh. A sure sign something was wrong. Which meant Drama Time. "I'm fine." The cheerful tone would have led anyone other than Jamie to believe her words. "I just miss you."

"I've only been gone since this morning," Jamie teased.

"I know. But you're so far away. And Newman's simply isn't the same without you."

"Mom—please. Don't go there."

Jamie heard an unmistakable sniffle—the sound that meant Mom tears were on the way—and guilt smacked her. Her mom didn't cry often, yet it seemed that over the past week, she'd shed an enormous amount of tears. Jamie's heart squeezed, knowing her situation and decisions were the cause.

"I understand why you left New York, honey," her mom said. "Really I do. But I hate that you'll be gone for such a long time. Who's going to help me balance my checkbook and do that online bill-paying thing you set up for me? You know what a financial disaster I am."

"I e-mailed you step-by-step instructions. I also wrote down all your passwords to access your online bill-pay account and a list of which bills get paid automatically and the ones you need to pay by check each month. You'll be fine. And if you can't figure something out, I'm only a phone call away."

Jamie drew a deep breath, then continued gently, "But, Mom, you can't call me every five minutes, okay? I need to . . . breathe."

Jamie could practically feel her mother's sadness oozing through the phone, and it filled Jamie with a guilt she didn't want to feel. "I know," Mom said. "I just miss talking to you. You're always so . . ."

"Bossy?"

"I was going to say decisive. And smart. And practical. You always know how to make things right."

Yeah, I'm a regular Ms. Caretaker Fix-it. She could solve everyone else's problems but not her own. Could see the cracks and flaws in everyone else's relationships, but not her own.

"Well, as I said, I'm only a phone call away. I need to go, Mom, but we'll talk soon. Love you. Don't forget tomorrow is trash day."

The instant the words left her mouth, Jamie cringed. She had to stop doing that. No wonder her mother depended on her so much—Jamie enabled her to do so. Her mom was smart—she'd figure it out.

The problem was that her mom had never *had* to figure out all the pesky little details that life involved, like remembering what day the trash was picked up, filing tax returns, and paying bills and making a household budget. Jamie's dad had taken care of all that, and upon his death, Jamie had stepped in. Maggie Newman had married young, gotten pregnant right away, and been a fabulous stay-at-home, never-miss-a-game/class-trip/school-outing mom who could whip up a batch of cookies at a moment's notice and whose artistic help always resulted in unusual and *tres* cool school projects.

But practical she was not. She could make her own curtains and decorate the hell out of a room, but had no idea how to pump her own gas, operate the lawn mower, or have the oil changed in her car.

Well, at the age of forty-six, she was going to learn.

Jamie's phone rang again and her lips pressed together in a grim line when Jack Crawford's name appeared on the caller ID.

"Brace yourself, Mr. Crawford. The Wrath of Newman is about to fall on you."

She answered with a brisk, "Hello, Mr. Crawford. Thank you for returning my call so promptly."

"What can I do for you, Miss Jamie?"

"There's been a mistake with my rental. The house you gave me the keys for is not the house I rented—the one pictured on your website."

"There's no mistake," came Jack Crawford's deep, slow—*reeeaaally* slow—Southern drawl. "You rented Paradise Lost."

"No," she said, with her usual outward calm. She'd learned long ago that even if she was raging inside, losing her cool accomplished exactly nothing. "I rented—and I'm quoting from your website—'a fully furnished, cozy beach cottage only minutes from the ocean where you can relax, unwind, and breathe in the fresh ocean air.'"

"And that's exactly what Paradise Lost is. Oh, she needs a little TLC, but you sure are lucky to have gotten her."

"The house requires more than *some* TLC—an Extreme Makeover is needed. The point is, it's *not* the house you advertised on your website."

"Well now, I'll admit those photos are a bit out of date," Jack said with a chuckle, "but that's Paradise Lost all right."

A *bit* out of date? Surely it broke about seven hundred laws to advertise with photos taken in, oh, 1972.

"I rented, and paid for, the house depicted on the website," she said slowly and distinctly, "and that is what I expect to have."

"And it is."

"No, it's not. The condition of the house is completely unacceptable. There must be something else available."

"There sure isn't. Every other house on the island—as well as every other beach in the area—has been booked for months. I sure am sorry Paradise Lost isn't all you wanted it to be, but there's no need for anything fancy here—life on the island is real casual. Different from what you're accustomed to, I reckon. Manhattan this is not."

Jamie doubted truer words had ever been spoken in the entire history of mankind. She could actually feel steam seeping from her ears. "You're telling me there's nothing else? *Nothing?*"

"Not a thing," he said cheerfully, as if that was fabulous news. "And even if there was—which there isn't—I can promise that you'd never find a last-minute, full-summer beach rental for the bargain price you're paying for Paradise Lost. Most houses here rent for a single week for what you're paying for the entire two months."

Jamie closed her eyes. No other accommodations on the is-land. Her Manhattan apartment sublet for the summer. Good Lord, if she didn't have rotten luck, she'd have no luck at all. "So I'm stuck here."

She hadn't realized she'd spoken out loud until Jack re-plied, "Best place in the world to be stuck, if you ask me."

Clearly Jack had never traveled. Anywhere. She drew a long, slow breath. "While remaining in this house for the next two months is not an option, it appears I have little choice but to spend the night. Which means there are two problems that need to be remedied *immediately*. First, there's no power."

"Oh, that's too bad. Paradise Lost has a new owner—Nick Trent bought the place only a few months ago. Could be he didn't pay the electric bill. And you'll need to take that up with him since Paradise Lost isn't actually a Seaside Cove Rentals property. I just let Nick list it on our website as a per-sonal favor."

Un. Freaking. Believable. That probably broke about seven hundred rental laws as well.

"How do I get in touch with this Nick Trent?"

"Shouldn't be too hard as he lives right next door to Para-dise Lost. Name of his place is Southern Comfort. Pretty fit-tin' name."

"Because we're in the South?"

"No, because . . . Well, I don't like to talk out of turn, but when you live in a community with only ninety full-time resi-dents, there are no secrets to be had, so you'll find out quick enough. Southern Comfort is fittin' 'cause it's a brand of whis-key and since Nick Trent took up residence on the island three months ago, he's been known to disappear for days at a time. Word is he goes off on benders. Either that or he's a hit man. Or a CIA agent. Ha, ha, ha. Just funnin' with ya. Nice enough guy, friendly to everybody, but he don't talk much about himself. One of those Men of Mystery types. Nobody's seen him for the past couple days. Most likely drunk as a skunk."

Jamie closed her eyes and pinched the bridge of her nose. *This day has to end. This day has to end . . .*

"If you look out your kitchen window, you can see Southern Comfort. If his truck is in the carport, that means he's home."

Jamie pressed her nose to the kitchen screen and looked across the weed-choked, untrimmed hedges that separated Paradise Lost from Southern Comfort. No truck, and not a single light glowed from any of the windows. Maybe Nick On-a-Bender/Hopefully-Not-a-Hit-Man/Maybe-a-CIA-Agent Trent had forgotten to pay the electric bill there as well.

"It doesn't look like he's home," Jamie reported.

"Could be he's at the Shrimp Festival over at Breezes Beach. It's a huge event around these parts—folks come from all over to attend. And it's especially big this year because it's the *Centennial* Shrimp Festival. In fact, I'll be heading that way as soon as we get off the phone."

"'Course the Shrimp Festival can't hold a candle to Seaside Cove's annual Clam Festival at the end of August," he continued in that unhurried drawl that in spite of its leisurely pace somehow didn't allow her to get a word in edgewise. "It is a sight to behold—a parade through town, arts and crafts, music at the pier, bonfires on the beach, and the best food you've ever tasted. My wife, Cecelia, makes a hot clam dip that could charm the scales off a fish. You have any good clam recipes, Miss Jamie?"

"Not really. About the power—"

"Oh, right. Could be it got knocked out by the storm that blew through last night. Have you checked the circuit breakers?"

"No."

"Bless your heart. You should do that. Do you know what a breaker panel box looks like? My Cecelia wouldn't know one if it jumped up and bit her in the butt. Bless her heart."

Hmmm . . . didn't sound like having one's heart blessed was necessarily a good thing. In fact, it pretty much sounded like it was interchangeable with "you're a dipshit." "Yes, I know what a panel box looks like. Where is it?"

"In the storage closet in the carport. The same key that unlocked the house opens the door."

"I'll check it. The other immediate problem is the smell in the house."

"Smell? Now that's just impossible. While Paradise Lost may be a bit run-down and worn, I can promise you it's clean. The Happy Housekeeping service was there just a few days ago and they're top notch."

"Well, the Happy Housekeepers must have missed something because the entire place stinks like fish."

Jack chuckled. "Well, you *are* at the beach, Miss Jamie. I reckon it smells like car exhaust in New York City, but not around here. Around here stuff smells fishy."

"Fishy is one thing. *Dead* fishy is quite another."

"Aw, it's probably just a forgotten clam. Seagulls drop clams on the roofs all the time to crack them open. Or could be something one of the island cats dragged onto the carport."

"Island cats?"

"Yes, ma'am. There're several colonies of feral cats on the island. Real good at keepin' down the mouse population."

"Who takes care of them? Who feeds them?"

"They take care of themselves, but they're monitored by a group of colony caretakers. Dorothy Ernst—she lives right across the street from Paradise Lost in Beach Music—heads up the Cat Colony Committee—she can tell you all about it. They trap any new ferals to the area and bring them to Doc Weston on the mainland, who gives them their shots and spays and ear-tips 'em for identification purposes for free. Then they're released back here at the beach. You'll see them wandering around like they own the place. As for feedin' them, well, just about everybody on the island leaves out food for them. Believe me, they never go hungry.

"But about the smell," he continued, "you'll need to take that up with Nick as well. Lucky for you, Milton's General Store and Bait Shop on the corner sells air freshener. They've got one called Blueberry Muffin that'll make the place smell like you've been baking all day. We use it in the rental homes all the time."

Yeah, lucky for me. 'Cause dead clam blueberry muffin is my favorite smell. "I'm afraid that's not good enough—"

"'Course, Milton's is closed up for the next two days, so you'll need to head to the Piggly Wiggly 'bout ten miles down Route 4 for any supplies between now and then."

"Excuse me?"

"Luther Milton, the general store's owner, is recuperating from gall bladder surgery and closed the store for a few days. But don't you fret, Miss Jamie, Nick'll be back soon. Paradise Lost may not be fancy, but I predict you're gonna fall in love with the place. It's sure to grow on you."

Yeah. Like mold on cheese. Before she could state that opinion, Jack said, "Try the circuit breaker—that's most likely the problem. If not, there's sure to be emergency candles and a flashlight in the house. No need to worry about air-conditioning—far as I know Paradise Lost doesn't have any. So just do what the locals do—open the windows and enjoy the ocean breezes. That'll air the place out and take care of your fish smell problem, too."

Had he just said no air-conditioning? Holy Freakin' Heat Wave. She was going to die here. In the dead clam inferno. "But—"

"Oh, and just in case you were planning a walk on the beach, don't go too far. Another frog strangler like the one last night is fixin' to blow through in the next little bit."

"Frog strangler?"

Jack chuckled. "A sudden, heavy rain—comes down so fast the frogs can't escape."

Jamie didn't particularly fancy herself a girly girl, but *yuck*. An image of hundreds of poor, struggling frogs being strangled by a wall of rainwater flashed through her mind. Damn it, who thought up that crappy expression? She'd probably have nightmares. "Uh, thanks for the warning."

"My pleasure. Oh, and a word to the wise—you might want to steer clear of your neighbor on the other side, Melvin Tibbs."

"Why? Is he an ax murderer?" Which would be just her luck.

"No. At least not that I know of. Ha, ha, ha. But he's as ornery and grumpy as they come."

Swell. But grumpy Melvin wasn't going to be a problem because she wouldn't be staying more than one night.

"Oops, the wife is callin'," said Jack. "I gotta get a move on. Welcome to Seaside Cove, Miss Jamie. There's no other place like it in the world."

Uh-huh. She didn't doubt that for a New York minute.

Chapter 2

After ending the call with Jack, Jamie slipped her phone back in her pocket, drew a deep breath, then headed toward the door. Since she was stuck in Casa Stinko for the night, there was a lot to do, and she made a mental list as she carefully maneuvered her way down the rickety stairs. Drag up the rest of her luggage she'd left on the driveway before the frog strangler (ewww!) hit. Check the circuit breakers—although she apparently didn't need to rush to do so because if that wasn't the problem, then she was apparently shit out of luck.

What else? Oh, yeah. Find emergency candles and flashlight. Locate source of fishy stench—not something she was looking forward to. Dispose of source of fishy scent—again, not looking forward to. Set up food, water, and a makeshift litter box for Cupcake since the general store was closed due to gall bladder surgery. Good thing there was lots of beach sand around here. Good Lord. Could this get any worse?

As if to answer her question, she heard an ominous rumble of thunder. "Perfect. Just freakin' perfect."

She heaved her three overweight suitcases—jeez, had she

packed anvils in them?—over the gaping hole caused by the two missing steps, up the stairs, and abandoned them in the kitchen. Grabbing the keys, she trotted down the steps again and crossed the carport to the storage closet door. At first the key didn't want to cooperate, then neither did the door. Sweaty, frustrated, and pretty much ready to scream, Jamie threw all her weight against the wooden panel. It burst open and only by grabbing the rusty knob did she manage not to fall on her face.

"'Cause busting my nose would have been the rotten cherry on this moldy piece of pie," she muttered. She picked her way around a washer and dryer of dubious workability, then over a pile of faded plastic beach pails and deflated inner tubes to reach the circuit breaker panel. The rusted metal door—was everything rusty around here?—squeaked in protest when she opened it. She leaned closer and saw that all the light switches as well as those for the stove and fridge had been tripped. Obviously last night's storm, rather than an unpaid electric bill, was the culprit. She flipped them all to the on position, then closed the panel.

After locking the storage room door, she hiked up the stairs again. "All these damn stairs better result in buns of titanium," she grumbled. She entered the kitchen, nearly gagging at the strong stink, and hit the light switch. The ancient fluorescent fixture in the ceiling hummed, sputtered, and blinked for several seconds, then flooded the room with harsh light that didn't do it any favors.

"Whoa, you are a lady best seen only in the dark," she murmured, running a fingertip over the worn countertop. She halted when she came to the sink, which, the light now revealed, held the source of the horrible stink.

A mesh bag filled with clams.

Very *dead* clams.

Jamie closed her eyes. "My life sucks."

A low growl of thunder sounded, making it official. Her life sucked and even the heavens agreed.

Doing her best to breathe through her mouth, she quickly searched the kitchen cabinets. The first one, in addition to assorted pots and pans, yielded three rusty cans of pork and beans that no doubt carried botulism. "Good to have on hand in case I feel the need to off myself," she muttered. Or someone else. Like Nick Trent.

She continued searching, finding cutlery, glasses, dishes, a roll of paper towels that had clearly gotten wet at one point, a yellowed roll of masking tape, three candles and a box of matches—that only contained two matches—a map of North Carolina dated 1962 (probably the same year those pork and beans came into the house), a phone book from 1978, three sand-encrusted pennies, and in the last cabinet, a stash of plastic grocery bags bearing the face of a smiling pig and the words Piggly Wiggly.

"At last *something* is going right," she said, pulling out a handful of bags. She tripled up three bags, shoved her hand inside, then used her free hand and her teeth to tie the handles at her wrist to fashion a makeshift glove. Grabbing a few more bags in which to put the clams and she moved to the sink and grabbed the mesh bag.

Oh. Dear. God.

Lifting the dripping bag released a whole new level of stench. Holding her breath, Jamie placed the mess inside several Piggly Wiggly bags and quickly turned on the faucet to rinse the sink. With her lungs starting to protest, she clutched the stinking bag of clams and hotfooted it across the kitchen, out the door, and down the stairs. She looked frantically about for the trash bin and nearly wept with relief when she found it on the far side of the house. She lifted the top, tossed in the offending bag and her makeshift glove, slammed down the lid, then sucked in a massive breath.

"Done," she gasped.

Now it was time to see to Cupcake, which meant fashioning a temporary litter box. Which meant a quick trip to the beach for sand. After grabbing two of the beach pails from the storage room, she headed down the block and across the street, toward the narrow pathway marked by a sign that read Beach Access.

The sandy path led between two oceanfront homes, one named Starfish, the other bearing a plaque proclaiming Sunset Delight. The muted sounds of laughter and music greeted her, growing louder as she neared the rear of the houses. The scent of grilling meat filled her head and she pressed her hand to her stomach. God, did that smell good. And damn, she suddenly realized she was hungry. Good thing she'd packed some snacks, although a hamburger sounded like heaven, especially since for the past week, after her life had gone down the crapper, the bulk of her nutrition had come in the form of brownies, Doritos, her two favorite guys Ben and Jerry, and an absolute shitload of peanut M&M's. Was there an M&M rehab? Probably she needed to look into that.

When she reached the rear of the houses, she saw that each had a party in progress. Both yards, as well as the huge wraparound decks, were filled with kids and adults. Starfish's yard had a built-in pool, where a raucous game of water volleyball was taking place. At least a dozen adults and several kids smiled and waved at her, greetings she returned. Shouts of "Mom—watch this!" and "Throw the Frisbee here, Grandpa!" tugged her lips into a wistful smile. A lump of emotion lodged in her throat as memories of childhood summer days spent with her mom and dad and Laurel flashed through her mind.

An image of her handsome, smiling father rose behind Jamie's eyes, and for several seconds it felt as if her chest caved in. In spite of the three years since the heart attack had ripped him away, there were times, like now, seeing a dad swinging his little girl up in his arms, the child squealing with delight, when the pain simply seized her, stealing her breath.

She forced her gaze from the father-daughter pair and continued. The pathway turned from sandy path to weathered boardwalk as she approached the rise of vegetation-covered dunes that she knew from the Internet site provided a natural barrier between the ocean side of the island and the marsh side. The sounds of the parties faded, replaced by the low swooshing hum of the ocean. She came over the rise and caught her breath at the endless stretch of dark blue water.

"Wow. Just . . . wow," she whispered. *This* is why she'd come here. For the peace and soul-healing serenity she'd always felt when looking at the ocean. It was the first place she'd gone after her father's funeral—just a one-day escape to Long Island—but staring at the endless stretch of water, listening to waves crashing, had somehow helped her, soothed her.

She hadn't been to the ocean since that day. Life and work

had consumed her time, gotten in the way of allowing her the solitude her soul sometimes craved. When she'd decided to get away from New York, to recharge her badly depleted spirit and reevaluate her life, there hadn't been any question of where she'd go. The beach. Thus began her Internet search for a summer rental—not easy to come by in late June, and damn near impossible since price was a factor. Anywhere on Long Island or the Jersey Shore had been financially out of the question. She'd finally, after hours of Internet searching, happened upon Seaside Cove.

Based on the bargain price, she'd suspected the accommodations might be a *little* rustic, but the deal had been too good to pass up. She was desperate to leave New York, and on a budget, beggars couldn't be choosers. Besides, how bad could any accommodations at the beach be?

As she'd found out, pretty bad.

No doubt about it, Paradise Lost definitely wasn't all she'd hoped for, but as she stared out at the long strands of waves breaking with gentle crashes, the white foamed water rushing up the wet sand trying to dampen the feet of a group of sandpipers that were much too quick, a sense of calm suffused her. She walked down the half dozen steps leading to the beach and slipped off her sandals. She groaned with delight at the sensation of her toes sinking into the soft, white sand, still warm from a day of sunshine. As she headed toward the water, she drank in the azure sky streaked with the first mauve ribbons of what promised to be a spectacular sunset.

Several dozen people still lingered, sitting in sand chairs, tossing balls to kids and dogs. A trio of youngsters built a sand castle, while a couple walked hand in hand toward the pier that jutted into the surf a half mile down the beach.

Jamie took a few minutes to stick her feet in the water and grinned. Just enough chill to make it refreshing. She couldn't wait to hit the waves tomorrow.

Her cell phone buzzed and with a sigh she pulled it out and looked at the caller ID. Her trepidation immediately faded when she read Kate Moore. Hearing from her best friend was always welcome.

"How's it going?" Jamie asked, twisting her feet to bury her toes in the cool, wet sand.

"Exactly what I called you to find out. How's the beach?"

"The beach is . . . perfect. Everything else, not so much."

"Uh-oh. Have Maggie and Patrick been calling you?"

Jamie huffed out a humorless laugh. "What are you, clairvoyant?"

"No, just your BFF. Tell me what's going on. You sound tired."

"I am." With the water washing over her feet, Jamie filled Kate in on her adventures thus far since arriving at Paradise Lost, concluding with, "So for now all I can do is wait until this Nick Trent gets home from his latest bender, and when he does, believe me, he's going to get an earful."

"Wow . . . I don't know whether to laugh or cry for you. I can just picture you with that bag of dead clams." Kate chuckled, then coughed to disguise the sound. "Laughing with you, kiddo, not at you."

"Uh-huh. Except I'm not laughing."

"You will—eventually."

"Maybe. But it's not funny now. Especially when faced with deciding whether or not to stay in the very non-paradisey Paradise Lost for the next two months." Jamie sighed. "With my apartment sublet, I don't really have much choice. At least not one that wouldn't break my budget."

"If you come back to New York, you know you're welcome to stay with Ben and me."

Jamie's heart cinched with love and gratitude. "That's very sweet and generous, and just like you, but you're a newlywed and need a houseguest for two months like you need a hole in your head." Her gaze settled on a pair of seagulls swooping toward the water, then soaring upward, wings spread, hovering in the breeze against a backdrop of the brilliant sky. "And even though Paradise Lost is a disaster, the beach is really great."

"Not that I'm backpedaling on my invite—which remains open," Kate said, "but the beach is also seven hundred miles away from New York—which, crappy house or not, is a huge point in its favor."

"True." Jamie blew out a sigh. "I don't want to even think about going back to the city. Not yet." A searing pain that felt like a knife plunging into her back hit Jamie between her shoulder blades. Tears pushed behind her eyes and she furiously blinked them back. Damn it, she refused to cry any more.

"I don't blame you," Kate said quietly. "And I know I've already told you this, but it bears repeating—especially since I hear those tears in your voice. I'm really proud of you, Jamie, for taking this time for yourself, especially given all the pressure your mom and everyone else at Newman's put on you to stay. You weren't just in a rut, you were in a veritable abyss. And now you're climbing out. You stuck to your guns, drew a line in the sand, and made a change. One that I think will be really good for you, even though it's difficult right now."

"Thanks. I needed that." Jamie pulled her feet from the sand and began walking slowly toward the pier. "And that's what this whole trip to Seaside Cove is all about—climbing out of that deep hole. Renewing, recharging, regrouping. Figuring out what *I* want. In a place where nothing's familiar. Where I don't know anyone, and no one knows me or about the humiliating crapfest my life had become. And best of all, where I'm not responsible for anyone other than myself. No demands, no stress, no pressure. Ha. When's the last time *that* happened?"

"Junior high maybe?" Kate suggested.

"That's about right. Paradise Lost is looking better and better."

"Exactly. The house might stink—"

"—literally," broke in Jamie with a grimace.

"But you don't have the stress of working every day with Laurel. Getting away from that toxic situation and relationship is the best gift you could possibly give yourself."

Jamie's throat tightened. "I know . . . but that doesn't mean Laurel's betrayal still doesn't hurt. And majorly piss me off. For cryin' out loud, rule number one of the Girl Code clearly states that ex-boyfriends are off limits—therefore, it should be obvious that *current* boyfriends are *really* off limits. *Especially* to one's own sister!"

"Absolutely," Kate agreed. "Bee-yotch should be beaten with her damn designer shoes."

"Then there's the other side of that extremely tarnished coin—not only did Raymond cheat on me with my sister, but with my *older* sister. Seriously, how many women get dumped for an *older* woman? And not just a month or two older, but *eight years*! Talk about insult to injury." Oh, yeah, she'd definitely reached a new low rung on the self-esteem ladder there.

"Just goes to show you what a shithead he is," Kate said. "She and Raymond deserve each other."

Jamie knew it. Yet the mention of Raymond's name still pissed her off, although at this point she wasn't certain if she was more angry at him for cheating on her, or at herself for so badly misjudging his character.

"Uh-oh," said Kate. "You've gotten very quiet, which can't be good. Repeat after me: Raymond's a shithead. Go on—say it."

A tired laugh escaped Jamie. "Raymond's a shithead," she repeated dutifully. Then she sighed. Over the past week she'd spent countless hours trying to figure out how she could have been so wrong about him, have allowed herself to fall in love with someone so lacking in integrity. Had the signs been there and she'd just ignored them? Had she really loved him—or had her head been turned by his wealthy lifestyle? And if so, what did that say about her?

Nothing she liked, that's for sure.

She'd always believed herself a fairly astute judge of people, but she'd really missed the mark with Raymond. Just more questions to ponder on this Seaside Cove Road to Rediscovery. In the meanwhile, maybe someday she wouldn't feel like whacking Raymond and Laurel upside their cheating heads with her cat carrier, but today was not that day.

"Good girl," Kate said. "Repeat as needed. And don't forget—the best way to get over a man is to get under a new one."

Jamie expelled a humorless sound. "I want another man like I want a flea infestation."

"I'm talking about indulging in a summer fling—nothing serious."

"Flings aren't my style."

"I know, but doing things that aren't your normal style is what this trip is all about."

"True. But I want to do them *alone*. I came here to get *away* from people."

"Just keep an open mind. Now tell me, seriously, how are you feeling?"

Jamie stopped walking and stared out at the waves. "I don't really know. Part of me feels empowered—because I took action and didn't cave to the pressure everyone, except you, put on me not to come here. That part is determined to make a change, to rediscover who I am and what I really want. Yet another part of me feels . . . lost. For the first time in years, my every waking minute isn't scheduled. My time is my own with no family drama or job stress, and as great as that is in theory, the reality is that I feel as if I'm dangling over a cliff without a safety net."

"I think it's the smartest thing you've ever done. Jamie, I've known you for twelve years, and in all that time you've always lived for other people. Your dad wanted you to work at Newman's, so you did. Since he died, you've given your life to that place to keep his dream alive. Your mom leans on you like a broken-down barn door, and you let her. You've picked up the slack for Laurel more times than I can count, especially with Heather. How your sister ended up with such a great kid is a mystery. Actually, it's not—it's undoubtedly because Heather spends so much time with you. You're always taking care of her—"

"I don't 'take care' of Heather—she's fourteen. I enjoy being with her."

"And she's very lucky that you do. You took a really brave, important step by leaving New York. Stop second-guessing yourself. The city, Newman's, your mom, Laurel, Heather—none of them are going anywhere. They'll still all be here at the end of the summer when you come home."

"This is why you're such a great nurse," Jamie said with a watery laugh. "You're very good at fixing broken spirits."

"You're not broken."

Jamie nodded. "You're right. I'm not. Just a little bruised. Thanks for the pep talk, Coach."

"Anytime. Now enjoy the beach. And that seven-hundred-mile buffer. And let me know what's going on. Love you."

"Love you, too. Bye."

Jamie slipped the phone back in her pocket, closed her eyes, and drew in a lungful of sea-scented air. "Everything's going to be okay." Her whispered words floated away on the salty breeze. Surely if she said them enough, they'd become true.

Recalling the main reason for her walk to the beach, she turned around. When she was once again in the soft, dry sand, she filled up the two plastic pails she'd brought, slipped on her sandals, then made her way back to Paradise Lost. She'd just made that doozy of a first step when a fat raindrop plopped on her arm. "The frog strangler cometh," she said and gave herself a mental high five for her perfect timing.

She entered the kitchen and set the pails of sand on the counter. The dead clam stink lingered, but at least it was no longer in the make-your-eyes-water stage. She rooted around in the lower cabinets and found a disposable foil roasting pan. It sported a few dents and the bottom was blackened from use, but it would do.

After filling the roasting pan with sand, she set it out on the screened porch, then went in search of Cupcake. Her pet was still cleaning herself on the Mets bedspread, working on her fluffy tail. Jamie scooped her up and nuzzled her cheek into Cupcake's soft fur. "You feeling better, baby?"

Cupcake graced her with a halfhearted purr, cat-speak for she *might* someday forgive Jamie for the plethora of indignities she'd suffered this day, but only if she was lavished with pampering and treats.

Jamie brought Cupcake to the screened porch and set her beside the roasting pan. "Here's your potty."

Cupcake blinked at the makeshift litter box, then looked up at Jamie with an expression that so clearly screamed, *WTF?* Jamie had to laugh. "Hey, I've been told that things are very casual here at the beach, and believe me, my bathroom isn't much better. It's the best I can do on short notice."

Leaving Cupcake to check out her facilities in private, Jamie reentered the house and headed for the kitchen. She opened the fridge and found it empty, but at least the interior was cooling off. When she checked the freezer, she discovered it was also empty—except for a sealed bottle of vodka. Finally, something useful in this joint.

Time to tackle the dead clam smell. Since she hadn't packed air freshener, she dug out her toiletries bag, then liberally sprayed the entire cottage with her favorite after-shower body spray. She was still spritzing the kitchen when Cupcake sauntered in.

"Everything come out okay?" Jamie asked. She crouched down, and after a few seconds of cat internal debating, Cupcake decided to bestow upon Jamie the honor of stroking her long white fur.

"See? That wasn't so bad."

Cupcake's expression indicated that, yes, it really was that bad.

"You'll feel better after a nice long nap. And don't be thinking you're going to collect that fifty bucks," Jamie added, scratching between Cupcake's ears. "I had to haul that dead clam ickiness down to the trash myself. But I refuse to be beaten. In fact, I'm thinking things might be looking up, Cupcake. The room smells more like vanilla sugar cookies than dead clam"—she drew a deep breath and her eyes crossed—"sort of—and the beach is fabulous. You've got food, water, and a place to do your business, there's a bag of peanut M&M's and a bottle of Diet Coke in my purse—not to mention a bottle of vodka in the freezer. And let us not forget that a beautiful seven hundred miles lie between us and New York. Yup, things are looking up."

A flash of lightning illuminated the interior of the house, followed immediately by a deafening boom of thunder that seemed to shake the house on its stilts. As was her habit during thunderstorms, Cupcake slunk off and bellied her way under the sofa.

More lightning and thunder crackled, this time followed by the sound of rain. "Things could definitely be worse," Jamie said to the tip of Cupcake's twitching tail visible from beneath the sofa. "At least we have a roof over our heads. And a good thing, too. It's really starting to come down hard."

Deciding to celebrate her small victory in style, she dug through her purse and pulled out the bag of peanut M&M's. Just as she ripped it open, a wet drop plopped on the back of her hand. Before she could react, another plopped on her head. She looked up. A huge water stain marked the kitchen ceiling. The center of the stain contained a growing wet spot. Another drop hit her chin, followed by several more that bombed her nose and forehead. Well, damn. They might have a roof over their heads, but a friggin' leaky roof it was. A howl of frustration rose in her throat, one she barely managed to swallow. Instead of screaming she closed her eyes, counted to ten, then slowly walked to the fridge—doing her damnedest to ignore the raindrops falling on her head. She pulled open the freezer section and slid out the bottle of vodka. Moving to the living area, she grabbed one of the folding chairs and positioned it so she could see the dark outline of Southern Comfort. Another raindrop landed on her head, but she was beyond caring. She sat, opened the vodka, took a delicate sip, then narrowed her eyes.

And waited for Nick Trent to return.

Chapter 3

The sound of pounding penetrated Nick Trent's comalike sleep. He pried open one eye and groaned when a shaft of sunlight stabbed his pupil. Damn. He'd forgotten to close the blinds again. How was anybody supposed to get any sleep around here? And who the hell was making all that racket?

He closed his eye, but the pounding continued, along with the added annoyance of someone ringing his doorbell. Add to that the dog's incessant barking, and it was a cocktail of headache-inducing cacophony loud enough to shake his brain inside his skull. He might have just slapped a pillow over his head, but damn it, now that he was awake—sort of—he'd at least have to quiet down the dog, who otherwise would bark nonstop until Christmas.

With a growl of annoyance, he pushed himself into a sitting position and stared with sleep-bleary eyes at the bedside clock. Seven twenty-five? *A.M.?* Jesus. He'd only crawled into bed less than two hours ago. No wonder he felt as if a truck had hit him. He glanced down and squinted. He still wore his jeans from last night—unbuttoned and unzipped. His Polo shirt, socks, and Reeboks rested in an untidy heap on the floor near his bare feet.

With an effort, he shoved himself to his feet, gave his fly a halfhearted yank, and made his way toward the door, wincing at the pounding and ringing and barking. Christ. That was one of the disadvantages of living in such a small community—everyone knew each other and there didn't seem to be any "you don't knock on your neighbor's door at the crack of dawn" boundaries. His last early-morning caller had been just a few days ago. Dorothy Ernst from across the street had wanted to know if she could borrow some half-and-half for her coffee.

Even though Dorothy had awakened him and the dog from a dead sleep—although with not nearly the noise that this morning's visitor was using—his annoyance had evaporated at the sight of her, tiny in stature and big on smiles that showed off sparkling dentures and creased seven decades worth of wrinkles around her twinkling eyes. She'd reminded him of a sweet, chipper bird, peering at him over her bifocals, another pair resting on her poof of snowy white hair—'cause she always needed an extra pair—and he'd felt like a total heel telling her he didn't have any half-and-half. The closest thing his fridge yielded was a quart of low-fat milk that had plopped in thick lumps into Dorothy's cup while filling the kitchen with a foul, sour stench. She'd laughed and said, "Typical bachelor," then left, her lime green rubber flip-flops thwapping against her heels. Later that afternoon Dorothy had stopped by again upon her return from the grocery store to give him a container of half-and-half—along with a chicken and rice casserole she'd baked.

And that was one of the huge advantages to living in such a small community.

The banging and ringing and barking continued until he entered the kitchen. He whistled to his chocolate Lab, who immediately turned and continued to bark, letting him know that someone was at the door.

Like with the pounding and ringing he hadn't figured that out.

"Godiva, sit," Nick said, simultaneously giving her the signal to stop barking.

Godiva's butt hit the floor—for a nanosecond—then she hurled herself at Nick in a tail-wagging, tongue-lolling frenzy of doggie adoration. Clearly more time was needed on her obedience lessons, but he found it impossible to be annoyed at a creature that loved him so profoundly and unconditionally.

"Good girl," he said, scratching behind her dark brown ears while Godiva slathered his forearm with kisses. He tapped her rump and pointed to the floor. "Lay. Stay."

This time Godiva obeyed, stretching out onto her belly, but her body quivered with excitement, her tail sweeping across the kitchen floor while pitiful whines emitted from her throat.

The banging and ringing had continued unabated, and with a growl of impatience, Nick yanked open the door. And stared. At an unfamiliar woman he judged to be in her mid-twenties who sported a scowl he bet matched his own.

"It's about time you answered the door," she said.

His scowl deepened. He didn't know who she was or what she was selling, but all that banging and now her attitude had definitely gotten him up on the wrong side of the bed. "I was asleep."

Her gaze skimmed over him and he could almost hear her cataloging as she went: *bad case of bed head, bleary eyes, three-day stubble, no shirt, wrinkled jeans, missing shoes.* He did notice that she lingered for several seconds on his unbuttoned Levi's. When her gaze again met his, pink stained her cheeks. "Wow, you really were on a bender."

What the hell? "Really? Well, you don't look so hot, either, whoever you are." Actually, that wasn't precisely true. In fact, she looked pretty damn good. Sure her honey-colored hair sported a finger-in-the-light-socket look, and her white tank top and tan pants that hit her midcalf looked as if she'd slept in them—something he could hardly throw stones at—but her eyes were gorgeous. They reminded him of caramel sprinkled with dark chocolate. Probably they'd be even prettier if they weren't filled with an expression that made it clear she'd like to thump him upside his head.

Even her thundercloud frown couldn't hide the fact that she was pretty damn cute, any more than those wrinkly clothes masked the fact that she had more curves on her than a black-diamond ski run. And those dimples flanking her full lips didn't hurt, either. But in his present mood, he didn't really give a damn how cute or curvy she might be.

At least not much.

He crossed his arms over his bare chest and glared at her. "*I've* been on a bender? Hey, black pot—kettle calling. You reek of vodka." Okay, maybe *reek* was too strong a word— but he definitely smelled a trace of vodka—and he damn well knew what it smelled like. But he also caught a whiff of something kinda good, something sweet he couldn't quite put his finger on.

"That's because I slept in a chair."

"Personally I find it pretty difficult to get good rest on a bar stool, but whatever floats your boat."

"Not a bar stool—a *chair*." Her tone indicated she thought he was three years old, which did nothing to soothe his annoyance. "A *folding* chair. Next door. At Paradise Lost. And let me tell you, it is really, really lost."

"Ah—so you're the renter."

"Yes. And you're the owner. I thought this place was supposed to ooze Southern hospitality."

"I'm not from the South."

"I'm picking up on that."

"Good. You want hospitality? Here it is: Welcome to Seaside Cove. Now go away and come back at a more reasonable hour. Like noon."

He made to close the door, but she slapped her palm against the wooden panel and wedged her curvy self in the opening. "I'm afraid not. We need to discuss this right now. After we've done so, believe me, I'll be more than happy to go away and leave you alone." She looked past him. "Is your dog friendly?"

He glanced over his shoulder at Godiva, who was inching her way on her belly toward them, tail still swishing, tongue still lolling, her soft brown eyes filled with curiosity about this new person she was clearly dying to sniff. If *Nick* had been feeling friendly, he would have assured her that the only thing she had to fear from Godiva was getting licked to death.

Since he was feeling particularly *un*friendly, he said, "She's unpredictable." Right—you never knew if you'd get a Godiva kiss on your arm or your leg or your neck. "Especially when she hasn't had her breakfast. So you'd better make this quick."

The door-pounding, bell-ringing renter didn't look completely convinced that Godiva might pose a threat, no doubt because Godiva's hopeful eyes and wagging tail and happy little whines practically screamed, *I love you! Who are you? I love you! If I don't lick you and smell you, I'll just die! You're my new best friend! Did I mention that I love you?*

She cleared her throat, then returned her attention to Nick. "The fact that you're the owner—that's why I'm here. To discuss the deplorable condition of your rental property."

An invisible lightbulb went off over Nick's head as understanding seeped into his sluggish brain. Obviously Princess Vodka here wasn't down with the rustic conditions. He should have known the renter would be someone who didn't understand what "as is" meant. "There's nothing deplorable about Paradise Lost. You didn't have to sleep in a chair—there are beds you know."

"Uh-huh. But none that look overly comfortable."

"Maybe not, but they're better than sleeping on a folding chair."

"Even after spending the night on a folding chair, I'm not necessarily convinced of that. Besides, I was looking out the window, waiting for you to come home."

Oh, great. She was not only a door-pounding, bell-ringing whiner, but a stalker as well. "I take it the accommodations aren't to your liking."

"That's putting it mildly. Those two missing bottom steps are a broken leg waiting to happen. Are you *looking* for a lawsuit?"

His gaze dropped to her legs, which looked long and curvy and definitely not broken. "Of course not—"

"And then there's the leaky roof. Water plopped on my head all night. No matter where I moved that folding chair, the damn drip seemed to follow. I'm lucky the ceiling didn't cave in on me. The furniture looks like something you picked up on the side of the road, the entire place doesn't look like it's been painted since the turn of the century, there's no dishwasher or air conditioner, and some idiot left a bag of clams in the sink."

Clams . . . Nick's memory kicked in. He'd stopped at Paradise Lost three days ago on his way home from his most successful clamming expedition yet and set down his catch while he'd fixed the dripping bathroom faucet. He'd put them in the fridge . . . hadn't he? Damn—had he left them in the sink? He'd couldn't recall, and he'd completely forgotten about them until just now. But thinking about the fridge suddenly reminded him about the bottle he'd left in the freezer—

"You drank my vodka," he accused, his voice filled with righteous indignation.

She looked at him as if he'd grown a third eye in the middle of his forehead. "Right after I tossed your clams. Believe me, I needed a drink."

"You *threw away* my clams?" Jesus. She really was the renter from hell. "Why on earth would you do that?"

For several seconds she didn't speak—just sawed her jaw back and forth as if she was chewing glass. Then she drew a deep breath, which she released very slowly, scenting the air between them with a trace of vodka and . . . peanuts? . . . and said through gritted teeth, "Because they were *dead*. And they stunk bad enough to make my *eyes water*." Each sentence grew in volume and added another layer of color to her cheeks. "And they were *dripping* that foul stench *everywhere*. It was *disgusting*. And in spite of wrapping my hands in *three* Piggly Wiggly bags, I may *never* get the *smell off me*."

Wow. No doubt about it, this was one pissed-off woman. She looked like Vesuvius about to blow. In fact, there might even be steam wisping from her ears. Normally he was smart enough to step away from any female with murder in her eyes, but he wasn't feeling particularly brilliant this morning. Especially toward a woman who was a clam murderer.

"Look, whatever your name is—"

"Jamie Newman. How is it that you don't even know the name of the person you rented your rundown, crappy shack to?"

Okay, curvy and cute or not, this chick was stomping on his last nerve. Just as she'd done, he drew a calming breath, then continued, "Look, Jamie, I'm tired, cranky, sleep deprived, and in need of an IV drip of caffeine—"

"Well, that's what happens when you go off on a three-day bender," she said without a lick of sympathy in her tone.

"What makes you think I was off on a bender?"

"Word gets around quick in a town this size. Are you saying you weren't?"

"I can't see how that's any of your business. Those clams, however, were *my* business. It took me hours to rake them, and they were fresh from the water when I put them in the fridge." At least he *thought* he'd put them in the fridge. "Why did you kill them?"

"*I* didn't kill them. They were dead when I arrived. And they weren't in the *fridge*, they were in the *sink*. Do you have any idea what dead clams smell like?"

In spite of his annoyance, he had to concede that she had a point—which only irked him further. That, and the fact that he'd apparently not put his catch in the refrigerator at all. "Yeah, I do." He cut his gaze toward Godiva, who'd bellied forward so her front paw now rested on his bare foot. "Godiva found one on the beach last week and rolled herself all over it in ecstasy. She thought she smelled swell, but it was gag worthy—and since that was from just one clam, I can imagine an entire bagful really reeked. So, sorry about that—my bad."

She appeared unimpressed with his apology and merely raised her brows. "You named your dog *Godiva*?"

Godiva woofed once and licked her chops at the sound of her name. "She's a chocolate Lab," Nick said. "And I like chocolate. You got a problem with that?" Yeah, 'cause if she did, he'd sic Godiva on her and Jamie Pain-in-the-Neck Newman would find herself slathered in doggie kisses.

Instead of answering his question, she asked, "Are you sober?"

"Are *you*?" he countered.

She blinked. "Of course. Why would you think I wasn't?"

"By your own admission, you stole my vodka and tossed back a few."

"I didn't steal it. It was in my freezer—which, by the way, wasn't even working, due to a storm the night before I arrived, until I flipped the breaker switch. You're welcome."

"Since I own the place, it's *my* freezer, and therefore *my* vodka."

"Well, then I'll be sure to see that your property is returned to you as soon as possible. In the meantime, I'm stuck here for now and I want to know, for starters, when you plan to fix the steps and the leaky roof."

"They're on my list of things to do."

"Terrific. When? Because before I arrived would have been great."

"You know, you're really demanding for someone who rented the place 'as is.' You knew up front it wasn't a Ritz Carlton, and that repairs would be ongoing during your stay."

A frown puckered her brow. "What are you talking about 'as is'? And what do you mean 'ongoing repairs'?"

"Did you *read* the rental agreement? All the terms were in there."

Her frown deepened. "Of course I read the rental agreement and I assure you there was nothing that mentioned the poor condition of the house, the words 'as is,' or 'ongoing' repairs. Nor was any of that mentioned on the Seaside Cove Rentals website."

She pursed her full lips and planted her hands on her hips. "And speaking of the website, you should be ashamed of yourself for so grossly misrepresenting the property there. Those photos must have been taken in 1972."

Now it was Nick's turn to frown. "What photos are you talking about?"

"The ones of Paradise Lost looking all freshly painted and charming and pristine, with decent furniture. With a yard that actually contained grass. And a shower curtain that actually hung from the rod. And a staircase with a full set of steps."

"I don't know what you're talking about. I've never seen any photos like that."

"Really? Well, how lucky that I just happen to have a print-out of the web page featuring them to refresh your apparently alcohol-soaked memory."

"You have a printout? Wow, you sure are anal."

She reached into her back pocket and pulled out a folded piece of printer paper, which she thrust at him. "No, I'm *organized*. And frugal. Which means I don't like wasting money on things that aren't what they're advertised to be."

Nick unfolded the paper and looked at a computer print-out containing half a dozen grainy images of the exterior and interior of a cozy beach cottage. On the last exterior shot, a plaque that appeared brand new hung over the carport, proclaiming the house to be Paradise Lost.

He thrust the paper right back at her. "You Photoshopped those."

"Right—because that's what I am—a photo forger whose fondest dream was to *pretend* that the cottage I rented for the entire summer was livable."

"All I can say is that the photos I e-mailed to Jack Crawford for the website ad were taken only a couple weeks ago—and showed Paradise Lost as she is today—warts and all. I only put the place up for rent at his urging, and he told me it would probably be taken by some crusty fisherman type who just needed a place to flop between boat trips. It never occurred to me some princess would move in for the summer."

Irritation and disbelief were written all over her face. "First of all, I'm *not* a princess. And secondly, warts and all is clearly *not* what was depicted on the website. Nor was there any mention of this 'as is' nonsense."

"That's impossible."

"Are you calling me a *liar*?"

Given the fact that if looks could have chopped off heads, her expression would have decapitated him—and for all he knew maybe she was an ax murderer—he decided a bit of diplomacy might be in order. "I'm saying there's clearly been a misunderstanding."

"Yes, there has. On *your* end. Do you have a computer? Let's check out the website right now."

Nick wanted to check out the website right now like he wanted a bad rash, but since it obviously needed to be done, he might as well get it over with. "We can use my iPhone. I'll get it." He considered closing the door on her while he did so, but a lifetime of good manners drilled into him by his mother had him stepping back and asking, "You want to step inside?"

She hesitated and then shrugged. "All right. Thanks."

She crossed the threshold, stepping around Godiva, who was sprawled on the linoleum floor like a big brown carpet, happily gnawing on a rawhide treat.

"Looks like a bomb landed in here," she commented, her gaze sweeping over the gutted kitchen, empty except for an ancient fridge.

"I'm renovating, making repairs. Putting in a new kitchen."

Her gaze moved into the living area, taking in the doors leading to the bedrooms and the sliding doors that led to the screened porch that ran the length of the front of the house. "This place is laid out the same as Paradise Lost."

"Most of the smaller homes on the island are this same shotgun style. There aren't many of them left—people have bought them just for the land, then torn them down and put up bigger, newer places to take advantage of the summer rental market here. Have a seat," he said, nodding toward one of the two wooden bar stools that stood where the snack bar used to be. "I'll be right back."

He entered his bedroom and, after closing the door behind him, rolled his shoulders and rubbed the back of his neck. Pesky woman. He should have slammed the door in her face. Told her to take a hike. But that printout she'd shown him and her insistence about there being no mention of Paradise Lost's "as is" condition on the rental site had a bad feeling tugging in his gut. He hadn't checked the site after sending Jack Crawford the info and photos. Actually, he'd only agreed to rent the place at Jack's insistence. He liked the Realtor—he reminded Nick of one of his favorite college professors, and he'd figured what the hell? The rental money would come in handy as there were so many repairs he needed to make to both houses. Nick hadn't believed anyone would want to rent Paradise Lost as it was, but Jack had assured him, "If you put it on the website, they will come."

Now where the hell was his phone? During his search he located his laptop. How had it ended up under a pile of laundry? Damned if he knew. It took him another few minutes to hunt up his phone, which he found under another pile of laundry.

Guess it was time to do some laundry.

With the phone gripped in his hand, he opened the bedroom door and stepped into the living area. And halted at the sight of Jamie Newman sitting on the plywood that was currently his kitchen floor, rubbing Godiva's belly. Godiva's hind legs twitched in delight and she was making her "Oh, please God, *never* stop doing that" noises while covering Jamie's elbow in adoring kisses.

"You are just the sweetest thing, aren't you?" Jamie crooned, sending Godiva into a state of complete canine euphoria by scratching behind her ears with one hand while still rubbing her belly with the other.

Nick found himself all but hypnotized by the sight of that rubbing hand . . . stroking, over and over. An image of that small, soft-looking hand stroking *his* belly suddenly popped into his mind and he realized with a slap of annoyance that he'd settled his palm against his own abdomen.

He jerked his hand away as if he'd burned himself. Damn annoying woman. An opinion that was magnified tenfold when she said to Godiva, "How did a sweet baby like you end up with such an annoying, irresponsible doofus?"

"Good news is, Godiva doesn't think I'm an annoying, irresponsible doofus," Nick said, walking into the gutted kitchen. "She doesn't judge people—something you might want to think about. And just FYI—it's not polite to denigrate a man to his own dog."

She gave Godiva a final pat and then stood. "Since you're so big on manners, it's not polite to greet guests with your pants unbuttoned."

"You're not a guest and I didn't invite you, so you're just going to have to deal with what you get when you drag a man out of bed at the crack of dawn."

Chalking up a mental point for himself, he opened the browser on his phone and pulled up the Seaside Cove Rentals website.

"Look under the New Rentals tab," she instructed, leaning in to peer at the screen.

Her bare shoulder brushed his bare arm and a bolt of heat that was surely annoyance shot through him. The faint scent of something delicious wafted up his nose and he found himself turning his head toward her and taking a few discreet sniffs.

Cookies. She smelled like *cookies*. Sweet, delicious, fresh-from-the-oven cookies. His stomach immediately rumbled and he pressed his lips together. Damn it, he *loved* cookies. And double damn it, he was hungry. And suddenly craving cookies. And there wasn't a damn cookie in sight. Except her. Jamie Pain-in-the-Ass Newman.

Who, he realized, had stepped away from him and was regarding him through narrowed eyes. "Did you just smell my hair?"

"Certainly not." He'd smelled . . . the area *around* her hair. Definitely not the same thing. He'd actually wanted to smell her neck, but based on the "eat shit and die" expression shooting from her eyes, that wouldn't have gone over well. But really, if she didn't want guys smelling her, she damn well shouldn't make herself smell like cookies!

His stomach rumbled again, and with a grunt of irritation, he turned his attention back to his phone. He tapped the New Rentals tab, and after some quick scrolling, saw the ad for Paradise Lost. A red banner proclaiming the property No Longer Available! bisected the ad, but it was still easy to see that the same photos Jamie had on her printout were featured on the web page. The bad feeling that had tugged his gut ballooned into a full-fledged *oh, shit* as he read the entire ad.

"Unbelievable," he muttered. As she'd claimed, there wasn't one mention of "as is" or ongoing repairs. And the only photos were those showing Paradise Lost looking like . . . well, paradise.

Crap. It was way too early in the morning for this. And without a cup of coffee in sight. He dragged a weary hand through his hair and met her gaze. "It appears you're right."

She raised her brows. "It *appears* I'm right?"

Great—he now knew what it felt like to have his blood pressure jump twenty points. "If you'd quit being sarcastic, you'd realize I'm attempting to apologize." He had to clamp his lips shut for several seconds to keep himself from adding *you pesky smartass* to the end of his sentence. "I sent Jack recent photos—where he found those other ones, I have no idea. I can't explain why the wording in the ad didn't state the house's condition. It should have, and I can only say I'm sorry it didn't. Clearly there was a miscommunication somewhere along the way between me and Jack. I'll call him later this morning to find out what happened."

He blew out a quick breath, then continued, "But at this point, I can't see that it really matters. Paradise Lost is the way it is. Given that it wasn't properly presented on the website, I can understand you being upset. If you want to leave, I'll fully refund your money."

He watched the expressions flicker across her face—surprise and confusion (obviously she hadn't expected an apology. Ha! Take that Miss Door Pounder), annoyance (no big surprise there), and finally distress.

"I can't leave," she said. "Where would I go?"

"Uh, back where you came from?" he said, unable to keep the note of hope out of his voice.

A look of pure horror came over her face and he suddenly wondered what had motivated her last-minute plan to spend the summer here.

"I can't. I sublet my apartment."

"Maybe you could stay with family?"

He actually saw a shudder shake her. And oh, Christ, were those *tears* filling her eyes? No, please, God, not tears. Jesus, he couldn't possibly deal with girl tears before he'd had coffee.

She blinked several times and he damn near swayed with relief when no tears fell. "Ah, staying with family isn't an option."

Hmmmm. Clearly a story there, but he sure as hell wouldn't be asking about it. Oh, no. He wasn't about to be sucked into her drama. He'd come to Seaside Cove to escape drama—not find it. "Friends? Hotel?"

"I can't impose on anyone for two months," she said, "and I can't afford a hotel for that length of time."

"Well, you could always suck it up, princess, and stay here." The instant the words left his mouth, he wanted to smack himself upside his own head. *What the hell are you saying, dude?* his inner voice yelled. *Let her go! Who needs this prissy princess living next door? Not you. She'll make your life a living hell if she stays.*

"In the cottage of horrors with the raindrops falling on me and the Stairs of Death? Not tempting."

Good. But then his damn conscience kicked him in the ass and he heaved a sigh. Clearly it was the lack of food and caffeine that had him feeling sorry for her. If he didn't get a cup of coffee and some food in him soon, he was going to black out.

"Look," he said, giving in to his sense of fair play, "the weather's supposed to be good for the next couple of days. I'll start work today on the stairs—shouldn't take me more than a few hours to make the repairs. Then I'll start on the roof."

She chewed on her lower lip, drawing his attention to her mouth. Damn, that was one gorgeous mouth. Full, pink lips . . . he was definitely a lip man. He was just contemplating whether those lips would taste like cookies when she said, "Well?"

He forced his gaze up to hers and her expression made it clear he'd dropped the conversational ball. "Well what?"

"You'll have the roof done before it rains again?"

"I can't predict the weather—all I can say is that I'll try."

"And the shower curtain?"

"I'll pick one up, along with the hanging things, when I hit Home Depot."

"There's a Home Depot around here?"

He couldn't recall ever hearing a woman sound so hopeful about a Home Depot. "Yeah. It's about ten miles down Route 4. Next to the Piggly Wiggly."

Interest flared in her eyes. He wasn't sure if it was directed at him or Home Depot or the Piggly Wiggly, but either way, heat zoomed through him. "You have a car?" she asked.

"A pickup. Why?"

"Looks like we're going to be neighbors."

Chapter 4

Jamie climbed into the passenger seat of Nick Trent's pickup truck—a vehicle she never would have believed was his given its spotless, shiny black exterior and equally pristine interior. She would've bet a month's rent his vehicle would have been in the same deplorable condition as Paradise Lost. Good thing she didn't like to gamble.

As he buckled his seat belt in preparation of heading to the shopping mecca that contained Home Depot—aka the store that would save Paradise Lost—and Piggly Wiggly—aka the supermarket that would save her and Cupcake from starvation and her pet from the roasting pan litter box—she found herself unable to stop taking surreptitious peeks at Nick from the corner of her eye. And she couldn't figure out *why*.

Men who looked like the morning after a rough night had never appealed to her before. She'd always been attracted to neat, orderly, clean-cut men. But for reasons she couldn't understand, Nick Trent had grabbed her attention the instant he'd opened his door, with his bare chiseled chest and rock-hard abs, and those darn unbuttoned jeans. Who answered the door like that? He'd looked like his bender had ended with a hedonistic orgy. For all she knew, there'd been some tramp sleeping off a hangover in his bed. All reasons for her to be completely turned off and to utterly ignore him.

Instead, even her righteous anger hadn't been able to keep her thoughts completely on the matter at hand, and throughout their conversation, part of her brain had uncharacteristically and really annoyingly kept wandering off track, distracting her with whispers of *Whoa, he is steaming hot!* and *Hmmmm . . . could his hair feel as thick and soft as it looks?* and *Wow—what a gorgeous mouth. Wonder if he knows how to use it for anything besides sucking down alcohol?* Her fingers had practically itched with the urge to reach out and pull his fascinatingly half-mast fly the rest of the way down, er, *up*. She meant up. Absolutely up.

The fact that he'd distracted her for even a nanosecond had royally irked her. He was Pain in the Ass Number One and she had every right to be pissed off at him and his unethical renting practices. Still, after his initial crankiness, he *had* apologized and offered her a refund, and if he was telling the truth, the miscommunication and misleading photos on the website were Jack Crawford's doing. Not that it did her any good. She sure as hell wasn't about to go back to New York, and even if she did, with her apartment sublet, she had nowhere to stay.

Thus she found herself in Nick's pickup, although if she hadn't been desperate for supplies and without a car, she definitely wouldn't be here. Nope. She absolutely didn't want to spend one more minute in his testosterone-laden company than was absolutely necessary.

After clicking the metal buckle into place, she stole another quick peek at him. She'd spent the fifteen minutes since she'd left his house washing her face, brushing her teeth, taming her electrocuted-looking hair into some semblance of order, and changing into a fresh tank top and shorts. As far as she could tell, the only freshening up he'd done during that time was to throw on a T-shirt. She assumed he'd fastened his jeans, but since he hadn't bothered to tuck in the T-shirt, she couldn't tell.

"They're buttoned," he said, sliding the key into the ignition.

She turned her head and found him staring at her with an expression that looked half amused and half . . . heated?

Yes, that was definitely heat simmering in his eyes . . . his intense green eyes that were framed by thick dark lashes every woman on the planet would kill for. They very nicely matched his slash of dark brows and his thick, wavy, sun-streaked brown hair that was several inches too long and looked as if he'd combed it with his fingers . . . those long, tanned, strong-looking fingers that were loosely curled over the steering wheel . . .

Jamie cleared her throat and hoisted one brow, favoring him with the withering look she reserved for unreliable restaurant vendors who didn't deliver their products to Newman's on time. "I beg your pardon?"

"You were looking at my crotch. I took a gamble that your superpower wasn't the ability to see through cotton, so I figured I'd tell you what you wanted to know. I'm fully buttoned and zipped."

While Jamie had always hated the fact that her chest and neck turned blotchy whenever she was embarrassed, she'd never hated it more than this very instant as she felt prickling heat flush her skin. God. She'd never met a more irritating, arrogant man in her entire life! The fact that he was sinfully good-looking only added to her irritation. The fact that he was so sinfully good-looking without putting forth even a lick of effort made her want to smack him with the ugly stick.

"I most certainly was *not* looking at your crotch," she said, inwardly wincing at her prim tone. Just another thing she hated about being embarrassed—she always ended up sounding like an uptight, three-hundred-year-old, virginal spinster. And she wasn't lying about looking—she'd merely stolen a *peek*. That was *so* not the same thing as looking.

A slow smile that could have melted an icicle during a snow storm curved his lips. "Whatever you say, princess."

For several seconds Jamie's lungs forgot how to work. Holy. Crap. That slightly lopsided smile was potent with a capital Po. She had to swallow twice to locate her voice. "I told you—I'm not a princess. And what's this nonsense about me having a superpower?"

"Everybody's got at least one—it's the thing that sets you apart from everyone else. Like Superman's ability to fly, and The Flash's superhuman reflexes."

Jamie instantly wondered what his superpower was. Probably the ability to stupefy with a single smile women who were pissed off at him. Or maybe it had something to do with other things that sinful-looking mouth could do. Her gaze flicked to his lips and her entire body tensed with awareness.

He shifted the truck into reverse, stretched his arm along the top of the leather seat, and sizzled a few more of her brain cells with another grin. "Relax, princess. It was a joke. Jeez. And I thought *I* needed coffee."

Since that damn grin of his had again stolen her ability to speak, she didn't reply. He backed down the driveway made of crushed shells, then headed toward the south end of the island. She cleared her throat and found her voice. "Isn't the bridge that leads to Route 4 in the opposite direction?"

"Yes. We're making a stop first."

"Where?"

"For breakfast. I need coffee and something to eat. I'm figuring you need the same. I know for damn sure you need some coffee, Miss Cranky Pants."

She shot him a glare that would have curdled milk. "Cranky pants? What are you, in third grade?"

"You're just proving my point. Not much of a morning person, are you?"

"And you are?"

"Depends."

"On what?"

"Who I'm with. And what happened the night before."

Before she could reply, he pulled the truck into a gravel parking lot and stopped in a space in front of a small building painted tropical green with bright yellow trim. A lighted sign in neon pink script that ran nearly the entire length of the building flashed the words—

"Oy Vey Mama Mia," Jamie read, peering out the windshield. "What is this place?"

"The best restaurant on the island—and the fact that it's the only one open for breakfast has nothing to do with it being the best. Believe me, you've never been anywhere like this."

They exited the truck and Jamie followed Nick up the short pathway leading to the entrance. To her surprise he actually held the door open for her, something she might have remarked upon, but every thought was driven from her head by the heavenly scent of coffee and bacon that instantly bombarded her.

In spite of the fact that the parking lot was nearly empty, there were at least two dozen tables filled with diners, and every spot at the counter was taken. Clearly folks renting out homes on the island liked to walk to breakfast, and really, why not, as everywhere on Seaside Cove was within walking distance.

The interior resembled a retro diner meets coastal beach town, combining a glossy, stainless steel counter with round, turquoise-vinyl stools. The walls were painted a soft Caribbean blue and decorated with hanging surf boards of every imaginable size, interspersed with seashells. A stone fireplace occupied the corner, its mantel decorated with sand dollars. Two tall glass revolving display cases showed off an array of delicious-looking desserts, and mini juke boxes that resembled 1950s automobiles sat at each booth and table. Jamie's restaurant-trained eye skimmed over the open stainless steel kitchen where three cooks toiled, one working the cooking area, one working the small prep area chopping onions like a pro, and the other plating dishes. The aroma of good food being prepared in such a fun atmosphere had her exhaling a sigh of happiness.

They were greeted by a pretty teenage girl with ebony hair that matched her soulful eyes. "'Morning, Nick," she said with a smile that included Jamie. "Two for breakfast?"

"Yeah, thanks, Rachel. This is Jamie Newman. She's renting Paradise Lost for the summer."

Rachel's smile widened. "Welcome to the island. You're going to love it here." She snagged two menus. "Inside table or the patio?" Before Nick could answer, Rachel leaned forward and whispered, "Grandma's working outside this morning."

Nick grinned. "Then definitely the patio."

Rachel laughed, then said, "Follow me."

They wove their way through a maze of brightly colored tables and booths filled with couples and families and a few lone diners, then through sliding doors that led outside. The patio overlooked the beach, offering a great view of the white sand and sun-dappled water. A red boat cruised beyond the breakers, a bright spot of crimson in the relentless blue. Rachel stopped next to an oval glass-topped wicker table and set down the menus. "Enjoy your breakfast. Nice meeting you," she added to Jamie.

She had barely settled herself on the beige-cushioned seat when a petite beaming woman Jamie judged to be in her mid-sixties approached their table bearing two canary yellow ceramic mugs and a carafe. "*Buongiorno*, Nico!" the woman said, setting the cups on the table. A bright scarlet dress with a beautiful embroidered design around the neckline encased her curvaceous frame, and her lipstick perfectly matched her outfit. Warm espresso-colored eyes dancing with laughter and curiosity shifted to Jamie as she poured fragrant coffee into both cups. "I see you bring us a friend this morning, Nico," she said in a lyrical voice that bore an unmistakable Italian accent.

"Maria, this is Jamie Newman," said Nick. "She rented Paradise Lost for the summer. Jamie, this is Maria Rigoletti-Silverman—the Mama Mia half of the restaurant."

"Nice to meet you, Maria," Jamie said, extending her hand and smiling.

"*Grazie*. Nice to meet you as well." She slid her gaze toward Nick. "I told you some crusty old fisherman wasn't going to rent the place. Ha!" She returned her attention to Jamie and gave her a speculative look, then jerked her head toward Nick. "So you'll be living next door to this one all summer, eh?" A hearty laugh escaped her. "*Bene*," she said, nodding. "It will be good for him. And for you, too." She leaned closer and tapped her temple. "I *know* these things. I *see* these things."

"Oy vey, Maria, stop with the crazy talk, *knowing* and *seeing*," came a deep voice filled with laughter. "They'll think you're meshuga."

Jamie looked around Maria. A rotund balding man with friendly hazel eyes that appeared magnified behind his oversized black-rimmed glasses approached them, wiping his hands on his apron emblazoned with the words "Reservations, Schmeservations—Eat at Oy Vey Mama Mia and Fuggetaboutit!" Jamie recognized him as the cook who'd been plating the meals. He slid his arms around Maria's waist and planted a loud smooch on her cheek. "Nice to see you back,

Nick," he said, then he smiled at Jamie. "Good morning, Nick's friend."

Jamie smiled and extended her hand. "Jamie Newman. New to the island. Renting Paradise Lost for the summer."

"Nice to meet you, Jamie. I'm Ira Silverman, the Oy Vey half of the restaurant."

"As if gefilte fish is a food," Maria said with an exaggerated sniff.

"As if pasta and cheese were the only two food groups," Ira replied with a grin.

"The only two that count," Maria said, winking at Nick and Jamie.

"I hate to steal away my bride," said Ira, "but she's needed in the kitchen. Trouble with the cacciatore that's today's lunch special."

Maria tossed her free hand in the air. "Whatsa matta for those boys in there, eh? If they've ruined my cacciatore, I'ma gonna whack them upside their heads!"

She hurried away, followed by a chuckling Ira.

"They've been married forty-two years," Nick said, handing Jamie a menu. "They met the summer before Ira graduated from Yale. His parents wanted him to spend a few weeks on a kibbutz in Israel, but he went backpacking in Italy instead. Stopped in a little café and took one look at Maria, who was working there, and in Ira's words, 'that was all she wrote.' He went back the following summer, they got married, and returned to the states."

He took a deep drink of his coffee, let out a satisfied *ahhhh*, then continued, "They used to come to Seaside Cove for a week every summer with their kids. Ira retired three years ago but within weeks was bored out of his mind. He and Maria came back to Seaside Cove for a visit that summer and never left. They bought a house on the island and decided to follow a lifelong pipe dream and open the restaurant. Their kids visit during the summer, and the grandkids work here during their visits."

"Nice story," Jamie remarked. "Very romantic. So how do you know so much about Ira and Maria?"

He looked at her as if she were nuts. "I learned their entire history the first time I ate here. I've lived on Seaside Cove for three months—that's like a lifetime in island time as far as getting to know the locals. Doesn't take long to find out everything about everyone who lives here full-time."

Jamie shook her head. "I've lived in the same apartment for four years and don't know the names of more than half a dozen people who reside in my building."

"That's the way big cities are. New York?" he guessed.

She nodded. "How'd you know?"

"You sound like a Noo Yawka."

She didn't think she had an accent at all, but whatever. "Where are you from?"

"Chicago."

Her brows rose. "This is a long way from home."

"This is home now." The finality in his tone hinted that he'd left behind a less than perfect situation—something she could certainly sympathize with. Not that she had any intention of sympathizing with him. Heck no. She was only sitting here because she desperately needed a ride to the Piggly Wiggly, and well, she wasn't about to complain about getting some breakfast. Especially at such an interesting, eclectic restaurant.

After several sips of the excellent coffee left her feeling quasi-human, she perused the menu. "Bagels and lox parmigiana with a schmear? Eggs Florentine with a schtickle of mascarpone?" Her gaze skipped to the lunch menu. "Pastrami with provolone on your choice of challah or semolina bread?" She couldn't help but laugh. "Those are some pretty creative food and cultural combinations."

"No doubt about it—some of them sound . . . well, not really kosher," Nick said.

"You mean like the matzo balls marinara?" Jamie asked.

"Exactly. But I've tried just about everything on the menu and haven't been disappointed once. As Ira would say, the food is 'to die for.' "

"Hmmm. No offense, but you look like the type of guy who would eat stale corn chips from under the sofa cushion and think you'd had a gourmet meal."

"Now why would I take offense at that?" he asked in a dust-dry tone.

Another pretty dark-haired teenager stopped at the table.

Nick introduced her as Ira and Maria's granddaughter Elizabeth. After she took their order, Nick refilled their cups from the carafe Maria had left on the table and asked, "You claim you're not a Photoshopper, so what do you do—besides pound on doors at the crack of dawn?"

"Ha, ha. As far as I'm concerned, you're lucky I didn't pound on your head. With your bag of dead clams."

"Ha, ha. My killer watch dog would have stopped you long before you ever got close to me."

"Yeah—she's obviously a real threat. About as much of a menace as Cupcake."

"Who—or what—is Cupcake?"

"My cat."

"Your cat's name is *Cupcake*?"

"I like cupcakes. You got a problem with that?" she asked, mimicking his question to her when he'd announced he'd named his dog Godiva.

"No—but I'm guessing Cupcake lies awake at night plotting your death for that name. I hope at least Cupcake is a girl cat."

"Yes. And she likes her name."

"I'm sure she'd tell you otherwise if she could talk. So— you never said—what do you do? I'm guessing teacher."

"Really? Why is that?"

"Two reasons. First, you're bossy. And second, you have the summer off."

"Well, you're wrong," she said, unable to keep all traces of smugness out of her voice. Thought he was so smart. Ha! "I manage a restaurant."

"You get fired?"

"Why would you ask that?"

He shrugged. "I've never heard of a restaurant manager having the entire summer off. Plus that whole bossy thing. Doesn't seem a far stretch that you'd have pissed off someone and gotten canned."

Warmth rushed into Jamie's cheeks, prickling irritation along her every nerve ending. "There's a difference between being bossy and being the boss. *Someone* has to be in charge. And for your information, I wasn't fired. I'd just saved up a lot of vacation and decided to take it all at once."

"And came to Seaside Cove for the summer."

"Yes.

He studied her over the rim of his coffee cup through intense green eyes that didn't give anything away. Finally he said, "Must have been a hell of a breakup."

Jamie froze as another wave of heat washed through her, and darn it, here came the blotches. "What do you mean?"

"I mean it must have been a hell of a breakup between you and your boyfriend to result in you abandoning ship for two months to lick your wounds. Either that or you committed a crime and skipped town to avoid prosecution. But if I was a betting man—and I am—I'm going with bad breakup."

"You fancy yourself a fortune teller?" she asked, her voice thick with sarcasm.

The way his eyes seemed to pierce into her soul gave her the uncomfortable sensation that he could see every emotion, every pain and heartbreak that had driven her away from the life she'd always known. "No. I just call 'em like I see 'em. I'd also bet you were the dumpee, not the dumper."

"And why is that?"

"First, because if *you'd* dumped *him*, if the decision had been yours, you would have stayed in New York, flipped him the proverbial finger, and continued on, business as usual. Second, when you remarked that Maria and Ira's story was very romantic, I detected a bit of a lip curl—like you'd bitten into a lemon and wanted to say 'blech,' which indicates a romance gone bad. Which leads me to believe the reason for the breakup was because he was cheating. Since you wanted to get away from New York, that makes me think he was someone you couldn't avoid. So that's my guess—he cheated, and he was in some way related to your job."

Okay, out of all the men she knew—many of whom she'd known for years—she couldn't name *one* who was in any way perceptive, yet this hungover stranger had hit every nail right on the head. It was weird. And uncanny. Totally unnerving. And really, really irritating.

"You're making an awful lot of assumptions for someone who's known me for"—she pursed her lips and made a big show of consulting her watch—"less than two hours."

"Maybe. But that doesn't mean I'm wrong."

"You sound more like a lawyer than a repairman."

Something flickered in his eyes, something that disappeared too quickly for her to interpret. Touched a nerve, had she? Good. And two could play at his game. "Since you seem to think you have me all figured out," she said, "now it's my turn."

She allowed her gaze to wander over him, then said, "You're the big kid who ran away from home. Black sheep of the family, your parents—probably your father—didn't approve of your lifestyle, and rather than keep fighting all the time, you just left. Probably there was a woman—or five— involved at some point who got tired of you going off on your benders. You decided you didn't need the hassle and moved away. You don't like people telling you what to do, you're not big on relationships or commitment, and you enjoy being your own boss. You took advantage of the down real estate market and managed to scrape together enough money for a minimum down payment on a couple of rundown places that were probably short sales or in foreclosure. You're up to your eyeballs in debt, but now there's no one to answer to but yourself."

"Now who's playing fortune teller?" he asked in a casual voice, but the muscle ticking in his jaw had Jamie giving herself a mental high five. *Ha, Mr. Smarty Pants. Hit a couple nails myself, didn't I?*

She was saved from answering by the arrival of their food. Jamie had ordered the eggs Florentine, and with the first bite, she closed her eyes in ecstasy. "Oh. My. God. I'm not sure if it's because I'm starving or that this is just that good, but I think these are the best eggs I've ever tasted. Ever."

"They're that good," Nick said. "Try this." He held out his fork, laden with a tempting morsel of his grilled challah bread toast topped with mascarpone and homemade raspberry syrup.

When Jamie hesitated, Nick rolled his eyes. "I haven't eaten off the fork yet. Jeez, you really are anal."

"No, I'm not. I'm merely . . . cautious."

"Got that. You want to taste this or not?"

The restaurant manager/foodie in her couldn't resist. She leaned forward and opened her mouth. Then once again her eyes slid shut at the burst of delicate flavors. As was her habit, especially when tasting new dishes, she chewed slowly, savoring the melding of textures and tastes. When she opened her eyes, she found him staring. At her mouth. She swallowed again, then said the only word she could manage.

"Yum."

Her voice seemed to yank him out of whatever stupor he'd fallen into and he scooped up another forkful of his breakfast. "I hate to say I told you so . . ." he said, then wolfed down a big bite.

"Somehow I sincerely doubt that, but I'm too in love with this meal to argue with you."

His lips curved up in that slow, lopsided grin. "So the trick is to keep you fed. Good to know."

Since that darn grin of his had stolen her ability to speak, she merely looked toward the ceiling and kept eating. She'd just mopped up the last of her eggs with a piece of perfectly toasted semolina bread when Maria stopped by the table to drop off their check. She eyed the empty plates and beamed.

"That's what I like to see—healthy appetites. You enjoy?"

"Best eggs *ever*," Jamie said, patting her stomach.

"A masterpiece, as always," said Nick.

"*Grazie*. You come back for dinner this week. The specials are my lasagna—she is the best you've tasted; I make the gravy from my grandmother's recipe—and Ira's brisket."

"Sounds delicious," said Jamie. "I absolutely love your restaurant, Maria—the food, the décor, the whole concept. It's eclectic and unique and fun, and the meals are seriously delicious."

Maria's smile could have lit the entire room. "*Grazie*, Jamie. The recipes are from my childhood, while the shells have been collected by family from beaches everywhere. But the sand dollars on the mantel are from Seaside Cove. I love them so much because they remind me of Roma."

"How do sand dollars remind you of Rome?" Jamie asked.

"It is because of the legend," Maria said. "In Roma, we have the Trevi Fountain. Legend says that if you throw a coin in the fountain, you will come back to Roma. Local legend here says that if you find a whole, unbroken sand dollar—which is very rare—you shall not only have great luck, but you are ensured a return visit to Seaside Cove. You see? The legend here is the same as that of my beloved Roma." She smiled at Nick. "Have you found one yet?"

"No. But I don't need one. I have no intention of leaving Seaside Cove."

"But it is a talisman of good luck, so you still must always look for the unbroken sand dollar."

"I'll keep an eye out," Nick promised. "Maria, did you know that Jamie manages a restaurant in New York City?"

Maria's eyes lit up. "No! Then I am doubly honored by your kind words, Jamie. Ira and I love Manhattan. So many fun things to do, so many great places to eat. What's the name of the restaurant?"

"Newman's." Just saying the name of the restaurant where Jamie had poured so much of her heart and soul filled her with a conflicting sense of pride and relief that she was here and not there.

"Ah, a family-owned restaurant," Maria said, nodding. "Just like we had back in Italy. That is the best kind. Where in the city is Newman's located?"

"West 44th Street, in the theatre district."

"We'll make it a point to eat there the next time we visit," Maria promised. Then her eyes widened and she clapped her hands together. "Oh, but this is perfect that you know so much about managing! Has the Clam Committee paid you a visit yet?"

"Clam Committee?" Jamie repeated. Uh-oh. This sounded like trouble.

"For the Clam Festival," Maria clarified, her brown eyes alight with excitement. "It's a huge event on the island—takes place the end of August, right before Labor Day. All the islanders volunteer. Ira and I have a food tent and we help decorate." She turned to Nick. "Aren't you helping to build the parade float this year?"

"I am." He grinned across the table at Jamie. "I'm sure the Clam Committee will have plenty for you to do."

Crap. She wanted to be on the Clam Committee like she wanted a hole in her head. Really, what she wanted was to be left alone. Seriously, why couldn't people just *leave her alone*?

"Oh, they will be so happy to have someone with your experience," gushed Maria, "especially since Walter Murphy is out of commission due to his hip-replacement surgery. You are *come il cacio sui maccheroni*!"

Probably that meant destined to die at the hands of the Clam Committee, Jamie thought darkly.

"She's like . . . cheese on macaroni?" Nick asked with a laugh.

"*Eccellente!*" Marie reached out and pinched his cheek. "You're getting very good at the translations, Nico! Yes, like cheese on macaroni—so, how you say—just what the doctor ordered."

Maria then grabbed Jamie's hand. "Oh! And you must put your name on the ballot for Clam Queen, Jamie." She leaned forward and lowered her voice. "I heard that *strega* Missy Calhoun"—Maria practically spit out the woman's name— "from Coastal Beach Island has been bragging that one of her daughters is going to win again this year. We need someone from Seaside Cove to win." Still gripping Jamie's hand, Maria turned to Nick. "She's *molto carino*—very cute, no?"

"No," Jamie interjected.

"Very cute," Nick agreed, completely ignoring the Stare of Death Jamie shot him. "Definitely has Clam Queen potential."

"Ah! It is settled then," Maria said with a beaming smile.

It totally *wasn't* settled, but Jamie didn't see any point in arguing about it with Maria. What the heck did she care if Missy What's-her-name's daughter won? It was really a nonissue as Jamie simply wouldn't put her name on the Clam Queen ballot, and she'd save all her refusals for the actual Clam Committee if they solicited her help.

Maria's gaze bounced between Jamie and Nick. "How long you two know each other?"

"It's been about two hours," Nick said.

"More like two and a half," corrected Jamie. "But it feels like five."

"More like ten."

"Years," Jamie said, nodding. "Ten years."

Maria laughed, a deep, throaty sound. "Ah, *amore*!"

Jamie nearly choked. She didn't know much Italian, but she certainly knew that *amore* meant love. "Uh, no. *Seriously* no. Not *amore*. In fact, pretty much the opposite of *amore*. Very much *un-amore*."

"*È stato amore a prima vista!*" Maria said, her eyes gleaming.

"What does that mean?" Jamie asked.

"It is, how you say, love at the first sight. The chemistry, the sparks—they cannot be denied. It was the same way with me and my Ira. You are both beautiful and it is *bellissimo* babies you will make." She blew them each a kiss, said, "Arrivederci," then sauntered away to visit another table.

Jamie pressed her fingers to her temples. "Holy cannoli. I feel like I just got hit by an Italian Mack truck." She glared across the table. "Since when did you turn into a mute? You didn't say anything to disabuse her of her crazy love-at-first-sight notions and all that *bellissimo* babies jazz."

"I learned a long time ago there's not much you can do to correct someone's wrong assumption about you other than to let time take care of it. And besides, I avoid arguing with women whenever possible."

"Because you know we'll win?"

"Because women base their opinions on emotions rather than facts. That makes arguing with them about as productive as smacking rocks against my head."

"Smacking rocks against your head . . . That could be arranged, you know."

"I'm sure it could. But you might want to remember that it's a ten-mile hike to the Piggly Wiggly."

Jamie sighed and opened her purse to extract her wallet. "I have *got* to arrange for a rental car."

"You can try, but I wouldn't plan on anything being available until after the Shrimp Festival." He smiled. "Looks like you'll need to be nice to me for the next couple of days, Miss No Car."

"I am being nice to you. Have I smacked you in the head with a rock?"

"No, but you've looked like you wanted to."

"*Wanting* to isn't a crime." She hoped.

He reached for the check, but she slipped her fingers on top of the bill and his palm came down on the back of her hand. "This one's on me," she said, dragging her hand and the check from beneath the warmth of his broad, callused palm, a move that for some inexplicable reason zoomed tingles up her arm. "For taking me to the Piggly Wiggly." He frowned at his hand that had been on top of hers for several seconds, then slowly pulled it back, flexing his fingers. When he appeared about to argue, she added, "And so I have something to hold over your head until my stairs and roof are fixed."

He studied her for the space of two heartbeats with an inscrutable expression, then one corner of his mouth tipped up. "If I'd known you were paying, I would have ordered the smoked salmon and linguini with lobster."

"I knew you would have—that's why I didn't tell you."

She left cash for the bill and tip, then slid out of her chair. Walking behind Nick, she found her eyeballs straying to his butt. How annoying was it that he looked as good leaving a room as he did entering it? Boy, it sure was a good thing he wasn't *at all* her type, otherwise she might find herself heaving a gushy sigh over him and his hotness.

And that nonsense Maria had said about chemistry and sparks? Ha! Any sparks she'd detected were purely from annoyance. A little voice in the back of her mind whispered, *Any kind of spark can start a fire.* Jamie frowned, but then shrugged off the words. She had plenty of things to worry about, but anything happening between her and totally-nother-type Nick Trent definitely wasn't one of them.

Chapter 5

Nick set the final trio of galvanized roofing nails on top of a new shingle and hammered them in place, the reverberations from each whack shooting a pleasant zing up his arm. When he finished, he covered the nail heads with roof cement, then wiped his dripping face with his T-shirt sleeve. Not that his grimy shirt was any drier than his face; after six hours spent in the broiling sun making repairs to Paradise Lost's roof, there wasn't a centimeter of him of that wasn't soaked with sweat.

He took a long swig from his water bottle and surveyed his rooftop handiwork. A damn good job if he said so himself. Of course, the big test to see if he'd patched all the leaks would come when it rained again, but he'd certainly fixed all the major problem areas.

Yesterday after the Home Depot run, he'd fixed the steps as well as the sagging screens on the porch and replaced the cracked windows—damn good jobs, too, if he said so himself—and gotten a head start on the roof repairs. Now that the roof was completed, the princess would get off his back.

Not that she'd been pestering him, he had to admit. In fact, he'd barely seen her since yesterday's return from their Home

Depot/Piggly Wiggly trip. She'd lugged home an enormous amount of bags filled with food, a forty-pound container of cat chow, and God only knows what else, and had disappeared inside the house. He noticed her leaving and returning yesterday afternoon on what he assumed was a walk along the beach, as she had in ear buds attached to an iPod. He hadn't seen her after her return, but he'd certainly heard her.

Since all the windows of Paradise Lost remained open, he couldn't help but hear the music she played. At least her taste in music was good—classic rock with some jazz tossed in. He'd even heard her singing along a few times. He winced at the memory. The woman couldn't sing for shit. If Godiva ever heard her, she'd start howling along.

She'd left the house a few hours ago, a big floppy hat shading her face, and carrying a canvas bag and a beach towel. His gaze had zeroed in on her toned, shapely legs, shown off to advantage in a short, bright orange dress—the kind women wore over their bathing suits. His imagination instantly shifted into overdrive, wondering what she wore underneath that little dress, and annoyance pricked him. What the hell did he care what she wore? She was nothing more than a bossy pest who couldn't sing worth a damn. When she returned from the beach, he'd be able to tell her the repairs were finished, and he'd be done with her. He'd spend the rest of the summer working on Southern Comfort, then, when the princess went back to New York, he'd start renovating Paradise Lost.

A sense of deep accomplishment filled him, something he hadn't felt in a very long time before pulling up stakes and moving to Seaside Cove. He'd left a great deal behind him, but he was slowly regaining ground, finding the part of himself he'd lost, that had gotten sucked dry by the life he'd been leading.

His gaze drifted to Southern Comfort and peace washed over him, like a gentle wave of incoming tide—the sort of tranquil calm he'd spent years struggling to find in his old life. It wasn't until he'd chucked it all and walked away without a backward glance that he'd finally felt, at age thirty, as if he'd started to live.

A huff of laughter rushed past his lips at the sight of Godiva sleeping in the shade of Southern Comfort's carport. She lay sprawled on her back in her cushiony outdoor doggie bed, all four paws dangling in the air. "Jeez, you really need to learn how to relax, Godiva," Nick muttered, chuckling.

With a sigh of contentment, he drained his water bottle and carefully swiveled around to face the beach. From his vantage point on the roof he could see the sun glinting sparks of gold off the dark blue ocean. Several boats zoomed along about a half mile out, small dots cruising through the water, leaving trails of white wake foam behind them. A trio of kites flew high in the sky, their colorful tails flapping in the salt-scented breeze. The soothing sound of the waves hitting the shore was muffled by the dunes, as were the excited shouts of kids playing in the sand and water—a background music he'd grown to love over the past few months.

A spot of bright orange caught Nick's attention. He pushed his Ray-Bans higher on his nose and saw Jamie emerge from the beach-access path and pause to look both ways before crossing the street. She wasn't wearing her floppy hat and her honey-colored curls floated in wild disarray around her shoulders. His heart lurched—like he'd just taken that first downward swooping rush on a roller coaster.

He frowned. What the hell was *that* about? Probably because he could now tell her he was done with the repairs and wish her a happy adios-have-a-good-summer-don't-call-us-we'll-call-you.

Yup, that was why.

He slipped his supplies back in his tool belt, made his way to the ladder, then climbed down. He'd just stepped off the bottom rung when she walked up the driveway.

"Roof's all fixed," Nick said.

"Great." Her gaze swept over him, taking in his dirty, sweat-stained shirt; faded, worn jeans; tool belt; and sturdy work boots. "You look hot."

"Thanks, babe." He slid down his Ray-Bans to give her a head-to-toe look. "You look pretty hot yourself."

Which she definitely did. Up close, he could see that the orange dress was made of some sort of lacy material that afforded tantalizing glimpses of a bright yellow bathing suit underneath.

And it suddenly felt about ten degrees hotter.

Color rushed into her cheeks. Damn, he couldn't recall the last time he'd seen a woman blush so easily.

"I meant hot as in *sweaty*," she said in the same prim tone she'd used on him yesterday—a tone that for some reason amused, rather than irked, him.

"That's what happens when you toil in the sun." He unhooked his tool belt and set it on the cement. "How was the beach?"

"Really nice. The waves were great. Got beat up by a few of them, but that's half the fun."

"You went swimming?"

She cocked a brow. "You sound surprised."

"I guess I am a little." Actually, more than a little. His experiences had convinced him that women favored pools. Beach trips usually involved a lot of complaining about the sand and the lack of bar service.

"I don't see why you'd be surprised," she said, shaking her head. "It's the *beach*. You know, the place where you swim, splash in the waves, body surf—that sort of stuff. I also built a sand castle and picked up some shells, but didn't find a sand dollar. I sure as heck didn't get this sand all over me and my finger-in-the-light-socket hairdo by lounging elegantly on a chaise."

Just another thing that surprised him. He couldn't recall the last time he'd been to the beach with a woman when she actually got her bathing suit, let alone her hair, wet.

"I'm definitely going to shop around for a Boogie board," she said.

"I have an extra you're welcome to borrow."

She blinked. "Oh. Well, thanks. That's very, um, nice of you. Very neighborly."

"I'm guessing you meant that as a compliment, but since you sounded so shocked that I'd do something nice or neighborly, it kinda lost some of its charm."

"I wasn't shocked."

Nick couldn't help but grin. God, not only could she not sing, but she was a horrible liar, too. "Yes, you were."

Her lips twitched. "Okay, maybe I was a *little* shocked." She hesitated, then said, "I'm dying of thirst. In keeping with this neighborly thing, may I offer you a cold drink?"

He had his own cold drinks at home—the place he couldn't wait to return to. To take a shower. To get away from her. Yet when he opened his mouth, the words, "Sure, that'd be great, thanks," came out.

He watched her dig her key from her beach bag, then followed her to the stairs so he could again check out the two new bottom treads. Yup, he'd done a really good job. He looked up from admiring his handiwork and stilled.

As far as he knew, he'd never been the guy who ogled a woman wearing a short dress as she climbed stairs—until right now, when a freakin' nuclear blast couldn't have unglued his eyeballs from her shapely butt as it swung from side to side with each step.

Damn. He needed more than a cold drink. He needed a damn cold shower.

After she disappeared into the house, he released a breath he hadn't even realized he was holding. Her voice wafted down from behind the screen door, and he found himself cocking his head to better hear her.

"Hey, Cupcake, how are you, sweet girl. Did you miss me?"

Apparently Cupcake performed some sort of cat maneuver that indicated she had indeed missed her, because Jamie laughed and said, "I missed you, too. Are you hungry?"

Cupcake let out a meow Nick bet was heard in the next county.

"Let's see what we have . . . Okay, would you prefer the tender turkey Tuscany with long-grain rice and garden greens, or the wild salmon primavera with garden veggies?"

Nick rolled his eyes. Sheesh. No wonder cats were so prissy.

"Here you go, baby," Jamie crooned. "I'm going to bring a drink to that pest Nick, then I'll be back. And you can tell me all about your day." The screen door opened and she stepped outside, carrying two bottles of water. And halted when she saw him standing at the bottom of the stairs. Nick liked that she wasn't wearing sunglasses and he was—definitely put him at an advantage as she couldn't see his eyes, which he knew held a combination of irritation, amusement, and worst of all, an avid interest in watching her descend the steps.

He settled one booted foot on the bottom tread, then braced his palms on the banisters. " 'That pest Nick' ?" he repeated, looking up at her. "And here I thought we were being all nice and neighborly."

Her cheeks turned bright red. By God, that absolutely fascinated him. Made him want to tease and embarrass her for three days straight just so he could see that wash of brilliant color stain her skin.

She hoisted her chin up a notch. "Eavesdroppers never hear good of themselves."

"I wasn't eavesdropping. I was standing."

"Listening to me talk to Cupcake."

"How was I supposed to know you were going to chat with your cat?"

She started down the stairs and his attention was riveted on the way the hem of that short orange dress flirted with her thighs. The next thing he knew she was standing on the next to the last step, there was less than two feet separating them, and his eyes were on the same level as her chest.

And speaking of chests, she slapped an ice cold plastic water bottle against his. "Here's your drink."

He lifted one hand from the wooden banister and took the bottle, purposely resting his hand over hers. "Thanks."

She snatched her hand away as if he'd scorched her and he had to fight the urge to grin. He could almost hear her debating the advantages of telling him to move out of her way versus remaining where she was on the second tread, which allowed her to look down at him. Clearly she opted for the latter because she merely unscrewed the cap of her bottle and took a sip.

He mimicked her actions, never taking his gaze from her, although given his dark lenses, she wouldn't necessarily know that.

She took another sip, then asked, "What's wrong with talking to my cat? Don't you ever talk to Godiva?"

"Sure. But all she hears is *blah, blah, blah, Godiva, blah, blah, blah.*"

"Cupcake would tell you that that's because cats rule and dogs drool."

"Shows what Cupcake knows. Godiva hardly ever drools."

Okay, that was a stretch—she drooled. A lot. But he wasn't about to let some soufflé-eating cat insult his dog. That's just what dogs did—drool. "So which meal did Cupcake choose? Personally I would have gone with the wild salmon primavera."

"She picked the chicken and cheddar cheese soufflé."

Figures. "They sure make fancy stuff for cats to eat. Bet that crap costs a fortune. Lucky for me, Godiva isn't picky." Damn right she wasn't. She'd eat gym socks if he put them in her bowl. Hell, she drank from the toilet every chance she got. "She'd scarf down that prissy cat food in a single gulp and not even know she was tasting tender turkey Tuscany. And by the way—you calling anyone a pest is like Cupcake accusing someone of having tuna breath."

She narrowed her eyes. "Is that your poetic way of telling me I'm a pest?"

"It was rather poetic, wasn't it? And yes, it is. And at least I'll tell you to your face, rather than saying it behind your back."

"First of all, Cupcake is sporting *chicken* breath, not tuna. And secondly, if you want me to tell you you're a pest to your face, fine. You're a pest. Happy?"

"Not really. I liked it much better when you told me I was hot."

Another shade of red stained her cheeks. Oh, yeah, life was good. Whatever she was about to say—and based on the look she skewered him with, it promised to be pretty scathing—was cut off when she suddenly looked over his shoulder and her eyes widened. Oh, yeah, like he was going to fall for the old "there's something/someone right behind you" trick. The second he turned around, she'd probably shove him aside and move off the steps, taking away his great eye-level view of what appeared to be a first-class rack.

"Um, what is Godiva doing?" she asked.

"Last I checked, sleeping in her dog bed on my carport. Why?"

"It appears she woke up. And is rolling around on the patch of weeds that's supposed to be my lawn. Is she okay?"

Nick turned, and sure enough, there was Godiva, right next to the decapitated flamingo, her tongue lolling, making orgasmic sounds as she writhed around like a happy pig in a mud puddle.

"Crap. The only time she does that is when she finds something really foul smelling." He whistled sharply. Godiva stilled, then rolled to her feet. She caught sight of Nick and ran toward him like she was shot from a cannon. She greeted him in a frenzy of tail-wagging canine joy that would lead anyone to believe she hadn't seen him in a decade.

"Holy Jesus, Godiva," Nick said, turning his head away from the horrific stench that rose from her fur in a noxious cloud of foulness. "What in God's name did you get into?"

"Ugh, I know that stink," Jamie said, covering her mouth and nose with her hand. "It's your dead clams."

"I thought you threw them away," Nick said, doing his best to avoid Godiva's rapturous attempts to rub her sides against his legs.

"I did. But according to the schedule I found in the kitchen drawer, the garbage isn't collected until tomorrow." Giving prancing Godiva a large berth, she disappeared around the corner of the house, no doubt to check her garbage bin.

Nick looked down at Godiva. "Sit," he commanded, pointing his index finger at the ground.

Godiva's butt hit the cement, and she looked up at him with worshipful, excited eyes that clearly said, *Don't I smell great? Don't you love it? Isn't it the best smell in the whole wide world? I did it just for you! 'Cause I love you!*

Jamie returned, her entire face scrunched into an expression that indicated the stench on the other side of the carport wasn't any better.

"Trash can's been ... well, trashed," she reported. "It looks like a clam crime scene over there—dead bodies all over the place." She looked down at Godiva and shook her head. "You think you smell absolutely fabulous, don't you, baby?"

Godiva gave a single bark and pelted Nick's jeans with her wagging tail.

Jamie raised her gaze back to Nick. "That is one stinky dog you have there."

He made an exaggerated gagging sound. "Yeah? I hadn't noticed."

She laughed, then planted her hands on her hips and shot Godiva a stern look. "You realize the only thing saving you is that you are massively adorable."

Godiva licked her chops and Nick nodded. "People say that to me all the time."

She raised her gaze and treated Nick to a look that was clearly meant to incinerate him where he stood. "I was talking to Godiva."

"I know. Doesn't change the fact that people say that to me, too."

"I'll bet. Just so you know, Cupcake would never do something like *that*." She indicated the clam crime scene area with a wrinkling of her nose and a vague wave of her hand.

"Right. Listen, we had a cat when I was growing up. He brought dead crap home all the time—birds, frogs, snails. He even left a dead goldfish on the porch once. God only knows where he got it. And then there were the hairballs—yuck. So don't be casting aspersions on my smelly dog like your cat wears a halo around her head."

To prove there was no way Miss Cat Owner was going to think that a little stink (okay, a gargantuan, steal-your-breath stink) would come between him and his dog, he reached down and gave Godiva's scruff a good rub. His eyes damn near crossed in his head from the stench, but hey, he'd proved his point—whatever the hell it was.

By the way her lips twitched, it was clear she knew the stench had about knocked him off his feet. "Now you both need a bath."

What they needed was a decontamination tank. "You realize this is your fault," he said, straightening and folding his arms over his chest.

Her brows shot upward. "How do you figure that?"

"You obviously didn't close the lid to your garbage can correctly."

"And you obviously didn't tie up your dog properly."

"I didn't tie her up at all—which has never been a problem until now—when certain people didn't close their trash cans properly."

"Well, the dead clams wouldn't have been in there in the first place if you hadn't left them in my sink."

Damn. She had a point.

"Which means *you're* the one who's going to have to de-stink *your* dog." She sniffed twice, then shuddered. "Good luck with that."

"We can do it—it shouldn't take more than an hour to give her a good bath."

The look she gave him indicated he was a few slices short of a loaf. "*We?* Who is this *we* you speak of?"

He smiled. "You and me."

"What on earth makes you think I'm going to help you bathe your dog?"

"That whole 'nice and neighborly' thing. It's the way things are done here in the South—so I've been told. Giving a seventy-pound dog a bath is a two-man job."

"I don't doubt it. But in case you haven't noticed, I'm not a man."

Oh, he'd noticed all right. In fact, he couldn't stop noticing. Or stop thinking about what she'd look like all wet, which she'd get if she helped him. He didn't really expect her to say yes, but since he couldn't resist trying to get a rise out of her, he continued, "Hey, if you had a dog that smelled like dead clams, *I'd* help *you*. Really."

"Yeah, right. More like you'd laugh your ass off while you hightailed it out of here."

"See, now 'hightailed' is a Southern expression—so you're catching on to island life. You know, island life—where neighbors help neighbors."

"Here's another Southern expression for you—I ain't doin' that no-how." She gave him a big, false smile and batted her eyelashes. "Bless your heart."

Nick pushed his sunglasses up onto his head and narrowed his eyes. "I've lived here for three months—I know what 'bless your heart' means."

"Congratulations. I knew what it meant after living here three minutes—ya big dumbass."

"That's exactly what it means."

"No shit."

He heaved a huge sigh. "Fine. Be that way." He looked down at Godiva. "Sorry, girl. Princess here thinks you're foul and doesn't want any part of you."

The woebegone look Godiva gave Jamie made it clear that this was the worst news she'd ever heard in her entire doggie life. Ever.

"No fair," Jamie protested. She glared at Nick. "You play dirty."

"I play to win," he corrected. "Always."

"How can you stand living with him?" she asked Godiva.

Godiva barked twice.

"That means, 'He's the best guy on the planet.'" Nick translated.

"Clearly she hasn't met every guy on the planet," Jamie said in a dust-dry tone. Her gaze wandered back to Godiva, who looked like she'd just lost her best pal, then she sighed and pointed at Nick. "If I help you bathe her, *you* have to clean up the clams."

"Deal."

Distrust was written all over her face. "*All* the clams. Every one of them."

"I'll bag them all up *and* correctly latch your trash bin—*and* I'll even put it out by the curb for you for tomorrow's pickup." He extended his hand. "Deal?"

Her gaze bounced between him and Godiva—who, gotta love her, was treating Jamie to her most angelic expression. After several seconds she caved and held out her hand. "Deal."

Their palms met and his hand engulfed hers. Her skin felt warm and smooth against his. The heat that sizzled through him from such an innocent touch surprised him. Confused him. And didn't particularly please him. The fact that her eyes widened slightly made him wonder if she felt the same spark. And if she did—what did he intend to do about it?

She withdrew her hand and his fingers involuntarily curled inward to retain the tingle her touch had left behind.

"There is one catch," he said.

She pursed her lips. Damn, she really did have nice lips. "I should have known," she said.

"Don't give me the evil eye. It's a good catch—something that will make the bath much easier."

"Easier for whom? Because I could make it a lot easier on myself by abandoning this entire project."

"Easier on all of us. I'll take Godiva to the beach first. Let her burn off some energy with a game of catch. The water will wash off some of the stink and all the running will tire her out so she'll be easier to handle—a win-win. Plus, you've never seen a dog in your entire life who loves to chase tennis balls more than she does. It's pretty entertaining. You're welcome to join us, or I'll just knock on your door when we get back."

She looked down at Godiva, who was quivering with excitement." "He had you at the words 'chase tennis balls,' didn't he?"

When Godiva barked, Jamie laughed. "Okay, I've seen what you can do with dead clams, so I guess I should see what you can do with a ball."

"I'll clean up the clams, then get her leash and be right back," Nick said.

"Okay. Do you have a special shampoo or soap you use to bathe her?"

"Just whatever's in my shower."

"I'll look in my toiletries bag and see if I can round up something a little more sweet smelling," she said.

"Are you insinuating I stink?"

"At the moment, yes, you do."

Since he couldn't argue with that, he whistled for Godiva and together they trotted back to Southern Comfort. Commanding Godiva to stay in the carport, Nick grabbed a couple of plastic bags from his storage closet and quickly gathered up the foul-smelling mollusks. After tossing them back into Jamie's trash can, he secured the lid, then wheeled the container to the curb. He took a couple minutes to dash into the house, wash his hands, and exchange his dirty, smelly, sweaty clothes for a pair of board shorts. He didn't bother to lock the door—anyone who wanted to steal his dirty laundry was welcome to it—and hurried down the stairs, confused as to why he was in such a rush. The prospect of hitting the beach with his clam-killing neighbor shouldn't have his heart thumping in anticipation, but there was no escaping that that's exactly what was happening.

But why? Yeah, she was cute, but so were a lot of other women. In fact, a lot of them were downright gorgeous. But it had been a long time since anyone had inspired such heat in him. And curiosity. He wanted to know more about her, but damned if he understood why. Probably it was just simply that she wasn't his usual type and she wasn't throwing herself at him. The old she's-different/hard-to-get scenario. Yeah, that had to be it. Because bottom line, she was a pest. A prissy princess—although he had to grudgingly admit that she wasn't proving to be quite as princessy as he'd originally believed. And bossy. She was definitely bossy.

Yet still his heart rapped against his ribs in a crazy, staccato rhythm.

Clearly he was an idiot.

He sure as hell wasn't looking for any entanglements— freeing himself from bad relationships had been one of his prime motivations in escaping to Seaside Cove. And getting involved with a woman who lived right next door, in a house she was renting from him, had Extremely Bad Idea written all over it.

Yet there was no denying his awareness of her. Or that sizzle when they'd touched. Which meant he had three choices— act on it, ignore it, or get the hell out of town for a couple days and hope it went away.

He knew which one his body wanted.

He knew which one was the smartest.

And he was pretty sure he knew which one he'd choose.

Chapter 6

Considering the fact that Nick Trent was a strong contender for the title of Least Charming Man She'd Ever Met, Jamie was both dumbfounded and highly irritated to find herself even momentarily charmed by him. But there was no denying that's what she felt as she stood next to him on the beach and watched him throw a tennis ball into the waves for an ecstatic Godiva.

In addition to feeling charmed, she also felt as if she were melting from the inside out—which unfortunately had little to do with the sun's hot rays and a whole lot to do with the fact that Nick looked like a freakin' Greek god in his board shorts.

How the heck did a guy who went off on regular benders manage to have perfect pecs and abs you could grate cheese on? Maybe he wasn't going off on benders at all—maybe he was modeling for those Calvin Klein underwear ads. Thank God she'd put on her sunglasses—she wouldn't want him to know she'd given him the onceover. *You've given him the onceover about forty-three times,* her suddenly number-conscious inner voice whispered.

Stupid voice. Where was a muzzle when she needed it?

But really, who could blame her? No one, that's who. At

least no one sporting two X chromosomes. Sure, every female knew that guys who looked like Nick Trent existed, but the average woman normally saw them only between the pages of magazines. Standing so close to one, in the flesh . . . such warm-looking, goldeny tanned, perfectly defined without being too muscular flesh . . . was wreaking havoc with her normally no-nonsense brain cells.

Which was crazy! She didn't even like the guy.

Maybe not, but darn it, she was pretty much in love with his dog.

Godiva was just so damn *happy*, her mood was contagious. Jamie laughed as the dog raced toward the water, kicking up sand behind her, then catapulted herself into the waves, a brown frenzied blur of canine joy. She grabbed the ball between her teeth, then ran back toward them.

"You might want to step back," Nick warned as Godiva approached.

"Why—?"

Her question was cut off when Godiva commenced a full-body shake that sprayed them with clammy-scented sea water.

"That's why," Nick said unnecessarily. With an unrepentant grin he picked up the wet ball Godiva had dropped at his feet. "Wanna throw it?"

Jamie eyed the wet, sandy ball. Clearly he didn't think she'd touch it. Clearly he didn't know who he was dealing with. "Sure," she said, taking the ball, then heaving it down the beach and toward the water. Godiva took off like a shot.

Nick gave a soft whistle. "That's a pretty good arm you've got there."

"I played softball in high school. Centerfield."

"Interesting. I would have pegged you more as the president of the debate club."

Humph. Showed what he knew—she'd been the *treasurer* of the debate club.

She was saved from replying by the return of a very wet and sandy Godiva, who proceeded to once again enthusiastically shower them with sea water.

"I'll have you know that Cupcake never sprays me like that," Jamie said, taking off her glasses to wipe them on the hem of her orange cover-up.

"Yeah, but can she do this?" He tossed the ball straight up. Godiva crouched down, then leaped upward, snatching the ball out of the air when it was still a good six feet off the ground.

"I'm sure she could if she wanted to," Jamie said with a sniff as she slid her glasses back on. "She just doesn't want to."

Nick laughed, then threw the ball once again, and a tireless Godiva gave chase. "You're being a good sport about Godiva showering you with doggie sea water."

"You sound surprised."

"I am."

"I don't see why. This is the beach, not a cocktail party. I'm wearing a bathing suit, not Armani. And I was already covered with sand and salt. What's a little water at this point?"

"*I* don't think it's a big deal, but I figured you would."

"Well, you figured wrong."

She sensed his gaze on her and turned her head. And found him looking at her. Even though she couldn't see his eyes through his dark lenses, she sensed the intensity of his regard. Awareness of him, of the sun glinting off his broad shoulders, walloped her like a steaming slap, shooting tingles to all her girl parts. Her avid gaze skimmed over him—for the forty-fourth time—taking in his toned arms and ridged abs, lingering on the fascinating happy trail that ran downward from his navel and disappeared into his waistband, before continuing on to his nicely muscled legs dusted with golden brown hair and ending at his sandy feet.

His very large, sandy feet.

You know what they say about men with large feet, Jamie.

Her gaze instantly zeroed in on his crotch. Hmmm . . . couldn't get a good read on things. Darn it.

"I'll show you mine if you show me yours."

Her gaze jerked upward. He'd pushed his sunglasses on top of his head and was regarding her through those unfairly gorgeous green eyes with an expression that made it very clear he knew he'd just been ogled with the sort of zeal a piranha would bestow on a hunk of beef.

Jamie's face ignited—oh joy, the blotches would appear any second. And because embarrassment always brought out her inner Victorian schoolmarm, she said in a glacial tone, "I'm not showing you anything. Ever."

He laughed. "Whoa, you can go from hot to icy in a blink. Can't figure out why that amuses me so much."

"Obviously there's something wrong with you." At least mentally. Because there was *nothing* wrong with him physically.

"Obviously," he agreed with a lopsided grin. He looked beyond her. "Here comes Godiva again. She looks like she's got three hundred gallons of water on her coat to shower us with. I don't know about you, but I'm going to make a run for it."

Before she could move, he tossed his glasses in the soft sand, then took off toward the water. Godiva immediately changed direction and headed toward him like a wet, brown laser beam.

Nick dashed into the waves, jumping over several before making a shallow dive beneath a third. Several seconds later he stood and Jamie nearly swallowed her tongue at the sight of him, rising from the foamy waves like a modern-day Adonis, sun glinting off his glistening skin, his board shorts clinging to him in a way that totally proved the big-feet premise, and totally *dis*proved the whole cold water/ shrinkage supposition.

Nick's presence in the shallow water sent Godiva into absolute doggie rapture. Jamie watched them for several minutes, laughing at their antics, and decided right then and there that as soon as her life was once again settled back in New York, she was going to get a dog.

"They're a lot more fun and a lot less trouble than a man," she murmured.

And speaking of fun . . . it was about time she joined in rather than standing on the sidelines. She kicked off her flip-flops, slipped her cover-up over her head, then set it and her sunglasses next to Nick's glasses and ran into the water. A wave broke on her thighs, splashing her right up to her forehead, and she laughed at the sheer refreshment of the cool water sluicing over her sun-warmed skin. She ducked beneath the next wave and surfaced in knee-high water about three feet away from Nick.

His gaze coasted over her yellow tankini and she totally blamed her suddenly hard nipples on the water temperature. He clearly noticed as his gaze lingered there for several seconds before taking in the several inches of bare skin exposed on her stomach. She stood up a bit straighter in an attempt to flatten out the roundness she'd picked up from eating about twelve million calories worth of pity-party Ben & Jerry's after Raymond had dumped her.

When his gaze met hers once again, he favored her with a crooked grin that made her heart flutter—either that or she was going into cardiac arrest. And given how ridiculously sexy he looked, heart failure wasn't outside the realm of possibilities.

"You look good all wet, princess." His eyes darkened and her lungs—which had worked perfectly well for twenty-six years—completely forgot how to function. Good thing a wave chose that moment to slap her in the ass and break her out of the trance she'd fallen into and suck in a breath, otherwise she might have passed out from lack of oxygen.

Nick's teeth flashed brilliant white in another grin and he nodded his chin toward the shore. "Now let's tire out my dog."

Jamie looked at Godiva. She stood on the beach, every muscle quivering, eyes bright with excitement, paws in the water, tail thwapping back and forth like a windshield wiper during a downpour, tennis ball clamped in her mouth.

"I'm thinking we'll tire out long before she does," Jamie said with a laugh, wading toward the dog. "She looks ready to run for about another two hundred miles."

"More like four hundred. Lucky thing you have a good throwing arm."

She paused and shot him a raised-brow look over her shoulder. "Dude. My throwing arm is way better than merely 'good.'" With that, she trotted to Godiva, who obligingly dropped the ball at her feet, and proved herself with a throw that would have done her old high school team proud.

They spent the next hour throwing the ball and splashing each other and Godiva. Nick and Godiva engaged in a playful tug of war over the ball that ended when Godiva suddenly opened her mouth and Nick fell flat on his ass at the water's edge. Jamie was already bent double with laughter while Godiva danced around her, loving this game, when a wave broke right behind Nick, completely engulfing him in foamy, sandy water.

With his gaze fixed on her, he slowly rose. "Are you *laughing* at me?"

"At you—and the piece of seaweed stuck in your hair—and the three pounds of sand that just got washed into your bathing suit."

He shook his leg, and sure enough at least a handful of sand plopped out of the leg of his shorts, dissolving Jamie in another round of giggles.

"God, I wish I had a camera," she managed to gasp out.

"Okay, that's it." He reached her in two strides, and before she could move, he'd scooped her up in his arms and walked purposefully back toward the water.

Although she was weak from laughter, she had enough of her wits about her to note that 1) he'd very impressively plucked her up as if she weighed no more than a daisy, and she was no flyweight, 2) his hard, muscular chest felt *really* nice pressed against her side, and 3) she was about to get tossed in the water.

She wrapped her arms around his neck. "Don't you dare."

He turned his head. His sand-dotted face was only inches from hers and for the first time she noticed the pale gold that radiated out from his pupils into his deep green irises like a sunburst. "Where I come from, laughter leads directly to retribution. And dares are *always* accepted."

"I dare you to put me down."

His gaze flicked to her lips, shooting sparks right down to her toes. "That the best you can do?"

Pretty much, yeah. Because given the way he was looking at her, at how close his lips were to hers, his skin against hers, his strong arms cradling her, she once again forgot how to breathe.

And a darn good thing, otherwise she would have taken in a lungful of water because in the next second he tossed her into an incoming wave and water closed over her head. She came up sputtering and narrowed her eyes at him. "You are in so much trouble."

"Hey, you dared me to put you down."

"I meant on my feet. On the sand."

"Oh. Bummer for you that you didn't make yourself clearer."

"You're going down," Jamie threatened.

"You'll have to catch me first."

She lunged for him, but missed. Godiva barked and danced on the shore, then galloped into the water to join the fun and an impromptu combination of tag, catch, and fetch commenced. Thirty minutes later, Jamie staggered out of the knee-deep water and flopped on her back on the wet sand.

"I give up," she said, breathing heavily from exertion. She felt a thump next to her and turned her head. Nick had dropped to his knees next to her. He was barely breathing heavy, damn him.

"You okay?" he asked, the water dripping from his body splashing on her arm.

"Swell. You happen to have an oxygen mask? Or maybe a morphine drip?"

"Sorry, fresh out."

Just then Godiva bounded out of the water and skidded to a halt beside her. She shook herself, spraying water like a sprinkler, then dropped the tennis ball next to Jamie's head and gave a questioning whine.

"Dear God, isn't she tired yet?" Jamie asked.

"Nah, she's good for at least another three, four miles."

Jamie groaned. Godiva gave her a sniff, then licked her cheek. "I need a minute. Or an hour. Maybe two hours." At least she now knew how Nick stayed in such primo shape. He didn't need a gym—he had the inexhaustible Godiva.

She looked up and saw a bird overhead. "Is that a vulture? Circling, waiting for me to breathe my last?"

"It's a seagull." He shot her a wicked grin. "Bless your heart."

A half laugh she was too exhausted to get all the way out rose in her throat. "I'll get you—and your little dog, too," she said in her best Wicked Witch of the West voice. "As soon as I regain my strength, that is."

"Like hell. As soon as you regain your strength, you're going to keep your promise and help me give my now very salty and sandy—although no longer clammy-smelling—dog a bath."

"Ugh." She flopped out a weak hand to lightly swat him and her fingers skimmed over firm, wet skin. She turned her head and saw that rather than his arm, she'd brushed her hand across his abdomen. Just south of his navel.

He sucked in a quick breath. "I'm not sure if your aim is really bad or really good."

Darn it, neither was she. Jamie's face caught fire and she snatched her hand away as if he'd turned into a blow torch.

"Sorry," she muttered, although she wasn't sure she really was. And if she *was* sorry, was it because she'd accidentally touched his happy trail—or because her hand hadn't brushed over him a few inches lower?

And did she even want to know the answer to that question? Probably not.

Due to her embarrassment, she suddenly felt revived, and—thanks to his beautiful eyes and steaming-hot body and gorgeous smile—as horny as hell.

She sat up and carefully avoided touching him as she stood. "I'm prepared to honor my promise."

They gathered their belongings, and with Godiva safely leashed, they walked back to Southern Comfort, where Nick turned on the hose. Amidst much grunting and laughter and spraying about of water and soapsuds, they managed to get a very excited Godiva soaped up and rinsed. While Nick turned off the hose, Jamie crouched down and wrapped a huge beach towel around Godiva and vigorously rubbed her wet fur.

"Does that feel good baby?" she crooned.

Godiva made happy noises in her throat, licked Jamie's chin, then flopped on her back and presented her belly, which Jamie obligingly rubbed.

"She'll give you three days to knock that off," Nick said from behind her.

Jamie looked at him over her shoulder. He stood several feet away, looking down at her with an expression she couldn't read. She gave Godiva a final pat, then rose.

"Cupcake enjoys having her belly rubbed, too. Must be a pet thing."

"Yeah. It's also a guy thing."

Her gaze dropped to his abs and an image flashed in her mind . . . of her fingers trailing over that taut belly, exploring all those fascinating ridges.

"Thanks for your help with Godiva, princess."

His voice yanked her from her heat-inducing thoughts. She jerked her gaze upward. There was no mistaking the fire kindling in his eyes. She locked her suddenly wobbly knees and swallowed to find her voice.

"You're welcome. And I'm not a princess."

A frown creased between his brows. "Maybe not," he conceded, although he looked both displeased and surprised.

"*Definitely* not." She held out his towel. "I, um, had fun."

He took the towel, and something that looked like confusion clouded his eyes. "Me, too," he said slowly, as if he couldn't believe he was actually saying the words. He studied her for several long seconds with an expression that made it clear he didn't quite know what to make of her. Then his gaze dropped to her mouth and all Jamie's girl parts went on red alert. Then his frown deepened and he took a slow step toward her, as if reluctantly being dragged closer, but unable to stop himself.

She went perfectly still. Holy crap, was he going to *kiss* her? That would be great, er, bad. Really bad. *Bad* idea. Yet it certainly looked like he was thinking about it. Which had her thinking about it. Which had her lips—among other things—tingling in anticipation of that oh so firm yet oh so soft-looking mouth touching hers.

A faint ringtone sounded. He blinked twice, as if emerging from the same lustful fog that had engulfed her. "That's my phone," he said in husky voice. "Excuse me."

He took the stairs two at a time. The screen door banged behind him, then she heard the low murmur of his deep voice.

"Saved by the bell," she murmured. "Literally." And thank goodness. Good grief, what was *wrong* with her? She was in full I Hate Men mode. Her mind and common sense and better judgment knew it—and wanted nothing to do with anything that had a penis—but apparently her libido hadn't gotten the memo and thought Nick Trent was the greatest thing to come along since triple-fudge brownies. With whipped cream. And a cherry on top.

Damn it, now she was hungry.

Kate's words suddenly popped into her mind. *The best way to get over a man is to get under a new one . . . I'm talking about indulging in a summer fling.*

Oh, no. That would be a really bad idea. Bad, bad, bad.

Wouldn't it?

Yes, definitely bad. Very bad. Bad, bad, bad.

The screen door opened and Nick stuck his head out, his iPhone pressed to his ear. He whistled for Godiva, who bounded up the stairs and pushed her way past Nick's legs to enter the house. When Nick looked at Jamie, all traces of heat were gone from his eyes.

"Sorry, but I'm going to be a while," he said in a voice as neutral as his expression. "See you around."

With that he disappeared back inside, the screen door slapping shut behind him.

See you around? "Not if I can help it," Jamie muttered as she walked back to Paradise Lost. She'd clearly lost her marbles for a few minutes there, something she'd put down to Hormone Overload Due to Unexpectedly Sexy Guy syndrome. But she was officially cured. Looks, as she well knew when it came to men, meant zero. Raymond was a perfect example, with his Upper East Side, Ivy League perfection. And he'd turned out to be a Super Shit.

While Nick wasn't handsome in that classical sense like Raymond, his brand of good looks was even more dangerous because he oozed sex appeal. The sort that made clothes just sort of fall off of their own volition—like too much tequila on an empty stomach. Raymond looked like a gentleman you'd want to go to dinner with at an expensive restaurant, while Nick . . . Nick looked like the sexy waiter who you'd want to drag into the pantry, press up against the vegetable bin, and beg to screw your brains out.

Well, there'd be no screwing. Absolutely not. She'd been screwed enough—and not in a good way. Her roof was fixed (hopefully); her stairs, windows, and screens were repaired; and she, therefore, required nothing further from Nick Trent. She'd gone above and beyond helping him bathe his zany but lovable dog, so it was peace out. She was going to pour herself a glass of wine, prepare herself a nice dinner, take a stroll on the beach, then read in bed. No drama, no family, no phone calls, no craziness, and nothing with a penis. Just her and Cupcake and a lot of peace and quiet.

And that sounded absolutely perfect.

Chapter 7

Jamie's first clue that peace and quiet might be harder won than she'd anticipated hit her like a hammer on her head the next morning when she was awakened by a raucous banging sound.

She blindly reached out and grabbed her cell phone from the bedside table, then pried open one eye to check the time. "Who the hell is banging on the door at ten to seven in the morning?"

Cupcake didn't even bother to raise her head from her spot at the foot of the bed. Jamie sat up and pushed her tangle of sleep-flattened hair off her face. The banging continued and she rose, snagged her plaid flannel robe to cover up her Bugs Bunny camisole and sleep shorts, then staggered from the bedroom, squinting against the bright sunlight pouring through the sliding doors that led to the screened porch.

She managed to stuff one arm into the robe, but couldn't quite manage the other arm. With the garment half hanging off, she peeked through the slats in the blinds covering the kitchen window to see who the hell was knocking this early. She'd half expected to see Nick—she wouldn't put it past him to enact revenge for the early-morning wake-up door pounding she'd treated him to the other morning—but instead of her sexy neighbor, three women stood crowded on the small landing outside the kitchen door. Two of them held Tupperware containers, and the other balanced an aluminum foil–covered pan.

Jamie unlocked and opened the door and discovered three pairs of curious eyes staring at her through the screen.

"Oh, dear, were you asleep?" asked the petite covered-pan lady who stood closest to the door. Her poof of snow white hair was adorned with a pair of bifocals—odd given that a pair also dangled dangerously close to the end of her small nose—and her skin was as tanned as shoe leather. She smiled at Jamie, showing off a set of ultra-white dentures that resembled Chiclets. "We're not too early, are we, dear?"

"Um, too early for what exactly?"

All three simultaneously lifted their Tupperwares and pan. "Breakfast," they chirped in unison.

"I'm Dorothy Ernst," said pan lady. "I live across the street. My house is named Beach Music. And this is Grace Cole," she continued, nodding at the attractive blonde behind her, "and Megan Richardson. They both live two blocks over, on Carolina Street. We would have stopped by sooner but we were all at the Shrimp Festival for the past few days and didn't return until late last night."

"We wanted to welcome you to Seaside Cove, seeing as how you'll be here the entire summer," said Grace, who was a good thirty years younger and a foot taller than Dorothy. "There aren't too many of us permanent residents."

"We heard you were from New York and thought you might enjoy a real Southern breakfast," added Megan, a smiling, gorgeous redhead Jamie judged to be in her midthirties, who in spite of the ungodly hour looked as fresh and dewy and perky as if she'd just stepped out of the Fifth Avenue Elizabeth Arden spa.

Apparently word really did travel fast in a small community. Neighbors arriving at the crack of dawn (at least it felt like it) bearing food—definitely not what Jamie was accustomed to, yet she was both touched and charmed by the friendly gesture. Blinking the sleep out of her eyes, she smiled at the ladies and opened the screen door. "It's very nice to meet you. I'm Jamie Newman. Please come in. I'm sorry I look like road kill."

"You look lovely, dear," said Dorothy, entering the kitchen and setting her foil-covered pan on the counter.

Yeah—said the lady who required two pairs of glasses.

Megan set down her Tupperware next to the sink. "We didn't mean to wake you."

Grace shot Dorothy a frown. "I told you it was too early to drop in on her."

Dorothy gave Jamie a sheepish smile. "I thought for sure you'd have been awake for hours already. Nick Trent assured me you were an early riser. In fact he stressed that if we wanted to catch you in, we'd best arrive before seven A.M. And that we should knock very loudly until you answered the door because you always had in your iPod earphones."

Coward. Sending the neighbors over to exact his revenge. She wasn't sure if that made him clever or a chickenshit. A bit of both, she decided.

"Wasn't that thoughtful of him," Jamie murmured. "When did he tell you this?"

"Last night, around eleven. He was leaving just as I was on my way in from the Shrimp Festival and we exchanged a few words."

"Leaving?" Jamie repeated.

"Him and Godiva. Nick had a duffel bag with him. Probably be gone a few days, as is his habit."

"No one knows where he goes," Megan chimed in, "but word is that he goes off on benders. After a few days away, he always stops in at Crabby's Bar. Bob Wright—Crabby's bartender—told Joey Morrison who told Todd Benton who told his wife Shari who told me that Nick always keeps to himself at Crabby's and seems down."

"There you go gossiping again, Megan," Grace said, shaking her head. She leaned closer to Jamie. "Some folks think he has a bunch of different women, while others say he has just one honey on the side. A *married* honey, which is why he goes off for days at a time—to meet up with her. Then, when he has to leave her, he's all sad."

"Now who's repeating gossip?" Megan asked mildly.

"I never repeat gossip," Grace said. Then she grinned. "So you'd better listen carefully the first time."

Dorothy frowned and shook her head. "I don't think he has a bunch of women. In fact, I think he's lonely."

"Men who look like that are never lonely," said Megan.

"Sometimes they are," Dorothy insisted. "Especially if they're nursing a broken heart. But regardless of his situation, I think he's a very sweet boy. Why, I only mentioned in passing that my doorbell was broken and the very next day he showed up and fixed it. Refused to let me pay him. If I had an unmarried granddaughter, I'd have her here pronto to check him out." She smiled at Jamie. "Shall I get a pot of coffee going, dear?"

Jamie snapped out of the fascinated stupor she'd fallen into while following the women's rapid-fire discourse about Nick. "I'll do it," she said, moving to the pantry to get a filter and the can of coffee.

While she counted out scoops of dark, rich grounds, her thoughts turned to Nick. So her pesky albeit sexy neighbor had taken off for parts unknown late last night. Well, good. She certainly wouldn't miss him. And his absence saved her the trouble of telling him what she thought of his sneaky send-the-neighbors-over-early revenge plan. Still, she couldn't help but be curious as to where he'd gone. And why.

A flurry of activity ensued, with Megan setting plates and utensils on the snack bar while Grace and Dorothy unwrapped the food and opened Tupperware. The savory scent of eggs and sausage wafted up Jamie's nose and her stomach growled.

"Smells delicious," she said, setting out four mismatched but serviceable coffee mugs.

"It's my breakfast casserole," Dorothy said, her voice tinged with pride.

"It goes great with my buttermilk biscuits and Megan's red-eye gravy," said Grace.

Cupcake sashayed into the kitchen and made her presence known with a loud yowl, then a squinty-eyed glare that simultaneously asked, *What's that fabulous smell?* and *Who the hell are all these people?*

While the ladies cooed over Cupcake, who graciously

allowed herself to be adored, Jamie served the coffee, then poured some of Cupcake's favorite crunchy fish-flavored treats into her bowl.

"Dorothy, Jack Crawford mentioned something about a Cat Colony Committee on the island," Jamie said as she returned the bag of kibble to the pantry. "What's that all about?"

"Me and six other local residents make sure the feral cats on the island are cared for, although dozens of families leave out food for them. You'll see the cats roaming around—you can identify them by their ears. The tips of their left ears are clipped. The committee uses the TNR method—that's trap-neuter-release. We humanely trap them and bring them to the local vet, who spays or neuters them and vaccinates them for rabies. They're then returned to the beach."

"But we also find strays on the island," Dorothy continued. "People hear about the island cats and they dump off litters of unwanted kittens." There was no mistaking the anger in her voice.

"You mean they abandon them?" Jamie asked, aghast.

"Sometimes right on the side of the road," Grace said, shaking her head. "They figure islanders will take them in, which we do."

"But that's a terrible thing to do to an animal," Jamie said.

"Yes," said Megan. "They don't all survive—either they starve before they can find food, or they're run over by cars."

"Aside from the clipped ear, how can you tell if a cat is abandoned or feral?" Jamie asked.

"Feral cats avoid human interaction and are actually happier living outdoors in their own environment," Dorothy explained. "Basically, they won't let you get near them. The abandoned cats are domesticated and will socialize with you. If you see any cats you think might be feral without clipped ears, let me know and we'll set a trap."

"Thanks, I will. And I'll put out food and water as well."

As the meal was all set out, they served themselves buffet style, then sat around the counter.

"To new neighbors and new friends," Dorothy said, raising her coffee cup.

Everyone touched mug rims and concurred. Jamie tasted a bite of biscuit and gravy and groaned in appreciation. "Wow.

That is delicious." Next she tried the casserole, which was an incredible explosion of luscious flavors on her tongue. "Fabulous. Any recipes you ladies are willing to share would be greatly appreciated."

"Always happy to share recipes," Dorothy said. "I bet you have some good ones from that restaurant you work in."

"I hear you're the manager," added Megan.

Clearly Nick's gums had been flapping. Not that her job was a big secret. She just didn't want to think about it. "I am, and yes, I do have a few favorite recipes."

"Anything with clams?" asked Grace. "If so, you need to make it for the Clam Festival. First prize is fifty dollars, which is, of course, nice, but the bragging rights for winning are priceless. It's a big deal around here."

Out of the corner of her eye, Jamie observed Cupcake's ears perk up at the word *clam*. Before she could answer, Dorothy said, "Nick told me that Maria Rigoletti-Silverman—isn't she a pip?—filled you in on the Clam Festival."

"Which is the other reason we're here," piped up Megan. "Aside from welcoming you, of course."

Jamie's fork froze halfway to her mouth. "Other reason?"

Dorothy smiled at her over the rim of her coffee mug. "Yes, dear. Grace, Megan, and I head up the Clam Committee. You can imagine our excitement when we learned an actual restaurant manager moved to the island. Especially since Walter Murphy is out of commission this year due to his hip-replacement surgery. Bless his heart."

Hmmm . . . she wondered if Walter Bless-His-Heart Murphy's hip replacement was due to dipshit behavior rather than simply natural aging. Jamie looked up from her breakfast casserole and stilled. Uh-oh. The Clam Committee was looking at her with very expectant expressions.

"We could certainly use your expertise," said Grace. "Walter has organized the entire festival for the past eight years, and while we have plenty of volunteers, without him here there isn't a whole lot of actual organizing going on."

Jamie vividly remembered a student meeting when she was a junior in high school—she'd excused herself for a couple minutes to use the bathroom and when she came back she found out she'd been put in charge of the prom committee.

This felt suspiciously similar.

"What exactly is involved?" she asked cautiously.

"Just making sure the vendors all have the proper permits filled out," said Megan.

"And coordinating the placement of the cooking and craft tents to make sure the foot traffic flows well," added Grace.

"Just basically organizing the volunteers and delegating duties—making sure everybody does what they're supposed to do," Dorothy said with an angelic smile. "Nick says you're real good at that."

Jamie cocked a brow. "Did he happen to use the word *bossy*?"

"He might have," Dorothy said with a dismissive wave, "but then my memory isn't what it used to be. If he did say bossy, I'm sure he meant it in the nicest way, seeing as how he's such a nice young man. He definitely said you were the right woman for the job."

Nice young man my ass. "I'm afraid I don't know anything about Clam Festivals—"

"Oh, it can't be much different than running a restaurant," Megan said with an encouraging smile.

"Certainly no more difficult than that," added Grace with an even more encouraging smile.

"It'll be as easy as clam pie," Dorothy assured her.

Jamie wasn't sure what clam pie was, but it sounded like something that would give her a massive stomachache. And she knew damn well she was being played like a Stradivarius.

Still, these smiling women were hard to resist, as was the delicious artery-clogging breakfast they'd brought. At ten to seven in the morning. Something like that simply wasn't done in Manhattan, at least not unless you wanted to be tasered or have a restraining order slapped on you. Seaside Cove was like a foreign country where she didn't understand the laws or the language.

Yet she understood, and appreciated, a friendly gesture, especially one involving food. She'd wanted a place, an environment that wasn't familiar, that was outside her comfort zone, and for better or worse she'd gotten it. And she was good at organizing, delegating, and coordinating—her position at Newman's depended upon it, and she'd always been proud of the job she'd done there. So she might as well embrace the opportunity to try to fit into this community she'd be calling home for the next two months. *When in Rome . . .*

"I'm happy to help out," she said.

"Oh, wonderful!" exclaimed Dorothy. "The next clam meeting is at my house next week. Everyone brings an appetizer-type dish for inspiration and I'll be serving Mojitos because . . . well, who needs a reason for a Mojito?"

"Not me," said Grace. "I've had a house full of rambunctious teenagers all week, so a night out with adults and Mojitos sounds like heaven." She turned to Jamie. "I have twin sixteen-year-old sons. Who between them have about eight thousand friends who love to hang at our house."

"*I* love to hang at your house," said Megan with a laugh. "Grace's place has a pool," she explained to Jamie. "*And* a finished terrace level. *And* a game room. It's like a resort over there."

Grace snorted. "Resort—ha! After a week with the teenagers, it looks like a dump. Your kids are still small. You have no idea how much food a gang of teenage boys can consume. Or how much laundry they make." She blew out a sigh. "When does school start again?"

"Not for another sixty-four days," said Megan, popping a bit of biscuit into her mouth. "Not that I'm counting. And even though mine are only three and eight, believe me, they eat plenty and are geniuses at getting stains on their clothes that even NASA couldn't find a way to get out."

"You'll be crying at the end of next summer, Grace, when those boys of yours go off to college," said Dorothy. "I cried buckets when my kids flew the nest."

Grace held up her hand. "Don't even mention it or I'll tear up. But in the meanwhile . . ." She looked at Jamie. "No kids?"

Jamie shook her head. "Nope. Just one niece. She's fourteen. I miss her a lot."

"Wanna borrow a couple teenagers for a month? Or two?"

Jamie laughed. "Sure, send them over. I'll bake them some cookies."

"If you do, they'll never leave," Grace warned. Then she grinned. "So, yes—why don't you bake a big ol' batch of cookies!"

When the laughter subsided, Dorothy said, "Maria Rigoletti-Silverman says you're entering the Clam Queen contest, Jamie."

Before Jamie could refute that, Megan piped in with, "That's great!"

"No, I'm not—"

"Fabulous," cut in Grace. "We need some new blood in that contest."

Dorothy frowned over the rims of her bifocals. "And we sure don't want that obnoxious Missy Calhoun's daughter to win. That girl's a skank." She looked at Jamie. "And before you ask, yes, I know darn well what a skank is. Got three granddaughters who keep me up to date on all the lingo. Even got me a Facebook page. I may be seventy-two, but thanks to those granddaughters, I'm on the cutting edge of pop culture. You need to know anything about Brangelina or those reality TV housewives, I'm your source."

Jamie couldn't help but smile. "Good to know. I'm on Facebook, too."

Dorothy beamed at her. "Fantastic. Send me a friend request."

"And go to the Clam Festival fan page—my sons set that up," added Grace. "Last time I looked we had over seven hundred fans!"

"Will do," said Jamie. "Now about the Clam Queen contest—not really my thing, I'm afraid. But I'll be sure to root for you ladies."

"Oh, we can't enter," said Megan. "It's for unmarried women only."

"Who are under the age of forty," added Dorothy, "otherwise I'd give you a run for your money." She made a disgruntled sound. "Bunch of age discrimination if you ask me. Been trying to get that changed in the town bylaws ever since I moved here forty years ago, but no luck so far. Folks don't like change, especially to a contest that's been around for more than seventy years. And since that old coot Melvin Tibbs is in charge of the contest, nothing will ever change."

"I've heard of this Melvin but haven't met him yet," said Jamie.

"Consider yourself lucky," Dorothy said. "He's been away visiting his brother in Florida. Good riddance, I say."

"Have you considered leaving the original contest as it is, but just adding additional categories? You could add a Senior Clam Queen or a Clam Empress—something where you have to be at least forty or fifty to enter."

Dorothy, Megan, and Grace all stared at Jamie, then Grace laughed. "Now why didn't we think of that? The committee could vote in something like that even without Melvin's consent because the original contest would remain intact."

"Exactly," agreed Dorothy.

"Maybe there could be a Clam King for younger men and a Clam Emperor as well for gentlemen over forty," Jamie continued, her mind whirling with ideas, especially as those ideas deflected the subject of her entering the contest. "A Mrs. Clam for married women. A Mr. Clam, too. Maybe even a Baby Clam for kids. There could be a fee to enter, which would raise revenue for the town, part of which could be specifically earmarked to help the island's cat population. The added categories would attract more people to the festival—especially if there was a cash prize for winning."

"I love that idea," Grace said.

"My youngest is three and a total girly girl," said Megan, her voice filled with enthusiasm. "She'd be all over a Baby Clam contest."

"Always good to bring in new blood to keep things fresh, and it looks like we've got ourselves a real winner with this one," Dorothy said, jerking her head in Jamie's direction. "Wait until grumpy old Melvin hears these ideas. He won't be able to say no."

Jamie's face warmed at the praise. "If you like, I can type up a draft of the idea and bring it to next week's meeting."

"Some chamber of commerce folks will be there, so that's perfect," said Dorothy. She raised her coffee mug. "Welcome to Seaside Cove, Jamie."

"You're already part of the family," added Grace, and Megan nodded.

A lump of emotion swelled in Jamie's throat. She'd wanted to get away from her old life, from everything familiar, but she hadn't anticipated making new friends. Hadn't expected such . . . acceptance. Especially from strangers. But it seemed there weren't any strangers in Seaside Cove. It felt odd. Unfamiliar.

But really good.

Once again they all clinked mugs. And a thin layer of the stress and sadness weighing her down was stripped away. There were still a lot more layers to go.

But it was start.

Chapter 8

After Dorothy, Grace, and Megan departed, Jamie set out a bowl of crunchies on the carport for the island cats. She'd yet to see any of them near the house, but she'd filled the bowl the last two mornings, and by evening it was empty.

Her gaze wandered to Southern Comfort, and as much as she didn't want to, she couldn't help but wonder where Nick had gone. And why he'd left so late last night. Was he really off on a bender as rumor had it? She supposed it was possible, but her gut told her there was some other explanation for his disappearances. She hadn't seen him drink anything other than water, nor had he smelled of alcohol. Not that that meant a whole lot, yet her instincts didn't buy the whole bender theory.

Could be his late-night departure involved something unsavory—like a married girlfriend. Or illegal. Or both. Could be . . . yet something told her no. Which pretty much annoyed her as she knew squat about him. *That's not really true,* her inner voice whispered. *You know he kept his word about fixing the steps and the roof. And he replaced the porch screens and cracked windows without you even asking. You know he's good to his dog. And that he has a great smile and a body that practically gave you whiplash.*

Humph. All true—yet not really good reasons to stop viewing him with a suspicious eyeball. At any rate, where he went and why wasn't her business. She didn't care, and she had no intention of getting involved.

She was about to head back up the stairs when a white pickup truck pulled into the driveway next door at Gone Fishin'. The door opened and a tall, silver-haired man she judged to be in his late sixties sporting a military buzz-cut emerged. Ah—this must be her neighbor, the infamous Melvin Tibbs. He wore a pristine white Polo shirt tucked into khaki pants with a razor-sharp crease, and brown Top-Siders. His posture was ramrod straight and Jamie found herself pulling her shoulders back lest she be caught slouching. As if he sensed her presence, he looked toward Paradise Lost. When he saw her, a scowl overtook his already-grim countenance. Yikes. This was one grumpy-looking dude.

Still, grumpy didn't scare her. Shooting him her friendliest smile, she walked toward him. "Hi. You must be Mr. Tibbs. I'm—"

"Newman," he cut in, his voice a brusque rasp. "Here for the summer. One of them New York types, I heard."

Jamie wasn't certain what a "New York type" was, but based on Melvin's tone, it wasn't good. Still, as she had no desire to make an enemy—unless it was absolutely necessary— she kept her smile in place. "Yes, I'm Jamie Newman, here for the summer, from New York." Ha—take that, Grumpy. And just to prove she wasn't ill-mannered, she added, "I was about to put on a fresh pot of coffee. Would you care to join me?"

His brows slammed together, turning his scowl downright ferocious. "Are you patronizing me, young lady?"

"Uh, no. I was inviting you to partake of a traditional breakfast beverage."

"I take my breakfast beverage at oh five hundred hours. Lights out is at precisely twenty-one hundred hours. I'll expect noise to be kept to a minimum after that." He narrowed his dark eyes at the bag of cat food she still held. "Another one of those bleeding-heart cat feeders, I see. Bah!"

Without another word he marched up the steps to his house.

Jamie blinked and resisted the urge to salute. "All righty

then," she muttered. So much for her first meeting with General Scrooge. Yet instead of annoying her, the encounter had piqued her curiosity as to why Melvin Tibbs had such a stick up his ass. And instilled in her a perverse desire to kill him with kindness, the same way she'd conquered Billy Holmes, her third-grade nemesis. She'd vanquished Billy with homemade chocolate chip cookies and bubble gum, eventually turning him from tormentor to buddy, and she didn't doubt Melvin Tibbs was nothing more than a grown-up Billy. *Heh, heh, heh, Melvin. You've met your match.*

When she reentered the house, she booted up her laptop, then set up a spreadsheet that clearly laid out for the committee members a budget of revenue and expenses pertaining to the addition of more clam contests to the festival. By utilizing different what-if scenarios, she illustrated the bottom-line possibilities with various entry fees and number of entrants. When she looked at the numbers, her brows shot upward. By charging even a nominal fee, the town could earn a lot of money. Anticipation tingled through her. She couldn't wait to show this to the committee at next week's clam meeting.

She shook her head. Clam meeting. Good grief. If anyone had told her even two weeks ago that she'd be making spreadsheets for a clam committee and shopping at a Piggly Wiggly and chasing a zany, smelly dog around, she'd have laughed herself into a seizure. Two weeks ago no one could have convinced her that she'd ever take an eight-week vacation from Newman's and escape seven hundred miles away.

Betrayal, she'd discovered, the sort that cut right to the bone, could change a lot of things very quickly.

After putting the finishing touches on her spreadsheet, she began an Internet search for local car-rental agencies. Google had just spit up a page of listings when a car door slammed directly outside.

Was Nick home? Her heart bumped against her ribs and she frowned at the reaction. She didn't care if he was home. Not a bit. And she certainly wasn't going to look to see if he was. Heck, no. But seeing the sun shining reminded her that it was far too nice to remain indoors. Time to grab her bathing suit and go for a swim.

She abandoned her car-rental search and rose. Before she could step toward the bedroom, however, she heard footfalls on the wooden steps leading up to her kitchen door. She was half a dozen feet away from the door when a face appeared behind the screen.

"Jamie?" asked a familiar voice, accompanied by a knock.

Jamie's steps faltered and for the space of several seconds her every thought was reduced to a single word.

Shit.

"Helloooo? Jamie?"

She had to clear her throat to find her voice. "Mom?"

Maggie Newman pressed her nose to the screen door. Her eyes widened at the sight of Jamie. "You're here. You're really here."

Jamie hurried across the kitchen. She opened the screen door and was immediately engulfed in a tight hug that filled her head with the delicate rose scent her mother always wore.

"I'm so glad I found you," her mother said, leaning back, but still holding her by the shoulders. "When I saw the run-down condition of the house and that decapitated flamingo, I thought I had the wrong address, but here you are." Her gaze shifted to take in the interior and her jaw dropped. "I thought you said the place was a palace."

"It's . . . rustic."

"It's . . ." Her mom's gaze took in the mail carton/plywood coffee table. "Yikes."

"It isn't fancy, but it's clean."

Mom looked at the Formica countertop and wrinkled her nose. "Are you sure? 'Cause it looks like it could use a good scrubbing."

"I'm sure. Mom, what are you doing here?"

Mom squeezed her hands and gave her a tired smile. "I missed you. New York isn't the same without my girl."

"That's sweet—and I miss you, too. But you could have called."

Mom shook her head. "I needed to see you. Talk to you in person." She set her purse on the counter, pressed her hands to her lower back, and stretched. "I'm sore from all that driving."

Jamie stared. "You *drove* here?"

Mom winced and stretched again. "I did."

"But . . . but you hate driving long distances."

"And this is why—my whole body aches from sitting for so long."

A sense of dread filled Jamie. Whatever her mom needed to say had to indeed be important for her to drive all the way to Seaside Cove. She scanned her mother from head to foot, taking in her Habitat for Humanity T-shirt, denim cutoffs, and flip-flops. Her shoulder-length light brown curls, which she'd passed along in the gene pool to Jamie, were pulled back in a haphazard pony tail. She wore no make-up, but she rarely did, normally only giving her lashes a swipe of mascara and her mouth a dash of lip balm—a habit also passed along to Jamie. At forty-six, Maggie Newman looked at least ten years younger—which Jamie fervently hoped would be passed along as well.

When her gaze finally settled on her mother's, Jamie's stomach knotted with concern. "Have you been crying, Mom?"

Mom's eyes immediately filled. "No."

Oh, God. Here came the drama.

"Yes, you have." Jamie took her hand and led her to the sofa. "Come. Sit. Can I get you anything? Juice, water, coffee?"

"No, thanks."

Once they were seated, Jamie asked, "Is this about the bill-pay stuff? Because if it is—"

"It's not." Mom dug in her purse and pulled out a wad of wrinkled tissues. "There's no easy way to say this, so I'm just going to say it." She looked at Jamie through watery eyes, drew a deep breath, then whispered, "I'm pregnant."

Jamie stared. Then blinked. Twice. She'd anticipated some sort of drama, but not anything remotely like this. She opened her mouth to speak, only to discover her jaw had already dropped. She forced out the only word she could manage. "Huh?"

Two fat teardrops dribbled down her mother's cheeks. "I'm pregnant. I just found out a few days ago."

"I . . . Wow." A dozen questions buzzed through Jamie's head as she studied her mom's distressed expression. "I don't know what to say, Mom. I didn't even know you were dating anyone." Which in itself was a huge shock—her mother was normally guilty of over-sharing. Jamie had never before known her to keep secrets.

Her mother's face turned crimson. "I've been seeing someone for a few months."

"You haven't mentioned him."

"I know. I wanted to, but . . ."

When her voice trailed off, Jamie asked, "Did you think I'd be upset?" Her mother merely shrugged and Jamie gently squeezed her hands. "Mom, it's been three years since Daddy died. I know you've been lonely." She raised their joined hands and pressed a kiss to the backs of her mother's fingers. "You're young and vibrant and loving and I would never begrudge you finding someone else. More than anything, I want your happiness. Surely you know that."

More tears left silvery tracks on her mom's cheeks. "Thanks, honey. But . . ." She briefly squeezed her eyes shut. "Good God, I'm *forty-six* years old. How did this happen?"

"Well, unless a test tube was involved, I'm guessing it happened the old-fashioned way." Jamie shook her head. "I can't believe I'm saying this to my *mother*, but weren't you using protection?"

"Of course—except for that one time. *One time!* But for God's sake, I honestly didn't think it would be a big deal. Do you know the odds of a forty-six-year-old woman getting pregnant? And by a one-time lack of a condom?"

"Not off the top of my head, but obviously, you didn't beat the odds."

A humorless sound blew past her mom's lips. "Obviously." She slipped her hands from Jamie's and dragged her fingers under her wet eyes. "God, I'm still in shock. At first I thought the reason I'd missed my periods was because menopause had kicked in. It wasn't until I started barfing my brains out every morning and my boobs swelled up and hurt like hell that I even thought of any other possibility."

Jamie wasn't sure which mental image was worse—her mother having wild monkey sex without a condom, or tossing her cookies with swollen boobs. *Thanks for those visuals, Mom. I'm now officially scarred for life.* "What are you going to do?"

"I . . . I just don't know. I've always been a go-with-the-flow sort of person, and as you know, practicality has never been my strong suit, but this . . . this has really thrown me. There's no way to be nonchalant about it, and I've had to force myself to think very seriously and consider all the ramifications as my decisions will not only affect me for the rest of my life, but the life of a child as well."

"Have you seen your doctor?"

"Yes. She explained that there are risks at my age, and extra precautions are needed, but many of the risks can be managed effectively. She prescribed prenatal vitamins and recommended testing to diagnose or rule out chromosomal abnormalities. She said that since I'm in excellent health, if the prenatal testing rules out chromosomal defects, the baby probably would be at no greater risk of birth defects than if I were younger."

She tucked a stray curl behind her ear, then continued, "On the surface, having a baby is wonderful and exciting and fun, but the hard reality is that the thought of raising a child on my own, at my age, is terrifying. And exhausting. God, Jamie, I'd be *sixty-four* at the high school graduation! Nearly seventy by college graduation. That's sobering, to say the least." She blew out a long, slow breath. "Yet the thought of ending the pregnancy is even more terrifying."

"Mom . . . you clearly haven't wanted to talk about the baby's father, but I have to ask—what about him? Why would you be raising the child on your own? What does he have to say about all this?"

When her mother hesitated, Jamie asked, "Does he know?"

She nodded, then a sob escaped her. "Yes."

Jamie's heart squeezed in sympathy as understanding dawned. "He's upset about the pregnancy and has left you to deal with it on your own." Bastard. She didn't know who he was, but he'd just taken over the top spot on her shit list. And the bottom spot as well. And he was all the shits in between.

Mom shook her head. "No, although he was definitely surprised. And he didn't leave me. I left him."

Jamie frowned. "Why?"

Her mother rose and paced the length of the room. "Because there are . . . problems."

Jamie forced herself to remain silent, to wait for an explanation, which was a shock in and of itself as Maggie Newman was normally a veritable chatterbox. She tried to recall an instance where she'd had to drag information from her mom, and came up blank.

Finally her mother said, "There are reasons why I haven't mentioned him."

"I figured as much. Do you want to talk about them?"

"I do. It's just . . . embarrassing."

"Is he married? Is that the problem?"

Mom's eyes widened with horror. "Of course not! How could you even ask me such a thing? I would never sleep with a married man. Unless, you know, I was married to him. No, the problem with Alex is . . . well, we weren't exactly dating. We were just . . . friends with benefits."

Jamie forced herself not to wince. God, she hoped her mother wouldn't suddenly revert back to character and embark on a bunch of over-sharing. Not that she begrudged her mother a sex life—not at all—but she seriously did not want to hear any details. Just the words "friends with benefits" coming from one's mother should be filed under Too Much Information. She could only pray her mom's next sentence wouldn't include the phrase "booty call."

Still, as this was clearly a crisis, she'd have to suck it up—just as she'd always done. After clearing her throat, she said, "I see. So you just have a sexual relationship with him."

"*Had.* A week ago I told him I didn't think we should see each other any longer. Three days later I found out I was pregnant." She paused in her pacing and faced Jamie. "I wanted to talk to you about it, but not over the phone. I was debating if I should come here or not, but then things came to a head yesterday and I had to get away. Had to see you. Talk to you."

"What happened yesterday?"

"Alex found out I'm pregnant."

"You hadn't told him right away?"

"No."

Something in her mom's voice made Jamie ask, "How did he find out?"

"He overheard me on my cell phone at Newman's speaking with the doctor."

"Newman's? He came to the restaurant to see you?"

"Not exactly. He . . . oh, hell." She wrapped her arms around herself. "He's been working there. You know the general contractor you hired to do the renovations at Newman's? Friends with Benefits Alex is Alex Wharton. The contractor." Before she could say a word, her mother added, "So now you know the basis for the problems."

Jamie raised her brows. "I do?"

"Yes. Do you not know who I'm talking about?"

"Of course. Alex Wharton. Contractor. Tall, dark hair, nice smile, always on time."

"And . . . ?"

"And . . . I don't know, Mom. Is he a criminal?"

Her mother shot her an are-you-kidding-me look. "I'm talking about his *looks*."

"What's wrong with them? I'm assuming you liked his looks since you got naked with him."

"You're being deliberately obtuse. Or maybe you really don't get it. Jamie—he's *thirty-two*."

"Last I heard, that's well beyond the age of consent, Mom."

"And I'm forty-six."

"Yes, I know. And yes, I can do the math. You're fourteen years older than him."

"Do you know what that makes me?"

"The envy of all your friends?" Jamie guessed.

"A cougar." Her mom frowned. "You don't look shocked."

"At what, exactly? That you'd find a handsome, younger man attractive? Hardly. That you'd sleep with him? Again, no. That you'd fail to use protection? Okay, that's surprising. That you're pregnant? Yup, gotta give you that one—you definitely stunned me there." In an effort to add some levity, she teased, "I mean it's usually the daughter who confesses to her mother that she's gotten knocked up by some stud."

"This is no time for jokes, Jamie. I'm in a terrible dilemma here."

"Sorry. So, what was Alex's reaction when he found out?"

"Well, he was stunned. And upset that I hadn't told him right away. And then he said he'd never wanted to break up in the first place. That he wanted us to get back together. And figure out this situation. Together."

"I see. And how do you feel about that?"

"I just don't know. I'm very confused." She dabbed at her eyes with her wadded-up tissues. "And these darn hormones aren't making things any easier."

"Why didn't you want to see him any longer? Was it because you didn't care for him? Or because you were beginning to care too much?"

With a sigh, her mother sank down onto the sofa beside her. "I . . . don't know. I think I care for him. A lot. Too much."

"Why too much? You said he didn't want to stop seeing you. Maybe he cares for you a lot, too. The fact that he said he wanted to get back together even after knowing you were pregnant has to tell you something."

"But where could our relationship go?"

"I don't know. I guess that depends on where you want it to go. On how much you care. And how much he cares. And what you decide you're going to do about the baby."

Her mom's troubled gaze searched hers. "What would you do?"

If Jamie had a nickel for every time her mom had asked her that question, she'd be cruising the Mediterranean on her three-hundred-foot yacht, hobnobbing with the Bill Gates/ Larry Ellison/Warren Buffet crowd. Most of the time the question involved nothing more serious than "seafood or steak for dinner?"

This, however, was not one of those times.

Aside from Laurel, this was another huge thing she'd wanted to escape—her mother constantly expecting her to make all her decisions for her under the guise of "what would you do?"

Well, she wasn't about to step into the huge hole of drama yawning in front of her. She therefore pondered for several seconds before saying carefully, "I'd think long and hard and very honestly about what I wanted, weighing all the pros and cons. And once I figured it out, I'd do everything in my power to get it."

"But what would you *do*?"

"It doesn't matter because that would only be what's right for *me*. You need to do what's right for *you*—and you're the only one who can figure out what that is, Mom. But I will tell you this: I wouldn't let a few years' age difference stop me from having what my heart desired."

Her mom gave her nose a gusty blow. "Fourteen years is a lot more than *a few*, Jamie."

"Okay, but I don't see why it's such an issue for you, especially as Daddy was sixteen years older than *you*."

"There's a difference between the man being older and the woman. Maybe there shouldn't be, but there is. At least to me. And fourteen years is a *big* difference. I'm afraid Alex is simply too young."

"For what?"

"A woman of forty-six."

"You obviously didn't think so when you started seeing him."

"I did. But he just proved . . . irresistible." She gave a helpless shrug. "It started out with just friendly conversation. Fun and flirty. I was flattered by his attention. It had been a long time since I'd felt any sort of spark with anyone, and when he asked me to dinner, I found myself saying yes. I knew he was younger, but I didn't know how much younger until we'd already slept together. And by then . . ."

"You were hooked?"

Mom sighed. "Completely addicted. I told myself it was just sex, so the age difference didn't matter. But sleeping with him was one thing. Having a baby with him, considering a future with him is something else entirely. When he's the age I am now, I'll be sixty."

"It's not as if he's a child, Mom. He's a grown man. He has his own company. From my dealings with him, I know he's professional, responsible, and does excellent work."

"So you think I should stay with him."

Jamie held up her hands. "I'm not saying that. Only you—and Alex—can make that decision. I'm not even saying the age difference shouldn't be a factor in your decision. All I'm saying is that I don't think it's the huge deal you're making it out to be. Men age, too, you know. And you're the youngest forty-six-year-old I've ever known. Age is a state of mind. And I'm guessing a younger man would, well, keep a woman young. Do you love him?"

Tears immediately filled her mom's brown eyes. "No. Yes. Maybe. I don't know."

A small smile curved Jamie's lips. "Decisive as always. You've always followed your heart, Mom. What's wrong with loving this man?"

"Would *you* want to be fourteen years older than your boyfriend?"

"Hell, no. He'd be twelve. And I'd be in jail."

"Ha, ha." Mom heaved a long sigh, then rose. "As you said, I have a lot of thinking to do. Can you help me with my bags?"

Jamie stilled. "Bags?"

"Don't worry, I packed light. Good thing, too, since this place is a lot smaller than you let on. Are the bedrooms through those doors?"

The reality of the situation suddenly hit Jamie like a sucker punch. Her much-needed life-reassessment, recharge, regroup alone time had just turned into a Rescue Mom—*Again*—scenario. She'd escaped New York and her family drama only to have New York and her family drama follow her here.

"Is there a washer and dryer?" her mom asked. "Because I only brought enough clothes for about three weeks."

Jamie's stomach dropped to her feet. *"Three weeks?* But . . . but surely you can't take that much time off from Newman's." *Please, God, tell me she can't take that much time off.*

"Don't worry, Nathan and Patrick have everything under control. Uh-oh," said Mom, holding her midsection. "Gotta barf. Quick—where's the nearest bathroom?"

Jamie pointed to the door leading to the empty bedroom and attached bath. Mom took off like an Olympic sprinter and seconds later Jamie heard the sound of muffled retching.

Damn, double damn.

Paradise, it seemed, was well and truly lost.

Chapter 9

The first deep purple skeins of twilight darkened the sky as Nick drove his truck over the bridge leading to Seaside Cove. He dragged one hand down his stubbled face and grunted out an exhausted sigh of relief. After three long days away, all he wanted was something to eat, then to fall facedown in his own bed and sleep until he wasn't tired anymore—which could conceivably be for the next five or six days.

A few minutes later he turned onto his street and found himself slowing down and craning his neck as he approached Paradise Lost. Which really irked him. 'Cause it made it seem as if he were looking for that princess. Which he absolutely wasn't. And damn it, given how tired, hungry, and grimy he was, he didn't need anything else to annoy him.

Godiva, who'd had her head stuck out the window for the entire drive home, turned toward him and started panting. Nick blew out a sigh. A man could lie to himself, but he couldn't lie to his dog.

"Yeah, she sort of has that same effect on me."

Damn it all to hell and back.

Or at least she had. But not anymore. No, these few days away had erased Jamie Newman from his mind. Absolutely.

Whatever mild attraction he might have felt for her was nothing but a blip on the radar screen. A complete aberration and now completely forgotten. The reason he was still craning his neck had nothing to do with trying to catch a glimpse of her. No, he was merely checking out the Honda parked in her carport. Guess she'd rented a car. Well good. Now he didn't need to offer to drag her ass to the Piggly Wiggly.

And speaking of her ass—

He hit the brakes and stared.

At her ass. Clad in faded denim shorts and hiked in the air as she knelt on a corner of the carport and leaned forward with one hand extended, trying to coax a fluffy black-and-white cat sitting near the bushes to come closer.

She wriggled a little closer to the cat and Nick actually felt his eyes glaze over . . . his eyes that felt superglued to her ass. Her very fine, very curvy ass. Had he thought he was hungry? Damn. Starving was a better word. Yet all thoughts of food had deserted him.

Wetness on his wrist pulled him from his stupor. He dragged his gaze from her butt and watched Godiva give his wrist another swipe of her tongue. "Okay, okay. We're going."

He lifted his foot from the brake and drove the remaining few feet to Southern Comfort, where he parked under the carport. Knowing Godiva's bladder was probably close to bursting, he reached over and opened the passenger door. She rocketed out and disappeared around the bushes separating Southern Comfort and Paradise Lost, barking for all she was worth.

Nick climbed from the truck, grabbed his duffel from the cab, and headed toward the back stairs leading up to his kitchen. Absolutely no way in hell was he going to chat with his neighbor. Before he reached the steps, however, he heard Jamie laugh. And to both his annoyance and disgust, he stopped and turned in that direction, drawn to the sound like a starving man to a banquet feast.

"You scared away the kitty, but it's impossible to be annoyed at you," came her voice from the other side of the hedge.

Before Nick could even think about what he was doing, he set down his bag and walked around the hedges. And found his faithful dog stretched out on her back, tongue lolling, paws dangling in the air, her left hind leg thumping in delight as she received a thorough belly rub.

"Do you ever get tired of this?" Jamie asked his dog.

"Never," Nick answered. "She'd let you do that until your arm fell off."

She looked up at him and smiled.

And Nick's stomach sank like a stone.

Shit.

One smile. That's all it took. And the unwanted attraction he'd only moments ago believed was an aberration roared back and walloped him where he stood. Which just really pissed him off. As did the fact that she'd somehow lured him over here with her sexy, husky laugh and sexy, curvy ass, making him forget all about being tired, hungry, and dirty.

"She's obviously got you well trained," Jamie said.

"Says the person who's still rubbing the dog's belly."

"I should be annoyed with Godiva—the cat I was trying to feed took one look at her and headed for Florida—but she's just too darn adorable."

Godiva made a sound that indicated she completely agreed with Jamie's assessment of her adorableness.

"That's why they call them scaredy-cats," said Nick. "But don't worry, your feline friend will be back. There's a whole gang of them that hang out around here." The fact that he stood there yapping, unable to drag his gaze away from her, instead of whistling for his dog and going the hell home, only served to irritate him further.

She gave Godiva a final pat and then rose. "I know. I've been feeding them. The feral cats are shy, but I didn't see a clipped ear on that one so I don't believe she's part of a colony. I think she's either abandoned or a stray and just frightened."

Even in the fading light he could see the pink tint of sunburn painted across her nose and arms left bare by her bright yellow tank top. Her honey-colored hair danced around her shoulders in a mass of loose curls his fingers itched to mess with. An inch of tanned skin peeked out between the bottom of her tank and the top of her shorts—a tempting bit of flesh he felt a sudden, overwhelming desire to explore. With his tongue. Combined with those cutoff short shorts that showcased her curvy, toned legs, and bare feet, she looked natural and sun-kissed and undone and good enough to eat. And damn it, he needed a good meal.

He forced his gaze back up to her eyes. "I'm sure she'll come back. I feed the island cats, too—although half the time Godiva gobbles up the food I leave out for them." He jerked his head toward the Honda in her carport. "I see you rented a car."

"No." Color stained her cheeks. "I, um, have company."

Something that felt exactly like jealousy, but of course couldn't have been, rippled through him. "Boyfriend?" He barely refrained from wincing. Damn it, he hadn't meant to say that out loud.

Her eyes widened, then she shook her head. "No. God, no."

Something that felt exactly like relief, but couldn't have been, replaced the it-wasn't-jealousy sensation. And he refused to acknowledge the jolt her answer—which made it pretty clear there was no boyfriend—gave him. Of course, her answer also made it sound like she hated men.

Not that he cared.

Nope, not a bit.

"My mother is here," she said.

You've solved the great who-owns-the-Honda mystery, so go home, his brain commanded his feet. His stupid feet remained nailed in place. "Is that . . . good?"

"She showed up three days ago. With half a dozen suitcases. And enough drama to sink a ship." Her gaze wandered past him to his truck. "What're in all those big boxes in your cab?"

Stop talking to her! "My new kitchen cabinets. Whitewashed oak. Really nice. It'll be good to have a kitchen again."

"You cook?"

He shrugged. "Depends on your definition of cooking. I can spread the hell out of peanut butter and jelly onto bread, pour cereal and milk into any bowl, and toast a bagel without burning it. Usually. And if something has microwave directions, I'm your guy."

"Impressive."

"Really?"

"Um, no," she said with a laugh.

Stop looking at her and get your ass home! his brain

yelled. Instead he crossed his arms over his chest and raised his brows. "And I suppose with all your restaurant experience, you're some sort of great chef?"

"I wouldn't say that, but I do like to cook. And by the way, dumping cereal and milk into a bowl does not constitute cooking."

"It does in my house. Ask Godiva. She thinks I'm a genius with Froot Loops."

"Uh-huh. I bet she drinks out of the toilet, too."

"Only when I forget to put down the lid." Which was all the time, but he didn't have to share *that* tidbit of info. And once again, instead of calling his dog, who was now sprawled out on her carport happily chewing a stick, and heading for home, he found himself asking, "How long is your mother staying?"

Jamie briefly closed her eyes. "I don't think she's ever going to leave."

A dry laugh caught in his throat. "Sounds like it's a good thing you never returned my bottle of vodka."

"Is that your not-so-subtle way of asking for it back?"

"Maybe." God knows he felt like he could use a stiff drink. Or two. Or twelve.

"That's not very neighborly of you."

"Maybe I'm not feeling particularly neighborly."

Which was the absolute truth. He felt hot. Tense. Edgy. And aroused as hell. And more than a little pissed off—at her for looking so soft and tousled and sexy and irresistible. All without even trying. God help him if she actually put some effort into it. But mostly he was pissed off at himself—for rapidly losing the battle to resist her.

He needed to go home. Now.

Instead he took a step closer to her.

He heard the faint snap of Dorothy Ernst's bug zapper across the street and his lips flattened into a grim line. He knew exactly how those poor fried bastards felt. They probably screamed, *Stay away from the light!* even as they flew right into it, unable to resist the tempting allure. Even knowing it was bad for them. Even knowing they were headed for doom.

It really rankled that he was apparently no smarter than a damn insect.

After being so tempted to kiss her four days ago while they frolicked with Godiva on the beach, he'd gotten the hell out of Dodge. Unfortunately the time away hadn't lessened his unwanted attraction to her. While he didn't know exactly what had brought Jamie to Seaside Cove, he strongly suspected she'd run away from a bad relationship. Which meant she was on the rebound—always a losing proposition in his experience. Plus, she was bossy. And had a prissy cat named Cupcake. Who the hell named their cat Cupcake?

Not only did he not have the time or the inclination to start a relationship—he'd had more than enough of having his heart and his gonads handed to him on a platter—there was no way he wanted to get involved with someone who lived right next door, who he'd have to see every day. Who'd have expectations of him.

Christ, he was so damn tired of people expecting things from him. Wanting, demanding. And the ultimate disappointment when he failed to live up to those expectations, and all the guilt that came along with that disappointment. That was his favorite thing about Seaside Cove—no one expected anything from him. The fact that the locals believed him nothing more than a decent enough guy who went off on benders was fine with him. That's the way he liked it. And the way he intended to keep it.

So what the hell was he still doing standing here?

And *really* what the hell was he doing taking another step closer to her?

Damned if he knew. Because it felt exactly like playing with fire. Still, he couldn't stop himself. Even though it felt as if he were burning.

Wariness flickered in her eyes and she took a step back. She looked decidedly unsettled. Grim satisfaction filled him. Good. Why should he be the only one off-kilter?

Her gaze wandered over him, making him aware of the fact that he needed a shower, a shave, and a change of clothes. She moistened her lips and his attention zeroed in on her plump mouth.

He took another step toward her. She hastily stepped back and her shoulders hit the outside wall of the storage closet.

He took a final step toward her and planted one palm on

the wall beside her head. A mere two feet separated them, and when he inhaled, his head filled with the delicious scent of cookies.

His jaw clenched and his hand fisted against the wood panel. Christ. What chance did a man stand against a woman who smelled like *cookies*? Seriously, there oughta be a law against that. He took another deep breath and bit back the groan that rose in his throat. She smelled so damn good and all he could think about was wolfing her down in a single gulp.

Her gaze flicked over the minimal distance separating them. When she looked at him again, he saw both annoyance and heat in her eyes.

He liked them both. A lot.

"Are you okay, Nick?"

"Why do you ask?"

"You seem . . . tense. And you're, um, crowding me."

Just to annoy her, he leaned forward to crowd her a little more. And was rewarded with another flash of heat and irritation in her eyes. "Actually, no, I'm not okay."

She lifted her chin and narrowed her eyes. Oh, yeah, she was definitely pissed. Excellent. Again her gaze skimmed over his rumpled, unkempt appearance. "So I see. Rough few days?" she asked with a decided sneer.

"You could say that. I've been busy."

"Yeah, well, whiskey doesn't drink itself."

He cocked a brow. "That's the word around town—that I've been off on a bender?"

"It's one of several theories."

"Really? What are the others?"

"I'm sure you've heard them."

"Actually I haven't—and I'd love to know."

He could almost hear her debating whether to tell him. Finally she said, "I've heard everything from CIA agent to you have a married lover."

"Interesting."

"Hit man is also making the rounds."

"How about that I'm visiting a crippled friend or helping the unfortunate?"

A snort of disbelief escaped her. "Not even in the top fifty."

Keeping his gaze steady on hers, he nodded slowly. "What's your guess?"

"It's none of my business."

"I agree. But I'd still like to know. Would you like a hint?" He leaned forward and his body lightly brushed hers. He heard a quick intake of breath, but wasn't sure if it came from him or her. "I don't have a lover—married or otherwise," he whispered in her ear.

He leaned back. She stood pressed against the wall regarding him with an unreadable expression. But the way her chest rose and fell with her rapid breaths and her dilated pupils let him know he wasn't the only one feeling this . ... whatever the hell it was.

She swallowed, then said, "Again, none of my business. The very fact that you'd think I was interested in knowing that makes it clear you've been drinking."

The whiff of disdain in her voice frayed his already tattered control. "Well, there's one sure way to find out, princess." He pinned her to the wall with his body. And settled his mouth on hers in a hard, demanding kiss.

For several stunned seconds, Jamie remained immobile under the onslaught of Nick's kiss. Damn it, he'd annoyed her. Goaded her. She absolutely shouldn't want this.

But, oh God, she did.

With a groan she couldn't contain, she wrapped her arms around his neck, arched into him, and parted her lips. Their tongues danced, circling, delving, exploring. He wasn't gentle and she didn't care. The overwhelming impatience and fierce need ripping through her would have shocked her if she'd had the ability to think clearly. But there was no thinking. Only feeling. Only pleasure. Only his tongue stroking hers. His hands molding her closer. His body hard and insistent. She pressed herself tighter against him to feel more. Take more.

With a noise that resembled a growl, he turned them so his back rested against the wall and spread his legs. She fit in the vee of his thighs and melted against him as if she were made of wax and he was fire.

He fisted one hand in her hair while his other hand skimmed down her back to cup her bottom. Her restless fingers tunneled through his thick hair, and she reveled in the warmth of his big hands urging her closer, the rasp of his stubble abrading her skin. God, he just felt sooo good. Big. Strong. And warm . . . He was so warm. Heat pumped off him like a furnace. And that gorgeous mouth of his? Oh, yeah, he definitely knew how to use it.

Her nipples tightened into aching points as her insides were reduced to liquid fire, spearing heat to her every nerve ending. The folds between her legs pulsed and she squirmed against him, desperately seeking relief. His hardness pressed her, oh, right there, and she groaned into his mouth.

But then, damn him, he raised his head. A moan of protest rumbled in her throat and she dragged open her eyelids. His palms still cupped her butt and the inferno in his eyes could have lit a match underwater.

"Well?" he asked, his rapid, choppy breaths matching hers.

She blinked. "You want *accolades*?" she asked, trying not to pant. "Sheesh. What an ego."

"Not accolades. Just the truth."

"Fine. It was a good kiss, okay? And this"—she lightly nudged her pelvis against his erection—"tells me you thought so, too."

"That's not what I meant. I meant, did you taste any whiskey?"

She froze as reality slapped her with an icy hand. She unplastered herself from him and stepped back several paces. She desperately wanted to rake her fingers through her disheveled mop of hair, but since her hands didn't feel quite steady, she shoved them into her pockets instead. A combination of humiliation, self-disgust, and anger brewed inside her. "So that's what that kiss was about. To prove a point."

He didn't move, didn't try to stop her from putting space between them, merely regarded her with an expression she couldn't read. "Did I prove it?"

She hadn't detected even the faintest trace of alcohol. No, all she'd tasted was heat. Passion. Desire. Raw need. And they'd tasted delicious. And left her hungry for more. One kiss and he'd completely stolen her self-control. It was humiliating. Aggravating. And given how reliable she'd always considered her self-control, pretty damn shocking. If he hadn't ended their kiss, God only knows what would have happened.

C'mon, Jamie, you know damn well what would have happened. You would have banged him like a screen door. You would have laid him like linoleum. You would have—

All right, all right, she got the picture. Jeez. Stupid inner voice. Where was duct tape when she needed it?

"Well?" he prodded. "Did I prove my point?"

She lifted her chin. "I don't know."

"Then maybe I should kiss you again. So you can be sure."

She favored him with the icy glare she normally used only on restaurant suppliers who thought she was a pushover because she was a woman. "Unless you want to sing soprano, I wouldn't suggest you try it. I don't like being used."

"I didn't use you. And for the record, that kiss was a whole damn lot better than just 'good.' " His eyes seemed to burn a hole in her. "Or are you going to try to deny that?"

God knew she wanted to. Unfortunately she was a lousy liar. And even if she managed to choke out the words, the moans and groans she'd emitted—to say nothing of her still hard nipples—would brand her a big fat fraud.

"It doesn't matter how good it *might have been*. The fact that you did it simply to prove a point means it was bad."

"Bad? Like hell. And I told you—I didn't use you."

"And I'm supposed to believe you?"

"I don't lie."

She rolled her eyes. "Give me a break. Everybody lies."

"I don't. Not anymore. I don't have to. I walked away from all that and I don't regret it for a minute. You should give complete honesty a try, princess. It's very liberating. I'll even give you a free lesson on how it's done."

He pushed off from the wall, and before she could react, he reached out and lightly grasped her hands, brushing the pads of his thumbs over her skin. In spite of the warmth that skittered through her, she was about to snatch her hands away when he said quietly, "I want to kiss you again."

Her gaze flew to his face and she stilled when she found him regarding her through very serious eyes.

"So badly I can barely think straight," he continued in a husky voice while his thumbs continued to draw slow, hypnotic circles on the backs of her hands, "although a small part of the not being able to think straight has to do with the fact that I haven't eaten since breakfast and I'm exhausted. But most of it's because of you.

"I didn't kiss you to prove a point. I kissed you because I couldn't *not* kiss you. Believe me, I tried to talk myself out of it. I knew it wasn't a good idea. For a whole slew of reasons. But in the end none of them seemed to matter." His gaze seemed to burn into hers. "That honest enough for you?"

Wow, wow, holy cow. Her head was spinning. She doubted she'd gotten that much truth out of Raymond during their entire eight months together. Nor had Raymond's hands ever felt like that on her—impatient and restless. Like he wanted to touch her everywhere at once. Nor had Raymond ever looked at her like this. Like she was Red Riding Hood and he was the big bad wolf.

"I know that kissing you again wouldn't be smart," he said.

She couldn't argue with that.

"Especially given how incredible the first kiss was."

She couldn't argue with that, either.

"But it's going to happen again."

That she could argue with.

The independent woman in her demanded she stare him down and say something in an arctic tone that included the words "you're an arrogant ass" and "over my dead body." Instead she had to swallow to find her voice at all. And when she did, all she managed to squeak out was, "Says you."

"That's right. Says me." He hoisted a brow. "You disagree?"

"Absolutely."

"Figures you'd argue about it."

She hoisted a brow right back at him. "Are you insinuating I'm argumentative?"

"No, I'm flat-out saying it. If I told you the sky was blue, you'd feel compelled to reply it was 'azure' or 'cerulean' or some crap like that."

"It was a rhetorical question."

"And besides that you're bossy."

"Okay, you obviously don't know what 'rhetorical' means."

She tried to pull her hands away, but he lifted them to his mouth and brushed his lips over her fingers. The fact that fire shot up her arm at the touch seriously irked her. How could she feel such heat for such a pest?

"But you're also cute," he continued. "And funny. And good to my dog. And for reasons I'm at a loss to explain, I actually *like* that you don't agree with me all the time—although agreeing with me *once* might be nice. Plus you're ridiculously, incredibly sexy. So even though I don't want to like you, I think I might. A little."

Okay, so a poet he definitely was not, and flowery compliments were obviously not his thing. But she didn't doubt he meant what he said. And she couldn't deny it was a heck of a lot more refreshing to hear a man say he might like her, a little, rather than having him say he loved her and totally not mean it and sleep with her sister.

"Oh, yeah?" she replied. "Well, you're arrogant and annoying and more than a little mysterious, which makes you *doubly* annoying." *Ha! Take that!* Yet given his honesty, she felt compelled to add, "But you're also good to your dog, and I like that you think I'm sexy." Okay, maybe that was *too* honest.

He touched his tongue to the center of her palm. "*Ridiculously, incredibly* sexy," he corrected.

Yikes. Okay, she'd just discovered his superpower. The ability to melt knees with his tongue. For self-preservation purposes she slid her hands from his and backed up a step. "Uh, yeah. Thanks. Too bad I think you're a troll," she added, proving her theory that everyone lied.

He laughed. "Good. That should make things easier between us. After all, one of us should stay in control, and I think I've proven it's not likely to be me."

Oh, great. If that was supposed to be her—what with Mr. Sexy, with his knee-melting tongue here—they were doomed.

Now that he wasn't touching her, her better judgment roused itself from the vacation it had apparently taken and smacked her in the head. *Not doomed!* Better Judgment intoned. *Get your shit together and set him straight. That kiss was a mistake and it's not going to happen again.*

Right. Annoyance at her lack of self-possession straightened her spine. "Look—the kiss was nice—"

"We've already established it was much better than 'nice.' "

"Now who's being argumentative? Bottom line is, I'm not looking for a relationship."

"Neither am I."

"I have enough unresolved crap going on in my life without adding to it."

"Well, God knows I wouldn't want to become anyone's 'unresolved crap,'" he said dryly.

She winced. "Sorry. I didn't mean that the way it sounded. But casual hook-ups aren't my style so I don't want to go down any path more kissing might lead to. Therefore—no more kissing. Got it?"

"Got it." A combination of heat and humor glinted in his eyes. "Guess that means a no-kiss quickie against the wall is out of the question."

An image of him taking her hard and fast against the wall, his flesh stroking deep inside her, flashed through her mind, followed by the words, *Yes, please.* "Out of the question," she forced herself to say. "Definitely."

He nodded. "I understand. And now, as much as I'd love to continue arguing and not kissing and whatever the hell else we've been doing here, I've gotta get some sleep."

Humph. Arrogant jerk. Just assuming *she'd* want to continue this tonight.

"No problem," she said in her breeziest tone. "I need to get back to my mom. No telling what sort of drama she's managed to involve herself in during the few minutes I've been out here."

"Okay." He whistled for Godiva, who jumped up and ran to him, knocking Nick back a step when her tail-wagging body collided with his legs. It was then that Jamie noticed just how exhausted and drawn he looked. And she wondered—for about the hundredth time—what he'd been doing for the past three days.

"Enjoy your rest," she said.

"Thanks." He turned to walk back to Southern Comfort, but after taking only two steps, he turned around. "I meant what I said."

She raised her brows. "Specifically what? You said a lot of things."

"Yeah. And meant all of them. But mostly that I think I might like you. A little."

"And I meant all the stuff I said, too. But mostly that I think you're annoying. And that there'll be no more kissing."

His lips twitched, damn him, as if he didn't believe her. "Whatever you say, princess."

With that he turned and walked around the hedge, Godiva trotting after him.

Jamie drew a deep breath. Thank God he was gone. She touched her fingers to her kiss-swollen lips.

Gone . . . but definitely, and unfortunately, not forgotten.

Chapter 10

The following morning, at precisely oh five hundred hours, Jamie began her Kill Melvin With Kindness campaign and climbed the stairs to Gone Fishin' bearing a carafe of freshly brewed coffee and a platter of her favorite frosted sugar cookies. Jeez, it was dark—like the freakin' middle of the night. Which it pretty much was. Who the heck ate breakfast at this time of day? Obviously people who had lights out at twenty-one hundred hours, which, thanks to Google, she'd discovered was nine P.M. Who the heck went to bed at nine o'clock? Obviously people who woke up at five A.M.

She was about to knock when the wooden door suddenly opened and Melvin glared at her through the screen door. "Newman. What do you want?"

Reminding herself that the emphasis was on *kindness* rather than *kill*, Jamie smiled. "Since I missed breakfast beverage time the day we met, I thought I'd stop by this morning with some coffee. I also baked some cookies."

His gaze shot to the platter she held. She thought she detected a flicker of surprise in his eyes, but it was so darn dark she couldn't be certain. Then he looked at her with a fierce frown. "Don't think I don't know what you're doing, young lady. Trying to butter me up over these newfangled ideas of yours regarding the Clam Queen contest before tonight's meeting. Well, it won't work. I've lived on this island longer than you've been alive and things are just fine as they are."

Wow—word did travel fast. "I'm sure they are," Jamie agreed. "So . . . I guess that means you're not interested in a cup of coffee and these cookies I baked while looking over the revenue projections I worked up." The printouts of which were conveniently in her shorts pocket. She lifted the platter of puffy, gorgeous, fragrant cookies so it was right beneath his nose.

His nostrils twitched, then his brows collapsed even farther. "I normally eat an egg-white omelet and Bran Buds for breakfast. Cookies aren't a breakfast food."

"I have to disagree with you, Mr. Tibbs. According to my grandfather, who is retired military, cookies are the best breakfast in the world."

His eyes narrowed. "Retired military, you say? Must have been in the Air Force if he liked cookies for breakfast."

"No, sir. Army. Infantry officer."

Jamie caught a definite gleam of interest in his eyes before he masked it. He seemed to conduct a brief internal debate, then said brusquely, "No sense in cookies going to waste. Come in."

Ah, the power of cookies.

Jamie stepped into Melvin's kitchen and the first word that hit her was *stark*. If she hadn't already pegged him as a military man, the sight of his home would have instantly done so. The interior was laid out exactly the same as Paradise Lost, but Melvin's house was pristinely clean and neat and as austere as an army barracks. Bare beige walls, plain blue sofa and chair, TV, coffee table. The only decoration was an American flag displayed in a triangular wood and glass case, set on top of a narrow bookcase.

Jamie set the carafe and the plate of cookies on the counter. As Melvin took two mugs from a cabinet and poured the coffee, she wandered into the living area to look at the bookcase, which contained a variety of military thrillers and biographies of famous army generals. And a single framed photograph. Of a young Melvin wearing his dress military uniform and an attractive, smiling brunette on what was obviously their wedding day.

"Your wife?" Jamie asked, studying the photo.

"Yes."

"She's lovely."

"Yes, she was." He set a container of half-and-half on the counter. "Died seventeen years ago."

Jamie turned back toward him and noted the muscle that ticked in his jaw. "The summer before we were married, she won the Clam Queen title."

Her heart squeezed, and with that single gruffly spoken sentence, she realized that Melvin had adored his wife. And that the reason he so adamantly didn't want the contest changed was because she'd once won it. Her gaze scanned his unadorned home. She also realized he was very, very lonely—and probably didn't even realize it. Or, if he did, wasn't about to admit it.

She offered him a smile. "Let's have some cookies and talk."

"I think that ornery old coot Melvin must be sick or something," Dorothy whispered to Jamie. They stood in Dorothy's kitchen, cutting thick slabs of the carrot cake Jamie had baked to serve at the conclusion of the clam meeting. "He didn't say boo when you put forth your suggestion about adding additional categories to the Clam Contest and he actually voted in favor of them!"

"I'm not deaf, you know," came Melvin's gruff voice from directly behind Dorothy.

Dorothy whirled around and pressed a hand to her heart. "You scared the bejeesus out of me, Melvin Tibbs."

"That's what you get for gossiping about people behind their backs," Melvin said with a glare.

Dorothy drew herself up and glared right back at him. "I wasn't gossiping. I merely expressed surprise that you didn't put up a stink about changing the Clam Queen contest."

"That's because we're not *changing* it—we're adding to it." He nodded toward Jamie but kept his gaze on Dorothy. "Newman here put together a clear, concise report containing all the pertinent facts, including the financial advantages for Seaside Cove, of which there are many. I may be ornery but I'm not stupid." He swiped up a plate of cake, grabbed a plastic spoon, then strode back into the living area much like a conquering hero onto a battlefield.

"Well, if that don't beat all," Dorothy said, staring after him. "That's the longest speech I've ever heard from that man."

Jamie pressed her lips together to hide her smile. "Maybe you've misjudged him. Maybe he's just . . . lonely."

Dorothy's head swiveled back and she stared at Jamie with a comical slack-jawed expression. "How many Mojitos did you drink?"

Jamie laughed. "Only one. You told me you thought Nick was lonely. Why is it so difficult to believe that a man whose wife died seventeen years ago might also be lonely?"

Dorothy's brows collapsed in a frown and her jaw sawed back and forth several times. Finally she said, "I guess it's not completely farfetched." Her gaze strayed into the living area, where Melvin sat by himself in the corner eating his cake while the other committee members congregated in small groups, laughing and talking.

"Looks like he might need another piece of cake," Dorothy said. "We have plenty left."

"And it shouldn't go to waste," Jamie agreed.

She took a big bite of cake to hide her smile as Dorothy headed across the room bearing two plates of cake.

Chapter 11

"What's that delicious smell?" asked Jamie's mom as she entered the living area from her bedroom and walked toward the kitchen.

Jamie immediately tensed.

In the two weeks since her mom had arrived at Paradise Lost, they hadn't seen very much of each other as Mom had spent most of her time in her room sleeping. When she was awake, she alternated between crying, barfing, and nibbling crackers—while crying. According to her doctor the barfing, while exhausting and unpleasant, was not abnormal, and Mom insisted a lot of the weeping sprang from rampant hormone upheavals rather than sadness. Still, Jamie knew her mom was distraught and confused, and it both saddened and worried her to see her normally vivacious, energetic, and smiling mother so wan and listless.

Yet, Jamie couldn't deny she'd also been avoiding her mom, so the fact that all she wanted to do was sleep was good. Because on the occasions they *had* talked, the conversation had always ended up with her mother once again asking, "What would you do?" or the similar but even worse, "What should I do?" or pressuring Jamie to return to New York sooner than she'd planned. Her mother had also complained about the changes to Newman's décor and menu Jamie wanted, insisting, as always, that everything at the restaurant remain the same as when Jamie's dad was alive. Jamie didn't want to upset her mother, especially now that she was pregnant, but those conversations made her want to run screaming from the room.

She prayed that this encounter wouldn't result in another blood-pressure-raising, stress-filled chat.

"Garlic bread, which is warming in the oven, and also fresh herbs for a pasta sauce I'm making up as I go," Jamie said. She set aside the basil she'd been chopping and wiped her hands on her apron. "How do you feel?"

"Better," Mom said. She rested her hands on her still flat stomach and actually smiled. "Given the . . . eclectic furniture here, my bed is surprisingly comfortable."

Jamie took her by the shoulders and nodded, relieved. "You look better. Rested."

"I should hope so," her mother said with a rueful chuckle. "I've done nothing but sleep the entire time I've been here."

"Not true. You've also barfed and cried a lot."

"Believe it or not, I haven't barfed since this morning. I haven't been as successful with the crying, but I'm trying. I don't know what I would have done without you, Jamie."

"I haven't done anything except brew you endless cups of decaf and watch you sleep."

"And barf and cry. But you're going to see me eat tonight because I'm starving."

"Excellent. I was planning to make linguini and shrimp, but I can cook something else."

"Don't you dare. That sounds like heaven. What can I do to help?"

"Feel like dicing some tomatoes?"

"Absolutely."

The area was small, and since Jamie and her mom had stopped sharing a kitchen when Jamie moved into her own apartment four years ago, some butt bumping ensued.

Jamie pulled out a dented frying pan from one of the lower cabinets and sighed. "I wish I had my own cookware here. Did I tell you I got that set of All-Clad I've coveted forever?"

she asked, hoping to keep the conversation from drifting to Newman's or pregnancy.

"No! Did you find it on sale?"

Jamie shook her head. "It was a gift. From Raymond. He gave it to me two days before I found out about him and Laurel. If I believed he possessed a conscience, I'd say the All-Clad was a guilt gift, but I think it just stemmed from him expecting perfectly cooked meals. If it wasn't the most magnificent set of pots and pans on the planet, I'd have thrown it in the trash."

"But hopefully not before hitting him in the head with it." Mom set a plum tomato on her cutting board and whacked off the end with a single stroke of the knife. "Cheating asshole."

A quick laugh escaped Jamie. Her mom might be drama-prone, but she was unfailingly loyal. "Well said. As for hitting him in the head—*soooo* tempting. But not only would I not want to dent those glorious pans, Raymond's not worth going to jail over for assault and battery."

"Honey, there's not a jury in the world that would convict you. In fact, you'd probably be awarded a metal."

"Well, he's Laurel's problem now." The knife of betrayal stabbed her between the shoulders at the thought. "They deserve each other."

"It just proves that money can't buy the things that really matter. Like integrity."

"Or loyalty," Jamie said, setting out another cutting board to mince the shallots and garlic she'd peeled before her mom came into the kitchen.

Mom attacked another tomato with the precision of a surgeon. "Raymond may travel in the same wealthy circles as Laurel, but neither of them know the true value of friendship or family or decency."

"And neither of them can cook worth a damn," Jamie added.

"Because they have cooks who do it for them. Where's the fun in that?"

"Beats me," said Jamie. "I can't imagine always letting someone else prepare my meals. How are the tomatoes coming?"

"I'm finished. What else do we need?"

"Lime zest."

"I'm on it. What's in this sauce you're making?" Mom asked, plucking a plump lime from the bowl on the counter.

"It started as a basic scampi, but I'm using lime instead of lemon, then adding those gorgeous tomatoes you chopped—which are from my new friend Megan's garden by the way—and a load of fresh herbs I found on my trek to the supermarket this morning. Who knew the Piggly Wiggly would carry such a great assortment of herbs?"

"The shrimp are beautiful," Mom said, looking them over where Jamie had set them on paper towels to dry after she'd peeled and cleaned them. "Did you get those at the Piggly Wiggly, too?"

"No. Believe it or not, I bought them from a man on the side of the road. Dorothy Ernst—she's the lady on the Clam Committee who lives across the street—told me about him. His name is Captain Pete and he goes shrimping six days a week. Then he sets up his little stand on the side of the road and sells his catch from his cooler. When he's sold out, he goes home. Dorothy and most everyone else at the meeting have been buying from Captain Pete for years and they swear his shrimp are the most delicious they've ever eaten."

Mom shook her head. "Shrimp from a cooler on the side of the road. We're not in Manhattan anymore."

"No kidding," Jamie said, rinsing the bunches of flat-leaf parsley, watercress, chives, and mint leaves she planned to use for her sauce. "The fact that the words 'clam committee' have become part of my everyday vocabulary and that I'm *on* that committee continues to surprise me. As does the fact that they liked my ideas for expanding the Clam Queen contest—and guess what—I'm now in charge of implementing those ideas. Me and my big mouth."

"You don't want to do it?"

Jamie frowned. "It's not that, not really. It's just being on a committee, involving myself with the activities and local residents, making new friends—actually *wanting* to fit in—I wasn't expecting any of that. I came here thinking I'd spend my time mostly alone." *Hint, hint, Mom.* "Walking the beach, reading, regrouping. Making decisions about myself and my future. It hasn't quite worked out that way. But I guess I should have known to expect the unexpected the instant I saw that decapitated flamingo in the front yard."

Her mom heaved a sigh, then turned and leaned her back against the counter. "I haven't spoken to Alex in the last four days."

Great. And here came the drama again.

"He's called and left messages and texted every day," Mom continued, "but I've avoided answering."

"You can't do that forever."

"I know. But I simply haven't been up to more of that last conversation. He pressured me to come home so we could talk things out in person, I said I wasn't ready to return to New York, lather, rinse, repeat. He doesn't understand that I need time and space to decide what I want, what's best for everyone involved. Nothing was resolved and he wasn't happy when we ended the conversation."

Cupcake chose that moment to make her presence known with a series of loud meows and Jamie could have kissed her pet for the timely interruption. "That means, 'Which one of you wenches whom I allow to live in my home and pamper me is going to serve my evening meal?'" Jamie explained.

Jamie scooped a can of wild salmon primavera with garden veggies into Cupcake's bowl and her mother asked, "What do you need me to do next?"

"The water's boiling, so if you'd add the pasta, I'll sauté the shallots and garlic."

They set about their tasks, and within mere seconds, a mouth-watering fragrance rose from the pan.

"That smells soooo good," said her mother.

"Whoever thought up the combo of garlic and olive oil is a genius," Jamie agreed. She added the shrimp to the sizzling pan, and said, "It was perfect timing that I arrived at Captain Pete's roadside stand when I did. He was nearly sold out, and three more cars pulled in after me."

Mom grinned. "You're a lucky woman."

"Given how beautiful these shrimp are, we're both lucky."

The shrimp cooked quickly, and once they were done Jamie slid them into a bowl and covered it to keep them warm. She was about to add another shot of olive oil and a pat of butter to the pan to make the sauce when a knock sounded on the kitchen door. She turned and stilled. Nick stood on the landing.

Nick—who she hadn't spoken to since their kiss twelve (not that she was counting) days ago. And there was her mother, eyes aglow with curiosity.

And she'd just called herself lucky.

Apparently not so much.

Jamie stood nailed in place in front of the stove, bottle of olive oil gripped in one hand, frying pan in the other, while her avid eyeballs drank in the sight of Nick through the screen door. Rumpled hair, bedroom eyes, three-day stubble. And let's not forget those lips that had all but kissed her into a lust-filled coma.

Although she had not spoken to him since that night, she'd known he'd once again mysteriously disappeared the morning after their kiss and then returned home from wherever he went four days ago because of all the hammering and saw buzzing going on at Southern Comfort. Not that she'd paid much attention. Heck no. She was ignoring him. Of course, it was pretty irritating to be ignoring someone who first wasn't home, and then never left his house. Naturally the fact that he was irritating didn't surprise her in the least. In fact, she'd hardly thought of him—except for those errant few (hundred) times. And even then it had been due only to all the construction-type racket going on over there. Definitely not because he'd blown her socks off with his kiss.

Oh, suuuuure, her inner voice sneered. *Jeez, it's a good thing you're not Pinocchio, otherwise your nose would reach from here to friggin' Europe. You know damn well that if Nick Trent had kissed you for even three more seconds, he would have blown off a lot more than your socks.*

Yeah. Like her panties.

She vaguely noted her mom looking in her direction. "I'll get that," Mom said. She walked to the door and smiled. "Hi. May I help you?"

"Hi. I'm Nick Trent. From next door. Is Jamie around?"

"She's right here. I'm Maggie Newman—Jamie's mother." She opened the screen door and held it with her hip.

"Nice to meet you, Maggie. I'd shake your hand but I'm covered in sawdust."

Mom smiled. "No problem. I'm covered in bits of basil."

"I was just wondering—oh, hey, there you are," he said, catching sight of Jamie, standing like a statue near the stove, olive oil and pan in hand. His lips twitched. "You look ready to cook the heck out of something." He sniffed the air and his eyes widened slightly. "Whoa. I take that back. It smells like you've already cooked the heck out of it—and did a great job."

Pulling herself from the stupor she'd fallen into at the sight of him—an effort because she was *so* ignoring him—she set down the oil and pan, then approached the door. "Hi, Nick," she said, all polite-I'm-ignoring-you coolness. "What can I do for you?"

Heat flared in his eyes. He muttered something that sounded like "Where do I start?" and Jamie's pulse took off like a horse slapped on the ass. "Do you have any cat food you could spare? Godiva sucked down the last of mine and there's a cat hiding under the bushes near my carport. I think it might be that same one you saw the other night. She looks hungry."

"Of course. I have plenty. C'mon in for a minute. I don't want Cupcake to get out."

Nick stepped into the kitchen, instantly reducing the area to the size of a postage stamp. She skirted around him to open the door to the small pantry. Staring at the shelves, she took several seconds to suck in a slow, deep breath she shouldn't have needed, but darn it, she did. When she turned around holding the bag of dry cat food, she once again stilled at the sight of him, this time hunkered down, one strong, tanned hand stroking Cupcake, who was rubbing herself against his denim-covered knees and purring so loud it sounded as if she'd swallowed a hive of bumblebees.

"So you're Cupcake," he said. "I've heard a lot about you. Most of it good."

"She's telling you there's nothing bad—that she's *purr*-fect in every way."

He gave the cat a final pat, then stood. "I bet Godiva would love to chase her around for a few hours and then slather some drool on her."

"Yeah, 'cause that's what every girl dreams of—getting chased and then slathered in drool."

Something kindled in his eyes—a warm, sexy something that made her knees feel like marshmallows. Damn him and his superpower! "Guess it depends on the girl," he said. "And who's doing the chasing."

Before she could think of anything to say, he plucked the bag from her. "Thanks."

She had to clear her throat to locate her voice. "No problem. I always have extra. And even if I didn't, I could whip up something for a hungry kitty."

His gaze flicked to the stove. "Is that what you're cooking— cat food? 'Cause I gotta tell ya, it smells way too good for pet food."

"Not pet food. Shrimp scampi."

"And you're actually *cooking* it? Like on the stove?"

"Uh-huh. Unless you think my superpower is the ability to heat food with my laserlike eyeballs."

He gave a quick laugh. "I meant it's not from the freezer section at the Piggly Wiggly?"

"Nope. And brace yourself—I even peeled the garlic and cleaned the shrimp."

"Jamie's an excellent cook," said her mother, whose presence Jamie had completely forgotten about. "Looks like you've been working hard, Nick. Were you the one doing all that hammering and sawing the past few days?"

Nick nodded. "Putting in a new kitchen. Just about finished."

"Oh, that *is* hard work," said Mom. "I bet it looks great."

"Actually, I think it does—if I may say so myself." His gaze bounced between her and her mom. "Would you like to see it?"

Jamie clamped her lips shut to prevent *I'd love to see anything you'd care to show me* from popping out. "We'd love to!" chirped Mom. "It's always such fun seeing renovations. But we're just about to eat dinner. Would you like to join us? There's plenty of scampi. Right, Jamie?"

Jamie barely held in the *oof* that popped into her throat when her mom's elbow jabbed her in the ribs. "Uh, yeah. Plenty." When Nick looked skeptical—yet undeniably hungry—she reiterated, "Really, there's enough shrimp to fill an aquarium. You're welcome to stay."

"Okay, thanks. I've been surviving on peanut butter and jelly, so a home-cooked meal sounds great. I'll just put out some food for the cat and then come back."

He flashed one of those darn killer smiles, then left, his footfalls thunking down the wooden stairs.

Jamie didn't realize she was staring at the spot where he'd been until her mom nudged her again. "So that's your neighbor," Mom said, her voice ripe with . . . something.

"Uh, yeah." Jamie frowned at the stove. "Do you think I should make more linguini? He eats more than twelve teenagers."

Mom's brows shot upward. "How do you know that?"

"Because we had breakfast together the first morning I was here and he packed food away like a linebacker. Humph. And not an ounce of fat on him. Totally not fair."

"I hope you don't mind that I asked him to stay."

She actually wasn't sure how she felt about it. The fluttering in her stomach felt exactly like anticipation. But it couldn't have been because, well, she didn't *want* to feel that. She *wanted* to forget Nick Trent Great Kisser even existed. How the heck was she supposed to do that if he was coming to dinner?

"I don't mind," Jamie said. "I'm used to you taking in strays—dogs, cats, neighbors." It was part of her mom's charm—and led to much of the drama that seemed to follow her everywhere.

"I didn't ask him to stay because I thought he was a stray."

"Oh? Then why did you?"

"Two reasons, actually. The first was the way you practically swallowed your tongue at the sight of him."

Yeah, Jamie—you know, your tongue? The one that was stroking his the last time you saw him?

Gawd! She *hated* that stupid inner voice!

"I was just surprised to see him. He's never stopped by before."

"Uh-huh. But then there was also the way he looked at you. Like he was starving—and not just for your scampi."

Heat swamped her face. Oh, crap—the blotches were on their way. "I'm sure you're mistaken," Jamie said in her schoolmarm voice.

"Honey. Please. Did you honestly not see the way he looked at you? Good Lord, it was enough to make *me* sweat."

"Those are the pregnancy hormones."

"Whatever. The point is, whether you saw it or not, he was looking. And whether you admit it or not, you were looking back."

"I *had* to look—he was standing at the door. Talking to me."

"There's a difference between looking and *looking* and you were *looking*. And so was he."

Jamie opened her mouth to argue, but before she could get out a syllable, her mother hurried on, "For heaven's sake, Jamie, there's nothing wrong with looking. Looking is good—it means you're on the road to recovery. And being looked *at* is also good. Enjoy it. In fact, enjoy it right now. Go watch that man who couldn't take his eyes off you feed the kitty. I'll grate the cheese while you're gone."

Do it, her pesky inner voice prompted. *You know you want to.* "Are you sure?"

"Positive. I'll also boil more water to make extra linguini. After all, we wouldn't want Nick to go hungry." Her mother practically shoved her out the door. "Go. Feed cat. Have fun."

"Okay. But only because I want to see the kitty."

Mom smiled at her through the screen door. "Of course, honey. Of course."

Jamie hurried down the steps and across the carport. As she neared the hedge, she slowed and proceeded on tiptoe so as not to scare the cat.

"Boy, you were hungry, weren't you?" came Nick's soft voice.

She peeked around the hedge. The same black-and-white cat she'd previously tried to coax from the bushes was eating ravenously from the bowl of food Nick had set out. Nick sat on the carport several yards away, his forearms resting on his bent knees.

"That's definitely the same cat I tried to feed," Jamie whispered, moving slowly so as not to scare the animal. She sat down next to Nick. "I don't think she's feral—her ear isn't clipped, plus she hasn't run away. I think she's just scared. Which means she's probably either lost or abandoned."

Jamie watched the cat eat, her heartstrings tugging at how hungry she clearly was.

"Nothing wrong with her appetite," Nick said. "Looks like the bowl needs refilling. You want the honors?"

"Sure." The cat watched her slowly approach, but didn't back away. Jamie sat on the cement and extended her hand. The cat stretched her neck, her nose quivering slightly. "C'mon, baby. I won't hurt you."

The cat took one tentative step toward her, but just then Godiva began barking inside the house. The cat jumped a foot in the air, then shot into the bushes as if she were fired from a cannon.

Nick winced. "Sorry."

"Not your fault. I'm sure she'll be back. Would you mind if we moved the bowl of food to my carport?"

"No, in fact, I think that's a good idea. I can tell you want to scoop her up and take her home."

"I'd like to reunite her with her family if she's lost. If she's abandoned—"

"I sense you'll be her new family."

"If she'll have me."

"If she knew you were cooking shrimp, she'd have you in a heartbeat." He stood, then held out a hand to help her do the same. When she hesitated, he raised a brow. "Not clean enough for you, princess?" He slapped his palm against his jeans a few times, then once again extended his hand to her. "How's that?"

Jeez. It was colossally annoying that she was so physically attracted to such a pest. And wasn't she supposed to be ignoring him? Frowning, she slapped her hand into his. Warm, strong fingers wrapped against hers, and before she could so much as draw a breath, he pulled her up with a heave-ho that had her crashing into him. Her palms flattened against his chest and his arms went around her to steady her. Her gaze collided with his and she discovered him looking at her with that combination of heat and lazy amusement that she was coming to like, er, loathe. Yes, definitely loathe.

Yeah, right. If only.

His hands skimmed down her back and settled at the base

of her spine, holding her lightly against him. "If you wanted a hug, all you had to do was ask, princess."

No doubt he expected her to push away. Well, she'd show him. She stayed right where she was. So there.

But she did narrow her eyes at him. "Has anyone ever told you you're a pain in the ass?"

"Actually, yes. Quite a few times."

"Notice I'm not plotzing with surprise."

One corner of his mouth quirked upward. "*Plotzing?*"

"It's Yiddish. Means 'to collapse in shock.'"

"Sounds like you've been chatting with Ira Silverman."

Jamie nodded. "I've eaten at Oy Vey Mama Mia twice this week. I highly recommend the brisket parmigiana—it's a lot better than it sounds—and the toasted challah bread bruschetta."

"Noted." Silence swelled between them for the space of several heartbeats, seconds during which Jamie completely forgot she needed to step away from him, a memory blip no doubt brought on by lack of oxygen to her brain because she'd sort of forgotten how to breathe.

"Unless you want to be kissed—which you've decreed you don't—you'd better stop looking at me like that," he said.

"Like what?"

"Like you want to be kissed."

This time her pride forced her to push against his chest. His arms dropped and she stepped back. "I wasn't looking at you like that." She hoped.

He laughed. "Okay. Whatever you say."

"You're very agreeable all of a sudden."

"I don't want to risk my dinner invite being revoked. Besides, you made your no-kissing rule very clear."

Crap. "Darn right."

He reached out and gently tucked one of her runaway curls behind her ear, a gesture that made her heart stutter. "Good thinking, 'cause if we kissed, we'd totally miss dinner."

"How do you figure?"

"Because our second kiss would last a lot longer than our first one."

Oh, my. "That's quite an ego you've got there."

"Just callin' it like I see it." His gaze shifted briefly to Paradise Lost. "Since it rained last night and you weren't banging on my door at dawn, I'm guessing you didn't have any roof leaks."

"None that I noticed."

"Good. The place needs a whole new roof, but as long as you're staying dry, it can wait until fall."

"Sure—fix the place up *after* I leave."

He cocked a brow. "It would take me at least a week to pull down the old roof and put up a new one. I didn't think you'd want the disruption of construction noises all day long."

"Like you haven't been making noise anyway?"

"All right. I'll try to get to it sooner rather than later."

"Maybe you could think about replacing the flooring as well. The peeling linoleum in the kitchen has got to go, and the carpet is older than I am. And some new furniture would be nice—you know, something that actually came from a store, as opposed to a yard sale."

He folded his arms across his chest, a move that stretched his dusty white T-shirt taut over his broad shoulders. A fine film of sawdust coated his strong forearms, clinging to the golden brown hair. He looked big and strong and capable and absolutely delicious. When had she developed this freakish attraction to the dusty/rumpled/unshaven/needs-a-haircut/been-working-with-his-hands-all-day look?

As soon as you clapped eyeballs on Nick Trent, her inner voice answered.

True. But weird. And confusing, as she'd previously always preferred clean-cut, white-collar types. Seemed everything in her life was changing.

"I already have flooring and carpet in mind for Paradise Lost, princess, but things need to be done in the proper order. Renovations first, then painting, then floors."

"What about furniture?"

"Dead last."

"You know, you could just move new furniture around during the renovations and cover it up when you paint. I believe that's what *drop cloths* are for. Plus, it would greatly please your renter not to risk getting splinters every time she sets her tea cup on that swaybacked piece of plywood that's posing as a coffee table."

A frown pulled between his brows. "You may have a point."

She widened her eyes as far as they would go. "Heavens. Are you saying I'm . . . *right*?"

His frown deepened, but humor lurked in his eyes. "Don't be a smart-ass. I'm saying you're . . . not completely wrong. I'll think about it. And now I'm going to grab a quick shower. I don't want to sprinkle sawdust on the scampi. Did I mention that shrimp scampi is my favorite dish?"

"No. But I have to warn you, this isn't traditional scampi— more something I made up as I went along."

"If it tastes even half as good as it smelled, I'll be in heaven. See ya in a few, princess." He climbed the stairs, a sight that once again distracted her from breathing. The screen door banged closed behind him, jerking her from the ass-staring stupor she'd fallen into.

Annoyed with herself, she stomped back to Paradise Lost, determined to make the best damn scampi she'd ever prepared. Not because it was Nick's favorite (*Yeah, right,* her inner voice sneered), but because the damn man continued to knock her socks off and it was about time she returned the favor.

Fifteen minutes later she heard his footsteps coming up the kitchen stairs. "Your date is here," her mom whispered.

Jamie nearly dropped her wooden spoon. "He's not my date," Jamie said in a horrified hiss. "And you can't whisper worth a darn—whenever you try, it comes out louder than if you just spoke normally, so knock it off."

"Sorry," Mom whispered with all the quietness of a sonic boom.

Jamie pointed the wooden spoon at her. "Behave yourself. No matchmaking. And *stop* whispering."

A knock sounded and Jamie called, "C'mon in, Nick."

The screen door opened and Nick stepped into the kitchen. And two words walloped Jamie like a wooden spoon to the solar plexus.

Whoa, baby.

Dressed in a clean white T-shirt and jeans that bore the sort of fade patterns that came with lots of wear rather than a designer label, he could be summed up in one word: wow.

Toss in his still-damp-from-the-shower hair and two words were needed: double wow.

Two other words ran through her mind: *no fair.* He went from yucky to yummy in less time than it took most people to wash their face. Although she had to admit his yucky was still pretty damn yummy.

"Hi," he said. "For you." Her gaze dropped to the single wild pink rose he held out to her.

Raymond had frequently bought her flowers—expensive, artfully arranged bouquets. But none of them gave her the heart tug she experienced from this single bloom.

"Thank you. So your superpower is the ability to make flowers miraculously appear?"

He smiled. "Nope. Turns out there's a rose bush in my overgrown backyard." He turned to her mom and held out an identical rose to her. "And one for you, Maggie."

Her mother accepted the flower. "Thank you," she murmured. Then promptly burst into tears.

Nick's smile instantly turned to alarm. "Crap. Shit. I'm sorry." He looked at Jamie with a panicked "help me" expression.

Her mom wiped her eyes with the back of her hand, then gave a shaky laugh. "You didn't do anything wrong and I'm the one who's sorry. It's the hormones. I'll be right back." She hurried into her bedroom, closing the door behind her.

Nick scraped a hand through his hair. "Hormones?"

Jamie nodded. "Mom's pregnant. She cries at everything. Yesterday she cried during a car insurance commercial."

"Is she . . . okay?"

"Aside from all the drama associated with an unplanned pregnancy, she's fine."

"I feel like I walked into the middle of a movie."

"My mother frequently has that effect on people."

He frowned at Jamie. "You're not going to cry, are you?"

"Nah. It's my mom who's knocked up, not me." A short huff of laughter escaped her. "There's a sentence I never thought I'd say."

"Or one I ever thought I'd hear." His gaze flicked to the door through which her mom had disappeared. "You sure she's okay?"

"Health-wise she's good. Emotionally, however, she's pretty much a mess, but not because of anything you said or did." She reached into the cabinet over the stove and pulled out a jelly jar. "Not much of a vase, but the best I can do."

"Well, it's not much of a flower, but the best I could do on short notice."

"It's beautiful. I love roses. And it was very thoughtful and gentlemanly of you."

He leaned his butt against the counter and casually crossed his ankles. "Glad you think so. But here's a tip on compliments, princess—they're a helluva lot more complimentary if you don't sound shell-shocked when you give them."

"I wasn't—" Her words cut off when she caught his look. "Okay, you surprised me. In a nice way." She added water to the jar, then set the rose inside. "I hope you're hungry."

"Starving. And it smells"—he closed his eyes and took a deep breath—"incredible in here."

Jamie's mom reentered the kitchen. She set her flower in the jar with Jamie's, then sent Nick a sheepish smile. "I'm so embarrassed. Sorry."

"No worries. Women take one look at me and cry all the time."

"I bet," Jamie said dryly. And she didn't doubt it for a minute. Any man who looked like him had to be a heartbreaker—something it would be really wise for her to remember. Because another heartbreak she did not need.

While her mom poured glasses of iced tea, Jamie served the plates and they all sat around the small snack bar area. She watched Nick take his first bite. His eyes slid closed and he made a sound in his throat that sounded more like sex than scampi and raised her temperature a good five degrees.

After he swallowed, he said, "Wow. Incredible. Makes me wish I was a poet so I could write something called 'Ode to Jamie's Shrimp Scampi.' "

Pleasure washed through her at the compliment. "Glad you like it, although I don't think the benchmark was too high considering you've been eating peanut butter and jelly all week."

" 'Like' doesn't really cover it, but I'm too happy to argue."

"Okay, *now* I'm plotzing. Note to self: Scampi makes Nick agreeable."

"Jamie, are you suggesting this hard-working, cat-feeding man who brought us roses is normally disagreeable?" Mom asked, her voice filled with mock horror.

Jamie snorted. "Suggesting it? No. Saying it flat-out? Yes."

Nick stabbed a shrimp with his fork. "Now that I know you can cook like this, I'll be a perfect angel."

"To quote the late, great Buddy Holly—that'll be the day."

Nick smiled at Jamie's mom. "She's crazy about me."

Jamie nearly spewed her iced tea. Before she could recover, her mother smiled back and said, "Just be careful with her. She's suffered enough recently. Bad breakup."

"Hey, no need to go into all that," Jamie said with a forced laugh. She shot The Look at her mother.

"She's not only a great cook," continued her mother, blithely ignoring The Look, as well as obviously forgetting there was to be no matchmaking, "she's smart, funny, a whiz at planning parties, great at her job, unbeatable at Scrabble, an extremely loyal friend, and a truly wonderful daughter." She batted her eyelashes. "Not that I'm biased."

"Thanks, Mom, but hey—enough about me." This time she shot her mother the evil eye. "How about those Yankees?"

"So this bad breakup—I guess that makes me the rebound guy?" Nick asked her mom.

"Hello, I'm sitting right here," Jamie said, waving her hand.

"I'm not sure rebound is the right word," Mom said, her brow puckered in thought. "I think for a rebound situation—"

"There's no situation," Jamie broke in.

"She'd need to be heartbroken," Mom continued as if she hadn't spoken. "And I believe she's more angry than hurt over the breakup."

"Happens when you get cheated on."

"She told you?" Mom asked.

"No, I didn't," Jamie said, leveling a murderous look at her mother. Mom, who seemed to have developed Teflon skin, continued to ignore her.

"No, she didn't," Nick agreed. "But I figured that's what went down. I know the signs."

"Someone cheated on you?" Mom asked, her voice filled with sympathy.

"Yup," Nick said, helping himself to another piece of garlic bread. "Do you live in New York, Maggie?"

Jamie chomped on her sautéed shrimp like she was chewing glass, and listened to them chatter on. After a few minutes, she realized a pattern had emerged in their conversation. Every time her mom asked Nick a question about himself, he'd answer with a noncommittal, short reply, then immediately change the subject by asking Mom something about herself. She recalled Jack Crawford saying that Nick didn't like to talk about himself, and clearly he was right.

Why not? And who had cheated on him? And when? Curiosity tugged at her, and although she tried to shove it aside, it remained right there, asking, *What's up with this guy?* What was he hiding? He didn't look like a hit man—or did he? What the hell did she know—she didn't know any hit men. Maybe he really was in the CIA. Or the witness-protection program. *Or maybe he's just a regular guy who doesn't like to talk about himself,* her inner voice whispered.

Maybe. But she wasn't used to that. Raymond had never been shy about regaling her with tales of his private school exploits, college days at Yale, skiing in Europe, beaching on St. Bart's. At first she'd been enthralled, but with the wisdom of hindsight, instead of interesting, he just seemed full of himself. Definitely not an attribute she could assign to Nick. But his closemouthed nature piqued her curiosity.

"Don't you think so, Jamie?"

Her mother's voice yanked her from her thoughts. "Huh?"

"That this would be a great evening for a walk on the beach."

"Is there a bad night for a walk on the beach?"

"Never," said Nick. He set his napkin beside his empty plate and patted his flat stomach. "Best scampi ever. Seriously. And I'm not just saying that because you saved me from another night of PB and J. If I knew how to cook, I'd be begging for the recipe."

"Jamie can give you some beginner cooking pointers," Mom said. "She's an excellent teacher. She gives lessons at the senior center twice a year. They were so disappointed when she canceled her session for August." Her tone made it clear she'd better not cancel again or the entire senior world would collapse.

No pressure.

Good grief. Why had no one ever invented a Mom muzzle?

Nick's gaze fastened on Jamie. "Teacher, cook, restaurant manager . . . is there anything you can't do?"

Yes. Get my mother to stop talking. "Yes—teach the dishes to clean themselves."

"I'll help," Nick said, rising. "It's the least I can do after that incredible meal."

They'd just finished clearing the table when a knock sounded at the kitchen door. All three of them turned. Jamie's mother whispered, "Oh, God," and grabbed Jamie's arm in a viselike grip.

Alex Wharton—her mother's baby daddy, aka Bringer of More Drama to Jamie's Supposed Sanctuary—stood on the other side of the screen door.

Chapter 12

Nick heaved a tennis ball toward the pier and Godiva took off like a rocket, kicking up sand behind her.

His shoulder bumped against Jamie's, sizzling an absolutely ridiculous bolt of heat through him. She walked next to him, her bare feet leaving prints in the wet sand in unison with his. He glanced down and inwardly shook his head. Damn, even her feet were cute—small and tipped with bright pink nail-polished toes. He really liked the way they looked strolling along next to his much larger feet. "You're unusually quiet," he said. "You okay?"

She shot him an assessing sidelong look. "Is that just a polite question to which I should just as politely answer 'I'm fine,' or do you really want to know?"

"I wouldn't want you to tell me you're fine if you're not."

"In that case, no, I'm not okay." She blew out a long, frustrated-sounding breath. "I came to Seaside Cove to get away from drama, yet it keeps showing up on my doorstep—first in the form of my preggers mom, who isn't shy about stating, and reiterating, her displeasure with my decision to stay here for the entire summer, and is pressuring me to make decisions for her that only she can make, and now in the form of her baby daddy. Twenty minutes ago I was eating scampi and now I feel as if I've been evicted from the place that was supposed to be my peaceful haven so my mom and Alex can talk. I know they have issues to work out, but jeez, can't they do it somewhere else? Like in New York? Where they belong?"

She raked her hands through her windblown hair. "And the fact that I'm thinking that way makes me feel rotten and guilty. Totally selfish and unsympathetic. But you know what? I have my own problems that I'm attempting to work through, and damn it, why *can't* I be selfish? Just this once? Where does it say that I always have to be responsible for everyone else and help solve their problems? Why can't I be allowed to just concentrate on *me*?"

She shot him a sheepish look. "Bet you're thinking, 'Sorry I asked.' "

"Maybe a little."

"And now you know what a selfish person I am."

"I learned a long time ago that if you don't take care of yourself, no one else will, so where you're seeing 'selfish' I'm seeing 'smart.' There's nothing wrong with taking time for yourself, Jamie. And it isn't as if you kicked your mom to the curb. In fact, it seems like you've been taking good care of her."

"Well, she requires taking care of. Ever since my dad died, she's been sort of high-maintenance and I usually don't mind helping her out. But in this instance the timing is less than stellar."

"Timing rarely is stellar. But maybe Alex coming here is good."

She turned to look at him. The setting sun glinted off her windblown curls, gilding the shiny honey strands. Her huge golden brown eyes reminded him of sweet caramel, and damn it, he loved caramel. The tip of her tongue peeped out to moisten her lips, a flick that filled him an overwhelming urge to stop walking, yank her into his arms, and kiss that beautiful plush mouth. But no way in hell was he going to give in to the craving. Next kiss was going to have to come from Miss No More Kissing.

"How do you figure?" she asked.

Damned if he knew—he'd looked at her mouth and completely forgotten what he'd said. "Figure what?"

"That Alex coming here is a good thing?"

Oh, right. He forced himself to look straight ahead and focus on Godiva, who'd momentarily stopped to gnaw on the tennis ball. "If they're able to work out their problems, then there'll be no reason for them to stick around. They'll head back to New York, and you'll have Paradise Lost all to yourself."

"And if they don't work out their problems?"

"Are you always so 'glass half empty'?"

"Believe it or not, no. Usually when life gives me lemons I—"

"Make lemonade?"

"Actually, I add cutlets and capers and make chicken piccata."

"Even better. But obviously not in this case because you're very"—he heaved the ball again for Godiva and searched for the right word, finally settling on—"tense."

"Jeez—ya think? Yes, I'm tense—and frustrated—because I planned this time away, and in spite of my intentions, it's not turning out at all the way I'd envisioned. This time was supposed to be for *me*. For me to fix *me*."

"What's wrong with you?"

"Now who's being a smart-ass?"

Nick shook his head. "I'm serious. I mean, yeah, you've got your quirks and faults and you're bossy as hell—"

"Wow, you really are a sweet-talker—"

"—but who doesn't? So what about you needs fixing?"

"What about *you* needs fixing?"

He grinned. "Aw, you don't think I'm perfect?"

"No." Godiva came back and dropped the ball at Jamie's feet. She picked it up and hurled it an impressive distance. "What you are is adept at sidestepping personal questions. You did it all through dinner with my unsubtly probing mother."

He shrugged. "I'm not comfortable being the center of attention."

"Or maybe you just like to keep people at arm's length."

Unable to keep from touching her, he skimmed his hand

down her back and said softly, "You've been closer to me than arm's length."

"Briefly. And only physically."

"Nothing wrong with physically." He paused and snagged her hand, forcing her to stop and face him. "Do you want to be closer to me than that?"

The question hung in the air between them and he wondered what in God's name had prompted him to voice it. What the hell was wrong with him? She'd made it perfectly clear she didn't want to get involved. And even more importantly, *he* didn't want to be involved. With anyone. Let alone this woman with her recent breakup and her pregnant mother and the mother's boyfriend and oh, yeah, she lived seven hundred miles away, and God only knew what else. But it seemed that he'd figured out Jamie Newman's superpower—it was the ability to make him say and do things that were the complete opposite of what he actually wanted to say and do.

She held back her curls with one hand and studied him through those caramel-colored eyes. "Do you mean do I want to be physically closer to you, as in have sex, or do I want to be closer to you more than physically, as in emotionally?"

When he didn't answer right away, she lifted her brows. "Are you listening?"

"Uh, no. 'Fraid not. My train of thought jumped the track when you said 'sex.'"

She blinked. "You didn't hear anything I said after the word sex?"

"'Fraid not." He shook his head to clear it of the mental image of them naked and sweaty. "Sorry." To keep himself from giving in to the temptation to yank her into his arms, he started walking again, and she fell into step beside him. "So finish telling me what about you needs fixing. I'm pretty handy."

"You are, but I'm not a leaky roof." A humorless laugh escaped her. "Although I feel like one."

"Which is why you came to Seaside Cove."

She turned to look at him. "And why you came here, I suspect. I'll tell you if you tell me."

"Sort of like I'll show you mine if you show me yours?"

She narrowed her eyes. "Are you talking about sex again?"

"Um, no?"

"I thought you said you didn't lie."

"Okay, then yes."

"Well, I'm not. No showing—just telling."

"I like my version better, but I'll play. You first."

"Why me first?

Nick looked skyward, then muttered, "Bossy *and* she questions everything."

"Part of my charm."

"I have no idea why I find you more charming than annoying."

"And there you go sweet-talking me again."

"I actually meant that as a compliment."

"Seriously? Here's a tip—your complimenting skills need some improvement."

"I'll work on it. You first."

She drew a deep breath. "Fine. You know my boyfriend cheated on me."

Nick nodded. "Yes. And for the record, any guy who would cheat on you is an asshole."

"Thank you."

"You're welcome. See? Told you I'd work on it."

"Noted. Anyway, he didn't just cheat—he cheated with my sister. My eight-years-older-than-me sister."

Nick winced. "Ouch. Triple whammy—you lost a boyfriend, a sister, and your dignity."

"Nail on head. Laurel's actually my half sister. Her mom and our dad divorced when she was six. My dad met my mom a few months later and it was love at first sight. I was born a year later. I adored Laurel the way I guess most little kids do their older siblings, but as I got older I sensed that she'd always resented me for coming along. That I, in her mind, stole our dad's affections and time."

Nick spied a sand dollar, but when he bent down to pick it up, realized it was broken. "She didn't see your dad?"

"She stayed with us every other weekend, and the entire month of July. Then, when she was nine, her mother remarried Martin Westerly."

Nick's brows shot up. "*The* Martin Westerly? As in Westerly department stores?"

"Yup. And in a heartbeat Laurel became a Park Avenue princess. You call *me* princess? Ha. Laurel could give Queen Elizabeth herself a few pointers. Exclusive private schools, designer clothes, all the trappings. None of that ever really interested me—just as well as my dad couldn't afford it. Laurel started looking at me like the poor relation."

"And what about the boyfriend?"

Jamie sighed. "He was from Laurel's lofty universe—private jets, trust funds, private schools, blah, blah, blah. Getting involved with a guy from that world of elite entitlement was a huge error in judgment on my part. Never again."

Nick glanced at her and noted her resolute expression. "It's not his fault he's from a rich family."

If looks could chop off heads, his would have been rolling in the sand. "You're *defending* him?"

"No. I'm merely saying that just because someone has money doesn't automatically make them an asshole. That's a distinction each person needs to earn on their own merit."

"Which Raymond did. In spades. But I met his family, I saw and experienced how they live, how they treat people, the subtle—and sometimes not so subtle—don't-you-know-who-I-am attitude. The expectation that their every wish, no matter how outlandish, would immediately be granted, and that there was always a loophole. I believe that deep inside him, Raymond just felt that rules didn't really apply to him, that there was always an exception, and he was entitled to that exception—a trait that resulted from his privileged upbringing."

"And yet you fell for the guy."

"I didn't realize that aspect of his character at first. And even after warning bells started ringing in my head and red flags began waving in the wind, I ignored them."

"Why?"

She huffed out a humorless sound. "One of the many questions I've been forcing myself to examine. And I haven't liked the answer."

"Which is?"

She hesitated, then said, "I got sucked into the lifestyle.

Getting into the best clubs, never having to wait for a table, car and driver at our disposal, VIP sections, quick jaunts by helicopter to his family's Hamptons estate. I didn't question things that I should have. Overlooked character flaws I'd deemed unacceptable in previous boyfriends. And I didn't like what that said about me."

"Sounds like you learned a lot about yourself."

"True. It was quite a jolt to realize I'd embraced so many things I'd previously thought of as shallow, activities I'd equated with Laurel, never myself. It's a situation I'll never let myself get lured into again."

"So . . . no more rich guys with helicopters for you."

"Exactly. I see one of those helicopter/private-plane/loophole guys again, I'm heading in the opposite direction."

Nick pondered that for several seconds, then asked, "How long were you together?"

"Eight months. He started sleeping with Laurel six months in."

"How'd you meet him?"

"At Newman's—Laurel had convinced him and some of his friends to stop by for dinner. She works there, too."

Nick whistled softly. "So that's why you took two months off seven hundred miles away."

"Yes. I needed a break."

"What does your sister do at Newman's?"

"Her official title is customer relations liaison. She's a networking whiz. Brings in lots of patrons and catering jobs from her wide circle of rich friends and social connections. As much as it pains me to say, she's very good at what she does."

"Which is schmoozing,"

"Yes. And boyfriend stealing."

"If he could be stolen he wasn't worth keeping."

"My mind, my common sense knows that, but my pride took a nasty hit. It's not easy or pleasant to lose your boyfriend under any circumstances. When you lose him to someone who's thinner, better looking, richer, and eight years older than you—who just happens to be your sister? Serious ego blow. The sort that makes you feel frumpy, dumpy, lumpy, and bumpy."

Nick shook his head. "She can't possibly be prettier than you."

Jamie laughed. "Okay, you're definitely getting better with the compliments, but that one crossed into bullshit territory."

"I don't bullshit."

She looked as if she wanted to argue, but instead she continued, "After we broke up I did a lot of soul searching, and while I didn't solve everything—thus my desire to get out of Dodge and come here—I came up with some interesting conclusions."

"Such as?"

They reached the pier and in silent accord turned around and headed back. She hesitated, then finally said, "This will probably sound crazy, but I felt like I missed out on being who I was supposed to be, who I wanted, deep down, to be, because I was so busy being the person everyone wanted and expected me to be."

"That doesn't sound crazy at all." In fact, he knew exactly how that felt.

"As much as I enjoy Newman's, it was never my dream to work there forever, but it sure was my dad's. It was more something I fell into, and as I got older, my responsibilities grew, and I just sort of became the manager. Then, after my dad died, the restaurant just overwhelmed my life. In the last couple of years, I've tried to make it more my own, put my personal stamp on it, but my mother won't hear of it. She wants everything to remain exactly the same as when my dad was alive. It's been a big bone of contention between us. I love Newman's, but . . ."

"It was your father's dream, not yours."

Jamie turned her head to look at him. "That sounds like the voice of experience."

Nick shrugged. "It is. So what's *your* dream?"

"I've always wanted my own dessert place—somewhere that specializes in cupcakes, cookies, pies, that sort of thing. Something small, intimate, maybe live music, great date place. Near the water. Something I've built from the ground up, decorated myself, everything handpicked by me."

"The way your dad did for Newman's."

She picked up a flat rock and skipped it into the waves.

"Exactly. It's been in the back of my mind ever since I was a teenager, but Newman's just sort of . . ."

"Swallowed you?"

She nodded. "Exactly. And that's it for me. Your turn. What's your dream?"

"Exactly what I'm doing now—owning a fixer-upper at the beach and renovating it."

"Are you planning to sell it once it's done?"

"Not Southern Comfort. That's . . . home. I think I'll probably keep Paradise Lost as well and rent it—*after* it's renovated."

"After renovation—good idea," she said dryly. When he fell silent, she prodded, "So keep going. What brought you to Seaside Cove?"

"A situation pretty similar to yours. Eldest son, heavy expectations to follow in my dad's footsteps—who followed in his dad's—to join the family business."

"Which is what?"

He hesitated. "They own a bed-and-breakfast in the Chicago area."

"And it was expected that you'd work there?"

"More like demanded."

Jamie nodded. "That pressure—it's hard to live up to."

"Especially when it's not what you want, when it's just what everyone wants you to want. And expects you to want. So, like you, I did what was expected of me, but I hated it. Hated being cooped up in an office, with meetings—"

"Oh, the meetings are the worst," Jamie agreed, tossing away a broken piece of sand dollar. "And the paperwork—yikes. Who taught you how do to carpentry work? Your dad?"

Nick barely managed to swallow the bark of laughter that rose in his throat. The thought of his father doing any sort of manual task other than raising a Cuban cigar or a cut crystal glass of one-hundred-year-old brandy to his lips was unimaginable. "A school buddy. I loved it from the first moment I held a hammer in my hand."

"And you moved to Seaside Cove to follow your dream."

"Yes. And I'm not going back. I've been happier here for the past three months, felt freer, than I have my entire life."

"And you're how old?"

"Thirty. It seemed a good time to reevaluate and make changes. You?"

"Twenty-six. And soon to be a big sister for the first time in my life—unbelievable. You said you're the eldest son?"

Nick nodded. "I have a younger brother." Who, in spite of them growing up together, he barely knew.

"He works at the B and B?"

"Yes. But as the oldest, it was expected of me to work there. But my brother's much better suited to it. He has the same killer instincts as our father."

Her brows rose. "I wouldn't normally associate killer instincts with a bed-and-breakfast. Must be a competitive field."

Guilt pricked him, but he shoved it aside. "More so than you'd think."

"What about your mom?"

"She died when I was nine. I have a stepmother." He didn't add that he'd actually had three of them and this latest one was only two years older than him. "I don't see my family much."

"I wish I could say the same about my family." They'd reached their beach access and they stopped to look out at the ocean. "I really like it here. I just wish all my uninvited guests would go home."

"I like it here, too." He turned his head to look at her. "Especially since I found out my renter is an excellent cook."

She smiled and turned to walk down the path leading back to the house. "And you haven't even tasted my cookies yet."

Desire hit him low and hard. "Is that an offer?"

Color flooded her cheeks. "No. Well, yes—but only for cookies."

Hoping to coax her skin to turn another fascinating shade, he teased, "Do you mean actual cookies or is that a code word for something else?"

"Like what?"

"I don't know. Nipples?"

She laughed—and he noticed that hers hardened. "No. Just cookies."

"Okay. Since I love cookies, I accept."

She blew out a long breath. "Now if I could only figure out what to do about my family, everything would be perfect."

"There's nothing to figure out—you just have to decide if—and then when—you're going to stop being a puppet."

She halted as if she'd walked into a wall of glass. "Excuse me? A *puppet*?"

He nodded. "You're allowing all these other people to pull your strings, dictate what you do."

She narrowed her eyes. "Are you trying to piss me off?"

A humorless sound escaped him. "No. I'm actually trying to get you naked."

"You're not on the right track, my friend."

"I can see that. I guess I'm out of practice. It's been a while."

"How long?"

"Long enough to forget that while women always say they want honesty, they don't necessarily appreciate it."

"I can't think of anyone who'd like being called a puppet." They'd reached Paradise Lost. She looked at the house and sighed. "I really don't want to go in there."

"That's exactly what I'm talking about. It's *your* house—at least for the summer. Stop letting other people pull your strings. As long as you allow it, they're going to do it. You're the only one who can stop it."

She shot him a withering look. "I meant I didn't want to interrupt."

"Fine. You can come to my place. I'll show you my renovations."

"Do you mean actual renovations or is that a code word for something else?"

Nick grinned. "One way to find out."

Chapter 13

Several minutes later Jamie turned in a slow circle in Nick's new kitchen, taking in the washed-oak cabinets—several of which had glass doors—speckled granite countertop, and stainless steel appliances. The hardwood floor gleamed beneath her feet. No doubt about it, he did very nice work.

"It's beautiful," she said, running her fingers over the glossy granite. She eyed the glass mosaic tile backsplash done in shades of blue from the palest arctic to the deepest azure. "That's gorgeous—it looks like the sea."

"Thanks. Took a long time for those tiles to come in, but I think they were worth the wait."

She nodded toward the living area, which looked like a construction zone. "What are you going to do in there?"

"Remove that old paneling from the walls and put up new sheetrock. Paint, extend the hardwood floor throughout. New furniture. After that I'll tackle the bedrooms and baths. Last I want to extend the screened porch."

"Sounds great. Are you planning to do the same for Paradise Lost?"

"That's the plan."

She nodded and turned her attention back to the kitchen. "I

love the sink—nice and big, and the high arc on the faucet is great. Makes it much easier to wash big pots and pans."

"Not that I have any pots and pans, but I liked it, too."

"No pots and pans? Are you kidding?"

She opened a cabinet and indeed found it empty except for a lone coffee mug. The sight of that single cup gave her a sensation she called a "heart owie"—a hollow feeling that invaded her chest for the span of a single heartbeat. That mug looked very forlorn and sad to her, and she vividly recalled Dorothy saying she believed Nick was lonely. Which was completely different than alone. People could choose to be alone (and in her case, choose it and fail to achieve it), but no one would ever choose to be lonely. Lonely was what happened when you had no one. And that cup somehow represented lonely.

"Nope. I tossed the ones that came with the house—they were either rusted or dented or stained with crud. Not that I ever used them. I'm a bachelor. Who needs pots and pans when there's take-out?"

"Don't you even cook eggs?"

"I don't really like the taste of charred eggs, so no."

"Boil water?"

"I don't really like the taste of boiled water, either."

"I mean to cook something. Like pasta."

"Nope. Never made pasta."

Jamie shook her head. "Unless you've had a personal chef at your disposal your entire life, that's just ridiculous. And even then, you're an adult—you should know at least how to cook eggs and make pasta."

"If that's an offer to teach me, I'm willing to learn."

"Well, even *I* can't cook without some pots and pans."

"You have any suggestions as to what I should buy?"

"Definitely. You tell me your budget and I'll help you outfit your kitchen."

"Deal. Since you're avoiding your company, how about I get my laptop and we go online shopping?"

"Picking out kitchen supplies while spending someone else's money is my favorite thing to do."

His gaze dipped to her mouth. "Can't say it's *my* favorite."

When his eyes met hers again, her breath caught at the fire burning in the glittering green depths. "But I'll play along."

He entered the bedroom and returned a moment later with a laptop that he set on the granite snack bar. Jamie settled herself on a stool and started pulling up several of her favorite kitchen supply sites.

"Would you like a drink?" Nick asked. "'Fraid I can only offer you bottled water. I would offer you vodka, but someone stole my only bottle."

"Water's fine."

He handed her a cold bottle, then straddled the stool beside her. "Whatcha got here?"

"Any of these three sets will do nicely for you—they all contain the basics and are good, dependable brands. You just need to decide how much you want to spend."

"Which one would you get?"

She clicked on the photo of the All-Clad set. "This is what I have. It's absolutely top of the line, and what most professional chefs and restaurants use. It's the most expensive option, but it's the only set of pots and pans you'll ever need. You'll be able to pass these on to your grandkids and they'll still be perfect."

"Then that's what I'll order. Done. What else do I need?"

"Don't you want to see the cheaper versions?"

He reached out and brushed a single fingertip over her cheek. "I only want the best."

Jamie's heart stuttered. "Stop looking at me like that."

"Like what?"

In that smoldering, I-want-to-eat-you-up way. In that way that could easily make a girl's panties fall off. Darn it, how was it that only moments ago she'd been thoroughly irritated with him and now she wanted nothing more than to take him up on that look? He thought she was a puppet, an assessment she didn't like one bit. Just as she didn't like *him.*

Oh, for God's sake, Jamie, her inner voice whispered. *You do like him—you just don't want to. And that puppet thing? Maybe that's a lot closer to the truth than you want to admit as well.*

She didn't like that stupid voice, either.

Or the fact that Nick confused her. Because God knows she didn't need any more confusion. But the way he was looking at her . . . *Whew!* It made her feel as if her skin had shrunk.

A car door slamming broke through the lust-filled fog surrounding her. "That sounded like it came from next door." She scooted off the stool and walked to Nick's screen porch and looked down.

"Oh, God, that's not good."

"What's wrong?" Nick asked, coming up behind her. "Is that Alex? Taking a suitcase out of his car?"

Jamie briefly closed her eyes and nodded. "Yup. Looks like my company isn't going anywhere anytime soon."

Chapter 14

Nick smoothed the sandpaper over the wooden railing he'd just finished nailing into place on the Clam Festival float, relishing the deep sense of satisfaction that filled him at the progress the committee had made on the project. If all went well, the float would be finished by the end of next week and ready for the decorating committee to paint and work their magic upon.

Noise surrounded him and he glanced around the huge chamber of commerce parking lot at the dozen float workers. Some hammered, some sanded, some made use of the level or saw, but all were involved. Nick noted Dorothy exchanging scowls with Melvin, while Megan and Grace served cold drinks to the workers while their husbands were busy measuring wood. A sense of community, of belonging filled him, one that satisfied his soul in a way he'd never known until he came to Seaside Cove. Which served only to prove that some things couldn't be bought.

He'd just wiped away the sawdust from the rail when a familiar voice came from behind him, "Looks like the float is coming along really well."

He briefly closed his eyes and absorbed the little jolt his

heart performed at the sound of Jamie's voice. He turned around and his heart gave another, bigger leap at the sight of her. Damn. One look at her and any hopes he'd harbored that not seeing her for the past week and a half would dampen his attraction to her zoomed away like a gull caught in a stiff breeze. She walked toward him and all he could do was stare. Jesus, the woman in motion was an engineering marvel of perfectly moving curvy parts that could stop a train in its tracks.

Her tight black athletic shorts showcased a full, rounded ass his palms itched to cup—right after his fingers traced over the several inches of tanned stomach peeking out between the top of her running shorts and a matching half tank top. Her hair was pulled back in a haphazard ponytail from which several curls had escaped, and in spite of the sweat glistening on her skin, he bet she smelled like cookies.

He wanted to grab her and take a great big bite.

She waved in the direction where he'd seen Megan and Grace standing. "Out for an early-morning run on the beach?" he asked, eyeing the sand clinging to the edges of her Nikes.

"'Run' is an overstatement, at least for the last mile, which is better categorized as a slow, gasping, painful jog." She pushed her sunglasses onto her head and wiped her brow with the back of her hand. Godiva trotted over and flopped on her back in a shameless plea for a belly rub.

Jamie obliged and continued, "Unfortunately I'm not one of those people who can't eat when stressed. Instead I bake. And eat. Even though my common sense knows what brownies and cookies can do to thighs, I just keep on baking and eating. Which results in many calories. And with many calories must come much jogging-related suffering."

His gaze skipped down to her legs. "If that's what brownies and cookies do to thighs, all I can say is keep on baking and eating."

She smiled. "You've really gotten much better with the compliments, but clearly your eyesight is going. I feel like I've gained a hundred pounds in the ten days since Alex arrived."

She gave Godiva a final pat, and after the dog settled next to Nick's feet and resumed chewing on her rawhide treat, Jamie continued, "I've officially renamed Paradise Lost. It's

now Tension Central and I've been cooking—and eating—
like a maniac. I would have happily shared a few hundred
thousand calories with you, but you haven't been around to
pawn them off on."

"No." He'd left Seaside Cove the morning after their
scampi dinner. He could have returned several days ago, but
he'd forced himself to stay away. "I got back late last night."

"I know. I was sitting on the screen porch and saw you arrive. You looked tired."

"It was late. So your mom and Alex are still here?"

"Oh, yeah. Whatever else is going on, they *love* Seaside
Cove. Love the beach, love the town, love the weather. They
love it so much they may never leave. Mom's already let Patrick and Nathan know she won't be back for at least another
two weeks. When Alex found that out, he rearranged his
schedule to remain with her. They said they'd stay somewhere
else, but—as I found out when I arrived here last month—
there're no vacancies anywhere. So they're with me. Yippee."

"They getting along okay?"

"Hard to tell. Mom's not saying much, but part of that has
been me dodging her. I really don't want to get involved in
their situation—or bicker with my mom about Newman's,
which is pretty much the only thing she wants to talk about
other than Alex. They've had lots of arguments and intense
conversations. I try not to listen—there are some things a
daughter just shouldn't know—but it's hard not to hear things
in a small house. So I've been spending most of my time at the
beach and exploring the island. But I can tell you this—Alex
is absolutely nutsy, coo-coo, crazy in love with my mother."

"Is she crazy in love with him?"

"I think she is, but the fact that she's older than him really
freaks her out, as does the fact that she's pregnant. I *know*
she's afraid of being hurt. Of making a mistake."

Nick nodded. "Love is scary. And it's easy to make a
mistake."

"Singin' to the choir, dude." She walked to the edge of the
float and wrapped her fingers around the carved balustrade
he'd nailed into place earlier that morning. "Lots of people
here this morning. Could you use another pair of hands?"

He offered up a silent thank-you to his Ray-Bans, which

kept her from seeing the avid way his gaze roamed over her spandex-covered curves. "I guess that depends on the hands. And what they'd be used for. You volunteering, princess?"

A blush washed over her cheeks—like she needed to look more gorgeous. "I wouldn't know a nail from a screw."

Even as his mind screamed at him to stay where he was— namely a safe distance away from her—he hopped down from the platform and stood directly in front of her. And standing so close, he couldn't stop himself from reaching out and dragging a single fingertip down her glistening arm. "I'd be happy to teach you the difference between a nail and a screw."

More color rushed into her cheeks. She bit her plump lower lip, then gave a quick laugh. "Walked right into that one, didn't I?"

"Sure did. But the differences are easy to master." He took her hand and turned it palm-side up. "A nail has a broad head and a straight, smooth body"—he ran the pad of his thumb slowly up and down the length of her palm—"and is driven straight in." He pressed his thumb in a slow, steady pumping rhythm against her soft skin. "While a screw has a ridged body that enters with a circular motion." He demonstrated by drawing a trio of leisurely circles around her palm.

A tremor ran through her, one that urged him to forget the people around them, snatch her into his arms, and make her feel it again. Instead he forced himself to release her hand and step back. "Got it?"

Her tongue peeked out to moisten her lips, a gesture that had him gritting his teeth. "Uh, yeah. Got it." She cleared her throat. "Thanks. But I meant Alex. He's a general contractor and as much as he loves the beach, I think he's suffering from Home Depot withdrawal. I mentioned the float to him and he lit up like a sparkler."

"Uh-huh. And this has nothing to do with you wanting him out of the house for a few hours."

"That, of course, would be an added bonus. If only my mom liked to hammer nails, I might get some peace and quiet."

"Always glad to have another helper."

"Great. I'll let Alex know. What's going to go on there?"

she asked, pointing to a raised dais accessed by a wide curved step.

"Chairs for the newly crowned Clam Queen, Clam King, and all the other clams."

"Excellent. You need to enter for Clam King."

He laughed. "I need that like I need a hole in the head."

She eyed his head. "That can be arranged."

Silence fell between them. Her gaze searched his face and he could almost feel her curiosity, her wanting to ask him where he'd been. The urge to touch her, to bury his face in that sweet spot where her neck and shoulder met and find out if she still smelled like cookies, grew stronger with each passing second, and he wasn't certain how much longer he could resist. When she continued to simply look at him, he asked, "You need something else?"

She blinked, as if coming out of a trance. "Yes. Actually the reason I stopped to talk to you. A delivery truck arrived at Paradise Lost yesterday morning. But I'm guessing you know about that."

Hmmm . . . sounded like the princess wasn't pleased. Well good. That would certainly be a reason to dislike her, and God knows he needed a few. "Yes, I know. Is there a problem?"

"Only that I wanted to thank you but couldn't because you weren't home. The new furniture is absolutely beautiful. Thank you so much for getting it now rather than later."

"You sound shocked."

"To tell you the truth, I am."

"I told you I'd think about it, and I did. And you were right—no reason not to furnish the place now."

Her eyes widened and she made a big show of cupping her hand around her ear. "Excuse me, what was that I just heard? Did you say I was *right*?"

"Yeah—but obviously I should have said 'you're a pain in the butt' instead. Believe it or not, it was never my intention for you to be uncomfortable."

"Well, the place went from 'pig' to 'Pygmalion.' The sofa, chairs, tables, lamps, both bedroom sets—all gorgeous. And so comfortable. You have excellent taste."

"I'm glad you approve."

Once again silence swelled between them and he wondered if she had any idea how sexy she looked in those damn little shorts and sports top, without any makeup, her messy hair and sweaty skin. The urge to grab her and drag her to the ground and cover her body with his was approaching overwhelming—audience be damned—and he had to cross his arms over his chest to keep his hands to himself. He leaned his shoulders against the railing and asked, "Was there something else?"

"Are you trying to get rid of me?"

"Actually, yes. I have a lot to do and you're kind of distracting."

Something kindled in her eyes—a warm, teasing mischief that sizzled fire straight to his groin. "*Kind of?* That sounds pretty half-assed."

"Okay, you're *very* distracting. Especially right here." He reached out and traced a single fingertip along that enticing bit of bare midriff. Her stomach muscles contracted and she drew in a sharp breath. "If you're unconvinced, I'd be happy to demonstrate exactly how distracting you are."

All the mischief evaporated from her eyes, replaced by a heat that made it clear her body craved the same thing his did. But instead of yielding to temptation, she shook her head and stepped back. "Not a good idea."

He couldn't argue with that. Yet the desire lingering in her eyes let him know he could change her mind. But he kept his hands to himself. He'd vowed that the next time they kissed, it was going to be at her initiation. It was a vow he intended to keep. God help him.

Just to make sure his resolve didn't crumble, he stepped back onto the platform and picked up a handful of nails and his hammer.

"So what were you doing these last ten days?" she asked.

Ah. So that's what she wanted. He placed a nail and gave it a good whack. "What were *you* doing?"

"Aside from dodging my mom and Alex and exploring the island, I completed the paperwork for the additional Clam Festival contests and started organizing all the vendor booths, setting up a map for the site locations, and compiling all the key contact information. I attended a bonfire, where I met a bunch of the other residents. Dorothy, Megan, and Grace made sure they introduced me to everyone."

"Sounds like fun."

"It was. And remember the black-and-white cat? I saw a lost cat poster with her photo on it—her name was Tabitha—and called the number. The next day, using her name, I was able to coax her to come to me and I reunited her with her family."

"That must have made you happy."

"Yes. We all cried. The most fun I had was helping out at Oy Vey Mama Mia for three days. Maria had two wisdom teeth pulled and she asked me to fill in for her. It was an absolute blast. Ira is absolutely hysterical—I don't know when I've laughed so hard. His first lesson was teaching me how to take the wine order—'you want Manischewitz or Chianti with that?' "

Nick laughed with her. The way her eyes glowed tugged something in the vicinity of his heart that he didn't want tugged, but was apparently helpless to stop.

"Okay, I've shared mine," she said, "time for you to share yours."

A slow grin tilted up his lips. "Sweetheart, I'm happy to share mine anytime you want."

She shot him a glare. "I'm not talking about . . . *that*. I told you what I've been doing, so now you owe me."

"And I'm a man who always pays his debts. What exactly do you want to know?"

"Where were you? Where do you go when you leave Seaside Cove?"

"Hey, Nick, can you give us a hand over here?" came Melvin's gruff voice from behind them.

Nick turned and raised his hand. "Sure. Be right there." He turned back to Jamie, who regarded him with a disgruntled expression.

"I guess that translates to 'saved by the bell,' " she said.

He hesitated, debating, then finally said, "How about instead of telling you, I show you? This place I go—it's about an hour's drive and I'm heading back there this afternoon. Wanna come with?"

She narrowed her eyes. "What sort of place is it?"

He looked toward the sky. "Nothing nefarious, for cryin' out loud. Stop looking at me like I'd haul you off to some den of depravity."

She snorted. "Like it hasn't crossed your mind."

"And yours, too, Princess Glass House, so quit throwing stones. But the den of depravity isn't where I'm going this afternoon." He raised his hand. "Boy Scout promise."

Skepticism was etched all over her face. "*You* were a Boy Scout?"

"Jeez, do you have to pick *everything* apart?"

"I'm not picking—I'm detail oriented."

"Tomayto, tomahto."

"So were you a Boy Scout?"

Damn but she was a persistent pest. But damn, he liked it. Which meant he must have gotten dropped on his head when he was a kid. "As a matter of fact, I was."

"For how long?"

Only for a week, damn it. Not that he was about to admit that. "Long enough. So, you want to come or not?"

"Wow. Such a pretty invitation. But I need more details."

"Because you're detail oriented. As opposed to a picky pest."

"Right. So are you going to a bar?"

"No."

"How long are you planning to be gone—I'm not heading out on some ten-day jaunt with you."

"Right—'cause ten days with *you* would be such a picnic. We'll be home tonight—probably around ten or eleven. You in or out?"

"In. But only to satisfy my curiosity. And because it's a chance to escape Pregnant Mom/Baby Daddy/Tension Town for a few hours."

"Good to know it's not because you think you might enjoy my company for a while." He started walking toward Melvin, glad she couldn't see the smile tugging at his lips.

"Happy hammering. See you at noon."

He heard her sneakers crunching on the gravel and peeked over his shoulder. As he watched her jog off, his gaze nailed to her butt, he knew, deep down, that he was screwed.

The moment she disappeared around the corner, he held up a finger to Melvin to indicate he'd be there in a minute and pulled his cell phone from his pocket.

There was a quick call he needed to make before his trip with the princess.

Chapter 15

Glad to have escaped the Palace of Tension, Jamie sat in Nick's pickup, enjoying the sea-scented breeze whipping through the open windows almost as much as Godiva, whose head was stuck out the back window in ear-blowing bliss. "So where are we going?"

"A small town about an hour inland called Harmony Crossing."

"And what's in Harmony Crossing?"

"A friend's house."

Jamie's brows shot upward and she turned in her seat to look at him. She wasn't sure what she'd expected, but it hadn't been that. "Seriously?"

He flicked a glance her way. "Are you shocked because I'm really not dragging you off to some lecherous lair or because you don't believe I'd actually have a friend?"

"A little of both. Is this friend someone you met since moving to Seaside Cove?"

"No. I met Kevin our first year of high school. We became good friends and I spent a lot of time with him and his family during those four summers. Kevin's father owned a small home-building business. Kevin helped him when school let out and I pitched in. They taught me everything I know about building and fixing houses and instilled in me a real love of working with my hands."

"And you've remained friends all these years."

"Quit sounding so shocked."

"I'm not. I was actually thinking it was nice to have a friend of such long standing. My best bud, Kate, and I have been friends since junior high."

"Kate must possess the patience of a saint."

"Ha, ha. So now Kevin lives in Harmony Crossing."

"He's always lived there—it's where his family is from and where I spent those summers."

She frowned. "I thought you said you grew up in the Chicago area."

"I did."

"Then how did you meet a guy who's lived his whole life in Harmony Crossing, North Carolina in high school?"

He hesitated a beat. "Kevin had an aunt and uncle in Chicago. He stayed for the school terms."

"That's a long way from home for a kid."

"He was close to his aunt and uncle so it worked out well. It was during the summer between our junior and senior years, when we drove to Seaside Cove for a day at the beach, that I first discovered the place. I sort of forgot about it, but then during a visit a few years ago we hit the coast. We crossed the bridge to the island, and I . . . felt something. I can't explain it, but it just felt like a homecoming. When I made the decision to relocate, there was never a question as to where I wanted to go."

"And now you live there."

"I do. And I'm never going back."

She noted the way his fingers tightened on the wheel when he said that. She studied his profile for several seconds—and a damn fine profile it was, darn him—then asked, "You never told me who cheated on you."

Another quick tightening of his fingers. "Fiancée." He shot her a glance. Their gazes met for only an instant but there was no missing the emptiness in his eyes—as if he'd very carefully wiped his face clean of all expression, leaving his features as blank as his tone. After returning his attention to the road, he said, "Yeah, yeah, I know, you're shocked that some woman would agree to marry me."

Myriad emotions rippled through her—annoyance, sympathy, but mostly shame that she'd given him the impression that she thought so little of him when that wasn't the case. He might be a pest, but he was a *likeable* pest. At least some of the time.

Most of the time, her inner voice corrected.

Jamie shook her head in the hopes of dislodging that stupid voice. "That isn't what I was going to say."

"Maybe not in those exact words, but I'm sure that was the basic sentiment."

She made a sound like a game show buzzer. "Wrong. I was thinking that I know how much it hurts to be cheated on and it's not a pain I'd wish on anyone. And that I'm sorry something so hurtful happened to you." She paused, then asked, "How long ago did this happen?"

"Two years."

"Are you . . . still in love with her?"

Silence swelled between them. Jamie peeked at him from the corner of her eye and noted his stiff shoulders and the muscle ticking in his jaw. Oops—obviously she'd asked the wrong question. Which could only mean that yes, he was still in love with her.

Her heart seemed to lurch sideways, filling her chest with an ache she couldn't name, along with something else that felt oddly like jealousy, but of course wasn't. Probably indigestion. Yeah, that's what was causing the discomfort. Indigestion. She definitely shouldn't have eaten that spicy chili for lunch. She placed her hand on her stomach but experienced no relief.

"No," he said. "I'm not still in love with her."

Suddenly her indigestion felt exactly like . . . relief? Weird! "You sure? It took you like five hours to come up with that answer."

"I'm sure. And I knew the answer immediately. I just had to decide how much of it to say."

"How many parts of 'no' are there?"

"She cheated on me, but she didn't break my heart. Because she never really owned it. I never really loved her. Not the way you're supposed to love the person you're going to marry."

"Then why did you ask her to marry you?"

"Looking back, I think I must have suffered a blow to the head. There were all kinds of red flags that should have warned me that she didn't love me for me, but just like you with your boyfriend, I either ignored them or chose to believe her. We'd lived together for a year. Everyone expected us to marry, including her . . ." He shrugged. "I caved to the pressure. I reasoned that it was normal to question my feelings. Figured there's no way to ever *really* be sure, *completely* sure, that you're choosing the right person."

"How'd you find out?"

Again he paused, then said, "Three weeks before the wedding I saw pictures of her kissing another guy at a party—and I don't mean a peck on the cheek. When I confronted her, she confessed."

Jamie winced. "Yikes. Well, better you found out three weeks before than three weeks after."

"Amen to that. After that, I really started reassessing my life, thinking about what I was doing and why, deciding what would make me happy—and realizing I wasn't doing it. When I turned thirty, I decided it was time to stop thinking and start taking action. I began planning for my future, and basically for my . . . I guess *escape* is the best word. I sold or donated everything that reminded me of my former life, moved to Seaside Cove, and haven't looked back. Don't intend to. I'm exactly where I want to be, doing exactly what I want to do."

He stopped at a traffic light and looked at her. She felt the intensity of his gaze right down to her toes. "I know you were pissed at me for calling you a puppet, for saying you allow people to take advantage of you and pull your strings, but I look at you and I see myself ten, five, even two years ago. Sometimes it takes an outsider, someone who's not a family member or close friend, to give us a different perspective. Or that kick in the ass we sometimes need."

"I think you just like the thought of kicking my ass."

"Kicking it isn't exactly the right word." His gaze skimmed over her, leaving a trail of warmth in its wake. When his eyes met hers once again, her breath caught at the unmistakable heat burning in the green depths. "It's a really great ass, by the way."

To her alarm she felt flattered instead of annoyed at his comment, which surely she should find sexist. Even worse, she couldn't dredge up any indignation for him once again using the word "puppet" in relation to her actions. And worser— was that even a word?—she didn't understand why.

Because you're glad he likes your ass, Stupid Inner Voice informed her. *And because you know damn well, as much as you don't want to admit it, that there's a grain of truth in his assessment.*

Before she could find her voice, the light turned green and he returned his attention to driving. At the next corner, he turned right, then said, "We're almost there."

Jamie shoved aside her unsettling thoughts to examine later, and asked, "Does Kevin know you're bringing a guest?"

"Yes. I called him. But even if I hadn't, it would be fine. Things are very casual and down-to-earth at his place."

Seconds later he pulled into the driveway of a modest brick ranch. The front lawn was small but meticulously groomed, as were the flowerbeds, which bloomed in a profusion of cheery purple, pink, and white. Jamie followed Nick and Godiva up the flagstone walkway, noting the wooden ramp that had been built over the several steps leading to the porch. Nick gave a single knock to the screened front door, then opened it. Godiva nosed her way past them and dashed into the house. Nick walked in and held the door for Jamie, who followed him inside.

They stood in a small ceramic-tiled foyer that opened to the right into a living area furnished with a comfy-looking navy blue sectional and an entertainment unit complete with a large flat-screen TV and an obviously at-home Godiva, who lay sprawled in the corner, chewing a rawhide knot. Straight ahead was a dining area that Jamie could see led to the kitchen. A hallway led off the dining area, presumably to bedrooms.

"We're here. Where's the welcoming committee?"

The words were barely out of his mouth when an exceptionally pretty blonde with huge China blue eyes entered the room. She broke into a huge smile at the sight of Nick and rushed forward to give him a hug. After she stepped back, she said, "I know you just escaped us, but we're so glad you're back."

"Happy to be here." He grabbed Jamie's hand and tugged her forward. "Liz, this is my neighbor, Jamie Newman. Jamie, meet Liz Sheridan, my buddy Kevin's wife."

"Great to meet you, Jamie," Liz said, extending her hand with a warm, engaging smile. She jerked her head toward Nick. "Hope this one isn't giving you too much trouble."

Jamie returned Liz's smile. "He's trying, but I'm not letting him."

"Excellent. Just watch that grin of his—when he flashes it, it means trouble with a capital T."

"So I've learned. Sunglasses help block the dazzle. So does keeping food in his mouth."

"Uh, I'm standing right here," Nick said, waving his hand. "And speaking of food, what's for dinner?" He sniffed the air. "I don't smell anything."

Liz rolled her eyes. "That's because I haven't started cooking yet."

"Well, get to it, woman. I'm already hungry and I haven't even started working yet."

"Does he eat constantly at his own house?" Liz asked Jamie.

"Don't know, but based on the couple meals I've shared with him, he can put away enough food to sink a battleship."

Liz nodded. "Kevin's the same way. And he never gains an ounce. *So* unfair."

"Ridiculously unfair," Jamie agreed. "Meanwhile, it takes me seven months to work off three bites of brownie."

"Did someone mention brownies?" came a male voice from the hallway. Seconds later a wheelchair entered the living area, propelled by a handsome man with ebony hair and matching eyes, whose right leg was encased in a cast from his toes to his hip. He smiled at Nick. "Glad you're here, man— even gladder if your presence has resulted in brownies."

"Kevin, this is Nick's neighbor, Jamie Newman," said Liz. She then turned to Jamie. "My husband, Kevin—who loves brownies above all else."

"Not *all* else," Kevin protested. "I kinda like you, too."

Jamie smiled. "Nice to meet you, Kevin. If I'd known you liked brownies so much, I would have baked you some."

"Hey—you never offered to bake *me* brownies," Nick said.

Jamie shrugged. "I didn't know you liked them."

Nick rolled his eyes. "C'mon. Everyone likes brownies."

"Not *everyone*."

"Have you ever met anyone who didn't? Especially a guy?"

Jamie considered. "You have a point."

Nick's brows shot upward. "You're *agreeing* with me?"

She raised her brows right back at him. "It would seem so."

"Jesus. Where are my ice skates? I think hell just froze over."

He turned to Liz and Kevin, who, Jamie suddenly noticed, were observing her and Nick with very interested expressions. "Jamie's an excellent cook—which I know firsthand. I *hear* she's an excellent baker—but as I've never tasted any sort of dessert she's prepared, I can't comment."

Jamie barely resisted the urge to stick out her tongue at him. Instead she smiled at Kevin. "*Some* people deserve brownies."

"Like guys with broken legs?" he asked with a hopeful expression.

"Exactly." She shot Nick a pointed glare. "And some people do not."

Nick shrugged and adopted a bored expression. "I'm saying you're all talk and no action, and couldn't bake a decent brownie if your life depended on it."

"Whoa," said Kevin, looking up at Liz from his chair. "Did you hear that gauntlet being thrown to the floor?"

"Sure did." Liz looked at Jamie. "You going to let him get away with that trash talk?"

"Oh, no. I intend to pick up his gauntlet." She favored Nick with an overly sweet smile. "And smack him with it. I just haven't decided yet how hard to hit him."

When Kevin snickered, Nick shot him a frown. "Whose side are you on?"

"Will you really bake me brownies?" Kevin asked Jamie.

"Yes."

Kevin turned back to Nick. "Sorry, bro—my allegiance is with the one who bakes the brownies."

"Traitor."

"You'd do the same and you know it. You ready to get to work?"

"Depends," said Nick. "You gonna share your brownies with me?"

"Depends." Kevin cut his gaze to Jamie. "Will you bake an extra-large batch?"

Jamie's lips twitched. "Done."

Kevin turned back to Nick. "Yes. I'll share. *One.*"

"Fine." He nodded toward Kevin's cast. "How's the leg feeling today?"

"Better than yesterday, not as good as tomorrow. It's actually my ass that hurts—from all this sitting around. I can't wait 'til next Wednesday." He looked at Jamie. "That's when the cast comes off. And the physical therapy begins."

"What happened?" Jamie asked.

"Fell off a ladder on the job." Kevin shook his head. "Broke my leg in two places. Required surgery. Now I have a plate and more screws than I care to think about holding me together in there and I've been in this cast for six weeks. Next up is several months of physical therapy."

Liz reached for Kevin's hand. "We're lucky only his leg was broken. When I think about what could have happened . . ." She closed her eyes and a shudder shook her.

Kevin brought their joined hands to his lips and kissed her fingers. "It didn't happen so don't think about it. I'll be up chasing you and Emily around in no time."

"Speaking of Emily," broke in Nick, "where is the love of my life?"

"Taking her afternoon nap," said Liz. "She'll be waking up soon."

"Emily's our baby," Kevin explained to Jamie.

"And she's also my goddaughter," said Nick. "And The Cutest Little Girl in the World."

"I have to agree with that," Kevin said.

"And you're totally unbiased," Jamie said with a laugh.

Kevin grinned. "Totally."

As if on cue, Jamie heard a baby voice say, "Mama, Mama, Mama."

"I'm being paged via the baby monitor," Liz said, pointing at a device that looked something like a handheld phone on the end table.

"I'll get her," Nick said. He scooted around Jamie and turned down the hallway.

"I'm planning to grill steaks for dinner, Jamie," Liz said. "Does that sound okay?"

"Sounds great. I'm happy to help."

"Thanks—with Emily now awake, an extra pair of hands is always appreciated. She may be the cutest little girl ever, but she's also very curious and into everything."

"How old is she'?"

"Eighteen months."

"I remember when my niece was that age. So busy, so cute."

Just then Nick's voice floated through the monitor. "Hey there, sweetie. How's my favorite girl?"

His question was answered by a happy baby giggle and the words, "Uncoo Nic. Up."

"You're getting so big, I can barely lift you." Nick made exaggerated groaning sounds, as if he were lifting a boulder, followed by kissy noises and baby squeals of delight. "What's the big idea of napping when I'm around? That's not allowed."

A few seconds later Nick entered the room holding an adorable toddler with her father's ebony hair surrounding her cherubic face in soft ringlets and her mother's amazing blue eyes. She had one chubby arm wrapped around Nick's neck and two fingers of her other hand in her mouth.

She blinked at Jamie, clearly wondering, *Who the heck are you?* Jamie smiled, waggled her fingers, and said, "Hi there, Emily. You sure are a cutie." Emily pulled her fingers from her mouth and grinned, showing her tiny baby teeth. Then she saw Kevin and Liz, and her smile deepened, showing off a pair of deep dimples.

"Dada," she said, and reached for Kevin.

"Oh, my gosh, she's absolutely adorable," Jamie said.

"That's because she looks just like her mom," Kevin

said, settling his daughter on his good leg. He wrinkled his nose. "She may look really cute, but whew, she smells really bad."

"I'm on it," Liz said, plucking Emily up like a daisy, lifting her high and blowing on her tummy, an act that brought out a delicious baby squeal of delight. She turned to Jamie. "I'm not sure I have all the ingredients to make brownies from scratch. Would you be interested in checking the pantry while I change her?"

"As long as you don't mind me rooting around in your pantry."

"I'll show her where it is," Nick offered, then he laid a hand on Kevin's shoulder. "I'll meet you in the back room in a few."

Kevin and Liz headed down the hallway and Jamie followed Nick into the kitchen. Bright golden sunlight streamed through a window that offered a view of a neatly landscaped, fenced-in backyard complete with a child's playhouse, a sandbox that looked like a giant turtle, and a swing set. As was her habit with every first-time visit to any kitchen, Jamie turned in a slow circle, absorbing the details of the space—pale oak cabinets, gleaming coffee-colored granite countertops, tiled backsplash, center island, and stainless appliances.

"Lovely," she said. "Everything's up to date, and so beautifully done. And obviously new."

Nick nodded. "Kevin finished it not long before his accident."

"Did you help him?"

"Helped him finish. He was well into the project when I moved to Seaside Cove."

"And I'm guessing you built the ramp outside to accommodate his wheelchair?"

"The trip down the stairs would have been pretty bumpy without it. The last thing he needs is for his leg to be jarred."

Even though she'd suspected ever since he'd kissed her that he wasn't going off on drinking binges, it was now all perfectly clear. "This is where you've been when you're off on your 'benders.'" She made air quotes around the last word.

"Guilty."

"You're not out drinking, you're here working. Helping your friend."

"Hey, we toss back a few brews at the end of the work day."

Her memory kicked in and she frowned, and said slowly, "When we talked about the speculation as to where you went . . . you suggested you were helping a crippled friend . . . and you really are."

"Well, he's only temporarily crippled, but yeah."

"You told me the truth and I didn't even know it."

"I told you—I don't lie."

Something seemed to crack inside Jamie, then crumble to dust. *That would be your preconceived notions about this guy,* her inner voice whispered.

"How did the rumor get started that you go off on benders?"

Nick shrugged. "The first few times I came here, I stopped at Crabby's for a drink before crossing the bridge to go home. I guess I was pretty tired, bleary-eyed, and scruffy looking after a few days of much work and little sleep. Someone must have thought I was drunk, word got around, and boom— rumor started."

"Why didn't you try to correct the misconception?"

"By the time I heard the rumors, they were pretty firmly in place, and quite frankly, I didn't really care. Newcomers are always prone to gossip in small towns, so I figured actions speak louder than words and the longer I lived there, people would eventually figure it out. And as strange as it may sound, I found the situation kind of funny. I've always been regarded as something of a straight arrow, so I can't deny it amused me to discover this perception of me as a mysterious bad boy who went off on benders."

"So you didn't do anything to disabuse me of the notion that you were Mr. Bender."

"No. Yet it seems you've figured it out."

"What if I hadn't?"

"I knew you would eventually. You're smart, and I'm patient." He reached out and tucked a wayward curl behind her ear, a casual gesture completely at odds with the intense look in his eyes. His fingers lingered, tracing lightly around the edge of her ear, shooting a shiver of delight down her spine. "I'm willing to wait for what I want."

Her heart stuttered. "Don't you ever get tired of waiting? Aren't you ever tempted to just reach out and grab what you want?"

"Oh, yeah," he said, his voice a soft, husky rasp that instantly brought to mind naked bodies, tangled limbs, and rumpled sheets. "I'm definitely tempted."

His gaze wandered down to her toes and then back up, lingering for several seconds on her mouth. By the time he looked into her eyes again, she felt as if she'd been tossed into an oven set on *broil*.

He cupped her face in one large, callused palm and studied her with a half-heated, half-troubled expression. It was clear he wanted to kiss her, yet he made no move to do so. Jamie's pulse revved and she parted her lips, willing him to lean down and—

"All clean and fresh smelling," came Liz's cheery voice from behind Jamie, causing her to practically jump out of her skin. Heat filled her face—oh, great, here came the blotches—at being caught dying to be kissed in the kitchen of a woman she'd met ten minutes ago.

Nick's gaze lingered on hers for several seconds with a heated look she hoped meant *to be continued* before switching his attention to Liz and Emily.

Liz set the baby down and she immediately toddled to Nick, grabbed on to his jean-covered knees, looked up at him with an adoring grin, and said, "Up, Uncoo Nic. Up."

Nick immediately picked her up, lifted her over his head, and lightly tossed her several inches higher and caught her. Emily laughed, then demanded, "Up!"

"Good luck with that—she'll never want you to stop," Liz said. She turned to Jamie. "Did you check out the pantry?"

"Not yet. I was too busy admiring your kitchen." *And ogling Nick. And hoping, waiting to be kissed, something I shouldn't be hoping or waiting for at all.* "It's beautiful."

"Thanks. They did a great job. Let's take a look."

Liz opened double doors to reveal shelves that ran from the floor to the ceiling. "This is great," Jamie said, admiring the neat, well-stocked rows.

"Pull out whatever you need. If you're missing something

we can walk to the market—it's just up the road. Meanwhile I'll get Emily's after-nap snack going."

In one smooth motion she plucked her daughter from Nick, set her in her high chair, then waved Nick out of the kitchen. "Shoo. You're in the way and we have girl stuff to do in here. I'll bring you guys drinks and snacks after Emmie's fed."

"God knows I don't want to get embroiled in girl stuff." Nick shot Jamie a wink, then strode to the high chair and pretended to nibble on Emily's tiny hand. She squealed and kicked her legs, and then he disappeared down the hallway. Seconds later she heard his deep voice mingling with Kevin's.

"What are they working on back there?" Jamie asked, pulling the items she'd need for brownies from the pantry.

"An extension. It adds another bedroom, a playroom, and a bathroom. This house was a lot bigger before we had Emily." Liz set a handful of Cheerios on the high chair tray and Emily immediately popped one in her bow-shaped mouth. "For a tiny person she takes up a lot of room," she said, dropping a kiss on her daughter's shiny curls.

"We considered buying a bigger house," Liz continued while adding a few banana slices to Emily's tray, "but with the economy and real estate market the way they are, we couldn't be sure we'd be able to sell this house. Since Kevin can do the renovations himself, it just made better financial sense to add the extension. But then his accident happened, and things got crazy. It's been a real struggle."

Jamie set the items she'd selected from the pantry on the center island, then leaned her hips against the polished granite countertop and watched Liz feed an enthusiastic Emily spoonfuls of what looked like applesauce. The baby alternately ate, grinned at Liz and Jamie, and batted her hands on the tray, causing the few remaining Cheerios to bounce—much to her delight.

Jamie laughed as her heart squeezed at the sight of that beautiful, happy baby, and at Liz, who practically glowed with pride and motherly love. And in a single heartbeat, Jamie realized that the internal tug pulling on her was envy. Because this lovely, cozy house contained everything she someday wanted. A loving marriage. And a child that was a product of that love.

And it also reminded her that there *would* soon be a new baby in her life. "My mom is expecting a baby," Jamie said.

Liz looked up from feeding Emily and Jamie swallowed her chuckle at the surprise in her eyes. "Wow. You must have a really young mom. I was one of those 'late in life' babies, so that ship sailed long ago for my mother. Are you excited about it?"

"Excited and nervous—I've never been a big sister before, and I haven't spent much time around a baby since my niece was one and she's fourteen now. Seeing Emily has really upped the excitement factor."

"She's a lot of fun. And a lot of work. But mostly fun. And she's an absolute *angel* when she's sleeping."

The muffled sound of an electric saw floated in from down the hallway. "How soon before the extension is finished?" she asked, engaging in a game of peek-a-boo with Emily.

"By the end of September—fingers crossed. Kevin's accident came at an especially bad time. Summer is his busiest season. With the economic downturn, jobs are scarce and he couldn't afford to lose any that he'd already contracted for, plus he needed to land as many future projects as possible. I seriously don't know what we would have done without Nick's help. He's overseeing all the jobs, and working himself to exhaustion on them as well."

"That's really great of him," Jamie murmured.

"He's a really great guy." Liz studied her for several seconds. "But I guess you know that."

Jamie huffed out a breath. "I have to admit it wasn't my first impression of him."

Interest kindled in Liz's eyes. "That sounds like a story. What happened?"

She related the Dead Clam/Leaky Roof Saga. When she finished, Liz wiped tears of laughter from her eyes. "I am, of course, laughing *with* you," she said.

"I'm just glad I'm able to laugh about it now," Jamie said. "Funny now—*not* funny then."

"I'm sure it wasn't. I give you a lot of credit for sticking around. And for not maiming Nick with that decapitated flamingo."

"Believe me, not doing so required a great deal of fortitude and restraint."

"I guess things are better now, seeing as he invited you to come here with him." She smiled. "I'm glad he did."

Jamie smiled in return. "Me, too. Although he only extended the invite to prove he hasn't been off on benders."

"I wouldn't be so sure of that. He could have just told you. This is the first time he's ever brought anyone here."

An oddly warm sensation rippled through Jamie at that bit of news. "Well, I can't deny that over these past weeks I've begun to see that he's . . . not completely horrible."

Liz laughed, then her blue eyes turned serious. "He was expecting some crusty old sailor/fisherman types to rent Paradise Lost. So you were a big surprise for him. But that's good. He needed a jolt."

"Paradise Lost was a jolt for me, too."

"But you rose to the occasion. That says something about you."

"That I'm certifiable?" Jamie suggested.

Liz chuckled and wiped Emily's mouth. "Maybe. But in a good way. And you know what they say about two jolts—they cause sparks."

The words, combined with the speculation in Liz's blue eyes, made it clear what she meant. "Nick and I are just friends," Jamie said. Yet even as the words left her mouth, she found herself wondering how true they really were. She'd had plenty of guy friends over the years, none of whom had inspired the unsettling whirlwind of confusing emotions mixed with sexual desire Nick aroused.

"Nothing wrong with that," Liz said. "As Kevin and I can attest, Nick's a terrific friend." Her gaze shifted to the brownie ingredients on the counter. "Do we have everything you need?"

"For the brownies—yes. Do you have any cream cheese in your fridge? If so, I know a recipe for a totally kick-ass frosting."

"Don't have cream cheese, but must have kick-ass frosting,

so we'll walk to the market as soon as I'm done with the imp here."

"Kick ass," repeated the imp with a big grin.

Jamie gasped and covered her mouth. "Oh, no—I'm so sorry," she said through her fingers. "Clearly I'm not baby-proof."

Liz waved off her concern. "No worries. I said it, too. Kev and I still aren't completely used to watching every word we say, and Emily's getting to the point where she repeats everything. I'm just thankful her first word was Dada, because her second word—which thankfully no one ever asks about—sounded suspiciously like s-h-i-t"—she spelled in an undertone—"which I let loose after I dropped a container of blueberries and those suckers scattered all over the floor like confetti." She grinned at Emily. "Then Mama said a bad word and you said it right back."

"Mama," said Emily, slapping her hands on the tray.

Liz grinned at Jamie. "And just like that, we've moved on. So let's grab the stroller and walk to the market and pick up what we need for the, um, *yummy yum* frosting."

"Yummy yum," said Emily.

And just like that, Jamie felt as if she'd made a new friend.

Chapter 16

The full moon hung in the evening sky, a fat, luminous pearl resting on inky velvet, the foreground to a thick scattering of brilliant diamond stars. Nick drove toward the main road for the hour-long trip back to Seaside Cove. He flicked a quick glance behind him. Godiva stretched the length of the backseat, dreaming doggie dreams. Nick then glanced at Jamie and found her looking at him. With the oddest expression. As if she'd never seen him before.

He returned his attention to the road, then to break the silence that somehow felt thick with tension, he said, "Those were some incredible brownies you made. I think Kevin wants you to move in."

"No need. I wrote down the recipe for Liz."

"Kev will have her baking them every day."

"Well, you know what they say—the way to a man's heart is through his stomach."

"First—not necessary since she already has his heart, and vice versa. And second, I actually think the way to a man's heart is about twelve inches *lower* than his stomach."

She gave a husky laugh that arrowed heat twelve inches lower than his stomach. "That's most likely true."

"Wait a minute—did you just agree with me *again*? Twice in the same day?"

"I'll alert the media."

Silence once again swelled between them and he wracked his brain for something to say, other than the words that were lodged in his throat like dry breadcrumbs: *Let's get naked.*

"I liked Kevin and Liz a lot," she said.

Nick seized on the topic, giving himself a mental *thunk* on the head for not thinking to talk about the neutral topic of Kevin and Liz himself. "They're great people. And an equally great couple."

"How long have they been together?"

"Three years, married for two and a half of those."

"A whirlwind courtship."

"Very. But Kevin was a goner the minute he met Liz, and she felt the same way. Never saw anything like it."

"Where did they meet?"

Nick's lips twitched. "Believe it or not, they met at the Seaside Cove Clam Festival."

"Really? I had no idea the event was such a hotbed of romantic intrigue."

He laughed. "Kevin called me that night from the festival to tell me he'd just met the woman he was going to marry. I thought he was nuts."

"You don't believe in love at first sight?"

"No. Lust at first sight? Yes. But love? I think that takes more time. How about you?"

"Well, given that my parents were a classic 'love at first sight' story, I'd never discount it, although I think it's really more of a 'wow, I really click with this person' sucker punch to the heart. And the love blooms from that initial punch."

He considered for a moment, then nodded. "I never thought of it that way. For a long time I didn't believe that sort of love was possible. Except for observing Kevin's parents together during those high school summers, happy marriages weren't part of my growing-up experience. But seeing Kevin and Liz together now, how good they are together, how happy they are, has me thinking that maybe, with the right person, it's possible."

"I grew up around a happy marriage, so I've always believed it's possible, but the hard part is finding that right person. That's the key to the whole program."

"I think I just experienced a sucker punch myself because it appears we have—brace yourself—once again agreed on something."

"Holy crap, you're right. That makes *three* times. We'd better stop talking. Right now."

"Nah, let's go for a record."

"We've already set one. Let's not push our luck."

"So we disagree."

"Just like old times," she said with a laugh. "Glad things are back to normal."

More silence descended and *let's get naked* once again pounded through his brain with such force he winced. And seriously doubted his ability to get through the remainder of the ride without uttering them. He glanced at her and saw she was once more looking at him with that odd, puzzled expression. Then she blinked, and it disappeared, leaving him to wonder if he was imagining it.

"I don't think I've ever seen a cuter baby than Emily," she said.

"She took to you like a duck to water."

"Spending time with her reminded me of how much fun I used to have with my niece, Heather."

His mind filled with an image of Jamie playing in the backyard with Emily and Godiva while Liz grilled the steaks. He'd been installing sheetrock in the new addition, chatting with Kevin, when he'd chanced to look out the window and had seen Jamie roll a rubber ball on the grass to Emily, who picked it up and toddled away as fast as her chubby little legs would carry her, squealing in delight when Jamie gave chase, all while keeping Godiva from knocking over the baby. A feeling he couldn't name—because he'd never felt it before—had invaded his entire body at the sight of Jamie with his goddaughter and dog. "I didn't know you liked kids so much."

"C'mon—who doesn't like kids?"

"I've actually met quite a few people who don't. Not really. Sure, they *say* they like them, but I think they mostly like the *idea* of kids, as opposed to the diaper-changing, give-them-your-attention, get-spit-up-on-your-clothes, don't-get-any-sleep reality of kids."

"As far as I'm concerned, diapers need changing, *every-one* needs attention, spit-up washes out, and babies do eventually sleep—so that's when you sleep. I can't believe that six months from now my mom will have a baby I'll get to play with and be a big sister to."

"Based on today, you'll be great at it."

"Thanks. I was only twelve when my niece was born and we've always been close, especially the last few years. You know, 'cause I'm her 'cool aunt' as opposed to her mom."

"You see her a lot?"

"Yes. We share a standing date every Sunday morning. Sometimes we go out for breakfast, but most often we stay at my apartment and cook together. And talk. And laugh. And discuss her literary idol, F. Scott Fitzgerald. I do my best to keep us connected. My time and attention are the best gifts I can give her, and I try to be the friend and sounding board she needs. Because there are days when she reminds me of a wilted plant everyone forgot to water. And others when teen-age attitude, anger, and hurt ooze from her like an open sore."

"She's very lucky to have you."

"Thanks, but I feel like the lucky one. I have to admit I was a little weirded out by the whole 'my mom is preggers' scenario, but I've gotten used to it and now I'm excited at the prospect. And as for being great at it, right back atcha. It's obvious you adore that little girl and she adores you right back. You realize you turn into a great big gooey marshmallow when she flashes those dimples at you," she said in a teasing tone.

Nick laughed. "Can't deny that, although just looking at her pretty much turns me to mush."

"I noticed. It was . . ."

Her voice trailed off and he found himself tensing, waiting to hear her finish.

"Really sweet," she finally said softly. "When she fell asleep in your arms and you kissed her hair, it was just . . . a lovely image. It was interesting to see you play the part of uncle and friend."

Her last sentence chilled the warmth her earlier words had

suffused in him. "It's not a part I play. It's who I am. What's important to me."

His words seemed to vibrate in the air between them for several long seconds. Then she said, "I'm sorry. I didn't mean it that way. I'm having trouble finding the right words to express what I want to say. I saw a side of you today that was . . . unexpected. And I . . . liked it. The kindness and generosity and loyalty you've shown your friends—those are qualities to be proud of. And admired." She made a self-conscious sound. "*That's* what I meant, but said very badly."

Her words stilled him. He wished he could toss out a light-hearted, smart-ass reply, but nothing lighthearted or smart-ass came to mind. In fact, the only thing that came to mind was, "Thank you."

"You're welcome. I liked Liz very much. We had a great time on our walk to the market and it turns out we have a lot in common, including drama-prone mothers. Some of the stories she told me about her mom's wild, single lifestyle since divorcing her dad was enough to make my curly hair curlier. Definitely gave me a whole new appreciation of *my* mother, who's a veritable saint in comparison."

Nick nodded. "Always good to be reminded that no matter what your problems are, someone else's are worse."

"Very wise words."

"Did we just agree again?"

"Yes, but don't let it go to your head. Liz reminds me of my best friend Kate. They both have that easygoing, friendly warmth about them."

"Liz said the same thing about you." He shot her a grin. "I told her she wouldn't think you were so easygoing if she'd seen you the morning after the roof had leaked on your head all night."

"The fact that your lifeless body didn't wash up on the beach after the roof had leaked on my head all night proves how easygoing I can be."

Nick laughed. "Actually, that's pretty much what Liz told me." He reached for the bottle of water he'd taken from Kevin's fridge before they left. After taking a long swallow, he said, "Every time I'm around them, I—" He stopped and pressed his lips together, suddenly feeling foolish. And unsure why he felt compelled to share with her the unsettling thought that had niggled at him ever since he moved to Seaside Cove and saw Kevin and Liz frequently.

"You what?"

He drew a deep breath. What the hell. If she thought he was nuts, so much the better. Might help him keep that *let's get naked* mantra to himself.

"Whenever I see Kevin and Liz together, I'm really happy for them. Honest to goodness, bone-deep happy. Yet at the same time, I'm . . . envious. Seeing them makes me want what they have. A home. A family. Someone who looks at me like I'm the best thing she's ever seen, and who I look at the same way. There are times when the three of us will all be talking and laughing when they'll suddenly look at each other and . . ."

"It's as if you're not there? Like you've disappeared?"

"Exactly."

Jamie nodded. "I know what you mean. Same thing happens to me with Kate and her husband, Ben. They got married five months ago and are as happy as ducks in a pond. I'm totally thrilled for them, love being with them, yet sometimes no matter how much fun we're having, no matter how much I love them and know they love me, a tiny part of me feels like an interloper."

"A third wheel," Nick said, and realized she did indeed know exactly what he meant.

"Yes! And not because of anything they've said or done. It just all stems from wanting what they have. That intimate, emotional, profound connection. For a while that envy made me very uncomfortable. But I finally realized that just because you desire something, it doesn't mean you don't want someone else to have it. That sort of envy isn't bad because it doesn't take anything away from the people it's directed toward." She reached out and briefly touched his arm. "It's okay to want things for yourself, Nick."

That whisper of a touch rocketed a shocking flare of heat through him. Jesus, she'd barely touched him, yet he felt as if she'd set him on fire. What the hell would happen if she *really* touched him? *Really* put her hands on him—like she meant it?

Stupid question. He knew damn well what would happen.
Her touch did to him what a lit match did to gasoline.

Her words swirled around in his head, twisting until they
applied only to her and how she made him feel. Battering him
with truths he really didn't want to acknowledge. Like the fact
that what he desired, what he wanted for himself right now
was her. In his arms. Naked. Under him. Over him. Like that
he wanted her, and didn't want anyone else to have her.

No, he definitely didn't want to acknowledge those things.
But damn it, that didn't make them any less true.

"I see one of those twenty-four-hour convenience stores
coming up just past the next intersection," she said, jerking
him from his unsettling thoughts. "Would you mind stopping
for just a moment?"

"Sure. No problem."

He pulled into the parking lot and shifted the truck into
park. "I'll be right back," she said, unhooking her seat belt.

She opened the door and the interior light blinked on, re-
vealing that her cheeks resembled a setting sun. "Everything
okay?"

"Uh, yeah. I just remembered I need some . . . girl stuff.
Be right back."

She closed the door and hurried into the store. Nick
dragged his hands through his hair and shifted in an attempt
to relieve the strangulation occurring in his jeans. Damn.
He'd known bringing her to Kevin's place wasn't a good idea,
but he'd thought about her constantly while he'd been away
and hadn't been able to resist asking her to come along.

Plus, part of him had hoped she'd bomb out with his friends.
That Kevin and Liz wouldn't like her. That Kevin would give
him the "bro, this girl is not for you" look. That Liz would
subtly suggest fixing him up with an acquaintance—her way
of letting him know that Jamie was getting the thumbs-down.
That Jamie would be standoffish with them and the baby.

But instead, she'd received thumbs-up all around. She'd
charmed Kev with her damn delicious brownies, bonded with
Liz like glue to paper, and both Kevin and Liz had privately
told him they liked Jamie a lot and hoped he'd bring her back.

And instead of being standoffish with the baby, she'd gotten grass-stained palms and knees playing with her on the

lawn. Which meant his ingenious "my best friends will hate her, giving me the incentive I badly need to banish her from my thoughts so I can concentrate on something other than her" plan had royally failed.

Which confirmed his earlier thought that he was royally screwed.

He'd tried to stay away from her. And failed.

He'd tried to stop thinking about her. And failed.

He'd tried to stop wanting her. And failed.

The store's automatic doors slid open and she exited carrying a plastic bag. His heart tripped over itself at the sight of her and he groaned at the ridiculous reaction, while *let's get naked* again drummed through his head.

Damn it, he needed a new plan. And fast. But after spending the day in her company, his good intentions were shot to hell. As was his will power. And his memory, because although there were at least ten thousand reasons he didn't want to get involved with her, at the moment he couldn't recall even one.

She climbed into the truck and he swallowed a groan of longing when he caught a whiff of her cookie-scented skin. "Get what you needed?" he asked, gripping the wheel to keep from grabbing her.

"Yes. You okay?"

"Yup. Great." He pulled out of the parking lot and prayed he'd come up with a plan—or at least recall why getting involved with Jamie Newman was a bad idea—during the remaining ten minutes of the drive home.

Jamie didn't speak, and Nick forced himself to shut the hell up and concentrate on jogging his memory. It kicked in just as they crossed the bridge leading to the island. *She's on the rebound,* it reminded him. *And she's bossy. And a pest. A picky pest. A cat person. And a princess. Not to mention she's leaving in a matter of weeks and lives seven hundred miles away.*

Relief filled Nick. Right. *So* bossy. *Such* a pest. *Irritatingly* picky. Would surely end up with even *more* cats. A *total* princess. *Completely* geographically undesirable.

Then he frowned. Actually, she wasn't really bossy. She was . . . assertive. And confident. And he actually liked those traits in a woman. Damn.

And really, she wasn't a pest at all. In fact, she was pretty much the opposite of a pest. And as for picky, well, it was more that she paid attention to details. And he liked that, too. Double damn.

And he could hardly find fault with someone who loved animals, especially someone who loved his dog and who his dog worshipped. And Nick couldn't deny he liked Cupcake. Triple damn.

And those grass stains she'd gotten on her knees today were just further proof that she wasn't a princess at all. Quadruple damn.

She's on the rebound.

Well that at least was true. As was the fact that her stay in Seaside Cove was only temporary. Except he'd completely forgotten why that mattered. Which meant he'd run out of reasons not to give in to the fierce desire that had plagued him for weeks and at this moment was choking him.

Several minutes later he pulled into Southern Comfort's carport. He turned off the ignition and headlights, plunging them into shadowy darkness. After unclicking his seat belt, he turned toward her. And saw she'd unfastened her seat belt and turned toward him. And was regarding him through very serious eyes.

Before he could snatch her into his arms and put out this damn fire she'd started inside him, she said in a quiet voice, "I enjoyed meeting your friends."

"I think you just enjoyed getting away from your mom and Alex."

"I can't deny that was a side benefit, but the truth is I had a great time. With them. And with you. I know I said this wouldn't happen again, but . . ." She leaned forward and lightly brushed her mouth over his. Before he could react, she'd leaned back. "Thank you."

His heart, which had stuttered to a halt, slammed against his ribs hard and fast enough to bruise them. "You're welcome. But that isn't what you said wouldn't happen again. This is." He slid one hand around her nape, pulled her toward him, and covered her mouth with his in the deep, hungry kiss he'd been aching to give her since the moment their first kiss had ended.

His fingers fisted in her hair, and he shifted closer, cursing the console that separated them. One of them moaned—who the hell knew who?—and her lips parted. Nick didn't hesitate. He stroked his tongue into the luscious, silky heaven of her mouth and kissed her with all the pent-up want and frustration that had been building inside him for weeks.

Christ, she tasted good. Even better than he remembered. She opened her mouth wider, an invitation that drained the remaining blood above his neck to settle in his groin. And just like the last time he'd kissed this woman, his control vanished, filling him with a dark, raw hunger unlike anything he'd ever before experienced. A visceral, gut-wrenching need that made him want to fling her over his shoulder, drag her off to his cave, and simply devour her until they both passed out from sheer exhaustion. Then wake her up and start all over again.

Somewhere in the back of his blood-deprived brain it registered that he was exhibiting a definite lack of finesse here, but he couldn't stop. Not yet. And based on the way her impatient hands tunneled through his hair, then raced downward to slip beneath his T-shirt and glide up his back, she had no complaints.

His fingers tightened in her hair, tilting back her head, and he dragged his mouth down her neck, lightly sucking on her delicious skin. The scent of cookies filled his head—like he needed anything else to make him crave her.

He ran his free hand down her chest to cup her breast through her tank top, then slipped his fingers beneath the stretchy material to pluck her hard nipple. She gasped and arched into his hand, whispering his name in a long, husky groan that raised his temperature a good ten degrees.

He dragged his tongue back up her delicious neck, then leaned back, breathing hard. With one hand still tangled in her tousled curls and the other still palming her breast, he ran his avid gaze over her moist, parted lips and closed eyes. Her ragged, uneven breaths matched his and she looked undone and hard-nippled and sexy as hell.

He waited for her to open her eyes, and when she did, heat rippled through him at how glazed they looked.

He had to swallow to locate his voice. "Just so we're clear, *that's* what you said wouldn't happen again."

She moistened her lips, a gesture that tightened his already aching groin. "I stand corrected."

He slipped his hand from her tank top and brushed back the sun-streaked curls clinging to her flushed cheek. She leaned into his touch and released a breathy sigh. "Didn't we agree at some point that we weren't going to do this?"

Nick traced her plump lower lip with his fingertip. "You said it. I never agreed."

"Do you remember *why* I said it?"

"Not a damn clue."

"I was hoping that if we did kiss again, it wouldn't be as good as the first time."

"You saying it wasn't?"

"Yes. It was better." She grabbed his wrist and sucked his finger into her mouth.

Nick drew in a quick, hard breath that came out decidedly shaky, then ended on a groan when she swirled her tongue around his fingertip. The hell with getting out of the truck. He wanted, needed his hands on her *now*. Besides, he was too damn hard to walk.

He reached for her, intent on dragging her over the console, when Godiva stuck her head between them and panted hot doggie breath in their faces. Nick glared at his pet, whose tail thwapped against the leather of the backseat while her expression clearly said, *Hey guys! Whatcha doin'? Can I play? Please? I wanna play! Right after I pee! I gotta pee! Wow, have I got to pee! And I'm hungry! What's for dinner? Please, oh please, tell me it's dinnertime!*

"Maybe cats *are* the way to go," he muttered. He twisted around and opened the back door. Godiva catapulted from the truck and dashed to her favorite spot on the patchy lawn and commenced with her sniff-every-blade-of-grass ritual. Nick watched her for several seconds, taking the time to gather his badly scattered wits, and suddenly remembered the big reason, the real reason he couldn't get involved with her.

He turned to face her and dragged his hands down his face. "We both know where that kiss was leading."

She nodded. "I was about to jump on you like a Dalmatian on a fire truck." To prove her point she swung her leg over the console with the agility of an Olympic gymnast. A heartbeat later she was straddling him, her pelvis pressed against his erection, her hands sifting through his hair. His hands cupped her ass and hauled her tighter against him.

"You'd jump on me . . . yeah—right after I stripped you bare so I could lick you like an ice cream cone," he said, and proved his point by slowly dragging his tongue down the side of her neck.

She tilted her head to give him easier access. "God. You really are a sweet-talker. Literally. Can I hold you to that?"

"Absolutely. But there's a problem."

"This would be an extremely bad time to confess you really are a hit man."

"Not a hit man, and unfortunately not a good Boy Scout."

She leaned back and frowned. "Meaning what?"

"I'm not prepared."

She rocked herself against his erection. "Feels like you're very prepared to me."

He actually felt his eyes glaze over. "But not fully prepared. At least not until I hit up a drugstore."

She set her hands on his chest, pushed him back, and looked at him with an unreadable expression. "You don't have any condoms?"

"No." Damn it to hell and back.

"You mean you don't have one handy, or you don't have any in the house?"

"None. Anywhere."

"Why not?"

"Because I haven't been having sex and I wasn't expecting"—he gave her denim-clad ass a gentle squeeze—"this. You."

"But you always use a condom—right?"

"Of course. Always. You?"

"Always. So tell me—how long have you not been having sex?"

"A while. Not since I moved here."

Her brows shot up. "Really?"

"Really. Between working on Southern Comfort and helping out Kevin, I've been busy. Getting laid wasn't a priority."

"That's a sentence I never thought I'd ever hear any man utter."

He huffed out a laugh. "Well, it wasn't a priority until you showed up." He shoved aside the disturbing realization that he hadn't wanted anyone but her since she'd shown up.

"Still, it seems you'd at least have a supply of condoms on hand. You know, in case you got lucky."

"Sweetheart, the only store I've been to in the last four months besides the Piggly Wiggly and Milton's Bait Shop is Home Depot, and to the best of my knowledge, they don't sell condoms at Home Depot."

"They don't sell them at the Piggly Wiggly?"

"Don't know. Never looked."

"As for Home Depot—it seems like they might carry them in the plumbing aisle. Or in hardware. You know, with all the screws and nails."

"You're killing me." He leaned forward and lightly scraped his teeth over the outline of one hard nipple pressing against her tank top. She gasped and arched her back, and Nick cursed his poor planning. "Much as I'd like to continue this here and now, I need to find an open drugstore."

Again she pushed him back and looked at him through glittering eyes. "You might not have been a good Boy Scout, but I was a *very* good Girl Scout." She held up the plastic bag she'd carried from the convenience store and swayed it like a pendulum between them.

"What's in there?"

"Condoms," she said. "The party pack. Thirty-six of 'em. I'm a firm believer that a girl should always bring her own. Just in case."

Nick skimmed one hand into her hair and dragged her forward until their mouths nearly touched. "Thirty-six—that should get us through the night," he whispered against her lips.

"Still think I'm a pest?"

"Hell, no. I think you're . . ." *Magnificent. Incredible. Sexy as hell. And you've got me so hard I can barely think straight.* "A genius."

"There *are* some advantages to being detail oriented."

"Obviously." He slipped the fingers of one hand under the hem of her denim shorts and explored the lacy edge of her underwear. "There're plenty of details on you I'd like to—"

"Orient?"

"Among other things. How about you and me and our thirty-six new best friends head inside?"

"I thought you'd never ask." Then she frowned and her expression turned serious. "But first . . ." She hesitated, pulled in what seemed like a bracing breath, then continued, "You told me after our first kiss that you liked me a little. You also said I should give complete honesty a try, so here goes: I like you, too. More than a little." Then she leaned forward and whispered in his ear, "And just so you know—you had me at 'lick you like an ice cream cone.'"

Complete honesty. The words ricocheted through his brain, tempering his anticipation with a hard slap of guilt. While he hadn't lied to her, he'd omitted a lot of details about himself. About what he'd left behind. Right or wrong, he'd made the choice to keep his past, his circumstances to himself.

If you tell her, you know what'll happen, his gut whispered.

Yeah, he knew. Which was why he hadn't told her. And didn't want to. Because he knew she'd tell him to take a hike.

Maybe someday he'd tell her. But not now. She gently bit his earlobe and he gritted his teeth against the dark pleasure that shuddered through him.

Definitely not now.

Her revelation that he'd had her at *lick you like an ice cream cone* floated into his mind and he vividly recalled the first words she'd said to him, when he'd answered his door and discovered his disgruntled new neighbor glaring at him. And it suddenly dawned on him that it was very possible *she'd* had *him* at *It's about time you answered the door.*

Chapter 17

With Godiva leading the way, Jamie followed Nick up Southern Comfort's stairs. She glanced over at Paradise Lost and noted all the windows were dark. Hopefully her mom and Alex had spent their day alone talking out their problems and solving their issues. Which hopefully led to her mother relenting and allowing Alex into the bedroom rather than making him sleep on the sofa. Which would hopefully lead to a full-on reconciliation that would hopefully send them back to New York. Like tomorrow.

She returned her attention to climbing the stairs and was greeted by the sight of Nick's very fine jean-clad butt right in front of her. Darn it, if only her superpower were X-ray vision! Well, no problem—those Levis would be off him soon enough.

She tightened her grip on the bag containing the condoms and offered up a mental *thank God* she'd bought them. She'd only done so because as far as she was concerned, it was a woman's responsibility to see to her own protection. The fact that Nick didn't have any condoms because he hadn't had sex—for *months*—well, that suffused her with a warm, melty feeling she didn't want to examine too closely. Much better that she just concentrate on the sex and shove aside anything that smacked of emotion. This was a temporary fling with her sexy neighbor. Nothing more.

And speaking of the sex . . . God help her, she couldn't wait. While she would have waited for him to return from the drugstore, she was damn glad it wasn't necessary. Her skin felt about three sizes too small, as if she were an overripe fruit about to burst. She hadn't felt this primed, this edgy, this sexually needy in . . . ever. Like she wanted to claw off his clothes, shove him to the floor, and have her wicked way with him.

He unlocked the door and she followed him inside. The need to touch him, to be touched by him—*now*—struck her like a lightning bolt. She pushed the door closed with her foot, grabbed a handful of his T-shirt, and yanked him toward her. He obviously didn't have a problem with that because before she could even think *who the hell needs foreplay?* he'd backed her against the wall, his mouth was on hers, his tongue stroking and delving, and his hands . . . God his hands, those big, strong, callused hands were everywhere. Tunneling through her hair. Yanking her tank top over her head. Teasing her hard nipples. Unzipping her shorts. Shoving them and her panties to her ankles, where she kicked them along with her flip-flops aside with an impatient flick of her foot. All while kissing her to within an inch of her life.

Jamie's hands were just as eager and busy, plunging beneath the soft cotton of his T-shirt to coast up his smooth back, then forward to greedily glide over the fascinating hard ridges of his abdomen. Desperate for more, she broke off their frantic kiss, grabbed the ends of his shirt and gave it a hard, impatient upward tug. His gaze met hers and she damn near melted on the spot from the fire burning in his eyes.

After tossing his shirt aside, she attacked the button on his jeans, but her quest was derailed when he hooked a hand under her thigh. He raised her leg, settling it high on his hip, then cupped her sex.

Her head thunked back against the wall and a low groan that felt dragged from her soul rattled in her throat.

He teased her folds, then slipped a finger inside her. "You're wet," he said in a ragged whisper against her lips.

If she'd been capable of forming a full sentence, she might have said that her aroused state could hardly be surprising given that the entire last five weeks had felt like foreplay. But she wasn't capable, so she just gripped his shoulders, arched into his hand, and demanded, "More."

And holy moly, he followed directions well. His mouth covered hers in a searing kiss, his tongue moving in tandem with his fingers, his other hand teasing her taut nipples, driving her to the brink of sanity. He performed some sort of magic with his hand, and her orgasm screamed through her, pulsing white-hot shards of pleasure to her every cell, dragging a harsh cry from her throat. Aftershocks were still trembling through her when she dragged her eyes open. And found him watching her, his green eyes nearly black with arousal.

"Beautiful," he said. "Absolutely beautiful. Are you always that impatient?"

"Jeez, is that a complaint?" she asked, fighting to catch her breath.

"Hell no. I like you aroused and impatient." His scorching gaze raked downward to where his fingers continued to lightly caress her. "I even like you bossy—when you're naked."

"Good." She slipped her hand into his unbuttoned jeans and cupped his erection, enjoying his sharply indrawn breath. "Take off your jeans. Then douse this damn fire you started. Because it's far from out."

"Best news I've ever heard." Without taking his gaze off her, he stepped back. Jamie locked her knees so she wouldn't slither to the floor, her gaze avid and greedy as he toed off his sneakers, pulled off his socks, then lowered his jeans and underwear with a single impatient movement. Boxer briefs, she noted. Probably they looked damn good on him. But whoa, baby . . . he looked really damn good without them.

He grabbed the condom box, ripped open a packet, and sheathed himself. In the next heartbeat he stepped between her legs, grasped her bottom, and lifted her.

"You're gonna want to hold on," he ground out in a harsh rasp.

Jamie gripped his shoulders, wrapped her legs around

his hips, then gasped when he entered her in a single, heart-stopping thrust.

Their harsh, choppy breaths filled the room as he stroked her. Hard, fast, relentless. Propelling her toward another orgasm. Her climax engulfed her like a giant wave, drowning her in its intensity. Her arms and legs tightened around him, and she buried her face in the curve where his neck and shoulder met while her entire body convulsed with pleasure. With a ragged groan he thrust deep and joined her in his own release.

Still panting and clinging to him like wallpaper, Jamie managed to lift her head. And found herself looking into eyes that looked as glazed as she felt. Speech was beyond her. Otherwise, she would have told him that was amazing. That she hadn't felt like that since . . . ever, and she couldn't wait to feel that way again. That she now knew what his superpower really was—the ability to bring her to orgasm with ridiculous ease, and hot damn, how lucky could a girl get?

But there was no way she could string that many words together, so she said the only thing she could.

"Wow."

He rested his forehead against hers and gently squeezed her butt. "Yeah. Wow."

She was greatly impressed that he'd managed two words. She sucked in some much-needed oxygen, and when her heart rate returned to something close to normal, she managed to say, "Thanks. I needed that."

He huffed out a quick laugh. "Me, too. So thanks right back at ya."

She unlocked her ankles and her boneless legs slipped down and her feet hit the floor. Nick withdrew and took a single step back.

"Don't move," he said.

"Okay. Good thing you said that. Otherwise I would have run screaming into the night to get away from you."

His lips curved into a slow, wicked grin that didn't do anything to shore up her knees, which felt like overcooked noodles. He stepped into the kitchen, and after quickly disposing of the condom, he grabbed the box, then in a feat of strength and brawn that had her heaving a gushy sigh, he swung her up into his arms and strode toward the living area.

She wrapped her arms around his neck and pressed her lips to his jaw. "Where are we going?"

He entered his bedroom. "My den of depravity."

"Oh, goodie. Can I be bossy in here?"

"I'm counting on it. Bossy, demanding, whatever you want."

"Whatever I want? That sounds promising. How about what *you* want?"

"With thirty-five condoms left, I'm not worried." He shouldered his way into the bathroom, then set her on her feet. After turning on the shower he drew her into his arms. "Since hard and fast went so well," he murmured, nuzzling her neck with his warm lips, "let's take a shower, then see how we do with soft and slow."

"I've lost track of how many times we've agreed today," Jamie said, stepping over the edge of the tub, then moving beneath the cascade of warm water. Nick stepped in behind her and reached for the soap. She leaned back against his chest and luxuriated in the sensation of his big, soapy hands gliding with agonizing leisure over her skin, circling her breasts. Dipping into her navel. Then lower, to caress her folds.

"Spread your legs." The husky command whispered past her ear, shooting tingles of delight right down to her toes.

"Now who's being bossy?" she asked, lifting her leg and setting it on the edge of the tub.

"Me. That a problem, princess?"

His talented fingers slipped between her thighs and Jamie groaned. "Absolutely not. Bossy doesn't scare me."

No, it didn't. But as pleasure built in her once again courtesy of Nick's clever hands and mouth caressing her, it occurred to Jamie that maybe she should be scared. Scared that this encounter, which was supposed to be nothing more than lighthearted sex, might turn into something more. And that this man, who resided hundreds of miles from where she lived, might come to mean something more than a summer fling.

But then his talented fingers touched her *ooooh*, right *there*, and with a sigh of pleasure, she arched into Nick's hand, shoving aside the admonishing voice. She hadn't planned on a summer fling, but why not? She'd enjoy herself, enjoy his company while she was here, then in a few weeks, at the end of the summer, when she returned to New York, it would end.

Easy and simple. No strings. And unlike so many things in her life lately, absolutely perfect. Nothing could go wrong.

Absolutely nothing.

Chapter 18

Nick normally awoke to the sound of Godiva's *I've Gotta Pee!* morning whine accompanied by a pelting of hot doggie breath, tempered by a few dozen canine kisses to his jaw. This morning he was greeted by a swatch of warm sunshine slanting through his open bedroom window, the cheerful chirping of birds, and the tantalizing aroma of bacon and freshly brewed coffee.

He opened his eyes and took in the dented pillow beside him and the badly rumpled sheets. Images of the previous night flashed through his mind like a slow-motion slideshow. Jamie under him. Over him. Her mouth on him. His mouth on her. Discovering she smelled like cookies—everywhere. Raiding his kitchen for a much-needed middle-of-the-night snack. Feeding each other bits of cheese and crackers in his bed. Talking. Laughing. Learning.

And damned if he hadn't liked everything he'd learned. She enjoyed action movies, mystery novels, and bike riding. She was a lifelong Yankees fan, couldn't ice skate to save her life but was deadly in a snowball fight, was a horrible singer but loved to sing anyway, enjoyed dancing, and played a mean game of Scrabble. She'd never been snow skiing, had broken her arm when she was eight, and loved visiting the Central Park zoo, and her favorite way to while away her infrequent afternoons off was to wander through the Metropolitan Museum of Art, where she'd been a member since childhood. In keeping with their sudden spate of agreeing, he'd discovered that they shared many similar views on politics and world events.

And then there was the fact that she blew his mind in bed.

She'd proven to be just as generous, playful, exciting, bossy, and demanding inside the bedroom as she was outside the bedroom. Hell, he had no problem with a gorgeous, naked woman telling him exactly what she wanted him to do to her, and exactly what she planned to do to him in return. Which was exactly what had happened after their snack. Several times. He wasn't sure if they'd fallen asleep or passed out from exhaustion. All he knew was that he wasn't exhausted any longer. In fact, he was wide awake. And starving. And for a hell of a lot more than bacon.

After a quick stop in the bathroom, he pulled on a clean pair of boxer briefs, then opened the door leading to the living area. And halted. At the sight of Jamie, wearing the white T-shirt she'd ripped off him last night—and from what he could tell, nothing else—looking deliciously flushed and tousled and wielding his new spatula and frying pan like Julia Child herself. She looked completely at home in his kitchen, and Godiva appeared perfectly content sprawled out on the new hardwood floor, chewing on a piece of rawhide.

Nick leaned a shoulder against the doorjamb and watched Jamie slide an omelet that looked perfect enough to grace a magazine cover from the pan onto a plate that she then slid into the oven. Then she turned and caught sight of him.

For several seconds they simply stared at each other. Looking into those golden brown eyes, his insides performed some sort of crazy swooping maneuver—like when he was a kid and would jump off the high diving board. She blinked, breaking the odd spell that had seemed to hypnotize him.

And then she smiled.

It wasn't the first time he'd awakened to the sight of a barely dressed woman in his kitchen after a night of great sex. But it definitely was the first time one had ever cooked him breakfast—normally they just lounged around, waiting for their morning meal to be delivered and served.

It was also definitely the first time he'd so greatly anticipated seeing the previous night's lover the morning after. And the first time in a very long while he'd enjoyed a woman's company so much—not just the sex, but the conversation and laughter. Certainly it was the first time he could recall going from amusement to blinding, raw need in a nanosecond. And it was really definitely the first time he'd ever felt knocked flat on his ass by a simple smile.

"Good morning," she said.

He pushed off from the doorjamb and walked toward her, drawn to her and that smile like steel to a magnet, not stopping until his body was pressed against hers from chest to knee and he'd backed her into the countertop. He tangled his hands in her shiny tumble of curls and gave her a long, slow, deep, tongue-mating kiss. When he raised his head, smug satisfaction filled him at her dazed expression. "Good morning," he said. "It smells great in here."

She looped her arms loosely around his neck. "In spite of the meager offerings in your fridge, breakfast is ready. I let Godiva out and fed her, too, although she told me she'd much rather eat bacon and eggs than dog chow."

"Who wouldn't?"

She laughed. "So . . . I guess this is where we have that awkward morning-after conversation."

"I guess." He rolled his hips, pressing his erection tighter against her belly. "Except awkward isn't exactly what I'm feeling."

A combination of humor and arousal glittered in her eyes. "It would appear not."

He leaned in to touch his tongue to the delicious curve where her neck and shoulder met. "There's a surefire way we could avoid any chance of awkward conversation."

"By not speaking?" she suggested.

He skimmed his hands beneath the T-shirt she wore and filled his palms with her gorgeous ass—which, he was gratified to discover, was gorgeously bare. "By having sex again."

She moaned and tunneled her fingers through his hair. "Okay."

"I've lost count of how many times we've agreed."

"That's because you've been saying some really agreeable things. But we can't constantly keep having sex."

He moved one hand up to cup her warm, soft breast. "Why not?"

"Well, for one thing, we'll eventually get hungry," she said, arching into his palm.

"I'm already hungry." To prove his point, he lightly bit her earlobe. "And it's a true testament to your ridiculous sexiness that I think you smell better than that bacon and I want to taste you more than that scrumptious egg concoction you put in the oven."

"Thanks. Um, Nick . . . I need to tell you something."

A tiny sliver of his lust-fogged brain noted her suddenly serious tone, but it was hard to pay attention when she just felt so damn incredibly good pressed against him, and that tempting bit of skin behind her ear felt so damn velvety soft. "What's that?"

She planted her palms on his chest and leaned back. When he straightened, he realized she was regarding him through very serious eyes. "I'm in love."

For several seconds everything in him froze. Heart. Lungs. Pulse. Then they coughed back to life, his heart pounding so hard he could actually hear the beats echoing in his ears. A warm, dizzying sensation filled him, one he couldn't name because he'd never experienced anything like it before. It wasn't panic—he knew what that felt like. Nor was it fear—he was familiar with that one, too.

The words *holy shit* rippled through his brain, but shockingly not in a "holy shit I need to get her the hell out of my house and away from me" way. No, it somehow seemed to be more in a "holy shit . . . that's pretty amazing, and I think maybe I might like it" way.

Nah. Couldn't be.

But then what the hell was it?

Before he could decide, she continued, "With your All-Clad."

He blinked. Then frowned. "Huh?"

"I'm in love with your frying pan. Given the condition of the pots and pans at Paradise Lost, I may have to steal it from you."

Surely that was relief, rather than disappointment, washing through him. Jesus, of course it was. Whew! Dodged a bullet there. Last thing he needed was his temporary neighbor falling in love with him.

He cleared his throat to loosen the inexplicable tightness there. "No need to steal. Feel free to borrow it. It's not like I know how to use it." He brushed his thumb over her hard nipple. "Of course, I *will* demand some sort of payment."

"Name your price."

He decided right then and there that the ridiculous amount he'd paid for pots and pans he'd rarely use had been worth every penny. He feathered his mouth over hers. "It's gonna cost you."

She heaved a put-upon sigh. "I'll force myself to suffer through the torture."

"Excellent."

He traced her plump bottom lip with the tip of his tongue, debating whether to lift her onto the counter, which would be more expedient, or carry her back to his bedroom, which would be more comfortable. Plus, that's where the condoms were.

The bedroom it was.

Making a mental note to start always keeping a condom within easy reach, he scooped her up in his arms and started walking toward his bedroom.

"What about breakfast?" she asked, pressing very distracting kisses to the side of his neck.

Before he could answer, angry, raised voices floated through the open sliding doors that led to the screened-in porch. Nick paused and listened.

"I *said* I'd be right back with the money," came an angry female voice followed by a slamming car door.

"Take it easy, little lady. All I said was I'd walk you to the door."

"Do *not* tell me to take it easy, *quit* calling me little lady, and you are *not* walking me to the door," yelled the female voice.

"Now look here, there's no need to holler—"

"OMG, yes there is because you are so not *listening* to me! My aunt will give me the cab fare and I'll be right back."

"Oh, God," Jamie whispered. "It can't be." She pushed against his chest and wriggled like a fish on a hook. "Put me down."

Nick set her on her feet and she ran into the screened-in porch and looked down at the street below. "Heather!" she called, waving her arms. "I'm here . . . up here. Stay there. I'll be right down."

Jamie then dashed back inside, muttering, "Shit, shit, shit." She frantically snatched up her underwear from the floor near the door where he'd stripped it off her last night.

"What's going on?"

"That yelling is coming from my fourteen-year-old niece, Heather," she said, yanking up her panties and then bending to seize her shorts. "She's outside with a huge suitcase, a crap-load of attitude, and a very unhappy-looking cab driver who, based on what we just heard, I'm expected to pay. I can only hope she flew here and just took that cab from the local airport and not all the way from New York, otherwise I'll owe the guy my life, a few vital organs, and my first-born child."

"Why is she here?"

"Don't know. But I need to find out. I can't imagine it's good. If my mother is a drama queen, Heather is the Drama Empress."

"Can I help?"

"Thanks, but no. I'll handle it. Of course if the cab fare is eighteen thousand dollars, I might need a temporary loan." She shoved her feet into her flip-flops. "Sorry to leave so abruptly. Breakfast is in the oven. Thanks for last night—it was great. See ya." She grabbed her purse and then dashed out the door.

The screen door slapped shut behind her and Nick stared at it for several long seconds, wondering what the hell had just happened and what he should do about it.

You shouldn't do anything. She said she didn't need your help. You're off the hook. Be glad.

But he wasn't glad. He was concerned.

It's none of your business.

Yet there was no denying the protectiveness he felt toward her.

That's just the sex talking.

Maybe. But that didn't make it any less real.

It's good she's gone—consider yourself saved. You don't need her drama. Besides, you know how women get after you let them spend the night. All clingy and possessive and filled with expectations.

Right. A frown burrowed between his brows. Except tossing off a hurried *Thanks for last night—it was great. See ya* didn't exactly smack of clingy, possessive, or filled with expectations. In fact, it felt pretty much like a brush-off.

He felt a nudge against his knee and looked down. Godiva shifted her soulful gaze from Nick to the door, then back to Nick, as if asking, *Where'd she go and when's she coming back?*

He hunched down and gave Godiva's neck a good scratching, much to her tail-wagging delight. "She went home. But she'll be back."

He intended to see to that.

But no matter what, he'd see her soon. After all, it was only neighborly that he make certain everything was okay at Paradise Lost.

And besides, she'd taken his T-shirt.

He hoped like hell she was still wearing it when he got it back.

Chapter 19

After paying the cab driver eighty-seven dollars, Jamie led Heather, who pulled along a wheeled Louis Vuitton suitcase she recognized as Laurel's, one that undoubtedly cost more than Jamie's entire wardrobe, into the carport. Better they talk there than in the house where her mom and Alex were—clearly sound asleep (hopefully from a night of reconciliation sex) as they hadn't come outside to see what all the commotion was about.

"You came out of that other house," Heather said in a confused voice, pointing at Southern Comfort. "Which one is yours?"

"This one. I was just, um, having coffee with my neighbor." Jamie tossed her cash-depleted purse onto the rickety wooden picnic table, then turned to her niece.

And just as it had every time she'd looked into those soulful, espresso-colored eyes since Heather was an infant, a tiny piece of Jamie's heart seemed to break off, no longer belonging to her, but to Heather.

"Hey, kiddo," she said, softly. "What's going on?"

She opened her arms, and behind her black-rimmed glasses, Heather's eyes filled with tears, slicing off another sliver of Jamie's heart. She stepped into Jamie's embrace and a juicy sob escaped her. Jamie pulled her in close and stroked her hair and waited for the storm to pass, all while silently cursing Laurel because she didn't doubt for a moment that her self-absorbed sister was at the root of whatever problem had brought Heather to her doorstep. Heather . . . who seemed to have grown up overnight, morphing from a shy, tomboyish little girl who loved to read into a contradiction of whiplashing moods—sweet and loving one minute, sullen and sour the next, followed in a blink by mouthy and rebellious.

After a minute or so Heather's sobs tapered off and Jamie leaned back and offered her a smile. "Feel better?"

Heather pulled a wad of tissues from the pocket of the black hoodie she wore over a dark purple T-shirt decorated with the name of some band Jamie had never heard of and scowled. "No." She blew her nose, shoved the tissues back in her pocket, then flopped onto the picnic bench and hunched her shoulders. "My life sucks." She shot Jamie a mutinous glare. "Something I wouldn't have had to come all the way to this lame-o place with its stupid cab drivers to tell you if you'd stayed in New York where you belong."

Jamie cast a glance at Southern Comfort and suppressed a wistful sigh. Five minutes ago an aroused, nearly naked Nick had been carrying her to his bedroom, where, as she knew from the hours they'd already spent there, she was about to be made *very* happy. Multiple times. Instead she now had to deal with more drama, the source of which she strongly suspected was Heather's contentious relationship with Jamie's backstabbing sister. Jeez. The things she did for love of this kid. This kid who was currently giving her a crapload of attitude and trying to squash her with guilt.

She pulled her gaze away from Nick's house, plopped down next to Heather, forced herself to ignore the attitude, and spoke the same words she always replied to Heather's frequent claims that her life sucked—words that had become a private joke between them.

"My life sucks, too."

Usually that earned a grin, but not this time. Heather merely shook her head. "Mine sucks worse. Seriously."

"Bet it doesn't, but okay, you first. Then I'll spill, then we vote. Loser has to clean up the kitchen."

Heather considered, then nodded. "Fine. Whatever."

"But first some questions. How did you get here?"

"Airplane. Duh."

"And your mom was okay with you coming here by yourself?"

A guilty flush stained Heather's cheeks and Jamie groaned. "She doesn't know you're here?" When Heather shook her head, Jamie asked, "How did you buy your ticket?"

"Online. With the credit card Mom gave me."

"I thought that was for emergencies only."

The defiant gleam perfected by teenagers the world over glittered in Heather's eyes. "This *is* an emergency. And like Mom would care. She's too wrapped up in her own stuff to give a crap about mine."

"That's not true," Jamie said, her resentment toward Laurel reaching a whole new level for being forced to defend her in any way. *This is about Heather, for Heather. Not Laurel,* she reminded herself. Still, it really irked. "We've discussed this before. Just because your mom is busy with her own life doesn't mean she doesn't care about you."

"The only person she cares about is herself," Heather said, picking at the chipped dark blue polish on her short nails.

"That's not true." *She apparently also cares about my former boyfriend.* "She loves you." Which in her own self-absorbed Laurel way, Jamie knew was true. She just didn't feel like assigning *any* good qualities to her sister right now. "Where does she think you are?"

"With Lindsey's family in the Hamptons," Heather answered, referring to her best friend.

"Heather, you can't just take off like that."

Heather looked up from her polish picking and shot a resentful glare at Jamie. "Why not? You did."

"I'm not fourteen. And I told everyone where I was going." Which had clearly been a huge mistake. "You need to call her. Right now. And tell her where you are."

Resentment turned to mutiny. "I don't want to talk to her."

"Too bad. You don't want to have a three-hour chat with her—fine. But you have to tell her where you are." When it was clear Heather planned to argue the point further, Jamie forestalled her by raising her hand in a *stop* gesture. "*Now*, Heather. Otherwise we're getting in the car and I'm driving you right back to the airport. You can stay with me for a few days, but only if your mom knows where you are and says it's okay."

Heather's expression resembled a thundercloud. "Fine. I'll tell her," she grumbled. "Like she'll care."

Jamie watched her pull her cell phone from her pocket and a tidal wave of love swamped her. Unlike blond-haired, blue-eyed Laurel, Heather resembled her dark-haired, ebony-eyed father. Instead of her mother's tall, sinuous grace, Heather was petite and curvy. And wore glasses. And braces. She hated her thick curly hair, her burgeoning boobs and butt, and her full lips, which she scathingly referred to as a "trout mouth." Jamie thought she was adorable and knew in a few years she'd be drop-dead stunning, but of course in her teenage all-knowing wisdom, Heather disagreed.

Just as it seemed she disagreed with nearly everything lately. Jamie couldn't count how many times Laurel had lamented at the restaurant that she didn't understand her daughter, who eschewed fancy designer labels and shopping on Fifth Avenue and instead wore a steady uniform of black jeans, T-shirts, and sneakers purchased at flea markets. Her brainy daughter who read Shakespeare and F. Scott Fitzgerald rather than *People* magazine. Who dreamed of someday writing a book and spearheading her own version of Habitat for Humanity.

During those conversations Jamie tried to remind Laurel that Heather was her own unique person—and a pretty terrific one in spite of all the teenage sullen crap—not a Laurel Mini Me.

Heather looked at Jamie and rolled her eyes. "I got her voice mail—she's obviously *sooooo* worried about me. I'll leave a message." Seconds later she said into the phone, "Mom, it's me. Aunt Jamie said it was okay if I stayed with her at the beach, so that's where I am. Bye." She ended the call, then shoved the phone back in her pocket. "Happy?"

Oh, yeah, I'm thrilled that my drama-stricken niece arrived on my doorstep unannounced—costing me eighty-

seven bucks for her cab—interrupted what probably would have been the best sex of my life, and is now giving me attitude. "Thank you. Now tell me what's going on."

Heather's bottom lip trembled, and guilt slapped Jamie for her impatience. "My dad texted me from the hospital. His girlfriend had the baby. I have a new sister."

And with those few words Jamie understood. This new baby meant that Heather would see even less of her absentee father, Marco, the playboy son of a wealthy Italian businessman Laurel had fallen madly in love with during a trip to Rome when she was nineteen. They'd fallen just as madly out of love shortly after Heather was born, and since they hadn't married, they'd simply gone their separate ways. Marco supported his daughter financially with a generous monthly check. His emotional support consisted of an occasional awkward transatlantic phone call from Italy, where he lived with his latest very young, very beautiful heiress girlfriend, and hosting Heather's one-week visit to his villa on Lake Como every August, a trip Heather both anticipated and dreaded.

Jamie slung an arm around Heather's slumped shoulders. "A new sister—how do you feel about that?"

Heather shrugged. "They named her Butterfly." She rolled her eyes. "Whatever. At least he and Mom named me after a flower and not an *insect*. And it's not like I'll ever see her anyway. She's my sister, but I don't *feel* like a sister."

"You'll see her soon, when you go to Italy to visit your dad."

Heather shoved up her glasses with an angry jab. "I'm not going." The words shot out of her mouth and she pushed to her feet to pace in front of Jamie with quick, jerky steps, her fisted hands jammed in her pockets. "Why should I? He doesn't know what to say to me, I don't have anything to say to him, and his girlfriend ignores me. All they're going to want to do is oooh and aaah over their new baby and I'll just sit there with nothing to do and nobody to do it with."

She halted and Jamie's heart turned over at the angry misery shimmering in those big brown eyes. She didn't doubt for a minute the accuracy of Heather's prediction of what her time in Italy would be like.

"I told Mom *weeks ago* I wasn't going and she said I *have* to," Heather continued in a voice that throbbed with resentment. "I figured she just wanted me out of the way for a while so I told her I'd stay with Lindsey instead, but she still said no, that I *have* to go visit my dad and meet my sister. I said she can't make me, she said she could, and, well . . ."

"That's when the fight started?" Jamie deadpanned.

A short, harsh laugh escaped Heather and she pushed back her curtain of dark hair with an impatient flick of her fingers. "Yeah." She sat down next to Jamie once again and pressed the heels of her palms to her forehead. "She never listens to me, Aunt Jamie. Never! All she does is throw orders at me, like some drill sergeant, and expects me to obey. She looks at me like I'm a freakin' alien or something because I listen to music she's never heard of and I'd rather read or visit a museum or write in my journal than go to lame-ass Saks or some stupid party or get my nails done. She actually wanted to take my temperature last week because I didn't want to go with her to Elizabeth Arden for a facial." She turned to Jamie and shot her a pained expression. "Elizabeth Arden? Facial? *Really?* Pu-leeeeze."

Jamie inwardly winced at her sister's cluelessness regarding her own daughter's interests. Before she could reply, Heather rushed on, "She thinks that because she was Miss Perfect Popularity and had like a million friends when she was my age, I should, too. I can't stand the popular kids at school. Why isn't it good enough that I only have a few really close peeps instead of a bunch of stupid mean girls who can't talk about anything besides celebrities and boys and shopping?"

"It's good enough—"

"Mom doesn't think so."

Jamie sighed, and again shoved back her resentment of Laurel and forced herself to think only of Heather. "Look—I agree that while the invite to Elizabeth Arden maybe wasn't up your alley—"

"*Maybe?*"

"Okay, definitely. But the fact is she at least tried to include you, suggested that you do something together. I'm guessing you responded by stomping off?"

Another shrug and frown. "Kinda."

Jamie gave her a one-armed hug. "She'd offered you an olive branch. Granted, it wasn't a good one—"

"Ya think? It like totally sucked."

"Agreed. But still, give some credit where it's due. She tried. Did it ever occur to you to offer an alternate suggestion?"

"Like what?"

"Like maybe a movie? Or a walk through the park? You enjoy cooking with me—have you ever tried it with her?"

Heather made a snorting sound. "Oh, sure. Can you see my mom wearing an apron or chopping onions? I don't think so."

"Well, then how about an outing to the Met or the zoo? Frozen hot chocolate at Serendipity? Lunch?"

"Lunch?" Heather scowled. "Mom would want to go to the Four Seasons—"

"So would it kill you to eat a meal at one of the best restaurants on the planet?"

"—or to Newman's where she'd get involved with work and forget all about me." Heather shrugged off Jamie's arm and glared at her through eyes swimming with confusion and betrayal. "Why are you taking her side?"

"I'm not. I'm just trying to get you to look at things from a different perspective. If someone makes a suggestion you don't like, you have nothing to lose by offering up one that you *do* like. It's called compromise. And it's one of those life things everybody sometimes needs to do. Maybe tell your mom that you'll go to the Four Seasons this time if you get to pick the restaurant next time." Jamie nudged her with her shoulder and grinned. "Then go somewhere you know she'll hate."

Heather's lips gave a tiny twitch, then she shrugged for what had to be the hundredth time since arriving on Jamie's doorstep. "I'll think about it."

"Good. Remember—you catch more bees with honey than with vinegar. And you're not going to get your mom—or anyone else for that matter—to listen to you or respect you if you don't listen to them and respect them in return."

"Tell that to Mom. Right after you convince her that I'm not going to Italy."

Jamie shook her head. "Oh, no. I'm not getting involved in that."

Heather's gaze turned pleading. "*Pleeeeeze*, Aunt Jamie. She'll listen to you. If she won't let me stay with Lindsey, I can stay here with you instead."

The thought of her mother *and* Alex *and* Heather all cramped into what was supposed to be her sanctuary at Paradise Lost shivered a chill down Jamie's spine. "I can't talk to your mom about Italy, kiddo."

"Why not?"

Jamie hesitated. She had no idea what, if anything, Laurel had told Heather regarding their estrangement, but she had no intention of disclosing or discussing Laurel's betrayal with Heather. Choosing her words carefully, she said, "Your mom and I are having our own issues right now—things that have nothing to do with you. Just sister stuff. Believe me, having me as an advocate won't help your cause with your mom."

"It's because her new boyfriend Raymond is that guy you used to date, right?"

Uh-oh. Clearly she knew *something*. Jamie couldn't foresee any good answer to that particular question. Obviously anything that contained the words "your mother stole my boyfriend" wasn't appropriate. So what to say? God, why didn't teenagers come with an instruction manual? "Who told you that?" she hedged.

That earned Jamie another eye roll. "Jeez, Aunt Jamie, I have eyes you know. Did you think I wouldn't remember that afternoon I spent with you and him at the museum? When I asked Mom, she just said you weren't going out with him anymore, and since she liked him, now she was going out with him."

Jamie wondered if steam was actually coming out of her ears. "Yup, that's the way it went down." Give or take a few cheating-related details. But Jamie wasn't about to share those with Heather.

"I don't understand what the big deal is about him. That afternoon the three of us spent together? I thought he was a douche. I mean he said like two words to me the whole time." Another shrug. "It doesn't bother you that Mom's dating him? 'Cause I think it'd be weird."

Yes, it bothers me, and it damn well breaks every rule of sisters and girl code ever written, and yes, he is, as you so eloquently put it, a douche. "It's a little awkward, but no worries. I'm a big girl." *Who'd like to slap your mother and her boyfriend into next week.* Anxious to change the subject, she asked, "So what else prompted you to get on a plane to see me?"

"What makes you think there's something else?"

Because a blind man could see it from a mile away. "Just a guess."

She fidgeted with her hoodie zipper. "I'm not sure I still want to go to Princeton."

Jamie's brow shot up. Okay, this was serious. Heather had dreamed of going there ever since discovering her literary idol, F. Scott Fitzgerald, had attended. Unlike Fitzgerald, Heather planned to actually graduate. "Why not?"

"I think I'd rather go to UCLA."

"Oh? Which of your favorite authors attended UCLA?"

"None. But UCLA gives the gift of distance, you know?"

Realization dawned and Jamie nodded. "Yes, there is that." Of course, until someone uninvented airplanes, she could attest that distance didn't always work to keep one's family away. Still, it seemed that the drama storm had passed and they were cruising into smoother waters. "I wouldn't worry about it too much right now. You have plenty of time to decide."

"I guess. Besides, I have other stuff to worry about."

"Such as?"

Heather heaved a sigh. "I think I'm a lesbian."

So much for drama-free, smooth waters.

Not wanting to say the wrong thing, yet not having a clue as to what the right thing might be, Jamie asked carefully, "What makes you think so?"

"I hate men."

Jamie had to cough to cover up the laugh that bubbled up in her throat. "Oh, honey, there's not a woman on the planet who hasn't hated men at some time or another. Or even most of the time. Even the very best of them can be real pains in the ass."

"So . . . it's normal to hate men?"

"Absolutely."

"Even one you kinda maybe like a little?"

Her gaze flicked toward Southern Comfort. "*Especially* ones you kinda maybe like a little. If you think you're a lesbian, the question isn't 'do I hate men?' It's 'do I love women?' "

"You mean in *that* way?"

"Yes."

Heather considered, then shook her head. "Not a bit. But I still think men suck."

As if the mention of "men" summoned one to appear, the screen door over at Southern Comfort banged shut and Nick, followed by a tail-wagging Godiva, descended the wooden stairs. Dressed in board shorts and a blinding white T-shirt that stretched across his broad shoulders, his hair still shower damp, Ray-Bans resting on his head, with Godiva's leash dangling from his long fingers, her neighbor looked more delicious than triple-fudge brownies with rocky road ice cream on top.

And that was saying something.

Heather glanced over, then, to Jamie's amusement, did a double-take. "OMG. Who's the hottie with the cool dog?"

Jamie hiked up a brow and forced herself not to stare at said hottie. "I thought you hated men."

"I do. But since I don't know him, I don't hate him. And I def don't hate his dog."

"His name's Nick Trent. He's my neighbor."

Heather's eyes widened. "*He's* who you were having coffee with?"

Heat rushed into Jamie's face. Which meant . . . oh, damn, here came the blotches. "Yes."

Scarlet rushed into Heather's cheeks—clearly the embarrassing trait had been passed along to the next generation—and a giggle erupted from her. "Coffee? *Suuuuure*, Aunt Jamie." She giggled again, then whispered, "You hittin' that?"

Embarrassment turned the heat in Jamie's cheeks into all-out fire, bringing out the dreaded prim, schoolmarm voice. "What kind of talk is that?" she hissed.

"It means are you sleeping with him."

Sleep had absolutely nothing to do with it. "I know what it means. I *meant* that not only is 'hittin' that' not a proper way to refer to sleeping with someone, it's also a completely inappropriate question."

Heather rolled her eyes. "I know about sex, Aunt Jamie."

I thought I did, too—until I started hittin' that and my hot neighbor taught me some things that damn near stopped my heart. Any reply Jamie might have made was wiped from her mind when her gaze collided with that of her hot neighbor who stood on the other side of the hedges. The heat in his eyes stole not only her words, but her breath as well.

He lifted his hand in greeting. "How's it going, ladies?"

"Ooooh, he even *sounds* hot," Heather whispered.

"Good grief, lower your voice, he's not deaf," Jamie whispered back. Then she smiled at Nick. "Going great. Come meet my niece."

Nick ambled around the hedge, with Godiva trotting at his heels. When the dog spotted Jamie, she broke into a run, skidding to a halt at her feet, then flopping on her back for a tummy rub.

"As you can see, Godiva is very shy," Jamie told Heather with a laugh as she crouched down to comply. "This is her owner, Nick Trent. Nick, my niece, Heather Newman."

Nick stuck out his hand and curved his lips into that knee-destroying killer smile. Jamie bit the insides of her cheeks to keep from laughing at Heather's wide-eyed reaction. "Nice to meet you, Heather."

As if tapped by a magic wand, Heather transformed from sullen and ill-mannered to smiling, blushing, and uber-polite. Great to know she had some manners. Too bad she rarely dusted them off for people who weren't strangers.

"Nice to meet you, too, Mr. Trent. Your dog is beautiful."

"Thanks. Call me Nick. But your aunt was wrong—I don't own Godiva. She owns me."

"OMG, that is *so* sweet," Heather said in a breathless voice, tugging on several of the dozen or so spaghetti-thin, black rubber bracelets adorning her wrist. She dipped her chin, looking away from the gorgeousness that was Nick, then squatted down to join Jamie with the tummy rub—although Jamie suspected that the squat was more likely a result of her niece's knees melting.

With Heather taking over, Jamie rose and found herself standing next to Nick. Freshly showered Nick. Who'd also shaved. And smelled deliciously of soap. And warm skin.

And yummy, sexy man. Her fingers positively itched to reach out and ruffle through the thick waves of his still-damp hair. Then explore his smooth jaw.

"Everything okay?" he silently mouthed.

She nodded, and her heart swelled when he looked relieved—as if he'd actually been worried about her.

He cleared his throat, then said, "Godiva and I were heading to the beach for a run and then a swim. You ladies care to join us?"

"What do you say, Heather?" Jamie asked.

Heather stood and pushed up her glasses. "Sure. Sounds cool."

"Great." Jamie turned to Nick. "We need to change and grab some towels and sunscreen. We'll meet you down there in a little while."

"You're just avoiding going on the run," Nick said with a teasing grin.

"God, yes," Jamie agreed.

He gently tugged on one of her curls, a casual gesture at complete odds with the "I wanna get you naked" look burning in his eyes. Then he shot her a wink, smiled at Heather, and said, "See you soon." After clipping Godiva's leash to her collar, they set off at an easy jog toward the beach.

"OMG," said Heather, her gaze glued on Nick's departing figure. "How come none of the boys at my school look like that?"

"Because he's not a boy." No—he was a libido-igniting, breath-stealing, kiss-you-'til-your-panties-fell-off man who was capable of making her forget both her own name and the fact that knees were attached to her body. In other words, a menace.

She dragged her gaze from Nick and cleared her throat. "Listen—before we bring your suitcase upstairs, get settled, and head for the beach, I want to finish our chat and tell you why my life sucks."

Heather shot her a look of utter disbelief while pointing at Nick's disappearing figure. "You can't be serious, Aunt Jamie."

"Oh, I'm serious. My mom is here."

Heather blinked. "What's wrong with that? Your mom is cool. And fun. Def cooler than my mom."

"She's also pregnant."

"Who?"

"My mother."

Heather's eyes widened to saucers. "You mean, like having a baby pregnant?"

"Is there some other kind of pregnant?"

"No way!"

"Way."

"Isn't she like too . . . old or something?"

"Apparently not. Her boyfriend is here, too. Alex. You might have met him at the restaurant—the guy who did the kitchen renovations."

Heather frowned, then her jaw dropped. "Like Alex—the guy in charge? The kitchen hottie?"

"Well, I never heard him referred to as that, but yes."

"Alex the kitchen hottie is doing your mom and he's her baby daddy."

"Not the most delicate way to put it, but yes. You've summed it up very succinctly. She's been here for more weeks than I care to remember, doing pretty much nothing except barfing, pressuring me to come back to New York, expecting me to make decisions for her, and just generally driving me nuts. Alex showed up a couple weeks ago. They've been arguing and God only knows what else."

"What *else*?" Heather repeated in a horrified voice. She scrunched her nose. "OMG, Aunt Jamie. I'd be like so *mortified*. I mean, ewww. That's just gross."

Jamie laughed. "Oh, honey, you said a mouthful. So—who wins? The person who's being forced to fly first class to Italy for a week to stay at a luxurious villa on Lake Como, or the poor slob whose mother is preggers and barfing all over the place and fighting with her baby daddy?"

"Well, when you put it *that* way . . . fine. You win. Kitchen cleanup on me." Heather rolled her eyes. "Jeez, Aunt Jamie. You have so much drama in your life."

And again, the kid said a mouthful.

"On that note, I vote we change into our bathing suits. I'll show you the beach and we can hang with Nick and Godiva." She picked up her purse from the picnic table, grabbed the handle of Heather's suitcase, and walked toward the stairs.

Heather fell into step beside her. "So this thing with Nick—is it serious or is he just a hook-up?"

Wondering that very thing yourself, aren't you? her inner voice whispered. Jamie shot Heather a fulminating look. "I am *not* having this conversation with you."

Heather flushed. "I'm only asking because, well, if you're serious about him and he lives here, what's going to happen at the end of the summer when you go back to New York?"

And for the third time in as many minutes, the kid had said a mouthful.

"Because you *have* to come back to New York, Aunt Jamie."

She forced a smile. "Don't worry, kiddo. I'll be back. Nick and I are just friends."

Really? asked her very skeptical, very pesky inner voice.

Yes, really. Because that's all she wanted. Especially with a man who lived hundreds of miles away.

Just friends. Who'd had amazing, mind-blowing sex, and would hopefully do so again very soon. But still just friends.

And if she said it enough times, it would certainly remain true.

Just friends.

Chapter 20

"I have to thank you," Jamie said.

Sitting on a striped beach towel with salt water still dripping from his hair courtesy of their last round of body surfing, Nick turned from watching Godiva race down the beach after the tennis ball a laughing Heather had just thrown, to look at the woman he'd been doing his damnedest not to stare at every minute since she and her niece had joined him at the beach several hours ago.

All three of them had splashed in the waves, walked to the pier—where he'd treated them to a gelato—built a sand castle, and played with Godiva, and through each activity he'd had to actually force his gaze away from her. Had to actually say to himself, *For God's sake, stop staring at her!* Only his Ray-Bans had saved him from her knowing he couldn't keep his eyes off her.

Yet who could blame him? With her honey hair blowing wild in the ocean breeze, the sun bringing out every shade of gold and brown, her skin glistening with something that made her smell like a cool, tropical drink, her gorgeous smile, and her killer curves showcased in another one of those bikini bottom/tank top bathing suits that left those few tempting inches of toned tummy bare—this one in bright turquoise with white polka dots that made him want to play connect the dots, first with his fingers, then with his tongue—she was completely irresistible. For some inexplicable reason he found those mere two inches of bare skin completely, utterly erotic, in a way he'd never found a skimpy bikini to be.

Maybe it's not the bathing suit but the woman wearing it that turns you on so much.

Definite possibility. And no doubt if she wore a skimpy bikini, his tongue would roll out onto the sand.

Yet if keeping his eyeballs off her was difficult, keeping his hands and mouth off her had proven an exercise in torture. The urge to touch her, tunnel his hands through that wild tumble of curls and kiss her breathless had all but choked him since the moment she'd appeared on the beach. And if not for the company of her impressionable fourteen-year-old niece, that's exactly what he would have done. For starters.

He managed to tear his gaze away from her long enough to note that Heather was now a good, safe fifty yards away, running after Godiva, affording them a brief moment of quasi-privacy. Yet he knew if he gave in to the temptation to steal even a quick kiss, he stood in real danger of losing the tenuous grip on his control and it turning into a full blown make-out, devour-her session.

So instead of doing what he wanted, he clasped his hands around his upraised knees to keep from grabbing her, and asked, "Thank me for what?"

"Curing Heather of any thoughts she might have been entertaining about her sexual preferences."

"How'd I do that?"

She huffed out a laugh and buried her toes in the sand. "Pretty much just by standing there and breathing. That smile of yours, however, really sealed the deal. She may hate men—which means there's a boy she really likes—but apparently only in the way most women hate them at some point in their lives."

"Happy to help. You need somebody to stand around and breathe, I'm your guy. You have any doubts about your sexual preferences you'd like to put to bed?"

Her quick glance in Heather's direction confirmed what

he'd picked up on as soon as they'd joined him at the beach—
that she wasn't comfortable with any public displays around
her niece. Which instead of annoying him in any way only
made him admire her more. He knew plenty of adults who
didn't bother to consider how their words or actions might
affect their kids—his own father among them. Heather wasn't
even Jamie's child, yet she clearly loved her and was obviously being careful to set a good example.

Still, he couldn't help but wonder if there was more to her
keeping her distance than merely not wanting to engage in
any PDA in front of her niece.

The unsettling question had drifted through his mind
several times during the day. Maybe her lack of flirting and
the physical space she'd carefully maintained between them
meant she wasn't interested in picking up where they'd left
off. Maybe after her abrupt departure that morning, the heat
she'd felt for him had cooled and she was done. With what
they'd shared. With him.

A sense of loss walloped him. Done with him? The hell
with that. Last night had only served to whet his appetite for
her. The thought of not having a repeat reverberated a single
word through him.

No.

"I don't have any questions about my sexual preferences,"
she said in an undertone. "But thanks for the offer."

He frowned. Now what the hell did *that* mean? Somehow
her words seemed fraught with a deeper meaning. Or maybe
he was just losing his mind. He wanted to ask her, but Heather
was nearly upon them, so he kept his mouth shut.

"I think Godiva's finally tired," Heather reported, flopping
down on the towel next to Jamie. A tail-wagging Godiva trotted up, dropped the ball at Heather's feet, then barked.

"OMG, you can't be serious." Heather groaned.

"She's good for at least another four, five hours," Nick said
with a perfectly straight face.

"I'm gonna need some water," Heather said, ruffling Godiva's fur. "Godiva, too."

Jamie reached into the small cooler she'd brought and
pulled out a plastic bottle, which she handed to Heather. Nick
pushed off his towel, then knelt in the sand next to Godiva.

"Pour some of that in here," he said to Heather, cupping his hands together to form a bowl.

Heather did as he asked, refilling Nick's hands several times as they all laughed at the slurpy, splashy spray Godiva made lapping up the drink. When Godiva had had her fill, Heather took a swig from the bottle, then asked him, "Can I take a picture of you and Godiva?"

"Sure."

Heather slipped her phone—the same iPhone he had, he noted—from the denim backpack she'd brought with her. Nick slung his arm around Godiva and smiled. Heather took more photos—of Jamie, Godiva, the beach, then Nick used her phone to take pictures of her and Jamie and Godiva together.

"Thanks," she said, taking the phone from him with a shy smile. "I'm going to text these to Lindsey, then post them on Facebook."

"Lindsey is Heather's BFF," Jamie explained to him as Heather settled herself on her towel, her thumbs flying over the phone's touch screen.

" 'Fraid I'm not really up on the teenage lingo," Nick said.

"Best friend forever."

"Ah. So Kevin's my BFF."

"Right. Do you think of him like a brother?"

"Definitely."

"Then he's your BFADM," said Heather, not looking up from her busy typing. "Brother from a different mother."

Nick chuckled. "I'll tell him." He looked at Jamie and tightened his hold around his knees. "So what's on your agenda for the rest of the day?"

"Not much until the clam meeting at Dorothy's house tonight. Before I go I need to see if any more vendor applications have come in and adjust my figures. Make sure everything is up to date."

"Did you say *clam meeting*?" Heather asked, glancing up from her texting. "Do I even want to know what that is?"

"Oh, honey, you aren't in Manhattan anymore," Jamie said with a laugh. Heather listened to her explanation of the festival and all its activities with such a classic "you've got to be kidding me" expression, Nick could barely keep a straight face. Jamie concluded with, "There's even a clam mascot—

one of the locals wears the giant clam costume and mingles through the crowd all day."

"No way," Heather said. "Who would want to do that?"

"Apparently it's the hottest gig at the festival. There's actually a lottery held the week before to see who wins the honor of being the Giant Clam."

"I'd rather *die*," Heather proclaimed. "All that—for *clams*?" Heather turned to him. "Is this true or is she just yanking my chain?"

"Completely true. The float is going to be a work of art this year, if I may say so myself."

"Nick's going to compete for the title of Clam King," Jamie said.

"Not in a million years," Nick corrected.

Heather giggled. "OMG, Lindsey is going to *collapse* when she hears this," she said, her fingers flying once again. "She won't believe it without evidence. Can I see this float so I can take a pic to send her?"

"Sure," Nick said. "But it's a work in progress—and you know what happens when you get anywhere near a work in progress."

Heather shook her head and kept on texting. "No. What happens?"

"You get put to work—so progress happens."

Heather frowned. "What kind of work? I don't know how to build a float."

"The building part is almost done. Think you can handle a paintbrush?"

She considered for several seconds, then shrugged. "I guess."

"Great. I'll add you to the clam painting committee," Nick said, nodding solemnly. "Which is fitting since your aunt told me you're an F. Scott Fitzgerald fan. Obviously you know James Gatz was a clam digger on the shores of Lake Superior."

Heather's fingers stalled and her head snapped up. "That's right. When he was seventeen."

"Who the heck is James Gatz?" asked Jamie.

"Jay Gatsby—before he changed his name and invented his persona," Heather answered, although her gaze remained on Nick. "You like *The Great Gatsby*?"

He lifted one shoulder. "It's been a long time since I read it, but it made an impression when I did."

"You read it in high school?" Heather asked, setting down her phone and pushing her hair over her shoulders.

"College actually. It was pretty much required reading at the time."

"Where'd you go?" Heather asked.

"Princeton."

He noticed Jamie's brows lift, but Heather's jaw dropped. "That's where F. Scott Fitzgerald went!" she exclaimed.

He grinned. "Which explains why *The Great Gatsby* was pretty much required reading. Even though he didn't graduate, there's still a strong connection."

"You didn't tell me you went to Princeton," Jamie said.

"You didn't ask." He pumped his fist in the air. "Go, Tigers!"

"Well, aren't you just full of surprises," she murmured.

There was any number of surprises he wanted to share with her, most of which involved them getting naked—a factoid best kept to himself. For now.

"*I* want to go to Princeton," Heather said in a rush, making the sentence sound like one long word.

"It's a great school. I'd be happy to answer any questions you might have about it."

"Cool. Thanks." She took a sip of water, then asked, "Did you like it?"

"I did—but it took a while. I didn't want to go."

Her expression indicated he'd sprouted a second head. "Why wouldn't you want to go to Princeton?"

"Mostly because my dad insisted I go." An image of his stern-faced, cold-eyed father flashed in his mind. *You will attend Princeton, Nicolas, and that is final.* "He'd graduated there, and so had his father, which made me a legacy. It was just always expected that I would go there, too." He shot her a half smile. "Which, of course, meant I would have preferred to go *anywhere* else."

She giggled, then bombarded him with a series of rapid-fire questions, which he answered as honestly as he could while remaining age appropriate. When she asked what his favorite Princeton tradition was, he sure as hell didn't admit it had been the drinking game Robopound. He felt Jamie's gaze on him and he wondered what she was thinking as he extolled the virtues of the Ivy League and imparted a few G-rated anecdotes.

"Did you go to arch sings?" Heather asked. "They sound totally cool."

"What are arch sings and how do you know about them, Heather?" Jamie asked.

Before Nick could reply, Heather said, "Late-night a cappella concerts under one of the campus's arches. And I know about them because of Google. Duh."

"I went to a lot of them," Nick said. "Especially my freshman year when I roomed in Blair Hall."

"Were you in a bicker club?" Heather asked.

"I was," Nick answered, impressed with her knowledge.

"Bicker club?" Jamie repeated. "Now that sounds up Nick's alley—a club for arguing."

Nick laughed and Heather giggled. "You bicker to get into an eating club," Nick explained. "They're sort of a cross between a dining hall and a social club—"

"And hello, they're in these totally awesome mansions," broke in Heather, "that were the primary setting for Fitzgerald's *This Side of Paradise*. Seriously, Aunt Jamie, you need to make better use of Google. So which club did you bicker, Nick?"

"Cottage," he said, using the students' name for the University Cottage Club, figuring she'd know, courtesy of her apparently exhaustive Internet searches.

She drew in a quick breath. "Oh! Fitzgerald began *This Side of Paradise* in the library there."

"Yes, he did." He turned to Jamie and teased, "See how much you can learn with Google, Aunt Jamie?"

"Do you still have your beer jacket?" Heather asked.

"Beer jacket?" Jamie shook her head at Heather. "You are not wearing anything that has a beer logo on it, kiddo."

"It's nothing like that," Nick said. "It's a huge Princeton tradition—every senior class designs a jacket to wear to events and reunions. They were originally called that because they protected the seniors' clothes while they tossed back beer." He shot Heather a conspiratorial wink. "Better call it by its more formal name—senior jacket."

Heather had just asked him another breathless question about the school when her phone rang. She grabbed up the instrument, then looked at Jamie. "It's Mom. Can I let it go to voice mail?"

"No. You need to talk to her. And *listen* to her." Jamie squeezed her hand. "I'm right here if you need me."

After heaving the sort of dramatic sigh teenagers were known for, Heather rose to her feet and walked briskly toward the water while saying into the phone, "Hi, Mom."

"How do you think that's going to go?" Nick asked Jamie once Heather was out of earshot.

"Hard to tell. For sure it will go better if Heather doesn't cop an attitude."

Nick nodded. "Yeah, fourteen-year-olds have plenty of that. But she's obviously a great kid. And really smart. And lucky to have you as an aunt."

"Thanks, but I'm the lucky one. She really is great— especially when she's not being a mopey, eye-rolling drama queen. But that comes with the teenage territory, so I grin and bear it. I'm hoping my experiences with her will help me someday with my own kids."

An image instantly flashed in his mind—of a laughing Jamie, swinging a miniature version of herself into her arms. A miniature version that squealed in delight and said, "I love you, Mommy."

He blinked and the mental picture disintegrated, leaving a sensation he couldn't name in its wake . . . an odd brew of yearning and envy, mixed with a dose of jealousy toward the imaginary guy who'd gifted her with that child.

"So . . . Princeton, huh?"

Her voice jerked him from his crazy thoughts. "Yeah. You have something against Princeton?"

"Not at all. I'm just surprised."

"Why? Did you think I was a high school dropout?"

She made a self-conscious sound. "Of course not. I guess I just somehow pictured you staying closer to home and helping out at your family's B and B, learning all the ins and outs of the business in preparation of running it someday."

Guilt slapped him. Hard. He could understand the note of confusion in her voice. An Ivy League education certainly seemed like overkill for running a small-time family-owned bed-and-breakfast. "Well, as I told Heather, both my dad and grandfather were alumni, so attending was expected. And at seventeen I wasn't prepared to buck my father's wishes or family tradition. Even though I resented being told where I had to attend college, I was glad for the escape it offered me."

"Very expensive escape for a middle-class kid."

"You've never heard of scholarships?" This time guilt didn't merely slap him—it punched him right in his mouth, which had uttered that misleading question. Definitely time to change the subject. He shot her what he hoped was a convincing grin. "I'm a lot smarter than I look."

But she didn't smile back. Instead she said, "I owe you another thank you. You've been great with Heather all day— patient, sweet, amusing." She hesitated, then added, "I especially appreciate it because I brought her on a museum outing with Raymond once and he pretty much just ignored her."

Annoyance rippled through him at being compared in any way to her cheating ex. "I'm not Raymond."

Yet even as the words left his mouth his inner voice whispered, *No, but you do have something in common with him.*

Another punch of guilt walloped him and her words that he'd never forget filtered through his mind: *Getting involved with a guy from that world of elite entitlement was a huge error in judgment on my part. Never again.*

Damn. Based on her experience with Raymond, Jamie had made it clear that she had no use for men who came from wealth and privilege. Nick knew not telling her the whole truth was a bad idea. Yet he also knew the moment he told her, she'd tell him to take a hike. Either way, he was screwed.

And not in the happy-ending way.

No need to tell her something that's not important and doesn't matter, he assuaged his conscience. *Especially since she's leaving in a few weeks and you'll never see her again.*

"I didn't mean to imply you're like Raymond," she said quietly. "My comment sprang from concern for Heather. During the afternoon we all spent together, Raymond had no rapport with her whatsoever and I knew she was uncomfortable. With him now involved with Laurel, he's going to be a part of Heather's life . . ." She blew out a sigh. "I just meant that you were great with her and it was nice to see her smiling and laughing. And the fact that you went to her dream school? A yummy cherry on top of an already delicious sundae."

"Is that your roundabout way of saying you think I'm yummy and delicious?"

Scarlet rushed into her cheeks and he stifled a groan of want. The urge to brush his fingertips over that wash of color was damn near strangling him. She pursed her lips in that prim way of hers that often followed her blushes. It shouldn't turn him on, but it did. Fiercely.

"Noooo," she said in that schoolmarm voice that ridiculously rushed blood straight to his groin. "It's my way of saying thank you. Do you always fish for compliments so shamelessly?"

"I wasn't fishing. I was just asking for clarification. Because I think—" His intention to tell her that he thought *she* was yummy and delicious was cut off by Heather's return.

She stood in front of Jamie and thrust her phone at her, all belligerent attitude. "She wants to talk to you."

Nick saw Jamie stiffen. He knew damn well speaking with her sister was the last thing she wanted to do. Protective instincts he didn't even know he had rushed to the surface and it was all he could do not to grab the phone and tell her sister exactly what he thought of her and what she'd done to Jamie.

She drew a deep breath, then rose. Took the phone, and walked toward the water, not lifting the instrument to her ear until a good fifteen feet separated them.

Heather flopped down on her towel and scratched behind Godiva's ears. A full minute of silence passed, then finally she said, "Can I ask you something?"

Oh, Jesus. He hoped like hell it was something he knew the answer to. "Sure."

"You're a guy, right?"

Okay, that he knew the answer to. "Last time I looked, yeah."

She giggled, then cleared her throat. "So then can you tell me why guys are so dumb?"

"Dumb in general, or regarding something specific?"

"Specific. Namely girls."

Ah. Well, given he was currently painfully attracted to a

woman who 1) was on the rebound, 2) lived seven hundred miles away, and 3) he hadn't been completely honest with, he probably wasn't the best person to ask because he clearly didn't have a clue.

"I think women are just really, really smart, so we men can't help but seem dumb in comparison."

She kicked at the sand and mulled that over. "So you're saying it's because women are brilliant and opposites attract?"

He laughed. "Exactly. You know the title of the shortest book ever published?"

"No."

"*What Men Know About Women.*"

That earned him a half smile. "Why are boys so hard to figure out?"

"Maybe I only think this because I'm one of those dumb guys, but I don't think we're hard to figure out at all. In fact, I think we're pretty simple. And very basic. Food, clothing, shelter, a partner—done." Being conscious of age-appropriateness, he didn't point out that the clothing part was definitely optional, especially where the partner part was concerned. "Some boy giving you trouble?"

She looked down, hiding her face behind her dark curtain of hair, and shrugged.

He made a big show of cracking his knuckles and adopted his best Marlon Brando as the Godfather voice. "You want that I should kick this boy's ass?"

That drew a giggle. "Nah."

Just then Jamie approached them. One look at her tight lips and now pale face told him her conversation with her sister had upset her. He wanted nothing more than to jump up and wrap her in his arms, but as he didn't believe she'd welcome the gesture, he forced himself to remain seated. She pulled in a deep breath, then smiled as she rejoined them, but Nick could tell the smile was forced and obviously for Heather's benefit.

"What's so funny?" she asked.

"Nick was just telling me why boys are so dumb."

Jamie smirked. "Well, he would know."

"Hardee-har-har," Nick grumbled.

She handed Heather her phone. "How did your conversation with your mother go?"

Heather shrugged. "Okay. She was pretty mad about me coming here without telling her. What did she say to you? Can I stay?"

"She just wanted to make sure you were okay. I told her you were fine and could stay."

"Thanks, Aunt Jamie. Did you talk to her about Italy?"

"No. That's between you and her." She picked up her towel and shook out the sand. "I don't know about you two, but I've had enough sun and I'm starving. How about we head back to the house and I'll make some lunch?"

"I could eat," Heather said with her customary shrug.

"Thanks, but I think I'll stay here and hit the waves again," Nick said.

"You're turning down a meal?" Jamie asked. "Are you ill?"

No. Just sick and tired of fighting this overwhelming need to touch you. He forced a laugh. "I'm fine. Just in the mood for another swim before heading home. I'll catch you ladies later."

He felt the weight of Jamie's stare, but with her sunglasses hiding her eyes, he couldn't tell their expression. He watched them gather their belongings, then climb the half dozen wooden steps to the beach-access path. The instant Jamie's curvy ass disappeared from view, he sucked in what felt like his first easy breath in hours. Finally she was out of sight.

Unfortunately she was nowhere near out of mind.

Chapter 21

"Please tell me you'll share the recipe for this incredible dessert," Jamie said to Dorothy later that night. The clam meeting had concluded—her PowerPoint presentation had been a hit, as had her handouts—and now the dozen committee members packed into Dorothy's living area were enjoying their favorite part of every meeting—dessert. Tonight's offering was their host's homemade hummingbird cake, a Southern classic Jamie had never heard of but now ranked high on her Oh, God, That's So Yummy list.

"Happy to share the recipe," Dorothy said around a mouthful of the moist cake topped with a to-die-for cream cheese frosting. "Especially with the person whose ideas for the Clam Festival have generated so much revenue for Seaside Cove."

"Hear, hear," said Megan and Grace in unison, lifting their cake-laden forks.

Everyone else chimed in, and warmth flooded Jamie's cheeks at the praise and show of friendship, and she marveled at the fact that a mere five weeks ago she hadn't even known any of these people, yet now she considered them friends.

"Tastes different than the hummingbird cake I grew up

with," grumbled Melvin, although Jamie noted he was among the first to finish his slice.

"That's my grandma Ernst's recipe and it won her the blue ribbon at more county fairs than you can shake a stick at," Dorothy informed him tartly. She turned to Jamie and said out of the corner of her mouth, "Shoulda known giving that sour old coot some cake wouldn't sweeten him up any."

"I'm not sour, nor am I deaf," Melvin informed her.

"Seems I gotta give ya the deaf part, but I'm stickin' with the sour part," Dorothy said, throwing him a scowl that he returned with equal force.

He then turned his frown on Jamie. "Saw you got yourself a teenager staying with you now, Newman. Regular hippie commune you've got going on there with all them guests of yours. Hope she doesn't think she can play raucous music at all hours of the night. You'll recall it's lights out at twenty-one hundred at Gone Fishin'."

Jamie smothered a smile. "She's my niece and she has earphones, so there's no need to worry about loud music."

She enjoyed her last bite of the delicious cake, then helped Dorothy gather the dirty dishes. She hugged Megan and Grace good-bye, promising they'd meet at the beach the next day.

"The boys will be there with some friends," Grace said, "so Heather will have kids to hang with."

"That's great," said Jamie. "She's with my mom and Alex this evening, discovering the previously unknown wonders of Walmart."

Megan's jaw dropped. "She's never been to Walmart?"

Jamie shook her head. "They don't have a location in Manhattan. She was pretty blasé about it, you know, rolling her eyes and muttering, 'whatever,' but I'm thinking she's going to be hooked, just like I am."

"She'll want to go every day," Megan predicted with a laugh. "Looking forward to meeting Heather tomorrow and hearing all about it."

"See you tomorrow," said Grace with a wave.

They departed, with the other committee members trickling out with promises to see each other the following week for the annual potluck dinner the Clam Committee held for its members, until finally only Jamie and, to her surprise,

Melvin, remained. He was lingering, studying Dorothy's collection of shells and sea glass she kept in a big bowl on her coffee table.

"I think he's hoping for another slice of cake," Dorothy whispered to Jamie.

"Again, I'm not deaf," Melvin barked. "And if you're offering, I suppose I could force down another piece."

"Humph. I suppose you'll be wanting another cup of coffee, too," said Dorothy.

"If you insist."

Dorothy looked toward the ceiling, then turned to Jamie. "Good thing I made two cakes since I promised Nick a piece as well. Would you be a dear and bring it to him?" She lowered her voice. "I'd do it myself but it appears I have a *guest.*"

"Still not deaf," Melvin called from the other room. "Good Lord, woman, you can't whisper worth a whit."

Jamie pressed her lips together to keep from laughing and ignored the combination of anticipation and trepidation that raced through her at the thought of delivering Nick's cake. He'd turned down her lunch invite earlier today, and she'd sensed there was more to the reason than simply wanting to take another swim. *You scratched his itch and now he's done with you,* her inner voice whispered.

He certainly hadn't seemed done with her this morning, before Heather's arrival had interrupted them. But that was over twelve hours ago—plenty of time for his ardor to have cooled. No doubt he'd decided she and her high-maintenance family weren't worth the trouble. It's not as if a guy like him would have any problem finding a willing bed partner or as if they were anything more to each other than a quickie fling.

A pain that felt like a stab in the heart speared her and she shifted her shoulders to relieve the discomfort. "Sure, I'll deliver the cake to Nick." Then she leaned close to Dorothy's ear. "Do you want me to stay?" She straightened and shot a pointed glance toward Melvin, who was now studying a framed black-and-white photo of a youthful Dorothy.

"Nah. He doesn't scare me. Besides, it's almost twenty-one hundred—he'll be leaving soon. You go on, dear." She handed Jamie a Saran-wrapped paper plate holding a generous slice of hummingbird cake. "Tell that dear, sweet boy Nick I said hello."

"Will do."

"I'll bring you the recipe tomorrow morning," Dorothy promised with a hug. "Bright and early."

"Not *too* bright and early," Jamie said with a laugh. "'Night, Melvin," she called from the doorway.

Melvin jerked his head up from the photograph, and for a single heartbeat, Jamie thought she caught a softening in his usual dour expression. But then his brows dropped into his normal scowl and she decided it must have just been a trick of the light.

"Yeah, yeah, g'night, Newman," he mumbled.

Jamie descended the wooden stairs, then headed across the street to Southern Comfort. She skirted around Nick's truck in the carport and climbed the stairs. As soon as she knocked on the screen door, Godiva started barking and raced into the kitchen.

"Hey, girl," Jamie said through the screen. "How ya doin'?"

Godiva answered with a prancing, dancing, barking display. Seconds later Nick strode into view and halted at the sight of her. Their gazes met through the screen door and Jamie's lungs sort of forgot how to work. He wore a pair of faded jeans that hugged him in all the right places, and a black T-shirt that bore streaks of what appeared to be sawdust. His hair was rumpled and a hint of stubble shaded his jaw. He looked big and strong and sexy and gorgeous and he put everything female in her on red alert, especially when he began walking toward the door.

"Hi," she said as he silently approached. "Dorothy asked if I'd deliver this piece of cake she promised you." Good grief, she sounded positively breathless. As if she'd sprinted the entire length of the island rather than walked across the street. When he reached the door, he gave Godiva the signal to heel and she stepped back so he could push it open. "You were so sweet today, I figured it was the least I could do—"

Her words were cut off when in a single motion he took the cake and set it on the counter with one hand, while dragging her through the open door and pulling her against him with the other. Before she could suck in a much-needed breath, his mouth was on hers, and his hands were . . . God, they were everywhere, impatient and just a little rough, molding her against him like melted wax. Which was just fine because that's exactly what she felt like.

In some small recess of her mind, it vaguely registered that he'd kicked the door shut. That he'd lifted her straight up and, with his lips fused to hers and his tongue stroking deep inside her mouth, had walked her toward his bedroom. That somewhere along the way her flip-flops fell off. Then he kicked the bedroom door shut as well and she thought she heard Godiva give a mournful whine, but the sound was drowned out by the echo of her heartbeat pounding through her.

One second he was kissing her into a quivering blob and the next she landed on the mattress with a bounce. She gulped in some desperately needed air, but again he stopped her lungs when he whipped his T-shirt over his head and tossed the garment aside. With his hot, intense gaze zeroed in on her like a laser beam, he unbuttoned his jeans and pulled down the zipper halfway.

Wow, wow, holy cow. Dots swam before her eyes, no doubt from lack of oxygen. God help her, she didn't know where to look first. Her hungry gaze skimmed over his broad chest, then down his ridged abdomen and settled on his erection, straining against the white cotton of his underwear. Without a word he reached for her, and before she could even find her voice to utter *let's get naked*, those magical hands of his made her shorts, panties, and tank top disappear.

Then he dropped to his knees next to the bed, slid his hands beneath her, and dragged her to him. His mouth was *oooh*, right *there*, and his fingers, *aaaah*, right *there*—stroking, delving, teasing, caressing, relentless, propelling her toward climax at breakneck speed. Her orgasm struck her like a lightning bolt, dragging a sharp cry from her throat.

Aftershocks of delight were still rippling through her when she heard a tearing sound. She managed to drag her eyes open in time to see Nick impatiently shove his jeans and boxer briefs low enough to free his erection, then roll on a condom. In the next heartbeat his body covered hers, pressing her into the mattress. He entered her in a single breath-stealing deep thrust. Their groans mingled, and then his mouth once again covered hers and the magic began all over again. Jamie wrapped her arms and legs around him, meeting each thrust until her body tightened and she once again hovered on the edge of release.

Nick broke off their kiss and dragged his mouth across her jaw. "Come with me, Jamie. *Now.*" That command, spoken against her ear in that ragged, harsh whisper, pushed her over the edge into another shattering climax. He clasped her to him, and with a long groan, buried his face against her neck as shudders racked his entire body.

She lay beneath him, a panting, boneless heap. A good minute passed before she felt capable of speech. And even then she only managed a heartfelt, "Wow."

He lifted his head and she forced her eyes open. And found him looking down at her through slumberous eyes. "Yeah. Wow."

"That was some greeting. I was only expecting a hello. Maybe a kiss."

"Did I not say hello?"

"Um, no. As best as I can recall, the first words you actually spoke were 'come with me, Jamie.' For the record, they were pretty darn fantastic first words, and you'll note that I follow directions very well."

"Noted. And since I deprived you of the greeting you expected . . ." He lowered his head and gently touched his mouth to hers. This kiss was soft, lingering, and tender . . . the complete opposite of the demanding, impatient, devouring kiss he'd given her at the door. Where that kiss had made her heart race, this one . . . this one simply melted it. Especially when he raised his head just enough to whisper, "Hello."

The word blew warm and soft against her lips and something inside Jamie seemed to shift, leaving a yawning space that immediately flooded with an intoxicating warmth that made her feel as if heated honey ran through her veins.

"Hi." She raised her arms above her head and stretched beneath him, reveling in the delicious feel of his weight on top of her. "You really are full of surprises. This afternoon you were Mr. Sweet and Charming, and now tonight you're . . ." She heaved a gushy sigh. "Mr. *Oh, My.*"

He tucked a stray curl behind her ear. "I'd been thinking

about you and when you showed up, I just couldn't keep my hands off you."

"You didn't seem to have a problem keeping them off me at the beach."

He raised a brow. "Wanna bet? The effort damn near killed me."

There was no denying the relief that filled her that it wasn't just her who'd had to expend that effort.

His gaze searched hers, intent and serious. "But I picked up on a definite hands-off vibe from you—and in case it missed your notice, you never touched me all day, either. The question is, was it hands off because you didn't want any PDA in front of your niece, or because last night was all you wanted from me?"

Her life would certainly be much less complicated if she were able to write him off as a one-night stand and ignore these unwanted feelings he was stirring up inside her. But that definitely wasn't the case. "Hands off was for Heather's benefit. I didn't want her to feel as if she was interrupting or that I didn't want her there. She feels that sting enough at home. As for the other, I'd be branded World's Biggest Liar if I said I didn't want a repeat of last night. How about you?"

He expelled a short laugh. "You're asking a guy who pounced on you like he was starved and you were brisket parmigiana, who had you naked in under a minute, and who couldn't even wait to get his own clothes all the way off before making love to you. That answer your question, princess?"

"Yes. And for the record, I really, *really* liked being that brisket parmigiana. Which means once again we agree."

He nuzzled her neck with his warm lips. "That's getting to be a habit."

"Yes." And it suddenly occurred to her that *he* could become a habit. Yes, the way he touched her . . . she could definitely become addicted to that. Which was a scary thought indeed.

"Since we're in agreement, how about a nice, warm shower, then I'll show you that, all evidence to the contrary when you arrived, I'm actually capable of slow and easy." He lifted his head and offered her a lopsided grin. "Especially now that the edge is off."

"I can't spend the night. I don't think it would be right with Heather—"

He stopped her words with a kiss. "I understand. And I agree."

"Yikes. *Really* getting to be a habit."

"Yeah." His gaze searched hers. "I think maybe *you're* getting to be a habit, Jamie."

She blinked. "Is your superpower mindreading? Because I just thought the same thing about you."

"No." His gaze remained serious for several seconds, then fire flared in the green depths. "Wanna see what my superpower really is?"

"I already know. I'm not sure what you call it, but it involves your magical hands and that incredible thing you do with your tongue. Yowza." A shiver of delight rippled through her at the memory. "You truly are a Super Man."

"What if I told you that's not it?"

Her eyes widened. "You're joking. You haven't already showed me? There's *more?* It gets *better?*"

He rolled them so that she was on top. "Sweetheart, I haven't *begun* to show you."

"Be still my heart. You'll recall that I can't spend the night."

"I remember. And I'm leaving early in the morning to go to Kevin's."

Disappointment flooded her. "How long will you be gone?"

"A few days. How late can you stay tonight?"

"Another hour."

He tangled his fingers in her hair and dragged her mouth down to his. "Damn. That doesn't leave me much superpower time."

"Okay, two hours. But then I really need to leave."

"Then let's make the most of the short amount of time we have left."

Their lips met, and her last thought before she forgot everything else was that their time wasn't short just tonight. With her return to New York a mere four weeks away, they didn't have much time left at all.

Chapter 22

"Nick, you know I think of you like a brother, right?" asked Kevin.

Nick didn't look up from the bead of caulk he was running along the shoe molding in the new playroom. Once he finished, the room would be ready for painting. "Yeah. I'm your BFADM."

"Huh?"

"Brother from a different mother." He glanced at Kevin over his shoulder. His friend stood in the doorway, his weight balanced on his crutches. "We're apparently also BFFs."

Kevin scrunched up his face. "Big football fanatics?"

"Good guess, but no. Best friends forever."

"Where are you getting this stuff? Have you been reading Liz's *People* magazine again?"

Nick laughed. "No. Jamie's teenage niece caught me up on some of the lingo."

Kevin nodded. "Well, I'm glad you know I consider you my bro. So you know I'm asking this with manly affection and all that shit. When the hell are you going home?"

Nick set down his caulk gun and slowly rose to his feet. "Today, apparently."

Kevin raked a hand through his hair. "Look, you know how much I appreciate your help. No way could I have gotten through all this without you. My business would have fallen apart while I've been laid up if not for you."

"So obviously there's a 'but' coming."

"Right. But—you've been here a week and you need to go. Not because I don't want you around. But because you're here for the wrong reasons."

"Since when is helping a buddy the wrong reason?"

"It's not. And the first four days you were here I desperately needed the help with the Langston roof job and the Portermans' deck. But both jobs are finished so I could have pulled in one of my other guys for the last three days to do the renovation stuff here you've hung around to do. Which, again, I appreciate, but I know damn well you have a load of projects to do on your own place."

"Nothing that can't wait. Getting this addition finished for you and Liz and Emily is more important."

"Maybe—but that's not why you've hung around three extra days."

Nick crossed his arms over his chest. "If you wanted me to leave, why didn't you just say so?"

Kevin shook his head. "It's not that I want you to leave."

"Sure as hell sounds like it. So what's the problem?"

"The problem is that you're not staying here because this is where you want to be. It's because you don't want to be *there*. And you know why you don't want to be there?"

"No, but obviously you're going to tell me."

"Damn right I am. It's because you're avoiding Jamie. Because she's got you all tied up in knots. And instead of facing her, you're hiding out here."

The fact that Kevin's words hit the bull's-eye really irked. "So what if that's the case?"

"There's no *if* about it. And you know what that makes you? A big fat chickenshit."

Nick narrowed his eyes. "Yeah, I'm really feeling all the manly affection."

"Well, you should be, asshole, because all this yapping about feelings and shit is not my favorite thing to do."

"So who asked you to yap about it?"

Kevin's gaze wavered and Nick groaned. "Oh, Jesus. Liz put you up to this."

The guilty flush that stained Kevin's cheeks confirmed it. "I can't deny we've discussed it, but dude, even *I* noticed the sparks flying between you and Jamie, and I don't usually pick up on that sort of thing. So you wanna explain why you're cowering in my house instead of heading back to your own and fixing whatever the hell is wrong? Because you can stand there and glare at me all you want but I know you as well as I know myself, and you, my friend, are not yourself. The facts are pretty simple—you were happy the day you brought her here. You came back two days later without her. That was a week ago and you've been miserable since you walked in the door. You could have, should have, left three days ago, yet here you remain. Looking miserable."

"I'm not miserable—"

"*Miserable*, bro. Not happy. Not yourself. Looking like crap. And I've had it. So spill. What's going on and why the hell are you still here?"

Nick dragged a hand down his face, grimacing at the stubble that abraded his palm. "I guess I've been a little . . . out of sorts."

"No shit. Why?"

He pulled in a deep breath and tried to put into words what he'd been wrangling with since the moment Jamie had left his house a week ago. "I guess the problem is that . . . I think I . . . like her."

Kevin stared at him in silence for a good ten seconds. Then he closed his eyes, shook his head, pinched the bridge of his nose, and muttered something that sounded suspiciously like, "Sweet God in heaven, please give me patience with this moron."

When Kevin opened his eyes, he said, "You *think* you *like* her? Nick. You're a smart guy—got the fancy schmancy Princeton degree to prove it. But if you believe the problem is that you *think* you *like* her, then you've been whacked on the head with the stupid stick. But just for giggles, let's say that's what's wrong. Then explain to me why, if you like her, you're avoiding her as if she's poison ivy."

"Okay, fine. I *know* I like her. A lot. And that's the problem."

"Seems pretty unproblematic to me. Boy meets girl, boy likes girl. If he likes her a lot, even better."

"There are . . . complications."

"She married?"

"No."

"Engaged or otherwise spoken for?"

"No. Although she recently had a bad breakup."

"So you're the rebound guy?"

"Debatable. Based on time since the breakup, yes. But based on her level of brokenhearted-ness, no."

"Criminal?"

"No."

"Druggie? Financial disaster? Kicks old ladies? Steals from kids?"

"None of that. I wish she was."

"Because every guy dreams of meeting a drugged-out, old-lady-kicking criminal?"

Nick shook his head. "Of course not. Because if she had serious flaws like that I wouldn't be in this mess. The problem is that this . . . *thing* with her wasn't supposed to happen. I didn't even like her at first. I thought she was a real pain-in-the-ass princess-type. You know I can't stand pain-in-the-ass princesses."

"Who can? But she didn't strike me that way."

"Because, as it turns out, she isn't. And as I started figuring that out, I realized I sort of *did* like her. But it's only supposed to be a fling. *Can* only be a fling. Her life is in New York. Mine is here. And that was fine—figured we'd have some no-strings fun, she'd leave and no sweat. But . . . the night before I came here, we were together, and . . . I don't know. Something happened to me. Damned if I know what it was. I was looking at her and it felt like I got punched. Right in the heart."

He paced a few steps and then halted. "You're right. I'm avoiding going home. I feel like if I do, I'll be starting—or continuing—something I can't finish. Something that won't end well. It's as if I'm standing on the edge of an emotional canyon and I really don't want to fall in. And I'm afraid that as soon as I see her again . . ."

"You'll fall?" Kevin guessed.

"Yeah."

Kevin's eyes reflected both confusion and concern. "Would that be so terrible?" Before Nick could reply, Kevin continued, "I know you're gun-shy and with good reason. But Jamie doesn't know the whole truth—unless you've told her?"

Nick shook his head. "No. Not yet."

"I've seen you with plenty of women over the years that were with you for the wrong reasons. For money, for what you could buy them, what your family connections could do for them. You almost married one of them. But you took all that out of the equation. Jamie doesn't know you as Nicolas Trent the third, heir to Luxe hotels."

"Not the heir anymore," Nick reminded him. "I walked away from all that."

"True, but my point is, your whole life you were never sure if a woman cared for *you* or for who you were. That's not a problem here. So why are you so afraid?"

"Well, for starters, her ex came from the same background as me. He cheated, it ended badly, and she harbors a definite distaste for that sort of man. Me being Nicolas Trent the third and all that goes with that would *not* be welcome news."

"You're not that guy anymore, Nick," Kevin said quietly. "You never really were."

"I did a lot of things I'm not proud of."

"Show me a person over the age of twelve who hasn't. As far as I'm concerned, the only thing you did wrong was trying to please everyone except yourself. By trying to live up to your family's expectations and living the life they demanded of you, you lost yourself and were miserable. It took a lot of strength and integrity to walk away from a lifestyle that most people would kill for."

As it always did, Kevin's steadfast loyalty touched him. "Even if she's okay with who I am—"

"Who you *were*," Kevin reiterated.

"She won't like that I wasn't up-front about it."

"Dude, that's what flowers, chocolate, apologies, and make-up sex are for."

Nick paced to the wall and back, then stopped in front of Kevin. "What about the fact that she lives seven hundred miles away?"

"Last I heard there were airplanes. You should know that—your family owns a freakin' fleet of them."

"Knock it off. I no longer have a private jet at my disposal."

"Cry me a river. So fly coach like the rest of us. All the major airlines—and a bunch of minor ones as well—have daily flights from here to New York."

"I know that. And that's great in theory, but the reality is I don't want a long-distance relationship. Sure, it would be okay for a while, but it's really just two people leading separate lives, and at some point it wouldn't work any longer."

"Then there are moving vans. People in love use them to relocate themselves and their crap closer to the ones they love."

Nick actually felt the blood drain from his face. "Whoa, whoa, first of all, nobody said anything about *love*. And second, I'm not going anywhere. No way. And there's no way she'd consider moving. Her life, her family, her career, they're all in New York."

Kevin looked toward the ceiling. "Bro—first of all, we've been talking about *love* this entire time. And second, based on my own experience I can only tell you that if you love someone enough, if they love you enough, you can work that other shit out."

Nick shook his head. "I'm not in love. I'm just . . . deeply in lust."

"Uh-huh. Let me guess—you can't get her out of your head. She's the first thing you think about when you wake up in the morning, the last thing you think about before you go to bed, and she's pretty much there all the hours in between. Every time you see her, it's hard to breathe for a few seconds. You can't wait to get your hands on her—but you enjoy her company just as much out of bed as you do in it. She makes you laugh. She makes you think. And ache like you never have before—with wanting her, with missing her. And other than knowing you just want to be with her every minute, you're so damn confused you don't know which end is up. Yet somehow, at the core of that tornado of confusion is a calm center that just *knows*." Kevin cocked a brow. "Sound familiar?"

An uncomfortable prickly sensation raced through Nick—

as if Kevin had just read his most private thoughts. "Some of it. Maybe."

"More like all of it. Definitely." The rubber tips of Kevin's crutches made soft splat sounds on the plywood subfloor as he moved to stand in front of Nick. "Listen, I know the signs. I've *lived* those signs. I saw the way you looked at her. And the way she looked at you."

"And how did she look at me?"

"The exact same way you were looking at her."

Something that felt like elation—topped with fear—rippled through Nick. Still, he narrowed his eyes. "I thought guys were supposed to talk their buds *out* of this stuff."

"We are. When it's the wrong girl. Did you try to talk me out of Liz?"

"Hell, no. She's perfect for you."

The instant the words left his mouth, he realized his tactical error. Kevin smirked. "I rest my case. The question is—what are you going to do about it?"

"Damned if I know." Surely, contrary to Kevin's opinion, he wasn't in love. Definitely not. While he couldn't deny he liked Jamie a lot more than he'd ever anticipated, love—real, deep, abiding love—took time. Lots of time.

Kevin fell for Liz in about four seconds, his inner voice reminded him. *And it's not like you only met Jamie yesterday.*

True. Still, they hadn't spent nearly enough time together. He was just lost in a haze of sexual desire unlike anything he'd ever experienced. His hormones had gotten the best of him—a pretty embarrassing situation for a guy his age. He wasn't a damn teenager, after all. This was just the result of him not having indulged in a fling in a while. And that's all this was, all this could be. A fling.

So what if he'd had to force himself to stay here these extra few days? He'd done it. Maybe it was for reasons he didn't fully understand, other than to know that he'd needed to prove to himself that he *could* stay away. And he'd proved it. Right?

Right, his inner voice agreed. *You did great. Proved this is just a fling. Now get your ass home where it belongs. And where it wants to be.*

"I'm not convinced you're right about everything, but you

do have a point. I've been avoiding the situation, and I need to go home."

"Hallelujah. How soon can you leave?"

Nick couldn't help but laugh. "You have a hot date?"

"As a matter of fact, yes. My folks are taking Emily for the night, which means that for the first time in weeks, Liz and I will have the house to ourselves. Which means you've gotta go. The sooner the better."

"Sheesh. Subtle you are not. Can I take a shower first?"

"No. Go home and take one with your woman. Now that my cast is off, I intend to take one with mine the instant you're gone."

"Liz would kill you if she knew you'd said that."

"Liz is going to be much too busy screaming with pleasure to think of murder. Now get out. You can come back in a few days and finish up."

"Gee, thanks. Maybe I will. Maybe I'll bring Jamie along and she'll bake brownies and you won't get any."

"You're forgetting about these weapons I'm wielding," Kevin said, brandishing one of his crutches.

"Yeah—as if you could catch me. But I'm outta here. Enjoy your hot date."

Kevin grinned. "You, too. See you in a few days."

Nick nodded, anticipation filling him. He was going home. To the woman he really, really liked.

"You slept with him *more than a week ago* and you're just telling me *now*?"

Kate's incredulous voice came through Jamie's cell phone, the last word ending an entire octave higher than the first.

A wave broke, washing cool water and sand over Jamie's feet as she walked toward the pier, a welcome contrast to the hot late-afternoon sun blazing from a cloudless, piercing blue sky. "You and Ben were on your Caribbean cruise—I didn't want to bother you. How was the cruise by the way?"

"Terrific and quit changing the subject. Calling me to read the minutes from your last clam meeting would have bothered me. A call to report that you've had sex with your neighbor who you hated at first sight is cruise-interruption worthy. Besides, I've been home for three whole hours! Why didn't you call me sooner?"

"Between my mom, Alex, and Heather, it's nearly impossible to get any privacy around here. It practically took an act of Congress for me to slip away for a while."

"*Heather* is there? Good Lord. So much for getting away by yourself. Tell me everything."

Jamie filled her in on all the drama at Paradise Lost, and had just started in on the latest goings-on with the Clam Committee when Kate broke in.

"Clam stuff can wait. I want to hear about the sexy time with the sexy man. So—how was it?"

Incredible. Mind-blowing. "Pretty good."

"Pretty good as in 'I lost count of how many orgasms I had,' or pretty good as in 'eh—I've had better'?"

Jamie blew out a breath and reached down to pick up a shell. "Pretty good as in I lost count and I've never had better."

Kate's whoop nearly pierced Jamie's eardrum. "So what the heck are you doing talking to me? Why aren't you in bed with him right this minute? Please tell me you're not letting your uninvited guests screw this up for you."

"There's nothing to screw up because he's not here. I'm not in bed with him because he left." The words were accompanied by a heart owie. She quickly brought Kate up to speed on the day she and Nick spent with Kevin and Liz, then continued, "He went to their house the morning after our second, um, interlude. He said he'd only be gone a few days, and that was a week ago. A week is a lot more than a *few* days."

"He hasn't called?"

"We never exchanged cell numbers."

"So you think he's avoiding you."

Jamie picked up another small shell. "It's crossed my mind. He certainly wouldn't be the first guy who wanted to escape after sex."

"True—but that would make him a jerk, and I'm sensing you no longer think he is."

"I wish I did—it would make this so much easier. But darn it, Kate, I *like* him. Much more than I want to. Much more than is wise. And the more time I spend with him, the more I like him. And that scares me. I just got out of a relationship, which, as you know, ended badly. I don't want another one. I don't want to feel so strongly about any man, most especially one who I'll be leaving behind in three weeks when I return to New York."

"Jamie, honey, that's what airports are for. Maybe the timing isn't perfect, but you know what? I don't think it ever is. God knows I wasn't looking to fall in love when I met Ben. I'd just started working at the hospital, my career required all my attention, and boom—Mr. Right walked in the door. He still had the bar exam to study for and pass, so the timing sucked all the way around. Ben and I are proof that if you're both committed to making it work, it can happen."

"Yes, but you and Ben are in *love*. I'm just a little bit too much in *like*."

"Which is only a heartbeat away from being in love."

"But I don't *want* to be in love," Jamie wailed. "He lives seven hundred miles away. A long-distance relationship just isn't feasible. Once I return to New York—you know how things are at work. I'll barely have time to breathe, let alone be flying down here. Before I came here this summer, I hadn't taken a vacation in three years—not since my dad died. Things won't be any different when I go back."

"They could be—if you changed them."

"I've tried to change things at Newman's but my mother refuses."

"Then you need to change *her*. What happened to the strong, independent woman who went to Seaside Cove to reassess and recharge so she could take charge?"

Jamie paused and stared out at the ocean. "She got overrun by her family and confused by her feelings for a man who dazzled her and made her like him enough to get naked with him, and whom she hasn't seen since."

"I hate to ask, but is there any chance he didn't think the sex was as great as you did?"

"Not unless he gave an Academy Award–winning performance. Based on his, um, enthusiasm, he found it as good as I did."

"Yet you think he's avoiding you."

Jamie raked a hand through her windblown hair. "I don't know what to think. Maybe he *wasn't* as satisfied as I believed. When I left his house that last night . . . the way he looked at me . . ."

"How?"

"I don't know how to describe it. Sort of a combination of 'I don't want you to go' and 'holy crap, I can't wait for you to get the hell out of here.' "

"Ah-ha!" said Kate, her voice filled with triumph. "He *is* avoiding you! And not because he thought the sex was bad, but because it was stupendous."

Jamie frowned. "That doesn't even make sense. What sort of man avoids you because the sex is stupendous?"

"A man who is no longer viewing it as 'just sex.' A man whose heart is becoming involved."

Jamie halted as if she'd walked into a wall of glass and her heart began thumping in fast, hard beats. "You think?"

"Jamie, from everything you've told me, it sounds like he cares. And if this thing between the two of you scares *you*, isn't it possible it scares him as well?"

"He doesn't seem like the sort who scares easily."

"Well, neither are you. But here's a news flash—love scares everybody."

Jamie felt a strong need to sit down. "Who said anything about love?" she asked, unable to keep panic from edging into her voice. "I've been talking about *like*. Only like."

"Uh-huh. Which leads to love."

"Which leads to heartache."

"Or to happiness—as Ben and I can attest."

"Not for two people who live seven hundred miles apart, Kate. Sure, it sounds all romantic and possible, but the harsh reality is it simply could never work. I couldn't keep a relationship going with a man who only lived two subway stops away."

"Uh, that would be because he was a cheating asshole, not because of where he lived."

"We'd never see each other. The relationship would just die a slow, painful death." And that, she knew, would really break her heart. "I called you to talk me *out* of this impossible, can-only-lead-to-heartbreak relationship. I have to say, you're really not helping."

"Probably because I'm not convinced it's impossible and

I'd hate to see you give up on something that could be exactly what you've been looking for."

"What I've been looking for is peace and quiet. Have I found it here? Ha! All I've gotten so far is a bombardment of the very people and sort of drama I was trying to get away from, and a guy who has me totally bewildered and out of sorts."

"At least you enjoyed a bunch of orgasms."

"Yes—which is one reason I'm so bewildered and out of sorts."

"You never did say how many orgasms it was."

"A lot. And again—not helping."

Kate's sigh came through the phone. "Fine. I can't deny you have a point—long-distance relationships rarely work out. And a quick, final break is preferable to the slow, painful fading of feelings that occurs when a relationship dies."

"Thank you."

"Which means you have two choices."

"Right. I can cut this off right now—assuming Nick hasn't already decided to do so."

"Or you can just keep reminding yourself that this is only a temporary fling, quit worrying about anything beyond the next three weeks, and enjoy yourself for the time you're still there."

"And then say good-bye and resume my life in New York."

"Exactly. Just be sure you check your heart at the door."

"Great advice. Except . . . what if it's too late about the checking-my-heart-at-the-door thing?"

"Then you're shit out of luck. If it were me, I'd take my chances and go the fling route. Odds are just as good that instead of falling madly in love over the next three weeks, you'll find out your first impression was correct and he really is nothing more than a pain in the ass. Hell, it might only take you three days—or three hours—to decide that."

"That's true," Jamie said, brightening at the thought. "Assuming he ever comes back to Seaside Cove."

"If he doesn't, it's his loss and you'll know he's utterly foul. Feel better?"

"Yes."

"Good. So there's no need for me to come down there and kick your butt?"

Jamie chuckled. "No. And as much as I'd love to see you, there's absolutely no room for you. Now tell me about your cruise."

"Lots of sun, food, dancing, relaxing, and sex. And speaking of sex, my handsome husband just walked in the door after a hard day of lawyering, so I'm going to—"

"I don't need details," Jamie said with a laugh. "Have fun. Thanks for the girl talk. Love you."

"Love you, too. And that have-fun thing? Same goes."

Jamie slipped her phone into the pocket of her shorts and realized she'd walked much farther down the beach than she'd anticipated and Oy Vey Mama Mia was just ahead. Unable to resist the lure of the place, she headed toward the wooden stairs that led to the ocean-facing patio. As soon as she reached the top, she was greeted by a beaming Maria.

"*Ciao, bella!* How lovely to see you! It seems like forever since you were here." Maria engulfed her in a warm embrace, then kissed her on each cheek. When she pulled back, her eyes immediately filled with concern. "But what is wrong, *cara*? Something is troubling you." Before Jamie could answer, Maria shouted, "Ira! Jamie is here and needs an *aperitivo*. A *negroni, por favore*. One for me as well." She turned back to Jamie. "The *negroni*—it will make whatever ails you feel better. The restaurant is quiet—that lull between lunch and dinner, so we can talk. Come." She pulled Jamie to a table in the corner and sat. "Tell Maria what is happening and why you haven't been to the restaurant for so long."

Since she wasn't about to confide about getting naked with Nick, she forced aside all thoughts of him and said, "Nothing's wrong, I've just been busy with my visitors." She'd just finished telling her about Heather's unexpected arrival when Ira bustled outside bearing a tray holding two glasses decorated with slices of orange peel.

"Hello, my dahling," Ira said, setting down the tray on the table, then giving Jamie's cheek a smacking kiss. "I brought you ladies something to nosh on—a little whitefish salad, a little smoked salmon, and some prosciutto and Italian olives—I call it Israeli antipasto. Enjoy." He dropped a kiss on his wife's head, then returned through the sliding screen door into the main restaurant.

They each picked up their drink and Maria clicked her glass to Jamie's. "*Salud!*" she toasted, then tossed back a healthy mouthful.

Figuring *when in Rome*, Jamie followed suit. And her eyes glazed over as the drink slid down her throat, filling her with what felt like liquid fire. "Delicious," she proclaimed, "but potent. What's in this?"

"Gin, vermouth, and Campari," Maria said, taking another swallow. "Two of them and your troubles disappear."

"Two of them and I'll be unconscious," Jamie said with a laugh.

"*Mangia,*" Maria said, pushing the tray of food closer to Jamie. "And continue telling me about your niece."

Jamie continued, all the while sipping on the delicious, seductive *negroni* and nibbling on the noshes. Whether it was the alcohol, or Maria's gentle prodding, the next thing Jamie knew she'd told Maria all about her situation with Laurel. When she finished, she shook her head—which felt decidedly fuzzy. "Heavens. This *negroni* is like truth serum."

Maria laughed. "That it is. It is also good for putting you in the mood for the *amore*." She squeezed Jamie's hands. "It is a good thing you do for your niece. An unselfish thing. It speaks well of you, *cara*. As for your sister, I understand your anger toward her. I had a similar problem with my own sister when we both liked the same boy in our youth."

"What happened?"

"Lucia and I, we exchanged many harsh words. In the end, Paolo chose her. I was devastated. But this tragedy, it was a blessing, for six months later I met my Ira. For those six months my heart was closed to her. To everyone. It did not open again until I met Ira. My love for him let me lose my anger toward Lucia. Because if not for her, I would have been with Paolo, who *portare male gli anni*—he does not age well." She squeezed Jamie's hands. "My mama used to tell me that anger poisons the person who holds it. Forgiveness sets us free. Don't dwell on what Laurel did to you. Instead concentrate on finding your own happiness. And pity her, because now she is stuck with that *bischero*."

Jamie wasn't sure what a *bischero* was, but since it was describing Raymond, she knew it wasn't complimentary.

"You haven't mentioned Nico," Maria said with a hoisted brow. "Ah, I mention his name and your eyes, they light up *veloce come un razzo*—fast as a rocket. The same way his eyes lit up when I said your name to him an hour ago."

Jamie's fingers tightened on her empty glass. "An hour ago?"

Maria nodded. "He came in for a late lunch. He seemed anxious to get home." She smiled slyly. "To see you maybe?"

Jamie's heart leaped at the thought. "Not likely. But home is where I need to head myself. My mother, Alex, and Heather probably think I ran away."

"You did. For a little while. And that is allowed. You come back soon and bring your family. This week's dinner specials are rigatoni pesto and corned beef on rye."

"I'll do that," Jamie promised. "And thanks for the pep talk." After exchanging hugs, Jamie headed back to the beach for the long walk to Paradise Lost, convincing herself the entire way that the spinning in her head was courtesy of the *negroni* and had nothing whatsoever to do with the fact that Nick was back.

Chapter 23

Nick stood on his screen porch and looked toward Paradise Lost, where lights blazed in all the windows. In spite of the desire to go over there that had nearly choked him since the minute he'd arrived home, he'd forced himself to remain at Southern Comfort. After all, he needed to shower. Sort through his snail mail. Check his e-mail and pay a few bills online. Feed Godiva. Put out food for the feral cats. Yeah—he had plenty of stuff to do.

When he'd finished all that, he ate a peanut butter and jelly sandwich even though he wasn't particularly hungry. He'd even gone so far as to wash the plate and knife he'd used and to make his bed. Then he'd forced himself to stay at home another hour. Just to prove he could. That he didn't have to go racing next door to see her. After all, she hadn't raced over here to see him. She had to know he was home—there was no missing his truck in Southern Comfort's carport.

Unless . . . maybe she didn't know he was home. Because maybe *she* wasn't home. Maybe while he'd been hiding out at Kevin's she'd met some other guy. Maybe she was out on a date.

His every muscle tensed and a red haze seemed to fog his

vision at the thought of her being with someone else. She was *his* fling, damn it.

That's it—I'm done. He'd proven he could stay away from her, so what the hell was he still doing here? He strode into the kitchen and rummaged around for a minute, coming up with a six-pack of beer—for those old enough to drink and who weren't pregnant—and a bag of Doritos. Gripping his offerings, he whistled for Godiva and together they headed to Paradise Lost.

As he climbed the stairs leading to the kitchen door, Maggie's voice drifted through the screen. "The cake is cool enough to frost, Jamie. Where are the candles?"

She's home. He refused to examine the ridiculous level of relief that washed through him.

"I don't know, Mom," came Jamie's reply. "Where did you put them?"

"*I* didn't put them anywhere."

"You didn't put them away along with the other things you bought at Walmart?"

"I didn't buy candles at Walmart."

"Why not?" Jamie asked, a hint of impatience in her voice. "I'd written it on the shopping list."

"Is that what you'd written? I thought it said 'candies.'" Maggie gave a laugh that sounded forced. "So—no candles. Sorry. But there's a giant bag of peanut M&M's if you'd like some."

"Unless we can light them on fire, they're not really going to work."

"We don't need candles," came Heather's tight voice. "Really, you guys. It's fine."

Nick reached the top of the stairs. Through the screen door he saw Jamie, Maggie, and Heather standing in the kitchen, all staring at an unfrosted chocolate cake on a plate. Alex sat slumped on the sofa in the living area, his gaze glued to the TV, where a baseball game was in progress.

With his attention fixed on Jamie's profile, Nick knocked. In the back of his mind, it registered that four heads turned toward the door, but his gaze locked with Jamie's and damned if for a split second it didn't seem as if his lungs forgot how to work.

"It's Nick," Heather said, her voice sounding . . . relieved?

He watched Jamie approach the door and the heat and desire he'd managed to hold at bay for the last week rippled through him. Damn, he loved the way she moved. He could just watch the woman *walk* for hours. When she opened the door, he immediately noticed the strained look in her eyes. Stress radiated off her like laser beams. The smile she offered him appeared tired. "Hi."

"Hi," he said. "Godiva saw the lights on and wanted to stop by. You know, to see if you had any dead clams she could rub herself in. I figured I'd tag along." *You know, in case I could rub against you.* He held up the six-pack and the Doritos. "We brought snacks." When she hesitated, he added, "If this is a bad time—"

"Not at all. In fact, your timing is perfect." She sounded sincere and a bit of the tension in her eyes faded. She moved back so he could enter. "C'mon in. We're almost ready for cake."

He smiled. "Then we agree—perfect timing."

He stepped into the kitchen, followed by Godiva, who made a beeline for Cupcake's food and water bowls. She sucked up the handful of kibbles like a vacuum cleaner, helped herself to a few splashy slurps of water, then began a tail-wagging, sniffing exploration, no doubt looking for Cupcake so she could bestow upon her some kibble-scented drool. Good times.

Nick exchanged greetings with Maggie, who looked pale and exhausted, and with Heather, whose eyes behind her glasses were suspiciously bright, as if she were holding back tears.

Alex ambled in from the living area, and there was no missing the relief on his face. "Glad to have another guy in the house," he said, shaking Nick's hand. "I'm severely outnumbered around here. I mean even the *cat* is a female."

"Glad to help." Nick nodded toward the TV. "Who's playing?"

"Yankees and Red Sox. Yanks are up four to three in the fifth." Alex eyed the six-pack of beer Nick had set on the counter. "You sharing that?"

"You bet." He handed Alex a beer, then looked at the trio of females, all of whom were staring at him. He could actually see the tension shimmering in the air and wondered what the hell was going on.

He tilted his head toward the cake and waded into the awkward silence. "Special occasion?"

Jamie cleared her throat and smiled. "Today is Heather's birthday."

Nick turned to Heather and smiled. "Happy birthday." He handed her the bag of Doritos. "From Godiva. They're not much, but the best she could do on short notice."

A shy smile ghosted across Heather's flaming face and she dipped her chin. "Thanks." She looked up and tucked her hair behind her ear. "You were gone a long time. The float's nearly finished."

"Yeah? You been painting?"

Heather nodded. "Me and a bunch of other kids. It's pretty cool."

"I can't wait to see it." He sniffed the air. "It smells like a bakery in here." His gaze cut toward the cake. "And that looks delicious."

"It's not frosted yet," Heather said, sounding agitated. Her gaze bounced between Jamie and Maggie, then returned to Nick. "You want to help?"

"Sure—if you don't mind a crappy-looking birthday cake. The only thing I know about frosting is how to eat it."

"Then you're in the right place," said Jamie, with what appeared to be a genuine smile, "because we whipped up a double batch of it."

"Hey, hey, you ladies all have each other, so I'm calling dibs on the only other male company. C'mon, Nick, grab a beer and let's watch the game. You a Yankees fan?"

"Cubs."

Alex grimaced, but said, "At least you're not a Sox fan, so the invite stands."

"Thanks. I take it you're a Yankees fan?"

"Lifelong. Got the season tickets to prove it. You go to Wrigley Field often?"

"I went to a few games, when I lived in Chicago." He wasn't about to share that he'd viewed those games from the comfort of his own luxury box suite. Just one more thing he'd sold when he'd walked away from his former life.

"Go ahead," Jamie urged, shooing him out of the kitchen. "There's not enough room in here for you anyway. Too many cooks and all that."

"First time I've ever been called a cook, but fine. And I want extra frosting on my piece of cake." He looked at Heather. "Make sure I'm fixed up, okay?"

She giggled. "Done."

"I'll bring you the spatula to lick when we're finished," Jamie said.

He looked into her eyes and didn't make any attempt to hide the fact that he'd rather lick her—and that he had every intention of doing so at his first opportunity. Given the crimson that rushed into her cheeks, she saw the desire he knew burned in his gaze.

"I'll look forward to that," he said with a grin. Then he turned to Alex. "Be right there. First I need to see what Godiva is up to."

"I think she went out on the porch," Maggie said.

"Thanks." Nick crossed the living area. The sliding doors leading to the screen porch that ran the entire length of the front of the house were pushed open. He stepped onto the dark porch and waited several seconds for his eyes to adjust to the darkness. Then he grinned.

He looked into the house. Alex sat on the sofa, beer in hand, his full attention focused on the game. Maggie and Heather were busy frosting the cake. His gaze then settled on Jamie—who was watching him. His pulse quickened and he crooked his finger at her.

She crossed the room, then stepped out onto the porch. "Did you find—?"

"Shhh," Nick said, touching a finger to her lips and pulling her into the far corner of the porch where they couldn't be seen from the inside. He turned her so that she faced the opposite end of the porch, then stepped up to stand directly behind her.

"Look," he whispered in her ear, pointing toward the opposite corner, where Godiva lay sprawled on her side. Cupcake was curled against her, her head cushioned on Godiva's outstretched paw.

"Oh my God, that is so cute," Jamie whispered.

Just then Godiva lifted her head a fraction of an inch and licked Cupcake's head. The cat's purr filled the warm night air.

"Hey—your dog just licked my cat," she said, her whisper filled with suppressed laughter.

"Yeah, well it doesn't look like your cat is complaining."

He breathed in and the scent of cookies filled his senses. With a low groan he turned her around and pulled her flush against him. It required every bit of his will to hold back that part of him that wanted to press her to the wall and devour her in a single gulp.

He lowered his head and fire raced through him in anticipation of kissing her, but before he could, she settled her hands on his chest and leaned back. She hiked a brow and lightly nudged his pelvis with hers. "Either you're carrying a zucchini in your pocket or you're glad to see me."

"It's a zucchini. I was hoping we could have that cooking lesson you promised me weeks ago."

"I see." She eased from his embrace and cast a glance at the nearby open sliding door, through which a swath of light and the sounds of the baseball game drifted. "As I'm sure you can tell, this isn't the time. Or place."

"I know." His gaze searched hers. "Something's wrong."

She expelled a slow, heavy breath. "Just a lot of tension in there," she said, nodding toward the house. "Heather's been moody and upset all day. A birthday phone call from her dad didn't go well—he expects her to visit him next week and she doesn't want to go. A call from her mother didn't go much better."

She rubbed her temples as if warding off a headache, then continued in a whispered rush, "My mother is still a hormonal mess—laughing one minute, crying the next. I swear she's worse than Heather. Plus, my mom is, hands-down, the most indecisive person on the planet. She *still* doesn't know what to do about Alex, and even though I've repeatedly told her only she can decide, it's clear she still wants me to tell her what to do.

"Poor Alex deserves a medal for his patience. He needs to get back to his job in New York, but he doesn't want to leave here until things are settled with my mom. He actually doesn't want to leave her, period, which I find amazing because she makes me want to run shrieking from the house. One night he's sleeping on the sofa, the next he's in Mom's bedroom . . . it's like an emotional roller coaster I can't avoid because it's right in front of me. Then the stress of trying to shield Heather from all the turmoil—it's enough to give anyone a migraine."

Unable to not touch her, he reached out and linked his fingers with hers. "I'm sorry."

"Me, too. I laid down the law with Mom this morning and told her she needed to suck it up, set aside her problems for today, and put on a happy face for Heather's birthday. I know she's trying, but she doesn't feel well and she's upset with Alex for God only knows what reason, and with me because she feels I'm not being understanding. Heather's picking up on it all, so she's tense as well as moody."

She shook her head. "Personally, I like Alex's method of dealing with the tension—watch TV, drink beer, and try to ignore it all. If it wasn't for Heather, that's exactly what I'd do." After heaving a sigh, she shot him a sheepish smile. "Bet you're really glad you came over, huh?"

"Actually, I am." He gently squeezed her hands. "I missed you." He hadn't necessarily meant to say that, but the words slipped out before he could stop them. He pressed his lips together before anything else could fall out. Like *I thought about you constantly.* Or *I want you so badly right now I'm ready to just pick you up, carry you off, and to hell with all those people in there.*

She flicked another glance toward the open door. Then her gaze searched his. "You were gone longer than just a few days."

He clearly saw the questions in her eyes. And the confusion. And, unless he was mistaken, a hint of hurt. "There was more to handle at Kevin's than I thought." True—although far from the whole truth. "But now I'm back. And I'm here." He raised their joined hands and pressed a kiss to her soft palm. "And I'm hoping that's okay."

When she didn't immediately answer, an unpleasant sensation that felt like an all-over body cramp seized him. She was still looking at him in silence when headlight beams arced over them. She squinted in the sudden brightness and turned her head toward the street.

Nick looked as well. A yellow taxi stopped in front of Paradise Lost in the circle of light cast by the street lamp. The back door opened and a bright red high heel with a matching sole emerged, followed by a long, slim feminine leg encased in expensive-looking denim. The other leg followed, and seconds later a tall, willowy blonde stood next to the curb alongside a huge suitcase while the driver unloaded several more bags from the trunk.

"Oh. My. God."

Jamie's horrified whisper had him turning quickly toward her. Her hands were fisted and pressed to her midsection and her face looked ghostly pale as she stared at the woman who was now pulling one of her rolled suitcases toward the driveway.

He stepped in front of her and grabbed her by the shoulders. Concern filled him when he felt a tremor rack her entire body. "What's wrong? Who is that?" he asked, although he had a sinking feeling he knew.

"That," she said, sounding as if she spit the word, "is Laurel. My *loving* sister."

Chapter 24

With her heart beating in hard, painful thumps and feeling as if she were slogging through thick, invisible Jell-O, Jamie moved on leaden feet toward the open sliding door. She stepped into the living area. And halted. At the sight of Laurel entering her kitchen.

As always, her sister looked stunning. Tall, slim, and casually elegant in her dark skinny jeans and crisp white sleeveless top, her thick, straight, glossy golden blond hair brushing her shoulders, not suffering a bit of frizz in the humid summer heat. Her designer platform pumps added a good five inches to her already enviable height, made her legs look like they reached the ceiling, and undoubtedly cost more than all the shoes in Jamie's closet combined. Jamie wasn't up on the latest hot designer handbag, but she was certain the gorgeous mahogany leather purse hanging in the crook of Laurel's arm was one with a waiting list. She exuded wealth and status, and wore the Upper East Side mantle she'd been given at the age of nine by her stepfather as if she were to the manor born. Rich, gorgeous, tall, skinny . . . if Jamie hadn't loved her, it would have been soooo easy to hate her.

But Laurel's betrayal had irrevocably changed and damaged that love.

And now she was here. Invading the sanctuary Jamie had tried to create for herself. Bringing with her the drama she'd traveled seven hundred miles to escape. Resentment and anger bubbled inside her until she felt like a volcano on the verge of eruption.

Jamie pulled in an unsteady breath. She felt Nick come to stand behind her. He rested a hand on her shoulder in a silent show of support she appreciated and desperately needed. She did not want to lose her composure, but God, she was teetering on the edge of screaming. Of striding across the room and ordering her sister to get the hell out. If not for Heather's presence, that's exactly what she would have done. She could only pray that her love for Heather would win out over her anger toward Laurel.

It was going to be a very, very close fight.

As Jamie walked toward the kitchen, she took in the tableau before her. Her mom—face pale, frozen in place, glaring at Laurel with the look of a mother bear protecting its cub. Alex—his arm around her mother's shoulders, looking both concerned and uncomfortable. Heather—wrapped in her mother's embrace, her expression a dumbfounded, vulnerable combination of *Wow, I can't believe you're here!* and *Oh, God, why on earth are you here?* that twisted Jamie's heart. And finally Laurel, standing in Jamie's kitchen, hugging Heather as if she had every right to be there.

In an effort to locate her voice, Jamie cleared her throat. At the sound, Laurel released Heather, and her gaze collided with Jamie's.

Anger and hurt exploded in Jamie's chest. She fisted her hands in an effort to keep her voice calm. "What are you doing here?"

The words were indeed calm, but there was no missing the icy chill in her tone. The question hovered in the air between them for several seconds, then Laurel offered a half smile that appeared uncharacteristically uncertain. "Hi. I'm here for Heather's birthday." Her blue-eyed gaze remained steady on Jamie's, filled with an imploring expression Jamie had never seen from her sister before. "I know you weren't expecting me, but I hope it's okay that I came. I didn't want to miss Heather's special day."

Jamie barely swallowed the bitter *No, it's not okay* that rushed into her throat. And forced herself to remember what was really important. Heather. "Whatever makes Heather happy."

There was no mistaking the gratitude in Laurel's eyes—or the surprise that rippled through Jamie at seeing it there.

"Thank you," said Laurel. She turned to Jamie's mom. "Hi, Maggie." After a brief hesitation, she walked to where Jamie's mom stood like a statue and gave her a quick, awkward hug—one that wasn't returned. Laurel stepped quickly back and slid her hands into her jean pockets. "How are you? Patrick mentioned you'd come to visit Jamie. I hope you're enjoying your stay."

"I'm fine, thank you," Jamie's mom answered, her words clipped and frosty. "And yes, I'm enjoying my stay."

Silence swelled, broken only by the muted sounds of the baseball game. Laurel's smile faltered and her gaze shifted to Alex. Recognition, followed by surprise, dawned on her face. "Alex? Alex Wharton? You did the kitchen renovations at Newman's."

Alex nodded. The fact that he didn't appear confused at the thick tension permeating the air made it clear her mother had told him about Jamie and Laurel's strained relationship. "Hello, Miss Newman."

Laurel held out her hand. "Please, call me Laurel." After Alex shook her hand, Laurel asked, "What brings you to Seaside Cove?"

"He's Maggie's boyfriend," Heather said, charging into the electric silence. "And that's Nick," she added, pointing to where he'd moved to stand next to Jamie. His shoulder touched hers and his big palm rested on the small of her back, a firm, steadying heat Jamie greatly appreciated. "He lives next door."

Laurel approached Jamie and Nick, her gaze flicking down to take in his hand resting on her back. Something Jamie couldn't decipher flashed in her eyes—surprise, maybe. Then she offered him a friendly smile and extended her hand. Jamie stiffened, fighting the urge to slap away those perfectly manicured fingers.

"Hi, Nick. Nice to meet you. I'm Laurel—Heather's mom and Jamie's sister. You own the beautiful chocolate lab. I saw the photos Heather posted on Facebook."

Nick's left palm gave Jamie's back what she assumed was meant as a reassuring rub while he shook Laurel's proffered hand. "Hello. Yes, Godiva is my dog."

Laurel laughed. "Great name for a chocolate lab." Then a tiny frown burrowed between her brows and she tilted her head, studying him. "You look vaguely familiar. Have we ever met? Perhaps at Newman's?"

Nick shook his head. "I've never been."

"At a charity event maybe? Or a gallery opening? Party in the Hamptons?"

"Nick doesn't attend the sort of events you do," Jamie broke in, her tone just this side of icy.

Laurel shifted her attention to her. "My mistake," she said softly. She hesitated, then reached out and gave Jamie a quick one-armed hug that Jamie barely managed to endure without wincing. When Laurel stepped back, she offered Jamie a shaky smile. "It's good to see you."

Jamie greeted that remark with stony silence and a cold glare. Then she caught sight of Heather over Laurel's shoulder. Her niece's eyes were big and watchful behind her glasses, and once again recalling what was important, Jamie forced herself to say, "We were just about to have birthday cake."

Without another word she stepped around Laurel and headed toward the kitchen. She offered Heather what she hoped passed for a genuine smile, then asked, "Shall I put on a pot of coffee?"

"I'm good with beer," said Alex. "In fact, I think I'll have another one." He turned to Nick. "You want one?"

"Sure. But coffee sounds good with the cake."

"I'll stick with water," said Jamie's mom.

"Coffee's fine for me," said Laurel. She turned to Heather. "Milk for you?"

"I'm not a baby anymore, Mom. I can have coffee if I want," Heather challenged.

"Another coffee it is," Laurel said mildly.

Jamie busied herself with the coffee preparations and pretended her blood wasn't boiling. She scooped fragrant grounds into the filter, trying to concentrate on the task, but her attention was fixed on the conversation going on behind her.

"So what have you been up to, honey?"

From the corner of her eye, Jamie saw Heather shrug. "Just going to the beach and stuff."

"I brought you a present." Jamie turned and watched Laurel reach into her handbag. She withdrew a rectangular robin's egg blue box garnished with a white satin ribbon. The distinctive color of the box marked it as being from Tiffany's.

Twin spots of color stained Heather's cheeks. She took the box and frowned. "Thanks, Mom, but I don't need another bracelet."

"I know. But I'm hoping you'll like this."

Heather shrugged, then untied the satin ribbon and lifted the lid. And stared. "It's a . . . pen." Jamie didn't think her niece could have sounded more stunned. She lifted the slim writing instrument that was the same iconic Tiffany's color as the box it came in and ran her finger over the glossy enamel surface.

"I know how much you enjoy writing," Laurel said, skimming her hand over Heather's hair. "I wanted you to have a special pen. To write your special words. And since turquoise is your favorite color . . ."

Heather didn't say anything for several seconds. Then she very carefully put the pen back in its bed of satin and set the box on the counter. Then she leaned in and gave Laurel's cheek a quick kiss.

"Thanks, Mom. It's really cool."

"You're welcome." Laurel blinked back what looked to Jamie like tears, then smiled brightly. "Can I do anything to help?"

Jamie's brow shot upward. Anything to help? *Laurel?* Ha! Laurel who was accustomed to five-star service everywhere she went? Who lived in a ritzy Fifth Avenue apartment—the best her stepdad's money could buy? Jamie barely refrained from asking, *Okay, who the hell are you and what have you done with Laurel?*

Instead she said, "Sure. We need plates, napkins, forks, and spoons. I'll take care of the coffee cups."

Laurel's gaze flew to the shabby cabinets as if seeing them for the first time. "Okay. I, um, don't know where anything is."

"I'll show you, Mom."

Whether it was just to fill the silence or because she felt like sharing, Heather told Laurel about the clam festival and the float. Jamie took the opportunity to suck in some much-needed calming breaths. Keeping her back to the rest of the kitchen, she pulled three mugs from the mismatched collection in the cabinet above her head, then watched the last of the coffee brew. Just as the final drops plunked into the glass carafe, a warm hand landed on her shoulder.

"You okay?" Nick asked in a voice only she could hear.

She wasn't. She felt as if she were hanging on to her emotions by the thinnest of threads that was stretched to the breaking point. Her skin itched with the need to get the hell out of there. Out of the house that was supposed to be her getaway. But how could she get away when everything she'd tried to distance herself from was now here? Crowding her. Closing in on her. God, she felt as if she were trapped in a coffin upon which everyone around her was tossing shovelfuls of dirt.

She wanted to tell Nick she was fine, but knew she'd never pass that whopper off as even partially true. "I've been better."

"You're doing great. Hang in there."

Forcing a smile, Jamie poured the coffee. Stuck one of the emergency candles she'd found her first night at Paradise Lost in the cake. Lit the wick. Sang the traditional song. Ate cake. Tried to keep the conversation from lapsing into awkward silences by telling about her visit to Oy Vey Mama Mia and her introduction to the *negroni*. The minutes passed as if she were on autopilot—the words coming out of her mouth, but she didn't really know how.

"I like the sound of the *negroni*," Laurel said, setting down her empty plate on the snack bar. She turned to Jamie. "Maybe we could take your friend's recipe and make it a drink special at Newman's."

"We're not looking to add anything new to Newman's menu right now," Jamie's mom said to Laurel in a cold, stiff voice before Jamie could reply. "And as for taking the recipe—haven't you taken enough things that don't belong to you?"

Silence, as thick as quicksand and just as suffocating, descended. All the color drained from Laurel's face.

Heather slammed her plate and fork onto the counter. Twin flags of color rose on her cheeks as her gaze scanned everyone. "That's it," she said, her voice shaking. "What's going on here? What's *wrong* with everyone? Do you think I'm stupid? Or blind? You're all pretending that everything is fine but it obviously isn't. Aunt Jamie's talking like a robot, Maggie looks totally pissed off, Alex and Nick have barely said a word, and Mom—I have no idea what's up with you." With each word her voice grew louder until she was yelling. "I know you're all pretending for my benefit and I *hate* it! I'm not a baby!"

She fixed her gaze on Laurel. "What did Maggie mean? What did you take?"

Laurel shook her head. "Nothing. I—"

"Why are you really here, Mom? And acting so . . . *nice*?"

Laurel looked as if she'd been slapped. "It's your birthday—"

"Like you care!"

Tears swam into Laurel's eyes. "Of course I care, Heather! I'm your mother—"

"Who for months has been too busy for me. So why are you really here? Why aren't you with your boyfriend? Did he dump you or something?"

Laurel's face paled even further. She swallowed, then jerked her head in a quick nod. "Yes." Her gaze flicked to Jamie. "As a matter of fact, he did."

Another thick silence descended, although Jamie missed it due to the buzzing in her ears. Raymond had dumped Laurel. That was . . . karma. Sickly funny. Completely ironic. And unheard of. Men didn't dump gorgeous, skinny, rich Laurel. Either it was a mutual parting of the ways, or she did the dumping. Her mother muttered something that sounded like, "What goes around . . ."

She looked at her sister and was surprised to note Laurel's hands were shaking and her bottom lip was quivering.

"Now I get it," Heather said with a harsh laugh. "You came because you had nothing better to do."

Laurel sucked in a breath. "That's not true. I came because I missed you. Because I wanted to see you on your birthday."

She reached out to touch her daughter, but Heather backed away. Laurel slowly lowered her hand and briefly squeezed her eyes shut. When she opened them, she said quietly, "You're angry. I get that. I'd like to talk with you about it—see if we can fix this rift between us. But not like this, when you're being deliberately hurtful. And not with an audience." She paused for an audibly shaky breath, then asked Heather, "Can we go for a walk? Maybe on the beach? And talk?"

Heather's bottom lip trembled, but her eyes were filled with mutiny. "Why, Mom? Whenever I talk, you never listen. So what's the point?"

"I'll listen," Laurel said. "I promise. Give me a chance." She reached out again and this time touched Heather's arm. "Please?"

Once more Jamie was tempted to blurt out *Who the hell are you and what have you done with Laurel?* "Please" was not a word she'd often heard pass Laurel's lips. Jamie wasn't convinced her sister was sincere, although there was no denying she *sounded* that way.

Heather's gaze cut to Jamie, clearly looking for guidance. Jamie nodded and mouthed, "Go. Try."

Heather rolled her eyes and heaved a put-upon sigh. "Fine. Whatever." She shot a scathing glance at her mother's shoes. "Too bad you don't have flip-flops."

"I have a pair of sneakers in one of my suitcases," Laurel said. "I left my luggage downstairs." She turned to look at Jamie. "I tried to book a room, but couldn't find anything available online. Is there somewhere nearby you can recommend?"

Jamie looked into Laurel's eyes. The unspoken question hung between them, as loud as if Laurel had shouted it. *Can I stay here?* And Jamie had to wonder why she hadn't asked. Actually, she wondered why Laurel hadn't simply *announced* she was staying. She normally took what she wanted—as evidenced by Raymond. This hesitant, diffident Laurel— who'd been *dumped*—was someone Jamie was having trouble recognizing.

Still, here was her chance. Her opportunity to say, *Too bad, there's no room available here, either, you backstabber. Have your talk with your daughter, then get back on your broom and fly home to New York.*

But she couldn't say it. Maybe she could—to her sister, if they'd been alone. But she simply couldn't to Heather's mother—especially not in front of Heather. So clearly she'd have to take one for the team.

Shit.

But that didn't mean she needed to stick around and endure Laurel's company. She'd come to see Heather and Jamie wouldn't stand in the way of that, but that's as far as she'd go. There might not be another place for her sister to stay—but there was for Jamie.

"Everything around here is completely booked," Jamie said. "There are twin beds in Heather's room. You can stay in there with her."

"But then where will you sleep, Aunt Jamie?" Heather asked.

"Nick has a spare bedroom." She turned to him. "Mind if I make use of it?"

"Not at all."

She honestly expected Laurel to wrinkle her nose at the less-than-five-star accommodations, but instead she nodded and said quietly, "Thank you, Jamie. I appreciate it."

Jamie frowned. Seriously, who *was* this person? She could not recall ever before hearing those six words pass Laurel's lips. She gave her sister a long look and noticed for the first time the pale violet smudges of fatigue under her eyes. She looked tired and drawn—totally out of character for her normally inexhaustible sister, who could party hop and schmooze until the wee hours and then show up at Newman's the next day looking as if she'd just spent hours at a day spa—which she probably had.

Laurel's gaze bounced between Alex and Nick. "Do you think one of you guys could help me get my luggage up those stairs?"

Alex glanced at Maggie, who shrugged. "Sure. I'll give you a hand."

Needing a moment alone with her mother, Jamie turned to Nick. "Would you mind helping them?"

"Not at all." He gave her hand a quick squeeze and then followed Laurel and Alex outside, the screen door slapping closed behind them.

"This sure turned into a strange birthday," Heather grumbled. She looked at Jamie. "Is Mom acting weird or is it just me?"

Not just you. But in an effort to help her niece, Jamie said, "I think she's really trying to make an effort. So meet her halfway. She said she'd listen. So talk. Calmly. Tell her how you feel, everything that's bothering you. Then return the courtesy and listen to her. And try to remember—just because you disagree with someone doesn't mean you have to be disagreeable. She's your mom and deserves some respect, okay?" Jamie gave her a quick hug. "Love you, kiddo."

"Fine, whatever, love you, too," Heather mumbled, her face burning bright. "I need to grab my flip-flops and text Lindsey before the big mother-daughter beach walk. Yippee." She walked into the bedroom she'd shared with Jamie and would tonight share with her mother and closed the door.

The instant the door closed, Maggie turned to Jamie and said in her loud whisper that wasn't at all a whisper, "I can't believe you said she could stay here."

Jamie's last nerve stretched to the breaking point. "What was I supposed to do, Mom? She's Heather's mother and today's her birthday. And that comment you made about Laurel taking things that aren't hers—"

"Was completely true."

"I know. And I appreciate your loyalty, but please don't do it again. For Heather's sake. It's not your place, or mine, to say anything to drive a wedge between them."

"Laurel seems to have managed that all by herself."

"Yes. But it seems she's trying to fix that. For Heather's sake, I hope so. And for Heather's sake I don't want to interfere with that in any way."

"You're being extremely understanding about all this, I must say."

"No, I'm not. I'd like to toss her out on her skinny ass and tell her to never darken my doorstep again. My stomach's tied in knots, my head is pounding, my skin feels hot and blotchy, and I'm a heartbeat away from screaming and ripping out handfuls of my hair. But my love for Heather is stronger than my anger toward Laurel." She pulled in a shaky breath, then continued, "But I'm not staying in this house with her."

"So you're abandoning me? Why do *I* have to entertain her? I have enough of my own problems to deal with."

Jamie pressed her fingers to her temple to ward off the headache brewing there. "You don't have to entertain her. She'll be out with Heather and then they'll be sleeping on the opposite side of the house. Take your man and go to bed."

Her mom's lips tightened. "I wasn't planning to sleep with Alex tonight. We had a disagreement. Which I wanted to talk to you about. He's asked me to *marry* him. What do you think I should do?"

That question snapped Jamie's last frayed nerve and the composure she'd fought to hold on to disintegrated. "Here's what *I think*, Mom," she said, her voice low and throbbing with all the frustration she'd been holding in for what felt like forever. "*I think* I traveled seven hundred miles to take some much-needed time for myself. To solve my *own* problems. To get some perspective on my *own* life. And instead I've had to deal first with you and your drama, then your boyfriend, then a teenager, and worst of all, now my sister, who is the one person I most needed to get away from.

"*I think* that you've leaned on me so much since Daddy died that you've forgotten how to stand on your own. Do you have any idea how much pressure that puts on me? It's absolutely exhausting. *I think*—and I've lost count of how many times I've told you this since you barged into what was supposed to be my peaceful haven—that only you can decide what you want and what is best for you. I will support whatever that decision is, and frankly, I don't see what the hell is so difficult. If you love Alex, then be with him. If you don't love him, tell him so and let the poor guy go. And for God's sake, quit expecting me to make your decisions for you because I'm *done*."

Without another word she stalked to the door and hurried down the stairs. Alex, Nick, and Laurel were halfway up with Laurel's luggage, but she didn't pause. She squeezed around them on the staircase, mumbled good night, and kept going, praying that she'd make it to Southern Comfort before her shaking knees gave out and the tears thickening her throat and pushing behind her eyes burst through.

She took the stairs at Southern Comfort two at a time and

relief filled her that Nick hadn't locked his door. She let herself in and paced the length of the house, trying to corral the tumult of emotions battering her.

God, she felt so . . . frustrated. Tense. On edge. And so damn tired of dealing with everyone and their issues. She craved a reprieve. A break from the drama and stress.

Footfalls sounded on the stairs. The door opened and Godiva dashed in, followed by Nick. Nick, who'd offered support and friendship and concern. Whose steady presence had made the unbearable tension at Paradise Lost somehow bearable.

Their gazes met and a bolt of desire unlike anything she'd ever felt before struck her. The need to touch him, be touched by him, feel his hands and mouth on her, hers on him crashed over her, stealing her breath. With her gaze steady on his, she walked toward him. Based on the fire that flared in his eyes, her intent was obvious. And fine with him.

When she reached him, she wound her arms around his neck and pressed herself against him. And was gratified to note he was already hard.

"Want you," she whispered, grazing his neck with her teeth. "Need you. *Now.*"

Based on the speed with which he swept her into his arms and carried her to his bedroom, they were once again in agreement.

Chapter 25

The first thing Nick became aware of when he awoke was the lush feminine body fitted against him. With his eyes still closed, he shifted closer to the soft warmth and nestled his morning erection more firmly against the delicious curve of Jamie's bare bottom. He breathed deeply, filling his head with the delicious scent of fresh-baked cookies.

She stirred, and his arm automatically tightened around her waist. He skimmed his hand up her torso to fill his palm with the softness of her breast. His thumb lightly circled her velvety nipple, which instantly pebbled beneath his touch.

He briefly slit one eye open. Sunlight streamed through the windows, announcing the arrival of morning. The morning after another incredible night with Jamie. The intensity of their lovemaking had blown him away. He'd had great sex before. This was better than that. *More* than that. More . . . intimate. Even more so than the last time they'd been together, and that had been pretty damn spectacular. Yet last night had been even better. He couldn't explain how, he only knew it had been.

And now as he lay with her in his arms, listening to her deep, even breaths, the troubling thoughts he'd shoved aside last night came roaring back, and he knew they could no longer be ignored.

He had to tell her the truth.

With a sigh, he eased away from her and slid from the bed. Stepping over their scattered clothes, he unconsciously counted the empty condom wrappers littering the floor as he headed toward the bathroom. One, two, three, four . . . Jesus, five of them. And that fifth time . . . damn. That fifth time—so slow and lazy and deep—had left him shaking. And feeling as if he'd emptied his soul into her.

But he hadn't. There were parts of his soul, or at least his past, he hadn't revealed. And he needed to fix that. Before things went any further.

After making use of the bathroom and brushing his teeth, he slipped on a clean pair of boxer briefs, then made his way to the kitchen. Godiva greeted him with tail-wagging joy, and after giving her a good rubdown, he opened the door and she scrambled down the stairs and headed for her favorite patch of grass. He put on a pot of coffee, and as the kitchen filled with the scent of fresh-brewed java, he changed Godiva's water bowl and opened a can of her favorite dog food. When she gave a quiet woof at the screen, he let her in and couldn't help but grin when she practically inhaled her breakfast.

"You don't see Cupcake doing that," came Jamie's amused voice from behind him.

He turned and his heart kicked at the sight of her. With her tousled hair, eyes still a bit droopy with sleep, and wearing one of his white T-shirts, she looked sexy as hell.

He leaned his hips against the counter and folded his arms across his chest. "Cupcake doesn't eat?"

"Oh, she eats. But daintily. Not like a vacuum cleaner."

He pushed off from the counter and walked toward her. "Sometimes you're just so hungry for something, crave it so much"—he snagged her hand and yanked her against him—"you can't help but devour it." He buried his face in the warm curve where her neck and shoulder met and pressed his open mouth to her soft skin. Never had any woman ever smelled as good as she did.

"Hmmm . . ." she murmured, tilting her head to give him better access. "I can't deny you proved last night—several times in fact—that being devoured is a *reeeeeeally* good thing." She ran her hands down his back and slipped her fingers beneath the waistband of his boxer briefs to skim over his butt. "Definitely wouldn't mind being shown again."

And God knows he wanted to. But in the light of a new day, his conscience wouldn't allow him to be sidetracked—not until he'd told her the truth.

"Definitely looking forward to that," he said against her neck. Then he forced himself to raise his head. "But first, we need to talk."

Her exploring fingers stilled on his butt and wariness crept into her gaze. "Uh-oh. That doesn't sound good."

Since he was pretty sure she wasn't going to like what he said, he couldn't argue with that. Instead he gently eased her hands from inside his briefs, entwined their fingers, and led her to a stool at the snack bar. "Why don't you sit and I'll pour us some coffee."

"Oh," she said in a tiny voice. "So, um, it's not only that we need to talk, but I need to be sitting down *and* fortified with a caffeinated beverage?"

He laughed, but the effort sounded forced. He quickly poured the coffees, then carried them to the snack bar. After setting them on the counter, he sat on the stool next to her, swiveled until he faced her, then loosely linked their hands.

"There's something I need to tell you," he said, his gaze steady on hers. "I should have told you already but—"

"Oh, God." Her face went pale. "You're married."

"No. I'm—"

"Out on parole."

"No."

"You really are a hit man."

He gently squeezed her hands. "No. And if you'd stop with the crazy guesses, I'll tell you." After she pressed her lips together and nodded, he continued, "Remember I told you about my family's business?"

"The bed-and-breakfast."

"Right. Well, I sort of underplayed that. A lot."

She frowned. "What do you mean?"

"It's not exactly a bed-and-breakfast. It's more like an

exclusive luxury boutique hotel. And there's not just one. There're actually two hundred and eighty-four of them. Spanning sixty-two countries. And it's growing every year. You've probably heard of them—Luxe hotels."

Her eyes widened. "*The* Luxe hotels?"

"Yes."

"Where all the celebrities and uber-wealthy stay."

"Yes."

"You're telling me that your family owns Luxe hotels."

"Every one of them. Right down to the Egyptian cotton towels in the bathrooms." Since it seemed he'd robbed her of speech, he rushed on, "Everything else I told you was true— about not wanting to be part of the business, of wanting a simpler, quiet life, being away from the rat race, building something with my own two hands. Of walking away from an existence I found empty."

He looked down at their joined hands for several seconds, then returned his gaze to hers. "You're the first woman I've ever been with who didn't know me as Nicolas Trent the third. Who didn't know who my father and grandfather were. Who didn't know my net worth. Who didn't expect expensive gifts and lavish vacations. Who didn't want anything from me. This is the first time I didn't have to ask myself, 'Is she interested in me—or in my money?' And most refreshing of all, you're also the first woman who didn't kiss my ass."

She cleared her throat. "Actually, I believe I *did* do that. Last night."

A surprised laugh escaped him. He hadn't expected humor during his confession. "So you did. But you know what I meant."

"I do." Her gaze searched his. "You walked away from a great deal. That must have been very difficult."

"In truth, it really wasn't. Because I wasn't happy. Whoever said money can't buy happiness knew what they were talking about. I had a big house, but lived in it alone. I had a lot of stuff, but that's all it was. Just . . . stuff. None of it really mattered. Except for Kevin—who lived hundreds of miles away—I didn't have any close friends. Sure, there were tons of acquaintances and hangers-on and ass kissers, but not true, got-your-back-no-matter-what friends. I hated working in an office, sitting behind a desk. I felt like my entire life was a lie. My brother loves it, thrives on it, the wheeling-dealing, the constant travel, the nightly parties, but I grew to hate it. To me it was all just superficial bullshit.

"Things came to a head when I asked a woman I didn't really love and who didn't love me to marry me. And I foolishly would have gone through with it if she hadn't found someone richer and, as she put it, 'more ambitious' than me. After we split, I reevaluated my life, decided what I wanted, and it wasn't the life I was living. What I wanted was here. Doing what I'm doing now. The sort of life Kevin has. Has always had. I bought Paradise Lost and Southern Comfort, sold my big fancy house and cars, my various real estate holdings, donated a lot of stuff, packed up what was left, and came here."

"And no one here knows all this."

"No one. Except Kevin. And now you."

"And you didn't tell me before now because . . . ?"

He again looked down at their joined hands. And really liked the way her fingers looked linked with his. When he raised his gaze, he said, "I just wasn't ready to share my past. I didn't want to risk that maybe you'd look at me differently. But I really decided to keep my mouth shut when you told me about Raymond and said you'd never want to be with another guy from that world. And that's where I'm from." He brushed his thumbs over the satiny backs of her hands. "And I wanted you to be with me. Just me—Nick. Not Nicolas Trent the third."

She frowned and nodded slowly, clearly digesting everything he'd said. "Now the Princeton education makes sense," she murmured. "And the high school where you met Kevin— since he was from out of state I assume that was a boarding school?"

"Yes."

"Of the fancy, ritzy sort?"

"The fanciest and ritziest, I'm afraid."

"But you said Kevin's family wasn't wealthy. So how did he get in?"

"Scholarship." A grin tugged at his lips. "We were roommates freshman year. I'll never forget entering our room for the first time. He glared at me and said, 'I'm not one of you rich boys. I'm here on scholarship. You plan to give me any shit about that, asshole?' " Nick chuckled. "I was fourteen and no one had ever spoken to me like that. Certainly no one had ever called me an asshole, although I'd done plenty to deserve it."

"Like what?"

He shrugged. "I was your typical spoiled brat. I was also a late bloomer—really small and scrawny back then. Kevin was about eight inches taller and outweighed me by a good ninety pounds. No way in hell was I going mess with him—he could have kicked my ass into oblivion. During that first week of school, we pretty much stayed out of each others' way. Then one of the bigger kids cornered me in the locker room. Said some shit, pushed me around. Kevin came in. Threw one punch at the guy. That's all it took. Then he looked at me and said, 'You okay, roomie?' I wasn't—I'd just about crapped my pants, but I said, yeah, and thanks. He told me I needed to learn a few things about real life—starting with defending myself against bullies—and since we were roommates, he'd give me a few pointers. We've been best friends ever since."

"Sounds like me and Kate—without the punching and the ass kicking, of course."

He nodded. "When I met your sister last night and she thought I looked familiar—Jamie, it's definitely possible she and I attended the same event at some point. I don't recall ever meeting her, but our paths may have crossed. When she said that, I knew I needed to tell you. I'd intended to last night, but when I walked in the door you—"

"Ripped your clothes off, had my wicked way with you, and, um, kissed your ass?"

He gave a short laugh. "Yeah. Not that I'm complaining. But one thing led to another—five times, if I recall correctly— and then we basically passed out from exhaustion. And now here we are."

"Here we are," she repeated softly. "Me and Nicolas Trent the third." She narrowed her eyes. "You can't be *too* destitute—you bought two houses here. And you ordered that All-Clad cookware without batting an eye, plus all that furniture for Paradise Lost."

"I never said I was poor." And he wasn't. He just was no longer defined by his possessions and his bank balance. His gaze searched hers. "So now you know."

She nodded slowly. "Now I know. Thank you for telling me."

"You're welcome. I'm sorry I didn't tell you sooner."

"I'm sorry you were the proverbial poor little rich boy. Having it all yet—"

"Having nothing," he finished for her. "Or at least not the things that were important to me."

"That doesn't sound like fun."

"It wasn't." Since her expression wasn't giving any clue to her thoughts, he asked, "Are you upset?"

"About what? Your upper-crust upbringing in general or the fact that you didn't tell me until now?"

"Either. Both." His gaze searched hers. "Am I forgiven? Are we okay?"

She didn't answer for several long seconds and he realized he was holding his breath. Finally she said, "I told you I never wanted another guy who led that lifestyle, and that still stands. But you're not that guy." She squeezed his hands and smiled. "So yeah, I forgive you."

The amount of relief that raced through him was nothing short of ridiculous.

"And yes, we're okay," she continued. "I mean, I don't see any reason why the revelation that you grew up mega-rich should cause the premature demise of our fling."

Her words were exactly what he'd wanted to hear—yet somehow hearing her call what they'd shared a *fling* didn't sit well. Which was completely crazy, because that's what it was.

So he forced himself to smile. "Glad we agree. After all, there're still almost three weeks until . . ."

"We're flung?" she suggested.

"Right. Flung." The word weighed like a stone on his tongue.

She slid off her stool, stepped between his knees, and wound her arms around his neck. "Actually, I find it very difficult to imagine you as a rich boy. You're so . . . down-to-earth."

He slipped his hands beneath the T-shirt of his she wore

and cupped her bare bottom. "I think that's the nicest thing anyone's ever said to me."

"Really?" Deviltry danced in her eyes. "Bet I could say something you'd think was even nicer." She leaned in, brushed her lips against his ear, then whispered a suggestion that made steam pump from his pores.

"Nicer?" she asked, trailing her mouth along his jaw.

"Oh, yeah." He pulled her closer and was about to settle his mouth on hers when he heard someone climbing the steps.

They groaned in unison. "Damn. That's no doubt someone from Paradise Lost," Jamie said, her gaze flying to the screen door. She grabbed his hand. "C'mon!"

Together they dashed into the bedroom—not an easy run with a raging hard-on—and closed the door. Seconds later a knock sounded and they heard Godiva barrel to the door, barking for all she was worth.

"Aunt Jamie?" came Heather's voice. "Are you there?"

Nick reluctantly eased Jamie away from him and headed toward the bathroom. "Good luck."

"Where are you going?" Jamie asked, following him.

He shot a pointed look at the erection tenting his boxer briefs. "To take a cold shower. I'm not suitable to receive guests."

She wrapped her fingers around him and he sucked in a sharp breath. "Neither am I. I'm not even wearing panties."

"Don't remind me or you'll never make it to the door."

"Who wants to go to the door?"

"Aunt Jamie?" came Heather's voice, more insistent this time. "Where are you?"

"Crap," Jamie muttered. She released him and bent down to scoop up her panties from the floor, affording him a view that damn near stopped his heart. With a sigh Nick moved into the bathroom and turned on the shower while Jamie quickly dressed in the shorts and tank top he'd taken off her the night before.

"To be continued," she said, giving him a quick kiss.

"Can't wait."

He watched her hurry out to answer the door, and with a sigh, he stripped and stepped into the shower, gritting his teeth when the cold water hit him in the chest. Damn. Her family wasn't just driving *her* crazy—they were bringing him along for the ride as well.

Jamie exited the bedroom, closing the door behind her, then hurried toward the screen door, where Heather was trying to calm Godiva, whose excitement over seeing her was thwarted by the screen between them.

"Good morning," Jamie said, opening the door. "C'mon in."

Heather entered the kitchen and Godiva immediately flopped on her back to present her belly. "You are shameless," Heather said with a laugh, bending down to oblige. She looked up at Jamie. "I know it's early, but I saw Godiva outside, so I figured you were awake." She looked around, her gaze resting on the two coffee mugs. "Where's Nick?"

"Shower. What's going on? Everything okay?"

Heather stood and pushed up her glasses. Jamie noted she looked tired, but not upset. "I wanted to tell you about my talk with Mom." She rolled her eyes. "My really *loooong* talk with her."

"Sure. Did you eat breakfast?" Jamie asked, opening the fridge.

Heather nodded. "A huge piece of leftover birthday cake. Yum."

"Well, be happy you ate because, let me tell you, unless you want mustard spread on a moldy piece of bread, there's zilch to eat here at Casa Nick."

Heather giggled. "Thanks, I'll pass."

"Me, too." She closed the fridge, hiked herself onto a bar stool, and patted the one next to her. "Sit. Talk."

Heather seated herself and Jamie took a sip from the now lukewarm cup of coffee Nick had poured her earlier. After clearing her throat, Heather said, "We walked to the beach and sat in the sand. She asked me to tell her what was bothering me, and I did. I told her everything. How I hate that she's always blowing me off and trying to change me and how she just doesn't *know* me at all. How I feel like I'm last on her list and how she never listens to me and hardly talks to me except to lecture me." Heather picked at her chipped nail polish—bright green this week. "I kept expecting her to interrupt or yell or something, but she just sat there and listened. Just like she'd said she would. I was pretty shocked."

"Then what happened?"

Heather shrugged and red washed into her cheeks. "And then . . . and then she cried." She looked up, her expression utterly baffled. "Aunt Jamie, she just put her face in her hands and cried. I didn't know what to do. I'd never seen Mom cry before."

Jamie tried to recall the last time she'd seen Laurel cry and drew a blank. "Then what happened?"

"I just sort of patted her back and gave her a hug and she finally stopped crying. And then she said stuff I never thought I'd hear from my mom. She told me I was right. That she'd been selfish and focused on her own stuff and not there for me—not like she should have been—and how sorry she was. How she'd lost sight of what was important and how much she wanted things to be okay between us. Spend more time together. Really get to know each other. She told me she was never close with Grandma Cindy when she was growing up and didn't want that mistake to carry over to us.

"Then she told me about Raymond dumping her. Not only dumping her, but for one of her close friends. Can you believe that?" Heather shook her head. "That's really low. What a douche."

"I believe it," Jamie said dryly. "Happens all the time."

"She said she really loved him and thought he was The One. He really broke her heart, Aunt Jamie. It happened almost a month ago but she didn't tell me. Didn't tell anyone. She said the breakup made her do a lot of thinking and she realized she had a lot of regrets. And wanted to fix things. Like her relationship with me."

Heather looked up from her polish picking. "And with you. She said one of the things she regretted most was a fight with you. That she was really sorry for it."

Jamie kept her expression completely blank—not easy given the emotions careening through her. "I see. Did she ask you to tell me that?"

Heather shook her head. "No. She said she's going to tell you herself."

"Did she tell you what the fight was about?"

"Sort of. She said you were still with Raymond when she started dating him. That you were really hurt when you found out. I told her that was a totally shitty thing to do, especially to her own sister. And she agreed."

Heather hesitated, then said, "I don't blame you for being totally pissed at her, Aunt Jamie. But I know she's really sorry. I thought about it like all night long, and you know how sometimes good stuff comes from bad? Like lemonade from lemons? Well, it occurred to me that the totally shitty thing Mom did to you maybe turned out okay for you because in the end, the guy was a complete dirtbag."

Jamie stared at her niece, nonplussed. Once again the kid had said a mouthful. And this time a very unsettling one.

She was saved from replying when Heather rushed on, "And if you hadn't fought with Mom, you never would have come to Seaside Cove, which means you never would have met Nick. I know you guys really like each other." She dipped her head and shrugged. "So, you know, lemons and lemonade."

And yet another mouthful.

"I also wanted to tell you I've decided to go to Italy," Heather said.

Jamie blinked, needing a few seconds to grasp the rapid subject change. Then she reached out and clasped Heather's hand. "I'm glad, sweetie."

"Mom's coming with me. We're leaving tomorrow."

Jamie's brows shot upward. "She is? You are?"

Heather nodded. "When I told her why I didn't want to go, she said she'd come with me. That way I'd have somebody to hang with when I wasn't doing stuff with Dad so I wouldn't feel so out of place and alone. And it would give us a chance to spend some time together. She spoke to Dad early this morning—it's like five hours later over there—and made all the arrangements. Mom and I are staying together in the guesthouse at Dad's villa."

"And your dad's okay with that?"

"He said he was." Heather giggled. "Although I don't

think Mom gave him much of a choice. On our way home from Dad's, she's taking me to Spain for a few days—not to shop, but so I can visit some of Hemingway's favorite haunts. I told her that after we did that, hitting a few stores would be cool."

Jamie leaned over and gave Heather a hug. "It sounds like your talk went really well. I'm happy for you, kiddo."

"Thanks. Me, too. I feel better and I know Mom does, too." She slid off the barstool and stretched. "So are all of us going to do something today? Since it's my last day, I'd like to go to the beach for a while."

"I won't be able to meet you there until later. Tonight's the Clam Committee's big potluck dinner and I have a lot of cooking to do."

"I'll help," Heather offered. "That way you'll finish faster."

"Sounds good." Jamie's gaze scanned Nick's kitchen. "With all these fabulous new appliances and the All-Clad cookware . . . I'd love to do the cooking here. I'm going to ask Nick if it'd be okay."

"Ask Nick if what would be okay?" came his voice from behind her.

She turned and her stomach performed a swoop as she watched him walk out of the bedroom. Dressed in board shorts and a white T-shirt, his hair still shower damp, his face freshly shaved, he looked big and tall and totally yummy.

"To use your fancy new kitchen to cook my contributions for tonight's Clam Committee potluck dinner."

"I guess I'd be willing to do that. Provided there's some home-cooked food in it for me. Deal?"

"Deal—provided you help Heather carry all the ingredients I bought at the Piggly Wiggly over here from Paradise Lost while I grab a quick shower. She knows where everything is." And it was a perfect excuse for her to avoid going over there and facing her mother and/or Laurel.

"Consider it done."

Nick and Heather left, and Jamie took the world's fastest shower, then quickly dressed, all the while pondering what Heather had told her. She'd just left the bedroom to head back into the kitchen when she heard Nick and Heather climbing the stairs. She ran to open the door. In walked a smiling Nick, his arms laden with Piggly Wiggly bags. Next came Heather, weighed down with more bags.

Then Jamie stilled as Laurel climbed the stairs, followed by Jamie's mother, and finally Alex.

"They all wanted to help," Heather said as everyone filed into the kitchen. "Think how fast we'll get done and be able to hit the beach, Aunt Jamie. What do you say?"

Jamie's gaze shifted from Heather's hopeful expression to Laurel, who looked tired and wary, to her mother, who looked exhausted and unhappy.

Blech. With the tension gripping Jamie at the thought of sharing a kitchen with them, a happy outing this did not promise to be. No, more likely this would turn into a drama-filled disaster. But there was no way she could refuse that hope in Heather's eyes.

So she'd suck it up and take another one for the team.

"I say let's get cooking."

Chapter 26

Jamie turned to Nick and Alex. "You guys feel like peeling garlic?"

She had to bite the insides of her cheeks to hold in her laugh at the identical looks of horror that passed over their faces.

"Ah, as fun as that sounds—and really it does," said Nick, "you ladies probably don't need two clumsy men taking up a bunch of room in the kitchen, and I could use Alex's help digging out the area behind the carport where I'm going to build an outdoor grill." He turned to Alex. "Unless you'd rather peel garlic."

"I'd rather dig in the dirt," Alex said without hesitation. As they exited the house, Alex said, "Owe you big-time for that save," and Nick laughed.

"Figured the old 'wanna peel garlic' ploy would get them out of here," Jamie said with a smirk.

Her comment broke the tense silence and they all gave halfhearted laughs. "Could they have gotten out of here any faster?" Jamie's mother asked.

"Not unless they'd jumped out the window," Jamie said. Determined not to allow the tension she felt simmering in the room to explode into an unpleasant, awkward situation, she continued, "Now that we have more room, let's get to it. Mom, how about you chop the herbs—"

"On it," her mother said, reaching for the cutting board, clearly relieved to have something to do.

"And I'll puree the tomatoes for the sauce. Heather, you're on garlic duty and we need water to boil for the lasagna noodles. After we get the sauce cooking, we can start on the meatballs." She turned to Laurel and hesitated. Just to avoid being in such close confines with her, Jamie wanted to suggest that Laurel simply sit and watch—preferably from the other room—or better yet, go outside with Nick and Alex. The fact that her pampered sister possessed zero cooking knowledge was only more incentive to banish her. Still, Jamie would be damned if *she'd* be the one to prove unpleasant.

"Laurel, how about you wash the herbs before my mom chops them?" Jamie suggested, deciding that was an easy enough, damage-free task.

Laurel hoisted her brows and shot Jamie an "I don't think so" look. She calmly reached for the apron on the counter and tied it around her waist. "Maggie can easily do that. How about I chop the onions?"

Jamie stared at her. Okay, this had to be an act. This Laurel she'd seen signs of last night and who Heather had described couldn't possibly be the real deal. Still, Jamie never would have believed she'd see Laurel wearing an apron or hear her offering to help in the kitchen—yet there she stood, looking ready to chop the crap out of anything that wasn't moving.

"I'll do the onions, Mom," Heather said, with a nervous laugh, wading into the tense silence. "I don't want you to lose a finger."

Laurel lifted her chin. "I know how to chop onions. I also know how to make spaghetti sauce."

Heather rolled her eyes. "We're making it from scratch. Not opening a jar."

"I realize that. And I'll have you know that the last pot of sauce I made turned out pretty good, if I may say so myself— except for the burned part on the bottom, of course."

Heather folded her arms over her chest and shot her mother

a classic teenage "you've got to be kidding me" look. "Uh-huh. And where did you learn to make this fictional sauce?"

Laurel snatched an onion from the bag on the counter and applied herself to the peel as if her life depended on it. Jamie and her mother exchanged a glance, then stopped what they were doing and simply listened.

"I've taken a few cooking classes," Laurel said in a clipped voice.

Heather couldn't have looked more amazed if her mother had announced she was an alien. "No way. Where?" Heather demanded. "When? Why?"

"At a cooking school in the city. I've gone once a month for the last few months. As for why—I've always secretly been interested in cooking, but never pursued it. I finally decided to do so."

"But . . . but I've never even seen you put bread in the toaster!" Heather protested. "Rosario does all the cooking at home," she added, referring to their live-in housekeeper.

"Which is why I never had to learn—someone's always done it for me." Laurel's voice grew louder with each word and Jamie's brows rose at her sister's growing agitation. "You've never seen me cook because I do it when you're at school."

"How come?" Heather asked in a tone that sounded both bewildered and hurt. "You know I like to cook. Why wouldn't you do it with me?"

Laurel slapped the peeled onion onto the counter and regarded Heather through eyes that reflected anger and suppressed emotion. "You want to know why? Fine. I'll tell you. It's because I wanted to surprise you. For your birthday. I know you enjoy cooking with Jamie and so I wanted to learn so I could cook with you, too. I've only had a couple of lessons, so I'm still a novice, but I was planning to cook you dinner for your birthday. But then you came here and . . . well, that was the end of that."

She then turned to Jamie and said in a tight voice, "I hope you know how lucky you are that you grew up with Daddy and a mom who taught you how to cook rather than having to pay someone to give you lessons." She turned her head to include Jamie's mother when she said, "I may have grown up with a lot of money, but there are some things that money just can't buy. Things that both of you were fortunate to have."

Without another word, she set the onion on a small cutting board and carefully applied her knife to it.

Silence throbbed in the kitchen for several long seconds. Then Heather cleared her throat. "Mom . . . you were really going to cook me dinner for my birthday?"

"Well, I was going to *try*. No promises as to the results. Just lots of prayers I didn't poison us."

"Wow, Mom. I seriously don't know what to say. Except that that's really . . . cool. And that you're full of surprises lately."

"Good. I'd hate to think I'm boring."

No, Laurel definitely wasn't boring, Jamie decided, shaking her head. And she couldn't deny that she sounded sincere or that she'd heard that bleak note in her voice when she'd said there were things money couldn't buy. Growing up, Jamie had spent countless hours in the kitchen with both her mom and dad. She couldn't imagine not having done so. Not having those special memories. Memories Laurel didn't have.

They went about their tasks, and Jamie sensed a slight lessening in the tension—as if a storm had passed. The quiet was punctuated by the whirr of the food processor as Jamie pureed the ripe tomatoes she'd purchased at a farm stand near the Piggly Wiggly. Soon the scent of onions sautéing in olive oil filled the kitchen.

"Smells great in here already," Laurel remarked, sniffing the air. She watched Jamie add sliced garlic to the large pot, then stir with a wooden spoon.

"How do you keep the garlic from burning?" Laurel asked, moving to stand next to Jamie in front of the stove. "I keep ending up with brown, overcooked garlic."

"Your heat is probably too high," Jamie said. "The oil should barely sizzle. Then only sauté the garlic for about twenty to thirty seconds—that's all you need to release the flavor. After that you start adding your other ingredients and that keeps the garlic from overcooking on its own." She demonstrated by pouring in the pureed tomatoes. "Ready for the herbs, Mom."

Her mother slid the basil and oregano from her cutting

board into the pot. Heather added freshly ground pepper while Jamie tossed in a pinch of salt. After giving the pot a stir, she put on the lid and then wiped her hands on her apron.

"Done. We'll just let that cook while we get these other dishes going."

"Did I ever tell you about the first time your father made spaghetti sauce for me?" Jamie's mother asked.

Jamie and Laurel exchanged a quick glance. "I don't think so," Jamie said. "What happened?"

"Did it turn out good?" Heather asked.

Jamie's mom laughed. "God, no. It was an utter disaster. Tom forgot to turn down the heat once the sauce came to a boil. It burned on the bottom and tasted like scorched dirt. While trying to rescue the sauce, he completely forgot about the meatballs and they burned, too, which set off the smoke alarm." She chuckled at the memory. "Poor guy. It was our second date and he was trying so hard to impress me and everything went wrong. Since I knew next to nothing about cooking back then, I wasn't any help at all. The first time I tried to cook chicken?" A shudder ran through her. "I discovered that overcooked chicken tastes like cardboard and undercooked chicken tastes like bird Jell-O."

"Bird Jell-O?" Heather said. "Ewwww! That sounds gross!"

"Try tasting it," Jamie's mom said dryly.

"I've set off the kitchen smoke alarm a few times," Jamie said.

"I've set it off every time I've attempted to cook," Laurel said with a laugh.

Jamie's mom's gaze bounced between her and Laurel. "Obviously you're both your father's daughters."

Jamie's gaze flew to Laurel and she found her sister regarding her through serious eyes. A long look passed between them, then Laurel said softly, "Yes, I guess we are."

A heart owie fluttered through Jamie, one that filled her with the sudden urge to reach out and touch Laurel's hand, to make physical that instant of emotional connection she'd felt flow between them. But then she recalled Laurel's betrayal, the profound hurt, and she curled her hand into a fist and looked away.

"Meatballs are next," she said, moving to the fridge to take out the necessary ingredients. Jamie added the ground beef to a large bowl and mixed the ingredients with her hands while her mother and Laurel added eggs, bread crumbs, herbs, minced garlic and onions, and grated Romano cheese as Jamie asked for them. Heather, meanwhile, set the oven to preheat, then added the lasagna noodles to the pot of water, which had come to a boil.

"Grandpa Tom always used to tell me that food brings people together," Heather said, coming to join them at the counter. "I never really thought about that much, but"—she made a circling motion with her hand that encompassed the four of them—"it seems like he was right."

Laurel nodded. "I never really got it when he'd say that, but yes, I'm starting to see what he meant."

Heather guffawed. "Mom, you never got it because, until you started those cooking lessons just a couple months ago, the only thing you'd ever made in a kitchen was a mess."

Jamie thought for sure Laurel would take offense at her daughter's words, but instead she laughed. "True. But thanks to the cooking lessons, I'm now making even bigger messes in the kitchen." Just then the egg she was holding slipped from her grasp and fell to the floor with a wet splat. They all looked down at the gooey mess. Then they all raised their gazes and burst out laughing.

"See?" Laurel said, reaching for the paper towels.

"You sure timed that well, Mom."

Jamie's mother suddenly frowned and sniffed the air. "Do you smell something? Like something's burning—"

The screeching wail of the smoke alarm pierced the air. Jamie's gaze flew to the stove, but nothing seemed amiss there. Then she saw that the oven was on. Pulling her fingers from the bowl where she was mixing the meatball ingredients, she stuffed her hand into a pot holder and flicked on the oven's interior light and peered through the tempered glass. No flames—thank God, but there was something in there, on the rack. Something that looked like . . . paper? What the hell?

"Stand back, and someone turn on the faucet," she yelled to be heard over the deafening noise. She opened the oven door. A poof of smoke emerged, along with the pungent scent of burnt paper. She reached in and grabbed a booklet with curled, charred edges from which wisps of smoke rose. Jamie slammed the door, then immediately tossed the paper into the sink and directed the spray of running water on it.

The screen door burst open and Nick ran in, followed by Alex.

"What's going on?" Nick shouted.

"Everything's fine," Jamie yelled. She grabbed a dish towel and waved it vigorously beneath the smoke detector. Her mother, Laurel, and Heather grabbed towels and waved them as well. "Smoke alarm went off."

"Got that part," Nick hollered.

Just then the piercing noise stopped. Jamie blew out a sigh of relief at the sudden silence and lowered her arms.

"What happened?" Nick asked.

"Well, the good news is your smoke detector works," Jamie reported.

"Got that part, too," said Nick. "The question is why did it go off?"

"That's the bad news." Jamie moved to the sink, turned off the faucet and then lifted the dripping booklet with two fingers. "The operation manual for your oven has seen better days." She glanced at the charred front page and read the oversized, bold lettering, "Do not leave in oven. Remove immediately."

Heather clamped her hands over her mouth. "OMG. I never thought to look in the oven before I turned it on. I'm so sorry."

"No problem," Jamie said, dropping the soggy papers back in the sink. She shot a pointed look at Nick. "Wouldn't have happened if *someone* had taken the manual out of the oven when he installed it. Obviously you haven't used your new oven yet."

"Sweetheart, I don't even know how to turn the stupid thing on," Nick said, shaking his head.

Jamie shook her head. "Jeez. What the heck did they teach you at Princeton anyway?"

"Nothing about ovens."

"You *seriously* need that cooking lesson I promised you."

"Starting with the very basics," Nick agreed.

Jamie's mom started to laugh. "At least the sauce didn't

burn on the bottom and it wasn't the meatballs that set off the alarm."

Heather giggled, adding, "And at least it's not bird Jell-O."

Laurel joined in, and then Jamie, and suddenly none of them could stop laughing.

"OMG, you should have seen your face, Mom," Heather said, tears of mirth streaming down her cheeks.

"OMG, you should have seen *your* face," Jamie mimicked to Heather.

"It's almost like Tom was listening and decided to make his presence known," Jamie's mom said.

"In the noisiest way possible, which was just like him," Laurel added, brushing tears of laughter from beneath her eyes.

Nick turned to Alex. "You have any idea what the hell is so funny?"

"Beats me. I just hope we're not having bird Jell-O for dinner. But just in case, I'm gonna deaden a few taste buds. Want a beer?"

"Good idea."

That exchange set the four women off into more gales of laughter. Alex grabbed two long-neck bottles from the fridge, and after he and a clearly baffled Nick had once again headed outside, Jamie grabbed a wad of paper towels and passed them around so they could all wipe her eyes.

"Well, *that* was fun," Jamie said. She eyed the bowl of partially mixed meatball ingredients. "Think we can get these finished without any further catastrophes?"

"One way to find out," her mother said. With a devilish grin she picked up the box of breadcrumbs and sprinkled some into the mixture.

They all washed their hands, then resumed working. As Jamie formed the meatballs, she asked, "You know what Heather said about cooking bringing people together?"

"I was wrong," said Heather, draining the lasagna noodles. "It's smoke alarms that bring people together."

They all laughed. "Seriously, I bet ninety percent of the world's problems could be solved in the kitchen," Jamie continued. "Think about it. If political leaders would get out of the war room and into the kitchen—"

"Planet Earth would be a better place," said Laurel, nodding.

"That would be a lot of cooks," Jamie's mother said. "You know what they say about too many of them spoiling the broth."

"There're a lot of cooks in this kitchen," Heather pointed out. "Three generations of us. And we're doing pretty good."

"Exactly," said Laurel. "Instead of arguing about nuclear weapons, those political leaders could debate the virtues of paprika versus cumin—"

"Discuss whether Himalayan sea salt is superior to the Mediterranean variety," added Jamie. "You know, subjects that don't lead to wars and death."

"Mediterranean gets my vote," said her mom.

Jamie shot her mother a mock ferocious scowl. "I prefer Himalayan."

Mom scowled right back at her. "This means war."

More laughter filled the kitchen. As they began browning the meatballs, Jamie mused, "Cooking has always been like therapy for me. It relaxes me. Takes my mind off everything else."

"Although I'm new to cooking, I'm finding it affects me the same way," said Laurel, rinsing the used utensils and putting them in the dishwasher.

Jamie's mom nodded. "Me, too. The kitchen is always where I've done my best thinking. Except when it came to helping Jamie with her high school math homework. I remember us suffering through trigonometry problems in between baking batches of cookies."

"I remember you weren't much help in the sine, cosine, tangent departments," Jamie teased.

Her mom laughed. "No kidding. About all I could do was commiserate with you and keep your glass of milk refilled. I was fine helping with the math when you were younger, but all that algebra and trig—yikes. I barely squeaked through it when *I* was in high school. Who knew triangles could be so complicated?"

"We'd always have to wait for Daddy to come home from the restaurant to help me."

"And the two of you would eat your way through the entire batch of cookies while figuring out those problems and equations." A faraway look came into her mother's eyes. "I've never known anyone who loved cookies more than your dad." Her expression cleared and she smiled at Jamie. "Except you, of course."

"No doubt about it, I inherited the cookie chromosome." She looked at Laurel. "Dad passed it on to you as well."

"Oh, yes," agreed Laurel. "I could eat cookies for every meal."

"And you passed it on to me," chimed in Heather.

"You also inherited Dad's height," Jamie grumbled, glancing at Laurel. "Cookies don't show on you like they do on me."

"The hell they don't. I'm eight years older than you, and let me tell you, that metabolism peters out after thirty."

"And just wait until you're over forty," chimed in Jamie's mom.

"So you're both saying I need to eat my cookies now," Jamie said.

"Exactly," her mom and Laurel said in unison.

Jamie looked at Heather. "You, too, I guess."

Heather giggled. "Okay. Twist my arm."

Laurel cleared her throat and looked at Jamie. "I . . . I like talking with you about Dad. It's hard to do with other people because they clearly don't know what to say. It's uncomfortable for them to discuss someone who died, which I guess is understandable."

Jamie nodded. "I know what you mean. I'll occasionally mention Dad during conversations with acquaintances, but it's usually just a casual 'oh, yeah, I visited that museum once with my dad,' or 'my mom and dad and I used to do that, too,' sort of comment. But those people didn't know him. Didn't love him. Didn't know how special he was."

"I like talking about him, too," Jamie's mom added quietly. "Remembering things he said and did, the way he'd throw back his head and laugh."

"God, he had the greatest laugh," Jamie said, adding another splash of olive oil into the pan as an image of her handsome father flashed in her mind. "No matter how crappy a day I might be having, Dad could always get me to laugh with him."

"That laugh, along with his beautiful smile, are what first attracted me to him," said her mom. "One smile and *pow!* I was a goner."

An image of Nick and his *pow!* smile flashed through Jamie's mind. "That smile . . . it was Dad's superpower," she murmured.

"You mean like the way Superman could fly? Hmmm . . . I never thought of it that way, but yes, that's a good description." Her mom stepped between her and Laurel, and after a brief hesitation, put an arm around each of them. "I see that smile in each of you." She looked at Heather. "And in Heather, too."

Jamie's heart swelled, with the bone-deep love she felt for her mom, along with a nudge of guilt as well for the way she'd stomped off the previous evening. Clearly her mother was trying, and, for the first time Jamie could recall, was stepping up and acting as the problem solver—a responsibility that always fell on Jamie's shoulders. Maybe her mom had taken the words she'd said last night to heart.

Jamie's mom gave them each a squeeze, then casually took the wooden spoon from Jamie and stirred the sauce. "Do you girls remember the time your dad took us canoeing?"

"Remember?" Jamie asked. "We're lucky we lived to tell the tale. A canoe person Daddy was not."

"What happened?" asked Heather.

"It was during the summer," said Laurel. "I used to spend the entire month of July with your Grandpa Tom, Maggie, and Jamie every year. This particular summer I think I was fifteen—"

"You were, because I was seven," broke in Jamie.

"Right. Dad rented a canoe, tied it to the roof of the car, and drove us out to Long Island."

"You sulked the entire way because you said canoeing was 'hard work,' " Jamie told Laurel, laughing at the memory.

Laurel hiked a brow. "And was I right?"

A shudder ran through Jamie. "God, yes."

"I'll never forget the look on Tom's face the first time the canoe tipped over and he ended up in the water," Jamie's mom said, chuckling.

"And the second, third, and fourth times," Jamie added.

They continued with the cooking, adding more meatballs to the pan, then making the lasagna by layering the noodles, sauce, and cheese, all the while reminiscing, one story leading without pause into the next.

"Remember the time Dad brought us to Coney Island?"

"How about that tent he made for us by covering the dining room table with a huge sheet, then telling us ghost stories when it got dark?"

"Or the time he taught us how to make s'mores in the fireplace—"

"When he took us horseback riding in Central Park—"

"Skating at Rockefeller Center—"

"Body surfing at Jones Beach—"

"The Staten Island ferry—"

"Statue of Liberty—"

By the time the meatballs were cooked and the lasagna out of the oven, Jamie felt as if she'd relived her most precious memories of her childhood and her father.

"I haven't laughed this much in a very long time," Laurel said, untying her apron.

"Me, either," Jamie agreed. An even longer time since she'd laughed so much with her sister. Or her mother.

"It was great hearing all those stories about Grandpa," Heather said. She looked at all of them, then spread her arms. "Family hug!"

Jamie hesitated briefly, then put her arms out as well. Her mother and Laurel did the same. They formed a tight circle and gave a collective hug.

"Cooking really does bring people together," Jamie's mom said.

Everyone murmured their agreement. Jamie shared a little hip bump with Heather, who stood on her right, then looked at her mother, who stood across from her in their tight little circle. Her mother gave her a watery smile and mouthed, "I love you." Tears pushed behind Jamie's eyes and she mouthed, "Love you, too," in return. She then turned her head to the left and looked at Laurel.

Their eyes met and Jamie saw that Laurel's swam with tears. And it hit Jamie that her sister had indeed undergone some sort of transformation.

With her gaze steady on Jamie's, Laurel said, "This has been a very good day."

Jamie nodded. Things were far from perfect, but yes, it had indeed been a good day.

Chapter 27

"Want to take a walk down the beach?" Laurel asked.

Jamie's hands stilled at her task of gathering the extra plastic cutlery and plates that remained after the very successful potluck dinner, which was still in full swing but had moved to the bonfire pit, where kids and adults alike roasted marshmallows. She knew Laurel's question meant more than a simple walk—it was really her way of asking *Do you want to talk? Try to settle our differences?*

Leaving Jamie to answer the question, *Do I want to do that?*

She could say no. Could hold on to her hurt and resentment. Part of her wanted to. Felt justified in doing so. Who needed a sister who'd betrayed her like that? *I'm right, she's wrong, the end.*

But another part of her wanted to hear what this seemingly new and improved Laurel had to say. And then tell Laurel exactly what she thought of what she'd done. Without worrying about Heather or anyone else overhearing.

"Sure," she said, setting down the bag of cutlery on the folding table where the mountains of now consumed food had been set up. "A walk sounds good."

She scanned the group surrounding the bonfire, noting Heather laughing with Grace's kids; her mother laughing and sitting next to Alex, their heads bent close together; Dorothy chatting with Melvin, who appeared to be . . . *smiling?*—nah, must be a trick of the fading light—and Nick, who'd just chuckled at something Dorothy said. Just looking at him kicked Jamie's pulse into high gear, and anticipation filled her at the thought of spending another night in his bed.

As if he felt the weight of her regard, his gaze shifted and locked with hers. And for several seconds everything faded away . . . the people and their conversations, the crackle of the fire, the splash of the waves breaking on the shore, leaving Jamie feeling as if only the two of them stood on the beach, intimately connected in spite of the thirty-some-odd feet separating them. Heat flared in his eyes, spreading warmth right down to her toes and setting fire to all her girly parts. Jeez—what the man could do to her with a single look was nothing short of ridiculous.

She blinked to break the spell, then inclined her head slightly toward Laurel, who stood beside her. Nick's gaze flicked to her sister, then back to Jamie. She waved her hand to indicate herself and Laurel then used her fingers to pantomime walking. He nodded his understanding, then gave her a look that said without words that he wished her luck and would be here when she returned. Then she turned to Laurel and, hoping the tension knotting her stomach didn't show, said, "Let's go."

They walked to where the breaking waves washed up on the wet sand, then headed toward the pier.

"The potluck dinner was a huge success," Laurel said. "Everyone loved the lasagna and meatballs. There's not one scrap left over." She rested a hand on her enviably flat stomach. "I can't believe I ate so much."

Clearly Laurel wanted to ease into the subject that stood between them like a big steaming pile of manure, so Jamie played along. "Me, either. Be comforted by the fact that what I ate is going to hang around on my ass a lot longer than what you ate will hang on yours." So unfair!

"I wouldn't be so sure. I had *six* desserts—and that's on top of the heaping plate of food I downed. I just couldn't choose—

they all looked so good." She turned to look out toward the water. "This place is really nice."

Jamie nodded. "I have to admit I was pretty horrified when I first arrived." She briefly described the condition of Paradise Lost that first night.

Laurel laughed. "Wow. I give you credit for staying. I would have been in a cab on my way back to the airport."

"Believe me, it crossed my mind. The new furniture made a big difference. And now so many things that were completely alien to me a month and a half ago—like clam festivals and neighbors who stop by just to chat and bring you a casserole—are among my favorite things about Seaside Cove."

Silence swelled between them, one Jamie didn't feel inclined to break. Laurel had asked for this walk, so she'd wait for her sister to take the lead. Finally Laurel said, "I'm glad you found this place, Jamie. But I'm sorry, so incredibly sorry my actions are what drove you away."

Laurel paused and drew Jamie to a stop by briefly touching her arm. "There are things I want, need to say to you. If you give me the chance to do so, I promise I'll then listen to anything you wish to say to me. Deal?"

Jamie's heart thudded hard and fast. There was no doubt in her mind that whatever happened next would define the future—if there even was to be one—of her relationship with her sister. She nodded. "Deal."

Laurel drew a deep breath, then turned to continue slowly walking, and Jamie fell into step beside her.

"Growing up, there was a part of me that loved you," Laurel said, "loved you so much it hurt. Missed you when we weren't together. Yearned for those two weekends a month when I'd stay with you, Daddy, and Maggie. Counted the days until July when we'd be together for an entire month.

"But then there was another part of me that was so jealous of you. You were small and cute while I was too tall and gangly. You looked like Dad, while I got stuck with my mother's fair coloring. You got to be with Dad *all the time*. Your apartment was lively and relaxed, casual and filled with laughter, while the Fifth Avenue penthouse we moved into after my mom married Martin was sterile and perfect and quiet as a tomb. You got to have all the fun. I loved sharing that with you when I was there, yet hated that you got to continue enjoying it after I left."

She paused and tucked behind her ear several strands of hair that had escaped her ponytail. "Not only did I envy you having Dad all the time, I envied you Maggie—or at least I did once I stopped looking at her as the reason my parents would never get back together. She was so much fun—always laughing, always happy, irreverent, naughty, warm, and so generous with her hugs and kisses. My mother, as you know, is not the warm fuzzy type. For a long time I resented Dad for divorcing her, but as I grew older I finally understood why. She's like a gorgeous piece of artwork—beautiful to look at, but remote and untouchable. The total opposite of Maggie. When at last I realized just how incompatible Dad and my mother were, I couldn't help but wonder why he'd married her in the first place. I asked him once and do you know what he said?"

Jamie shook her head. "No."

"He said he couldn't help himself. He was young and impetuous, and she was so beautiful, he'd just lost his heart. But after eight unhappy years he finally realized she'd never really wanted his heart and had never given him hers and that they'd both be better off apart. As you know, a few months after the divorce was final, he met Maggie and fell head over heels in love—but with your mom his love was returned."

"You have to admit—they were great together," Jamie said softly.

"The best," Laurel agreed. "They had the sort of relationship everyone wants. When my mother married Martin, I suddenly had every material possession any kid could want. I certainly had more than you. Yet you were who I wanted to be. I wanted your house. Your mom. Our dad. Yet as much as I wanted it, as I became a teenager, I grew resentful of the time I had to spend with you. I was older and had my own friends. I came to love the luxurious lifestyle that came with the Westerly name and didn't like hanging with my kid sister who still played with Barbie dolls. Yet, I couldn't let go of Dad. I loved him. And so it went.

"I didn't need to work at Newman's, but I wanted to stay

connected to him. And Maggie. And to you as well. I loved you, but I guess there was that small part of me that still resented you. That somehow just always felt you'd taken something that should have belonged to me. I thought it had gone away, that I'd grown out of it. But then came Raymond."

The name seemed to hang in the sea-scented air, a heavy dark cloud that wedged itself between them. "I'd run into him at various functions here and there," Laurel continued, "and always had a bit of a thing for him. He was everything I looked for in a man—handsome, wealthy, charming—but the timing was never right. Either I was with someone or he was. Still, I'd given him my card and told him to stop by Newman's sometime. And then one night I saw him there. Sitting at the bar. Alone. I was thrilled and excited. I joined him and over drinks he told me that he'd been in twice the previous week for dinner, both times on nights I wasn't there. And that he'd met you. Just then you came over to the bar. Greeted me with a smile—and Raymond with a kiss. And I realized he wasn't there to see me."

Laurel bent down to scoop up a small shell and Jamie forced herself to remain silent, to not say the words that rushed into her throat. *Yes, he was there to see me. And you didn't care. You wanted him so you took him.* Her inner voice whispered, *But she couldn't have taken him if he hadn't wanted to be taken.* Jamie frowned and shoved the voice aside.

"Raymond and I ran in the same circles, and over the next several months, we bumped into each other at least a dozen times. Each time we saw each other, he grew progressively . . . flirtier, I guess is the best word, and I grew more and more attracted. At one particular party he grabbed my hand and led me off to a private room. I knew what he wanted. I wanted it, too. But before I let him pull me into that room, I asked him if he was still seeing you."

She paused and clasped Jamie's hand to halt her. Jamie stopped walking but pulled her hand away. When she looked at Laurel, she saw her blue eyes were bright with tears. "He said no. That he'd ended things with you. That he was free. I won't lie to you, Jamie—I can't swear I wouldn't have gone into that room with him even if he'd said you were still together. I was already halfway in love with him and I honestly don't know what I would have done. But when he said he was free, there was no decision to make."

All the hurt and betrayal Jamie had spent the summer trying to put into perspective and move past came roaring back. "We hadn't broken up," she said in a cold, clipped voice. "We may have had an argument—I don't know. I don't remember. But there'd been no breakup, or even talk of one."

"I didn't know, Jamie. I swear I didn't know."

The fury Jamie thought she'd buried struck her like a lash. "Maybe you didn't know that night—I'll give you that, even though I still think it's really shitty that you'd take up with a guy you knew at the very least I'd been dating twenty-four hours earlier. If you'd been even the tiniest bit concerned about my feelings, you would have at least discussed it with me first. But you didn't. And what about after that night, Laurel? What about for the next *two months* when you were sneaking around behind my back? You knew damn well we were still seeing each other *all that time*."

Jamie fisted her hands and forced herself to take slow, deep breaths to try to stem the rage welling up inside her. Her heart was pounding and her knees were shaking.

Laurel's face paled but she didn't look away. "I didn't know that first night, which turned into an entire weekend, but I found out on Monday when I saw you at Newman's. You mentioned you were seeing Raymond that night and I realized he'd lied to me. I was shocked. And hurt. And absolutely furious. I left work and confronted him. He apologized profusely. Said as far as *he* was concerned, you'd broken up. And that he'd make it clear to you that you were through. He told me he loved me. And wanted to be with me. I stupidly believed him. Because I'd foolishly fallen in love with him. And desperately wanted to be with him."

She raked a hand through her hair. "For the next two months, in order to avoid any potentially awkward scenes, I avoided you as much as possible at work, which given how busy you always were at Newman's wasn't difficult. You didn't look brokenhearted to me, but since you were never the type to wear your heart on your sleeve . . ." She shrugged. "He told me he loved me, that he was ending things with you, and since that's what I wanted to hear, I didn't question the rest."

"I had no idea there was someone else," Jamie said, proud that her voice barely trembled, "let alone that someone else was *you*, until I saw you coming out of his apartment that last morning—wearing the same clothes you'd worn at Newman's the night before. When I confronted him, he admitted the two of you had been together for two months."

"If it means anything, I was as shocked to see you as you were to see me. As you know that resulted in your breakup. Even though I was furious with him for not being completely honest with me, I forgave him." She shook her head, her eyes filled with disbelief. "I swear to God I don't know what I was thinking. I'd *never* allowed any man to treat me that way before. Ever. My only defense is that I honestly, truly, and very stupidly loved him. And I thought, even though he'd made mistakes, that he loved me as well."

Anger suddenly fired in her eyes. "I can't believe what a *fool* I was! Even though I felt horrible about what had happened with you, I consoled myself with the fact that at least I'd found my soul mate. And that when you returned to New York I'd try to mend our relationship. And then, four weeks ago, I decided to surprise Raymond with a visit to his apartment." Twin flags of color stained her cheeks. "I surprised him all right. Him and one of my good friends. I later found out he'd been seeing her the *entire time* he was seeing me."

Jamie blinked. "Wait . . . you mean he was cheating on *you* the entire time he was cheating on me with you?"

"Yes! That son of a bitch was cheating on both of us."

Jamie looked into Laurel's eyes, which positively spit fury. "Well, I'll be damned."

They stood facing each other and Jamie watched the rage slowly ebb from Laurel's eyes to be replaced by a weariness that tugged at her heart. "I know I hurt you and I'm sorry, Jamie. From the depths of my soul, I'm sorry. And deeply ashamed. I've done a lot of selfish things in my life, things I'm not proud of, but being with Raymond . . . it was worse than just selfish, it was *wrong*. In every way.

"I've spent the entire last month thinking," Laurel continued, "about my life. About the sort of person I am versus the sort I want to be. The sort of mother I want to be. And the sort of sister as well. To my chagrin I realized I was falling far short in an appalling number of areas. And I want, more than anything, to fix that. Have been *trying* to fix that. I want to be a person I can look at in the mirror and be proud of. I want to be a mother who is there for Heather and sets a good example for her. And I want to be the kind of sister who appreciates what a great sister she had . . . and hopefully still has."

Laurel regarded her through solemn eyes. "I can't promise you I'll never do or say anything stupid again, but if you'll forgive me and give me another chance I *can* promise you that a man will never come between us again. And I'll try to be the best sister I can be."

After a brief hesitation, Laurel slowly held out her hand.

Jamie looked at it with her heart thudding in thick, fast beats, and realized that hand was a bridge. To a new beginning. All Jamie had to do was decide if she wanted to cross it.

Maria's words from the previous day drifted through her mind: *Anger poisons the person who holds it. Forgiveness sets us free.*

Yes, she'd been hurt, but not maliciously, as she'd believed—Raymond had lied to Laurel as well. He'd hurt both of them, yet in truth, he'd hurt Laurel worse because she'd been in love with him, whereas Jamie had really only been in love with the *idea* of him—of being swept off her feet by a rich, handsome, charming man.

She wanted to be set free. She didn't want the poison in her life any longer.

Hot moisture pushed behind her eyes. Instead of taking Laurel's hand, she opened her arms. Tears filled Laurel's eyes, and with a half laugh, half cry—a sound that Jamie echoed—Laurel stepped forward and into her embrace.

Chapter 28

The next morning, after everyone had eaten breakfast together at Nick's—cooked amid much laughter at Southern Comfort because, after all, Nick had the All-Clad pots and pans—Jamie and her mother walked to the beach for one last look at the ocean before her mom and Alex began their drive back to New York.

As they stood at the water's edge, allowing the cool water to lap at their bare feet, her mom murmured, "I've been thinking about what you said."

"Anything in particular? I said a lot of things."

"About coming here to get away from me. About all the pressure I've put on you."

Jamie let out a slow breath. "I'm sorry, Mom. I didn't mean to hurt your feelings. I was angry and frustrated when I said that."

"That doesn't mean it isn't true." She turned to face Jamie. "I want you to be honest with me, Jamie. Have I driven you away? Because you must know, that's the last thing I would ever want to do."

Jamie pressed her lips together and took a few seconds to gather her thoughts, because while she wanted to be completely honest, she didn't want to be hurtful. "I know, Mom. But the unvarnished truth is this—I love being included in your life, and having you in mine, but since Daddy died, you've become too dependent on me. It's been three years, yet you're still leaning on me as much as you did when he first passed away. Three years ago I understood it, but now . . . now it needs to stop. You're a smart woman, perfectly capable of doing things for yourself, yet you want me to make your decisions for you. And I can't. You need to make your own decisions, based on what's right for you. And I need to make mine, based on what's right for me. And you need to respect those decisions. And not put so much pressure on me."

There. She'd said it—the words she should have said months ago. Or at the very least, when her mother first arrived at Paradise Lost. A sense of calm and peace suffused Jamie, one she hadn't experienced in a very long time. She felt as if a huge weight had been lifted from her shoulders.

Her mom reached out and took her hands. Gave them a gentle squeeze. "You're right. Absolutely right. I haven't been able to think of anything else since you stomped out the other night saying you were done."

"I'm sorry about leaving that way—"

"Please don't be. I admit what you said was a slap, but it was one I desperately needed. I also have to admit that when you left New York, I was angry with you. It seemed to me you'd abandoned all your responsibilities—and over a man who wasn't worth even one of your tears. But mostly I was upset because I felt like you'd abandoned me—just when I needed you the most."

"I left Newman's in good hands," Jamie reminded her. "Nathan is a very capable manager—"

"I know. But this whole situation with Alex . . . I needed *you.*"

"As long as we're being so honest, Mom, I'm glad I didn't know about your situation at that time, because if I had, I might not have come here. And I desperately needed to get away. To recharge myself. Because what I was doing, how I was living, the decisions I was making, none of it felt good anymore. Nothing felt *right.* I needed a change. And not just a little one. A catastrophic upheaval was called for."

"I know that—now. But at the time, I'm afraid I was awash in hormones and only thinking about my own problems, and for that I'm very sorry. They say change is good—of course, I don't know who 'they' are, and I'm not sure they're right. I do know, at least for me, change is *hard*. And very scary. And since your father died—my life has been nothing *but* change."

She drew a deep breath, then continued, "The worst change is that I feel like you and I have . . . lost each other a bit."

The truth of her mother's words, as well as the catch in her voice, shamed Jamie. "I guess we have. And it's mostly my fault. I allowed work and my relationship with Raymond to take over my life." How many times while she was dating Raymond had her mom invited her over for dinner and she'd said no?

A lot.

How many times had Jamie purposely avoided conversations with her mom because she didn't want to be involved in any drama or listen to her mom discuss her grieving process— because talking about her dad was hard?

Again, a lot.

But, standing in Nick's kitchen while they'd prepared the food for the potluck dinner, she'd realized that while listening to her mom talk about her dad was hard, it was also . . . cathartic.

"I know I've leaned on you a great deal since your dad died," Mom said quietly, "but—"

"We leaned on each other, Mom. When Daddy died, it was a terrible time for me, too."

"I know, but I've continued to lean, and for a very long time now. You've had to take on so many things I didn't know how to do. I should have kept up with all the financial stuff— the investments, the bank accounts, the tax returns, running Newman's—but your dad always took care of all that. I was still trying to adjust to empty-nest syndrome when he died."

Her eyes glistened with unshed tears. "After you graduated from college and moved into your own apartment, I was truly happy for you, and so proud of the wonderful young woman you'd become. How well you transitioned into the role of managing Newman's. But a part of me felt . . . so lost. My little girl was all grown up and on her own. I wasn't needed as a mom anymore."

Jamie's heart felt as if it slipped from its moorings. "I'll always need you, Mom."

Her mom shook her head. "But not in the same way you did growing up—which is completely normal. I understand that there's a natural growing apart, that the mother-daughter relationship changes as we both grow older. My mind knows that, but even though I love being your friend, I still clung to the past because it just *hurts* when your child grows up and away from you. And it's not really something you can understand until it happens to you.

"But then, only six months after you moved out, your dad died. And not only was I not a mom any longer, I wasn't a wife—the two roles that had defined me for more than half my life."

She let out a shaky breath. "What I'm trying to say, is I really appreciate how much you've helped me with everything. You always have—even as a kid—but especially after your dad died." She gave a watery laugh and looked down at her midsection. "And here you are, once again helping me. Taking care of me. You came here to sort out your own problems, and I swooped in with mine. I shouldn't have"—a pair of tears streaked down her cheeks—"but I really needed my best friend."

Jamie's breath hitched and she pulled her mother into a tight hug. And for the first time since her mom had shown up at Paradise Lost, Jamie was glad she'd done so. "Mom. I'm always here for you."

"I know. And I'm always here for you, too. You're just better at stuff than I am."

Jamie shook her head. "Not true. You're a great mom."

"I'm glad you think so."

"I *know* so." She leaned back and shot her a teasing grin. "Look how great I turned out."

"You did. I couldn't have asked for a more wonderful child."

"And I totally hit the parent lottery."

"Even though I don't know how to file a tax return?"

"Phooey. That's what accountants are for."

"Even though I suck at trigonometry?"

"Yup. Mom—you were good at the important stuff. Hugs and kisses and listening and sitting with me when I was sick and being proud of me and always making me feel loved. Even when I was a pain in the ass."

"You were never a pain in the ass."

Jamie cocked a brow. "You've obviously blocked out the moody teenage years."

Mom laughed. "Okay, maybe you were a pest one or two times."

"More like one or two thousand times, but it's very sweet—and just like you—to love me anyway."

"And just like you to love me even though I've been a drama-prone, demanding mess."

"Hey—that's what best friends are for."

"You're going to make me cry," Mom said, wiping her eyes.

"Yeah—like *that's* hard to do," Jamie teased with an exaggerated eye roll.

Her mom smiled, then sobered. "A few months ago, I was browsing a self-help book and came across this proverb: When the winds of change are blowing, some people are building shelters and the others are building windmills. Those words struck me like a bolt of lightning and I realized that ever since your dad died, I'd been building shelters—protecting myself against the changes his death wrought, refusing to accept that my life was different and would never be the same."

"I know it's been difficult for you, Mom."

"There are days when it still is, although my grief support group helped a lot." Her eyes grew misty. "I not only lost your dad, but the life we'd planned to share. I thought we'd grow old together. Even though your dad was older, I never truly envisioned being here without him. The adjustment's been . . . God. Brutal. I told myself I never wanted to go through anything like that ever again—no more changes. No more heartbreak. If I just kept my head down, and kept moving forward, one step at a time, I'd survive. And that's what I was doing. And doing it well, I thought, although with a lot of help from you. And I could have done that forever—

just plodded along in the little rut of non-change I'd carved out for myself."

She pulled in a deep breath. "But then, right around the time I read that proverb, I met Alex. And suddenly I was laughing and feeling things I hadn't felt in a very long time. Things I never thought I'd feel again. I figured, 'He's young, he's fun, why not flirt a little?'"

"You decided to come out of your shelter and build a windmill."

"Yes."

"That was brave of you."

Mom huffed out a laugh. "I didn't feel brave. I was scared to death." Her gaze filled with both confusion and unmistakable pride. "As much as I hated that you left New York, I can't deny it was a very brave step to take."

A humorless sound escaped Jamie. "Not really. It's not as if I left permanently. I just took vacation time I'd been due forever. I'll be going home soon." Those words tied an uncomfortable knot in her stomach, one she refused to examine, at least not right now. "What you did by getting involved with Alex—I imagine that felt like jumping off a diving board without knowing if there was water in the pool."

"Exactly. It was supposed to be fun and easy, and it was. I started to really care for him, which I hadn't planned on. And then when I found out I was pregnant—it all became so incredibly complicated, and the whole time I've been here I haven't been able to think clearly. But that talk we all had while cooking for the potluck dinner made the proverbial lightbulb go off over my head, and I finally realized what was bothering me."

"And what was it?"

"I was paralyzed with the fear of forgetting your father, of his memory fading until I wouldn't be able to recall him any longer. But being in that kitchen, cooking with Tom's two daughters and his granddaughter, I realized that he lives on through the three of you. You, Heather, and Laurel all have something of him in you, and he'll never be lost to me because of that. After that, I recalled something you'd said—something that condensed all my worries, all my fears, all my scattered thoughts down into one simple sentence, and it struck me just as hard as the windmill proverb had."

"What did I say?"

"That you didn't see why my decision was so difficult—that if I love Alex, then I should be with him, and if I don't, I should tell him so and let him go. When I thought about it that way, I realized I'd been agonizing over something that was really a no-brainer." Tears filled her eyes. "I love him, Jamie. I want to be with him. And have our baby with him. He's told me all along that he loves me—even before he knew about the baby, he'd told me. The fact that he rearranged his life to come here, to stay with me all this time, and didn't dump my pesky ass has proven to me that, miraculously, he means it. I . . . I accepted his proposal last night. We're planning a November wedding. Something very small. I didn't want to announce it at breakfast—I wanted to tell you privately first."

Jamie smiled and pulled her mom into her arms for a long hug. "I'm really happy for you, Mom. Both of you. And so proud of you. You figured out what you wanted all on your own. And you're going to be a fantastic mom. Again."

"I certainly hope so."

Jamie leaned back and teased, "And I'm going to have the hottest stepdad on the planet."

Her mom laughed—erasing any worries Jamie may have had that she wasn't secure in her decision—then heaved a gushy sigh. "He really is great, Jamie."

"And very lucky to have you."

"That's what he says."

"Good. And he better keep saying it, or I'm going to whack him upside his head. And I have the All-Clad pans to do it with."

Her mom's gaze turned serious. "What about you? Even though I've been immersed in my own drama, it hasn't escaped my notice that you and Nick have become . . . close."

Heat flooded Jamie's face. Darn it, she could actually feel the blotches creeping up her neck. "We're . . . enjoying each other's company."

"I like him very much."

Jamie smiled. "I like him very much, too." And she meant it. So why did the words feel like a lie? *Maybe because you more than 'like him very much,'* her pesky inner voice whispered.

"You're heading back to New York in just over two weeks' time," her mom said. "What happens then?"

An unpleasant cramping sensation gripped Jamie. She gave what she hoped passed for a carefree laugh. "Then we won't be enjoying each other's company anymore."

Saying the words out loud gave her a heart owie that continued to linger the entire time she and her mom walked back to Paradise Lost. But no matter how much the heart owie hurt, Jamie knew she'd just have to suck it up. Nick's life was here. He'd made it clear he'd never leave Seaside Cove. Her family, her job, her *everything* was in New York. And in little more than two weeks from now, their time together would be over.

When they arrived back at Paradise Lost, her mom went directly to Alex, and with their hands joined, they announced they were getting married. Congratulations and hugs were shared all around, then a flurry of activity commenced as Alex loaded Jamie's mother's car with their luggage, and Laurel and Heather's bags were moved downstairs to await the arrival of the taxi that would drive them to the airport for their flight to Italy.

"We would have driven you," Jamie's mom said to Laurel, "but there's no way we could fit everyone and all the luggage as well into my car."

"Definitely not my luggage," Laurel agreed with a laugh. "A light packer I am not."

Nick gave Jamie's hand a light squeeze. "I need to get something from Southern Comfort. Be right back."

While he was gone, Jamie and Heather returned to the house and performed a quick check through each room to make sure none of their belongings were left behind. They'd just finished and were about to head back downstairs where the others were waiting when Nick entered the house holding a Piggly Wiggly bag.

"For you," he said to Heather, handing her the bag.

"You're giving me groceries?" Heather asked with a giggle.

"No—I just don't have any wrapping paper."

Still giggling, Heather looked in the bag. Then gasped. Her eyes widened and her gaze flew to Nick's. "No way," she said, then pulled a black jacket bearing a formidable-looking tiger from the bag. "But . . . but this is your Princeton beer jacket," she said, tracing the bright orange numbers that denoted the year Nick graduated. "I can't accept this."

"Sure you can. Consider it a belated birthday present."

"But what will you wear to your reunions?"

"Only alumni who are out of school four years or less wear them. After that the class designs something new. So if I decide to go to a reunion, I wouldn't wear my beer jacket anyway." He shot her a conspiratorial wink. "When you tell your mom what it is, be sure to call it a senior jacket."

"I will, I def will," she said in a breathless voice. She dropped the Piggly Wiggly bag and shrugged into the jacket. It was way too big on her, but she quickly rolled back the sleeves, then held out her arms and asked in an awed voice, "What do you think?"

"I think it looks a lot better on you than it ever did on me," Nick said with a laugh.

"OMG, Lindsey is just going to *die* when I text her!" She launched herself at Nick and gave him a quick hug, then, with her face resembling a ripe tomato, she stepped back. "Thanks, Nick. It's the coolest present ever. Seriously. I can't wait to show everyone."

"You're welcome."

She dashed from the house, and as the screen door banged shut behind her, her excited voice floated through the window, "OMG, Mom, wait 'til you see what Nick gave me!"

Jamie turned to Nick and her heart . . . God, how many owies could it take in one day? It was one thing for him to be nice to her, but quite another for him to make her niece look like she'd just been given the moon and stars. "That was really nice of you."

He set his hands on her hips and urged her forward until their pelvises lightly bumped. "I'm a really nice guy."

Yes, he was. And the idea of saying good-bye to him—

She ruthlessly cut off the thought and shoved it as far down as it would go into the Cross That Bridge When I Get There abyss. "So I've noticed. I don't think I've ever seen her so excited. Especially over something most teenagers wouldn't be caught dead wearing."

"Speaking of stuff you wouldn't wear . . ." He slipped a single finger beneath the thin strap of her tank top, eliciting a delighted shiver from her. "I'm looking forward to you not wearing this top." His other hand slid down to cup her bottom. "Or these shorts. And as soon as all these people leave—"

His words were cut off by the honking of a horn. "Sounds like they're ready to go."

"Good. Because as much as I like them, I'm ready for them to be gone."

Jamie couldn't help but laugh. "Me, too."

They joined the others downstairs, and amid much hugging, laughing, and a few tears, Jamie's mom and Alex piled into the car, while Laurel, Heather, and their mountain of luggage squeezed into the taxi, then both vehicles drove away. Jamie and Nick waved until they'd turned the corner and vanished from view. The instant they did, Nick swung her up in his arms and walked purposefully toward the stairs.

"In a hurry?" she asked in a prim voice—as if she wasn't.

"Yeah." He paused at the bottom of the stairs and treated her to a deep, fierce, tongue-mating kiss that made steam pump from her pores. When he raised his head, he looked into her eyes and said, "We only have about two weeks left, so I'm not inclined to waste any time. That okay with you?"

Since his kiss had stolen her ability to speak, she merely nodded. *Two weeks left. Two weeks left.* And as he climbed the stairs with her cradled in his arms, she shoved those words right down into the Cross That Bridge When I Get There abyss to reside with the depressing thought of saying goodbye to him.

Chapter 29

"What's all this?" Nick asked, looking at the array of ingredients and cookware set out on his countertop.

"We're ready for your cooking lesson."

"What are we making?"

"Three things—first are frosted sugar cookies."

Nick nodded his approval. "Excellent. I love cookies." To prove it he stepped in behind her, wrapped his arms around her waist, then lowered his head to nibble on her neck. "Yum."

She laughed and wriggled out of his reach. When he reached for her again, she snatched a wooden spoon from the counter and brandished it like a sword. "Back off, big boy. Cooking is serious business. Don't make me get rough with you."

Nick grinned. "Rough? Oooooh, baby. This gets better and better." He made a rolling motion with his hand. "Carry on. What else?"

"While the cookies are baking, I'll teach you the other basics I promised—how to boil water for pasta, and how to cook eggs."

"How long do the cookies need to bake?"

"Eight minutes. This recipe makes three batches, so we'd better get—hey! Where are you going?"

"Be right back," he said over his shoulder as he walked out of the kitchen. He returned less than a minute later. "You forgot an ingredient." He set his contribution on the counter.

Jamie glanced down, then cocked a brow. "Condoms?"

"We have to do *something* for those eight minutes while the cookies bake."

He watched color bloom on her skin and couldn't resist smoothing his fingertips over her velvety smooth cheek. Damn but he loved that blush. And was amazed she still could do so after the countless hours they'd spent naked together.

"And since it's only eight minutes," he continued, "we'll need a head start." He flicked open the button on her denim shorts, pulled down the zipper, and with a single tug, they landed around her ankles, leaving her dressed only in her white tank top and black lace panties. "Now *that's* what a cooking teacher should wear."

Her lips twitched. "I'll remember when I give my next lesson at the senior center."

The subtle reference to her life in New York knotted Nick's insides. With the same effort he'd put forth every day of these last two weeks, he ruthlessly shoved aside all thoughts of her leaving and forced himself to concentrate on the present. On this special moment. Because they were nearly out of moments.

She eyeballed his jeans. "So how come I'm the only one in my underwear?"

In the blink of an eye, he'd rid himself of his jeans—and his T-shirt as well. And had snatched her into his arms. "Now we're cookin'," he said, nuzzling her neck.

She laughed and pushed back against his chest. "I can see that baking cookies with you is going to take all day."

He palmed her breast. "I sure hope so."

She laughed again—damn, he loved that husky sound—then adopted her schoolmarm voice—another sound he loved. "Behave yourself or there'll be no cookies for you."

He heaved an exaggerated sigh and let her go. "Fine. Show me what to do so we can get these suckers in the oven. I have plans for those eight minutes."

Amidst much laughing and kissing and leaving floury
fingerprints on each other, she taught him how to preheat
the oven—which worked like a charm now that the operat-
ing manual wasn't inside—how to cream together butter and
sugar, operate a hand mixer, roll out dough, and use a cookie
cutter. It was fun—but only because she was there. He sure
as hell couldn't imagine himself baking cookies without her.
Which made this but one more in a very long list of things
that were special because of her. Things, moments, he'd never
forget.

After they slid the cookie sheet into the oven, she showed
him how to set the timer. The instant she was done, he yanked
down her panties, jerked her tank top over her head, swooped
her into his arms, and carried her to the nearest chair—
snagging a condom on the way.

All amusement, all playfulness vanished as the need to be
inside her, to feel her wrapped around him, nearly strangled
him. He set her down long enough to shuck off his underwear
and roll on the condom, then sat, pulling her down so she
straddled him. With her gaze on his, she lowered herself, engulfing him in her tight, wet heat. When he was fully, deeply
inside her, they both stilled.

With her beautiful caramel-colored eyes looking deeply
into his, he reached up to frame her face and realized his
hands weren't steady. Emotions collided in him, a jumble of
feelings he'd been trying for these last two weeks to figure out
how to express. A thousand words that needed to be said, yet
in the end they all boiled down to just one word. The word
that had drummed through his brain for the past eight weeks,
gathering speed as the days zoomed by, careening forward
until now . . . when they had only this day, then one more.
And then there would be no more days.

"Jamie."

Her name passed his lips in a fervent whisper that ended in
a groan when she rocked against him.

With her gaze still on his, she captured his hand and
pressed a lingering kiss against his palm. "Nick."

Gazes locked, they moved together, slowly at first, each
stroke pushing him toward a climax he didn't want to reach.

He wanted to prolong this day, this moment, never let it end. But need, desire built and soon, much too soon, they climaxed, shuddering against each other, holding tight. He'd barely caught his breath when the timer beeped. Still joined, their gazes met. The sight of her—tousled and flushed, her lips moist and swollen from his kisses—touched something inside him that he hadn't even known was there until she proved its existence.

With the incessant beep piercing the silence, she whispered, "We're out of time."

And his heart ached with the knowledge that she was right—and it had nothing to do with cookies.

The morning after their lesson, Jamie awoke in Nick's bed. Lying on her side, she felt his warmth pressed against her back and took a moment to simply drink in the feel of him. God, she loved waking up in his arms. Falling asleep with his naked body pressed against hers. The sensation of his skin on hers. She glanced down and her heart constricted at the sight of his large hand splayed against her abdomen. It looked so right there. Felt so right.

And it was about to end.

Because today was her last day in Seaside Cove.

Stifling a sigh, she opened her eyes and looked at the small bedside clock. Seven A.M. Time to get up and start getting ready for the Clam Festival. Then, after the festival, she'd spend her final night with Nick. Then wake up early to catch her morning flight back to New York. To the hectic pace of the city. To everything that was familiar, that she'd known her entire life. To her family and Kate and all her other friends. To her apartment and her job and the restaurant her father had built. To her life.

Where she belonged.

Her insides ached with the knowledge that there were so many things she'd miss about Seaside Cove. The neighbors who'd become friends. The cats that wandered the neighborhood and cleaned out the food bowl she filled twice a day. The gorgeous sunrises. Walks on the beach. Buying shrimp on the side of the road. But what she'd miss most of all was Nick. How was it possible that her time here had passed so quickly? Especially the last two weeks since her family had departed. Two blissful weeks spent with Nick.

Nick . . . She'd spent every day with him and each day, each hour, had proven more magical than the one before it. Lounging on the beach, splashing in the waves, playing with Godiva, walking hand in hand along the shore, talking, laughing, kissing. She'd accompanied him to Kevin and Liz's house twice on day trips, and both times she'd loved spending time with the couple and Emily.

She and Nick had enjoyed several meals at Oy Vey Mama Mia, and one night Jamie cooked a big spaghetti dinner for Megan and Grace, and their families and Dorothy Ernst. She'd also invited Melvin, who, to her surprise, had brought her a small bouquet of flowers as a hostess gift. "Don't get many dinner invitations, Newman," he'd said gruffly as he'd shoved the blooms toward her.

They'd spent hours exploring the quaint beach towns surrounding Seaside Cove, discovering one particular store called Seas the Moment that was like the Home Depot for beach-themed items. Nick asked her for help in choosing some lamps and wall prints for both Southern Comfort and Paradise Lost, and they'd laughed as they staggered out to his truck with his numerous purchases.

They'd devoted several days with the other volunteers to finishing the float, and when it was finally done, the entire committee headed to Oy Vey Mama Mia for the lunch special of bagels and lox with a side of melon-wrapped prosciutto. Jamie completed her paperwork for the vendor submissions and layout and felt a real sense of accomplishment and pride when, during the final clam meeting, everyone applauded her efforts. The camaraderie and team atmosphere of the committee reminded her very much of Newman's—except without the stress of turning out thousands of meals a week.

Evenings were spent enjoying the nightly bonfire. Several times she and Nick rented movies and they'd snuggle on the sofa with Godiva and Cupcake and a huge bowl of popcorn. They rarely managed to make it to the end of a movie, however, as Nick had wandering hands and lips and Jamie found him far more interesting than anything on the screen.

And the nights ... they'd spent every night together. Exploring. Learning. Laughing. Making love. The way he touched her left her breathless. Sated, yet aching for more. Never in her life had she felt so in sync with anyone.

Especially yesterday during their cooking lesson.

The way he'd made love to her while the cookies baked had lodged a lump in her throat. There'd been so many things she'd wanted to say, to express how much their time together had meant to her, but the only word she'd been able to manage was his name. Just ... Nick. Yet somehow, that had said it all.

And now it was about to end.

Nick stirred behind her and she briefly squeezed her eyes closed as the words that had haunted her for the last several days once again drifted through her mind.

How was she going to say good-bye to him?

God help her, she didn't know.

Any more than she knew how she'd ended up sleeping with a guy she hadn't even liked when she first met him. Or when what was supposed to be nothing more than a light, no-strings fling had started to feel so very ... not light.

Slowly, so as not to awaken Nick, she sat up in the bed. Turned to look at him over her shoulder. And found him regarding her with an indecipherable expression.

"Hi," she said softly. "I didn't mean to wake you."

"You didn't. I've been awake for a while." He took her hand and gently tugged. "Come here."

The teasing warmth she was accustomed to seeing in his eyes in the morning was gone, replaced by a solemn intensity that heated her right to her core. She snagged a condom from the supply on the bedside table. He wordlessly took the packet from her, sheathed himself, then settled his body between her splayed thighs. With her gaze locked on his, she glided her hands over his torso, his back, memorizing again every inch of the skin she'd endlessly explored these past few weeks. Her orgasm overtook her, and with a cry, she absorbed every shudder. Nick's strong hands gripped her hips, and with a final deep thrust, he found his release.

Aftershocks still rippled through her when she pressed a kiss against his neck. His pulse thumped hard and fast beneath her lips and for several seconds she savored the sensation. Until reality returned, along with those depressing words.

How was she going to say good-bye to him?

For Nick the Clam Festival passed by in a blur. With Jamie's palm snug against his and Godiva's leash in his other hand, they'd visited every one of the dozens of craft booths. She'd done a great job arranging the layout, and he lost count of how many times they were stopped by Seaside Cove residents who echoed that sentiment.

At her urging he bought several kitchen gadgets he knew he'd never use but that she insisted every well-stocked kitchen had to have. He didn't even know what "zest" was, but by God, he now owned a thingamabob that would zest any lemons he might buy. He figured he'd keep it in the drawer with the cookie cutters—something else he couldn't conceive of ever using again. Because she'd be gone.

One booth sold enamel trinket boxes inlaid with crystal, running the gamut from flowers to fish. One in particular—a delicate pink flamingo—caught his eye. After purchasing it he presented it to her with a flourish.

"Even though this flamingo has its head attached, I hope it will remind you of Paradise Lost. And me."

Instead of smiling as he'd expected she would, she'd pressed the box against her heart, then softly kissed him. "I don't need anything to remind me of Paradise Lost or you—you're both unforgettable. But I'll treasure this. Always. Thank you."

They sampled food from several vendors, washed down a dozen baked clams with ice-cold beer, and had their photo taken with the giant clam mascot. Jamie bought two copies and presented him with one. "To remind you of me," she said.

He looked down at the photo, of the two of them and Godiva, their arms around each other, smiling, standing next to that silly giant clam. They both looked so happy . . . so happy together. So *right* together. Like she belonged there beside him. A perfectly matched puzzle piece—one he hadn't even known was missing until she'd filled the space, proving it had been empty before she got there.

And it suddenly hit him, like a fastball to the chest. The thing he'd refused to examine too closely, had refused to admit to himself, but could no longer deny.

He loved her.

God help him, he loved her. Loved being with her. Talking to her. Laughing with her. Loved her sense of humor. Her integrity and loyalty. He loved her in bed. Out of bed. Anytime.

All the time.

Damn. So much for his fancy Ivy League education giving him any sort of smarts. Because falling in love with her was the stupidest thing he could have done.

And yet that's exactly what he'd done.

And wasn't that just a colossal pain in the ass? Jesus. She'd made it clear from day one that her time in Seaside Cove was temporary. That her life, her job, her family, her everything was in New York. That that's where she belonged, where she wanted to be, and where she'd return at summer's end.

He'd known it. Had known feeling anything deeper for her than mild affection was the height of idiocy. And yet, here he stood. Painfully in love. With a woman who was leaving tomorrow.

He lifted his gaze from the photo and looked into her beautiful eyes. And had to clear his throat to dredge up his voice.

"I don't need anything to remind me of you—you're unforgettable," he said, mimicking her earlier words. "But I'll treasure this. Always. Thank you."

The day marched on, with the early afternoon marking the crowning of all the clams. Dorothy Ernst was crowned Senior Clam and proudly took her place on the clam float with the other winners, one of whom was Megan's three-year-old daughter who won Baby Clam. No other Seaside Cove residents were crowned, but Nick figured that was good—if locals won all the titles, people would assume the contest was rigged. After the parade, Nick and Jamie wandered down to the beach to watch the fireworks display.

Then Nick remained by the bonfire and watched as Jamie said good-bye to all her Seaside Cove friends. Watched her embrace Megan and Grace and the other members of the

Clam Committee. Ira Silverman lifted her up and spun her around, then gave her a smacking kiss on the cheek. Maria held her close and whispered something in Jamie's ear that brought tears to her eyes. And the entire time he watched her say good-bye to all those people, all he could think was, *How am I going to say good-bye to her?*

God help him, he didn't know. Other than to know he didn't want to.

Which meant he couldn't let her go without at least trying to convince her to stay.

After she'd said good-bye to Dorothy and Melvin, Jamie joined him by the fire. "Guess what?" she whispered.

I love you. I want you to stay. Don't go. He drew her into his arms, buried his face against her neck, and breathed her in. And knew that for the rest of his life, he'd think of her every time he ate a cookie. Which, given how much he liked cookies, didn't bode well for ever being able to forget her. "Don't know."

"Melvin asked Dorothy for a date."

"Oh. Yeah, that I know."

She planted her hands on his chest and leaned back. "You know? How?"

"Melvin told me."

"When?"

"A few hours ago."

"And where was I?"

"Waiting in that ridiculously long line for the ladies' room."

"What did he say?"

"Um, that he'd asked Dorothy for a date."

"Details," she demanded. "What else did he say?"

"He's taking her to Oy Vey Mama Mia tomorrow night. He told me he hasn't taken a woman to dinner since his wife died seventeen years ago and asked if I had any advice."

"Did you?"

"I told him a bottle of Chianti wouldn't hurt, especially if he keeps himself to one glass and Dorothy to several. And that if he senses an argument coming on, the best way to forestall it is to lay a kiss on her—one that'll make her forget all about arguing."

Jamie laughed. "Good advice. I hope he takes it."

She was still chuckling when he lowered his head and kissed her—a long, slow, deep kiss that he wished could go on for days and made him wish like hell they were alone.

"Wow," she said, when he lifted his head. "Not that I didn't enjoy that, but in case you didn't notice, I wasn't arguing with you—I was agreeing with you."

"Good. What do you say we go home and get naked?"

She wrapped her arms around his neck and pressed herself against him. "And once again, we agree."

Chapter 30

The next morning Jamie ran her hand along Southern Comfort's shiny granite countertop. She'd come to some profound realizations in this kitchen with regards to her sister and her mother and ultimately herself. And now as she looked at her packed suitcases standing by the door next to the cat carrier, which contained a very unhappy Cupcake, she came to another realization.

She did not want to leave here.

Yet on the heels of that realization came another one.

She had to go.

Nick entered the living area through the sliding doors leading to the screen porch. "The taxi just pulled up."

Which meant it was time to go. Her time was over. She and Nick had made love for the last time. Showered together for the last time. Eaten breakfast together for the last time.

He walked into the kitchen and took her hands. "I don't mind driving you to the airport."

"I know. But I don't want you to. I hate airport good-byes. I'd rather say good-bye here." A hitched breath escaped her and she looked at the floor. "Actually I'd rather not say good-bye at all."

"Then don't."

Her head snapped up. And she found him looking at her with a grave expression she'd never seen on his face before. "What do you mean?"

"You don't want to say good-bye—so don't say it." His green gaze bored into hers. "Stay."

Stay. Stay. Stay. One single word. One that seemed to echo in the air, so tempting, so enticing.

So impossible.

A lump lodged in her throat and she could barely speak. "I can't stay, Nick. I want to, but . . . I can't." She swallowed, then added softly, "Maybe we could try a long-distance thing . . ."

The suggestion evaporated when he shook his head. "We could, but we both know it wouldn't work. Not really. Not for any length of time. And it would just wind up ending badly. As you've said—my life is here. And your life is there."

He was right. Her life was there. Her job wouldn't allow her to keep coming here. It was better to make a clean break. Now. Right this minute. Before she fell apart.

"Thank you," she whispered. "For the best summer of my life."

He cupped her face between his hands, brushed his mouth over hers with a tenderness that welled tears in her eyes. Then he rested his forehead against hers. "Back atcha, sweetheart."

The sound of a horn honking broke the silence, and without another word, Nick carried her luggage down the stairs while Jamie followed, carrying Cupcake. Godiva clamored after them, and after her belongings were loaded in the cab, Jamie crouched down to give Godiva a final belly rub.

"You take good care of Nick," she said. "He didn't quite master cooking eggs, so don't let him feed you too many burned ones." After a final pat, she rose. Then feeling as if she were experiencing some sort of out-of-body, numb dream, she gave Nick a final hug, clinging to him for a few extra seconds to imprint the feel of him on her. A final soft kiss to his beautiful mouth. One last look at Paradise Lost, with its decapitated flamingo.

Then sliding into the cab. The door closing, the sound like that of a crypt slamming shut. The taxi moving slowly away. Watching Nick and Godiva through the rear window until the cab turned the corner. And then they were gone. She thought she'd cry the entire way to the airport, but instead she just stared out the window, dry-eyed.

When the cab stopped in front of the terminal, she still felt as if a fog engulfed her. She opened her purse for her wallet and stared. At a palm-sized square box on top. With shaking hands she lifted the top and caught her breath. Inside lay a perfect sand dollar, accompanied by a tiny card that simply read *Love, Nick.*

And the tears she'd been unable to shed filled her eyes and ran unchecked down her cheeks.

Twelve long, draining hours later, after the sun had set and stained the sky with the first dark mauve streaks of twilight, Jamie once again slid into the rear of a taxi.

"Where to?" the cabbie asked her.

"Home," she said in an exhausted voice. "Take me home."

Chapter 31

Nick sat on the dilapidated picnic bench on Southern Comfort's carport and listlessly tossed Godiva's tennis ball between his hands. Godiva lay at his feet, her head resting on his sneaker. She heaved a heavy sigh, then looked up at him with mournful eyes.

"Yeah, I know exactly how you feel."

Jamie had left twelve hours ago—actually twelve hours and forty-eight minutes ago, not that he was counting—and by damn, they'd been the worst twelve hours and forty-eight minutes of his life. He felt . . . gutted. Eviscerated. Empty.

"This sucks, Godiva."

Godiva heaved another sigh, gave his ankle a halfhearted lick, then flopped her head back on his sneaker.

Another painful minute passed—bringing the count to the worst twelve hours and forty-nine minutes he'd ever spent—and Nick shook his head.

"That's it. I'm done." He pulled his iPhone from his pocket and accessed the Internet. "I'm such an idiot. Damn it, I should have told her how I felt. Should have at least given the long-distance thing a shot. Maybe it would work. Maybe if she knew I loved her, she'd want to stay. Or maybe if I gave it

more time and she fell in love with me . . . I don't know. All I
know is that this whole 'she's there, I'm here' thing definitely
isn't going to work. And I need to tell her. In person. End of
summer is a great time to visit New York."

But then a thought occurred to him—one that had him
jolting upright. He turned it over in his mind a few times, then
said slowly, "You know, Godiva, as much as we love Seaside
Cove, there *are* beaches—and beach houses—in New York."

Godiva raised her head at that news and looked at Nick
with a "tell me more" expression.

"I think while we're in New York we should go and check
it out," Nick continued, nodding. "Yeah. I mean, I know I said
I'd never leave here, but that was before we met Jamie. And
there's just no way around it—I'd rather be there with her,
then here without her. You'd be just as happy on a New York
beach, wouldn't you?"

Godiva jumped to her feet and pranced, clearly saying, *I
don't care what beach it is as long as I have you! And Jamie,
too! And what's for dinner? Please tell me it's dinnertime!*

Nick laughed and barely resisted the urge to thump himself on the head. "Yup, definitely an idiot. I think I'm going
to demand a refund from Princeton. Either that or they need
to start offering a course called How to Not Screw Up Your
Love Life 101."

He accessed his favorite travel site, and in less than ten
minutes, the transaction was done. "We're going to New
York," he told Godiva. "Tomorrow."

Godiva thumped her tail and Nick drew his first easy
breath in what felt like weeks at the knowledge that he'd be
seeing Jamie tomorrow. And that he wouldn't leave New York
until they'd come to some sort of arrangement. Until she knew
he loved her.

"C'mon girl. Flight leaves early in the morning. Let's go
pack." He stood and Godiva jumped to her feet. They were just
heading for the steps when a car stopped in front of Southern
Comfort. Nick turned and stilled at the sight of the taxi. The
rear door opened and Jamie emerged, holding a large shopping bag.

With his heart pounding hard enough to crack a rib, he
hurried toward her, stopping when only an arm's length sep-

arated them. He wanted to grab her, but forced himself not to. Forced himself to wait and hear her out. Because once he grabbed her, he wasn't letting her go.

"Hi," she said, reaching down to give a prancing Godiva an affectionate pat.

"Hi." His gaze flicked to the shopping bag, and he frowned when he noted the Seas the Moment logo—the shop they'd discovered during their explorations the previous week. "What's going on?"

For an answer she held out her hand. The sand dollar he'd given her rested on her palm. "Where did you get this?"

"I found it on the beach a few days ago. I hoped if I gave it to you, the legend would come true and you'd return to Seaside Cove. Seems it worked."

She nodded, then cleared her throat. "When I saw it, I made some pretty amazing realizations. Realizations I might have made before I left, if not for you, by the way."

"Me? What did I do?"

Color rushed into her cheeks, and her lips pursed in that prim way that never failed to both amuse him and set him on fire. "You distracted me. Very badly. And almost constantly."

He crossed his arms over his chest and hiked a brow. "I didn't hear you complaining at the time."

"Of course not. There's nothing to complain about—unless there's serious thinking to be done. And there was. A lot of it. And I couldn't do it. At least not until I got away from you. When my head finally cleared from that glazy-eyed fog you put me in and as Larry here was unloading my bags at the airport"—she jerked her head behind her to indicate the cabbie, who gave Nick a thumbs-up—"it suddenly hit me. I just didn't want to leave. I mean I already knew I didn't want to leave, but when I contemplated getting on the plane to actually leave, I knew I couldn't. So I told Larry to stop unloading my bags."

"Pretty bossy she was about it," Larry chimed in with a grin.

"I realized that my mother is settled with Alex, Laurel and I have mended our fences, and Heather and I can always text each other to death. I called my mom and told her I wanted to stay here, and after assuring her I'd come back for the wedding, she gave me her blessing. But even if she hadn't, I was staying here—no more letting anyone pull my strings, except me. I phoned Newman's and spoke to Nathan and together we worked out a schedule and he's going to start interviewing for new managers right away. I then called Maria and officially accepted the offer she made me last night at the bonfire—to manage Oy Vey Mama Mia as she and Ira would like more free time. She also told me that the storefront next to the restaurant will be coming available in about four months. It would make a perfect dessert bistro—the exact sort of place I've always dreamed of opening.

"And then, there was you. I told you a number of times that my life was in New York, and maybe that was true. But it turns out my *heart* is here. With you. And you can't have a life without a heart, right? So I told Larry to take me to Seas the Moment."

"Told me to get her there as fast as I could," Larry added from the driver's seat. "Kept telling me she wished my superpower was the ability to fly. I told her I wished it was, too."

"Why did you want to go there?" Nick asked.

"To get this." She handed him the huge bag. "I would have been here sooner, but this took a while."

"Hours," Larry said. "It took *hours*. But she wasn't going to leave without it."

"What is this?" Nick asked, taking the bag.

"One way to find out."

He untied the bag and pulled it away. And found himself holding a beautiful oval wooden house plaque like the ones that adorned all the homes on Seaside Cove. This one depicted a flamingo wading in shallow water near a beach where a perfect sand dollar rested in the sand while the sun set in the background. The letters spelled out—

"Paradise Found," he read, tracing his fingers over the raised letters. "It's beautiful."

"And very true." She set her sand dollar on the cab's rear seat next to Cupcake's carrier, then moved closer to him, and he set down the plaque so he could take her in his arms. "I know you didn't specifically ask me to come back," she said softly, "but you did give me the sand dollar, and since you asked me to stay, I'm hoping you don't mind."

"Mind?" He snatched her against him and took what felt like his first deep breath in more than twelve hours. "Just so you know, if you hadn't come back, Godiva and I were going to New York. I'd just finished booking the flight for tomorrow morning. We decided we'd rather be there with you than here without you."

She leaned back in the circle of his arms, and her eyes searched his. "You mean you'd *move* to New York?"

"If that's what it takes, yes. Maybe we can look at getting a beach house in New York and splitting our time between both places. Here, there, as long as we're together, I don't care." He cupped her face in his hands. "I thought Seaside Cove was my home—"

"I thought New York was my home. But home—"

"Is where *you* are," they said unison.

Tears filled Jamie's eyes. "In case you haven't figured it out, Mr. Smart Guy, Princeton, Ivy League, I'm wildly, crazy in love with you."

"Thank God. Because I'm wildly, crazy in love with you." He settled his mouth on hers and the area surrounding his heart that just a few minutes ago had been empty and aching filled to overflow. His hands impatiently pressed her closer, but an insistent, "Excuse me . . . excuse me, you two . . . *excuse me*," broke through the haze of love and lust engulfing him. Bemused, he lifted his head, and realized Larry was staring at them.

"I'm real happy for you folks, but it's late and I'm tired."

"Sure, Larry," Jamie said. Then she looked at Nick. "Um, you're happy to see me, right?"

He nudged her with his pelvis. "You can't tell?"

She gave a smothered laugh. "I can. And I'm very glad. Because there's a slight problem. It, ah, concerns my cab fare. I'm *reeeeeally* hoping you meant it when you said you weren't poor."

Nick raised his brows, then looked at Larry over her shoulder. "What's the damage?"

Larry glanced at the meter. "Five hundred seventy-two

dollars and thirty-five cents." When Nick whistled softly, Larry added, "I'll have you know I took her off the meter during our lunch break."

"That was very nice of you, Larry," Jamie said.

Nick returned his gaze to Jamie. "I take it you're in need of financial assistance in settling your bill."

"I'm afraid so. The plaque pretty much maxed out my credit card."

"You realize you'll be in my debt."

Her eyes glittered. "Oh, yeah."

"For a very long time."

"Even better. I'm thinking it'll take me at least a few weeks to pay you back."

"Longer than that, I'm afraid."

"Oh yeah? Like how long?"

He cupped her face in his hands. "I'm thinking about fifty years. At least."

Her lips curved slowly upward, until the most beautiful smile he'd ever seen bloomed on her face, and he found himself looking into eyes filled with all the love he could ever hope for.

"Fifty years," she repeated. "And once again, we agree."

Turn the page for a preview of
the next contempoary romance featuring

Seaside Cove
by Jacquie D'Alessandro

Coming soon from Berkley Sensation!

Laurel Newman pulled in a steadying breath she wished she didn't need. Wished she wasn't wracked with nerves. Plagued with doubts. Wished her palms weren't sweating, or her heart pounding in hard, uncomfortable knocks. It was crazy to be so nervous, so unsure of herself, but as many times as she'd tried to change it, she always felt this way when faced with the unfamiliar. The best she'd ever been able to accomplish was the ability to hide her jitters—a task she'd mastered. She was an expert at camouflaging her discomfort, of always appearing calm, cool, collected, and confident on the outside. None of her friends or family had ever suspected that her unruffled exterior hid a chronic worrier who, all evidence to the contrary, rarely let down her guard. Not that she needed to worry any longer about her friends discovering her secret.

Because they weren't her friends any longer.

No, they were gone. Just as everything familiar to her was now gone. So much loss, so much pain. Her entire existence lost down a twisting path that had, after much chewing, spit her out here, in Seaside Cove. And brought her to this marina, to this building that overlooked the white-capped bay and grassy marshes of North Carolina. Where she was about to do something she'd never done before.

Apply for a job.

"C'mon, Laurel," she whispered in her best pep-talk mode. "You can do this. People apply for jobs every day. First time for everything. Nothing to be afraid of."

Except she was afraid. Because for the first time in her life she *needed* a job. Needing a job, applying for a job, uncertain about the future, uncertain about . . . everything. So many firsts.

God, she hated firsts.

How had her life changed so drastically in such a short a period of time? Less than a year ago she'd been financially secure, a card-carrying member of New York City's elite—with the black Amex to prove it.

And now . . . now it was all gone. The wealth, the luxury, her home, her security. All gone.

A breeze ruffled her hair and she wrinkled her nose at the underlying whiff of three-day-old fish—a scent she recognized as one the Seaside Cove locals called "low tide."

Chanel it was not.

"Oh, how the mighty have fallen," she muttered.

Yes, she'd fallen, but she was determined to rise. Not just for her own sake, but for Heather's. She'd let her daughter down too many times in the past. She wasn't going to do it again. She hoped.

So these desperate times called for desperate measures. And God knows she was desperate. A humorless sound escaped her. Desperation. Another damn first. One she really, really disliked.

Straightening her spine, Laurel knocked on the door whose plain black lettering let her know she was at Griffin's Marina and Custom Boat Building. Only muffled music reached her ears. She knocked again, and when no one answered, she turned the knob and pushed the door open.

The scent of freshly cut wood hung heavy in the air. Light from the weak February sun fighting through the thick cloud cover seeped through the tall paned-glass windows, illuminating the partial wooden hull of a boat. Classic Aerosmith blasted from somewhere near the back of the hull, loud enough to awaken the dead. A pair of dusty jeans and work boots indicated someone stood back there as well. Probably Griffin, the person who'd posted the job ad. Since he couldn't see her and he'd never hear her entering over the racket of music and whine of some sort of power tool, she headed toward him. Her boot heels tapped against the cement floor, a welcome change to all the wood decking she'd encountered in Seaside Cove. Decks and docks and boardwalks everywhere. Hazard of a coastal town, she supposed.

In contrast to the rustic outside, the interior of the building was immaculate. Long rows of steel shelving ran the length of one wall, filled with gizmos and tools she couldn't name, but she recognized the pristine organization. Clearly this Griffin was neat and tidy. Maybe even to the point of being anal. The thought of working for an anal boss didn't thrill her, but beggars couldn't be choosers. Given that this was off-season in Seaside Cove, jobs weren't plentiful. In fact, they were just about non-existent. She'd have to take what she could get. So far she'd gotten nothing. So anal boss or not, she wasn't leaving here without a job. And she certainly wasn't going to let the fact that she knew zilch about boats stop her.

She rounded the back of the boat and found herself looking at a broad back covered by a faded plaid flannel shirt. Her gaze drifted down, taking in faded Levi's hugging long legs that ended in work boots so scuffed they must have traveled the planet. The cacophony created by Aerosmith and the power saw buzzed through her skull, so loud she could feel the reverberations in her chest. She didn't want to scare the guy—that saw looked like it could take off an arm.

"Hello," she shouted.

Steven Tyler and the saw screamed on.

She gingerly moved around the table saw so the man could see her and waved her arms. "Excuse me," she bellowed.

His gaze flicked up and she saw annoyance flash in his eyes behind the safety goggles he wore. The saw stopped with a fading wheeze, and he reached out to turn off the radio with an impatient flick.

"Hi." She smiled, ignoring the ringing in her ears. "Are you Griffin?"

"Yeah," he said, his tone as impatient and forbidding as his expression. Not to mention his size. She was five-nine

in her socks, hitting six foot with her boots, a height many
men found intimidating. But not this man. He had a good
four inches on her and sported a glower that no doubt would
have sent someone less determined than her slinking away.
Stubble shaded his square jaw, shadowing features that might
have passed for good-looking if they weren't in the running
for the title Mr. Seriously Pissed Off. His ebony hair was
thick and rumpled and a few inches too long. Everything
about him screamed big, rough, and Get Lost. If she wasn't
desperate, she would have done just that. His dark-eyed gaze
flicked down to her boots and his frown grew more pro-
nounced. "Who're you?"

Oh, joy. Anal *and* grumpy. Yippee. Definitely not looking
at all happy to see her. Which didn't bode well for this interview. Which frankly annoyed and confused her. He was the
one who'd left the voice mail on her cell setting up this meeting. She swallowed her irritation and offered another smile,
along with her hand. "Hi, Griffin. I'm Laurel Newman."

The frown he sizzled at her outstretched hand was clearly
meant to incinerate it. Instead of shaking her hand, he shoved
his safety glasses on top of his head and folded his arms
across his chest. "I'm not sure how you got in here—"

"I used the door."

"It was closed."

"But not locked. I knocked. Twice. You didn't hear me."

"Because I was working." His tone made it abundantly
clear that she'd interrupted him and he wasn't happy about
it—as if his pointed glare hadn't already made that obvious.
"Look, if you're here to talk to the dockmaster about renting
a boat slip—"

"I'm not," she broke in, lowering her hand and fighting to
keep her voice calm. Anal, grumpy, *and* insufferably rude. If
she wasn't desperate, she'd tell this hulking buffoon what he
could do with his power tools—in an anatomically specific
way—then get the hell out of there. "I'm here about the job.
Laurel Newman," she repeated, because he clearly wasn't the
sharpest knife in the drawer. "You scheduled an interview
with me at one o'clock."

"I didn't—" His words broke off, then he muttered what
sounded like an inventive combination of curses. After drag-

ging his hand down his face, he said, "I didn't set up an appointment with you."

"You said you're Griffin—"

"I am. But I'm not the only Griffin. There's my brother. Evan Griffin. I'm Ryan. Evan must have set up your interview."

Hope filled her. Maybe Evan was the sunshine to this guy's thundercloud. "In that case I apologize for disturbing you. Can you tell me where I might find Evan?"

"He's not here."

Clearly a man of few words. She knew—and disliked—the type. Getting more than five words out of them required infinite patience, which she currently didn't have much of, and a nuclear blast, which she was fresh out of. "I don't mind waiting."

"No point. He's gone for the day."

Great. Just freakin' great. He didn't look any happier about it than she was. "Will he be back tomorrow?"

"Don't know." He blew out a long breath. "Guess that means I'm stuck with this." He pinned her with a hard, assessing look. "Did Evan tell you about the job?"

"We didn't actually speak—only left messages on each others' voice mail. According to the ad in the newspaper, you're looking for an office manager. It's a position I'm well qualified for." She opened her oversized purse and pulled out a copy of her resume. Making a resume—another first she could have happily lived without ever experiencing.

He took the proffered paper without a word and perused its contents. When he looked up from the resume and met her gaze there was no missing his you've-got-to-be-kidding-me look. "Wanna explain how cochairing some debutante shindig, serving on a committee for some artsy-fartsy fund-raiser, and overseeing customer relations for a New York City restaurant qualifies you to work at a marina and boat-building business? There aren't any debutantes here—except for you."

Years of practice dealing with ill-mannered louts allowed Laurel to hold on to her temper. "It's been many years since I was a debutante, Mr. Griffin," she pointed out mildly. "And those positions I held required finely honed organizational skills—which I'm sure you'll agree are important when managing an office. Whether that office is attached to a restaurant, an art museum, or a marina."

"What do you know about boats?"

I know that at this time last year I was sunning myself on the deck of one in the French Riviera owned by a fashion designer who used to call me his muse and who no longer takes my calls. "I know they float and that they're your business—one that needs an office manager."

"There's a lot of catch-up that needs to be done," he said, his frown still in place. "Bills to be paid, invoices to send out, supplies to be ordered, filing, checkbook balancing, not to mention handling the phone calls." As if to prove his point, she heard the muffled sound of a phone ringing.

"All of which I'm perfectly capable of." She hoped. Just because her accountant had always paid her bills and she'd never sent out an invoice or balanced her checkbook in her entire life didn't mean she *couldn't* do it. She'd just never had to before. But now she did. So she'd figure it out. She was smart. How hard could it be?

"Since when do debutantes send out invoices and do filing?"

"As I said, Mr. Griffin—I haven't been a debutante for a long time."

He glanced down at her resume. "According to this you were working in a New York restaurant until just a few weeks ago. Why'd you leave?"

A tidal wave of painful memories threatened to swamp her. She forced them back into the dark abyss from which they'd arisen and then said, "The restaurant suffered an economic setback and my position was eliminated." Not exactly true, but the only explanation he was going to get.

"Why not stay in New York?"

"It's very expensive to live there. I wanted to try somewhere new."

"Why Seaside Cove?"

"I spent some time here last summer and fell in love with the island."

"So you moved here? Just like that?"

"Yes." *I had no where else to go.* "My sister's fiancé owns a rental on the island. I'm staying there until I get a place of my own." Rent-free, thank God.

"Which house?"

"It used to be called Paradise Lost, but they've renamed it—"

"Paradise Found. That's Nick Trent's place."

"Yes."

His frown bunched deeper. "He's a good man."

"I agree. And he's engaged to my sister." A fact she didn't hesitate to reiterate since Mr. Frowny Face apparently liked Nick. She wasn't above exploiting a connection to get her foot in the door.

He kept that unwavering narrow-eyed regard on her, clearly trying to read her, as if she were some kind of book—one he hadn't enjoyed the first chapter of and was debating whether or not to keep turning the pages. Well, he was destined to fail. She didn't wear her thoughts or emotions on her sleeve—a lesson she'd learned the hard way.

"The office opens at eight thirty, closes at five, Monday through Friday. Lunch is noon to one." He mentioned an hourly salary that wouldn't add up in a week to what she'd normally spent on a single night out in New York. *Those days are over, Laurel.* "You'd need to go to the bank once, maybe twice a week to make deposits. That a problem?"

Probably not a good time to mention that she didn't have a car. Since she'd always had a limo and driver at her disposal, she hadn't needed one. Especially since she didn't even know how to drive. "Absolutely not a problem." Hell, that's what taxis were for. Or sneakers—if the bank was in walking distance.

Once again a muted ringing phone sounded and his gaze swiveled to a door at the far end of the building. She wouldn't have thought it possible, but his frown seemed to grow fiercer. He swiveled his gaze back to her and she felt pinned in place by the intensity and obvious frustration brewing in his eyes.

"When could you start?" he asked.

In spite of the fact that the prospect of working for Mr. Congeniality here wasn't appealing, relief rippled through her, and she had the sense that she'd been saved, literally, by the bell. "Right now, if you'd like."

He gave a terse nod, muttered, "Follow me," then headed toward the door behind which the phone continued to ring. His long-legged stride would have left a shorter person in the dust, but she kept pace with him, her boot heels tapping a staccato rhythm on the cement floor. When they reached the door, he paused with his hand on the brass handle.

"Let's see what sort of order you can bring and how much you can accomplish in the next four hours." He winced. "And for God's sake, handle that phone. Impress me and you're hired."

Oh, she had every intention of impressing him. Even if it killed her. Just to prove to him that she could. Because he clearly didn't think she'd be able to.

"Be prepared to be impressed, Mr. Griffin."

"If you're hired, no more fancy high-heeled boots," he said, shooting her footwear a fierce scowl. "Sneakers or deck shoes or work boots only. Got it?"

"Got it."

His only answer was a grunt. She crossed the threshold and the door closed behind her.

The instant Ryan closed the door, he headed swiftly back toward the saw, but he wasn't quick enough to miss the debutante's gasp. Not that he could blame her. He knew damn well what the office looked like—a mess of papers and coffee cups and open files. An inbox that overflowed onto the desk, the windowsill, two chairs, then continued onto the floor. Somewhere hidden in that disaster area was the phone that never seemed to cease ringing. Damn it, he was boat builder, not a secretary. And Griffin's needed a secretary. Badly. They'd been without one for over a month, and between the mounting administrative stuff, the ongoing dock repairs, and the custom boat he was two weeks behind on, he was ready to lose his mind. Problem was, it was nearly impossible to find anyone during the off-season. Miss Debutante was the first—and only—person to answer the ad.

He shook his head. If even one other person had expressed interest in the job, Ryan would have escorted that glamorous piece of fluff right back out to the parking lot. Jesus, she looked as if she'd just jetted into town between modeling assignments. She looked more out of place at Griffin's than he would have at a one of those silly debutante balls. God, he should have known better than to leave Evan in charge of the hiring. His younger brother was an expert at bringing trouble to the door, then disappearing as he'd done today—and Ryan was frankly exhausted from cleaning up the messes. And there was no doubt that Laurel Newman would be trouble. Any woman who looked like her meant Trouble with a capital T. And that rhymed with P and that stood for Problem.

And more problems he didn't need.

Turn the page for a preview of
the historical romance featuring

The Ladies Literary Society of London
by Jacquie D'Alessandro

Seduced at Midnight

Available now from Berkley Sensation!

The latest Ladies Literary Society of London read is a ghost story that propels Lady Julianne Bradley into the greatest adventure of her life . . . with the Bow Street Runner her heart cries out for, but who can never be hers.

"You shouldn't have come out here, Lady Julianne." Even the darkness couldn't disguise the heated intensity of his gaze. Dear God, the way he was looking at her . . . as if he were a starving beast and she was a tasty morsel he'd happened upon. And the way he made her feel . . . as if she were gasping for air and he was the last bit of oxygen on earth.

Holding her breath, she stood in an aching jumble of desperate want, need, apprehension, and anticipation, unable to move, waiting to see what he'd do next.

Just when she thought his hot scrutiny would incinerate her where she stood, his gaze shifted to study each of her features. When he came to her mouth, he lingered for several breath-stealing seconds before slowly raising his gaze back to hers.

"You should return to the house," Gideon said.

Julianne had to swallow twice to locate her voice. "Yes," she whispered.

She should return. She knew it. But apparently her feet did not as they remained firmly rooted in place. Maybe perhaps she might possibly have convinced her feet to move, but then he touched a single fingertip to her cheek. And the only thing fleeing the garden were any thoughts of her leaving.

His finger followed the same path his gaze had just traveled, painting feather-light strokes over her face. The tip of his finger was hard. Blunt. Calloused. Not that of a gentleman. Yet infinitely gentle.

She watched him as he touched her, noting the avid way his gaze followed his finger. The muscle that ticked in his square jaw. With his finger lightly circling the outer curve of her ear—a bit of skin she'd had no idea was so sensitive—he leaned in. Brushed his cheek against her hair.

In an agony of anticipation, Julianne remained perfectly still, terrified that if she so much as breathed he would stop. End this wondrous adventure. She heard him take a slow, deep breath, one he released in a ragged stream of warmth against her temple.

"Delicious," he muttered. "Bloody hell, I knew you'd smell delicious." The last words ended on a low groan. "What is that scent?"

How could he possibly expect her to answer questions? With an effort, she managed to say, "Vanilla."

"Yes . . ." He pulled in another deep breath. "You smell like the bake shop. Warm. Sweet. Scrumptious." His lips brushed over her hair, and he groaned again. "You really need to return to the ball, Julianne. Now."

The intimacy of that gravelly voice saying her name, without the formal use of her title, touched something deep inside her. She could no more have left the garden at that moment than she could have held back the tide. She'd longed for a moment like this—free of the suffocating constraints of society and away from the ever-vigilant eye of her mother who was determined to see her married off to a duke. Dear God, if Mother suspected Julianne was alone with a man, let alone a man like Gideon—a Bow Street Runner, a commoner—she'd fly into the boughs and never allow Julianne out of her sight for an instant.

But this was the man who'd haunted Julianne's dreams for months, who'd set her dreams and imagination on fire. A man who could never be hers for longer than this stolen instant in time. She'd longed for a chance like this and nothing her common sense or conscience screamed at her could deter her.

"No," she whispered. "Not now."

JACQUIE D'ALESSANDRO

Tempted at Midnight

Lady Emily Stapleford never dreamed that the burden of saving her family from financial ruin would rest on her lovely, resourceful shoulders. Since she's willing to marry only for love, and not money, Emily pens a story she hopes will bring her fortune—only to have it rejected by every publishing firm. After all, what respectable reader would dare embrace a vampire heroine?

Not to be dissuaded, Emily decides to stir public interest by creating false vampire sightings. Overnight, London is abuzz with the news. With renewed interest in Emily's book, she's guaranteed success—if it wasn't for the mysterious American Logan Jennsen. He's onto Emily's duplicity, and he has every intention of using it to his advantage. If only he wasn't falling in love with this unabashedly creative woman. And if only he didn't have a scandalous secret of his own—one that's putting both their lives in danger . . .

penguin.com

Also Available From *New York Times*
Bestselling Author

Jacquie D'Alessandro

Seduced at Midnight

*The Ladies Literary Society of London gathers
again for a ghost story...*

Lady Julianne Bradley has always longed to indulge in a wild adventure. Unfortunately, the man with whom she wishes to share her fervor can never be hers. Tormented by her desire, she's preparing for a suitable marriage when she witnesses ghostly occurrences straight out of her latest read. To protect Julianne, her father hires the very man her heart cries out for.

M376T0211